Leonardo's Flight

Leonardo's Flight

PHILIPPE BLAIS

Gates & Bridges, Inc.

LEONARDO'S FLIGHT. Copyright © 2000 by Philippe Blais. All rights reserved. No part of this book may be used or reproduced in any manner whatsoever without written permission except in the case of brief quotations embodied in critical articles and reviews.

Library of Congress data available.

Printed in Canada.

Distributed by Independent Publishers Group, Chicago.

ISBN 1-929953-00-3
Fiction

Gates & Bridges, Inc., Lexington KY

1

No Time, No Space

*T*sss...

A small spot of light suddenly widened into a flash that filled the monitor. Its glow illuminated the surrounding darkness. The eletronic canvas lit up to show a sky-blue corporate logo.

<<SPARO AERONAUTICS>>

The logo moved to the top left corner of the screen, diminishing in size as it climbed. The line

<<PROJECT SPEAR M40>>

filled the center of the screen and followed the path of the corporate logo.

<<ENTER ACCESS CODE>>

With every touch on the keyboard, the corresponding letter appeared on the monitor.

"MAVIS"

<<ENTER USER ID NUMBER>>

"58367"

<<ENTER PERSONAL PASSWORD>>

"☐☐☐☐☐☐☐" The screen replaced each letter with a box.

<<HI NED! HOW ARE YOU? HAVE YOU HAD YOUR COFFEE YET?>>

The personalized greeting confirmed that the computer had accepted the password. After a few seconds, it was replaced by a menu of activities.

<<WHAT DO YOU HAVE IN MIND TODAY?

    1.   DATA ENTRY

    2.   SIMULATIONS

    3.   PRINT REPORT

    4.   E-MAIL

    5.   WORK ORDERS

    6.   WORK SCHEDULES

    7.   RETURN TO SA-COLLINS PROGRAM

    8.   EXIT SYSTEM>>

Using the arrow keys, the operator moved the cursor to item number three and confirmed the selection with the return key.

<<ENTER REPORT SELECTION>>

"SM40-EC"

<<PRINTING ON LPT3>>

The operator's fingers tapped nervously on the desk while waiting for the printout.

A new message flickered in red lettering on the bottom left corner of the screen.

<<Incoming E-MAIL>>

The operator acknowledged the message and returned to the main menu. He moved the cursor to item number four and pressed the return key.

<<E-MAIL MENU>>

    1.   SEND E-MAIL

    2.   NEW MESSAGES

    3.   E-MAIL FILING

    4.   RETURN TO SYSTEM >>
The cursor stopped at item number two. Click.
The e-mail message appeared on the screen.

SPARO AERONAUTICS

DATE:	August 30, 1988
TO:	SACOL-OP
FROM:	HOLD245
SUBJECT:	SAM MOD

In absence of SAM-DAD, advise of status of SAM-MOD A.S.A.P.
Security breach suspected. Teacher, monitor student. Must patch
leak. Fade-out time - 30 seconds.

The computer operator reached for the page in the printer, turned it over
and copied the key words on the back of the printout: SACOL-OP /
HOLD245 / SAM-MOD / SAM-DAD.
The message faded from the screen and disappeared.

University of Caldwell

August 1988
It was the first day of the Fall semester. Rodney Blake, his thick jet-black
hair, still wet, combed back, wearing cowboy boots, denim jeans and jacket
with a golf shirt, scanned the classroom. The cracks in the wall; the
decaying paint; the tired desktop-chairs; nothing had changed since last
April. The urban cowboy smiled. He found an empty seat in the front.
"It's good to see that the increase in my tuition fees has been put to good
use."
    "What do you expect?" a voice boomed from the back. "They've used
the money to organize a two-week all-expense-paid administration

convention in the Bahamas where the deans of the various faculties will discuss, during their golf games and over many bottles of Rémy Martin and Dom Perignon, the ways to reduce costs and to increase next year's tuition!"

Rodney recognized the voice. His smile broadened as he shrugged and looked up to the ceiling.

"Damn!!" he exclaimed. "This school will do anything to collect tuition. They..."

"Yeah, their criteria for passing are pretty damn slack," the voice from behind interrupted. "Rod, jeez ... if you can pass... well I guess that proves it! The world's gone to the dogs."

"Aaah-oooo-oooh!" Rodney howled.

Some of the classmates who overheard the conversation were laughing. This was a typical scenario. A voice broke through the rumble.

"That's all we needed. Mutt 'n Jeff in the same class again," the voice sighed. "To think I was looking forward to this year!"

From behind, the voice thundered again.

"Hold on to your panties, Marty. If you play your cards right, maybe you and me can go steady this year."

More laughs from the audience. Wishing he'd remained silent, Marty turned his back to the voice, his light skin turning the same red as his hair.

Rodney was absorbing every word with delight. Then, he felt a hand on his shoulder. He cocked his head back to look at the tall strong figure of the man who stood behind him. Although, Charles Durkin was towering in stature, nothing attracted attention more than his steely blue eyes. They conveyed an air of confidence as well as a zest for life.

"What's up buddy?"

Rodney stood up and extended his right hand into his friend's. His five feet ten inches were half a foot short of the other's height. "Charles, my man, it's good to see you. I see they still haven't put you behind bars."

Charles lifted one foot onto a seat beside Rodney's, resting one elbow on his thigh and gently stroking his chin with his hand.

"Actually, Rodney, me boy, I prefer standing in front of a bar and throwing back a few pints. In fact, I don't remember meeting a beer I didn't drink."

Charles took his foot off the seat and lowered himself into it. He grabbed the table in front of him and rocked the swivel seat back and forth, which resulted in a deafening screeching noise.

"Ah! It's good to see that some things don't change," he said with a smirk. As he balanced himself on the seat and looked around him, he noticed that his actions were not meeting with everyone's approval. This observation prompted him to increase the tempo of the rocking.

"I see you still love to live at peace with your environment."

"Hey when you've got charm, you use it!" Charles retorted.

"By the way, who teaches this course? I hope it's not old humorless Collins."

Charles tried to contain his smile. "Bingo! Your good old pal himself. But he may be replaced. No one's seen him since..."

"Speaking of the devil..." Rodney interrupted, nodding towards the door.

William Collins, a man in his late fifties, balding, half-moon bifocal glasses perched on his narrow triangular nose, dressed in well-pressed wool pants and a tweed jacket, bow tie, was the stereotypical University professor. Clutching an old weathered briefcase in his right hand, a beige trench coat folded over his left arm and an umbrella dangling from the wrist, he was flushed and walked with slight hesitancy.

He peeked over his specs and examined the familiar faces in the classroom as he deposited his accessories on the desk in front of him. His dark eyes lacked sparkle. He opened his class planner and fumbled through its contents until he reached the desired page. His body swayed slightly, almost imperceptibly, but it was obvious that the professor was drunk.

"The Class of 1988. I welcome all distinguished seniors to another semester. I'm sure you all share my enthusiasm for the captivating subject, *The Physics of* Aerodynamics."

Muffled laughs. The students looked at each other, sharing knowing glances.

"Well now. My words have not fallen on deaf ears. This is quite a change from last year. A summer of sunshine may have done some of you good after all." His comments generated a few laughs of approval. "There may be some hope for you people yet."

"There's something wrong here," Rodney whispered astonished. "This can't be the same guy we had last year. This guy has a sense of humor!"

"This guy is loaded to the gills!" Charles seemed disturbed. Rodney noticed his friend's expression of concern.

"What's the matter Charles?"

"Nothing. It's just that I'm surprised to see Collins here, that's all... with his resignation and all."

"What do you mean?"

"I worked with him this summer. You know, I interned at Sparo. Collins is involved in the fighter project. He's a great guy. In fact, I think the guy's a genius."

"You mean, Collins, the jerk you despised, has become your idol?"

"There's more to him than meets the eye."

Rodney shook his head.

"Shhh! Could you guys be quiet? Some of us are listening," a pretty brunette sitting in front of them interrupted. "Do you mind?"

"No we don't mind at all. You can listen to us anytime you want, sweet Debbie," Rodney teased.

"Come on, guys. You know what I mean," she said, trying to hold back a smile.

"No, but I'm ready to listen," Rodney added, mocking the voice of Groucho Marx. "Your place or mine?"

Debbie rolled up her eyes and turned back towards the front of the classroom shaking her head, not believing that she'd fallen into that same trap again. "*I should know better*," she thought, smiling nonetheless.

Rodney hadn't seen her come in, but now that her intervention had caught his attention, his eyes were riveted on her back. Like no other girl, she had stirred something inside him from the first time their eyes had met. In fact, on occasion, he'd felt clumsy in her presence, a feeling that made him uneasy. They had worked together on group assignments in the past, but other than his usual teasing, their exchanges had always been academic, from one student to another. Debbie had always been very pleasant and approachable with most of her fellow students, but she remained distant on the social activities level. Although the thought had often occupied his mind, Rodney had never mustered enough courage to ask her out on a date.

Professor Collins continued his instructions: "...weekly assignments should be handed in on Wednesdays before class starts. As you are well aware, any late papers are not accepted, no matter what the reason." He paused and looked at his notes and instead of lecturing on, reached down and pulled up his briefcase. He took out a small flask, poured some of the contents into a small glass and drank it.

The students gasped, all of them shocked by this surprising display. Their collective reactions blended into a rumble. The professor looked at them and smiled. He burped.

"Pardon me. Where was I? Hmmm. Ah yes. I have been asked by many of you to try to integrate the personal computer into my course. Assisted by... one of your peers, I have prepared a course- ... enhancing program which will be of grrr... great use to those who want to further their knowledge. The information is available on diskettes for the modest sum of fifteen dollars."

A young woman raised her hand.

"Yes, Miss Crabton," Professor Collins acknowledged her presence.

"Sir, I believe it's unfair to have a system that will give an advantage to the people who own a computer. We don't all have the means to buy one," she protested in a whining tone. Her comment caused murmurs of disapproval among the students.

"I don't think your argument has much foundation." He poured another drink from his flask, drank it and sighed. "The Faculty has many PC's available for your use. All you have to do is reserve a time with the attendants," he argued.

There was a murmur of approval.

"…and if you don't want to use it, I don't give a damn."

"I can't believe he's started drinking again!" Charles said, manifestly upset. They were following their classmates out of the auditorium. "I guess that explains his disappearance."

"What are you talking about?"

"It's…it's a long story. I'll tell you all about it later," Charles tried to evade the question.

"I'm ready to listen now."

"Later!" Charles sighed and tried to regain composure. "Let's talk about something else. So what's new with you, Rod?"

"S.O.S." Rodney decided to respect his friend's need to change the subject.

"Same old shit, hey? Somehow that sounds good to me," Charles responded wistfully.

"By the way, the boys and I are throwing a party on Friday night. You're invited."

The walk down Anderson Avenue, Oscar Maxwell could do with his eyes closed. Even though he'd opted not to move in with his childhood friends, he was always accepted with open arms... and a cold beer. Oscar shared many things with the four residents of 230 Anderson Avenue, also known as Club 230. Born and raised in the same town, they had grown up together and lived many of the same experiences. Their parents were also close friends.

Anderson Avenue was in the old part of Caldwell. On the same island as the campus, it blended the rich Victorian architecture of its houses and buildings with the youthful appearance of its inhabitants. The houses had once belonged to middle and upper class people, and at the turn of the century, had been part of an exclusive neighborhood. Nevertheless, time had taken its toll. The once prestigious buildings had lost their appeal for the new generations of homeowners who had opted for newer homes with big backyards in the suburbs. The University of Caldwell had therefore bought a good number of the old houses and rented them to its senior students. The carefree and sometimes destructive habits of their youthful residents had accelerated the deterioration of some of the residences. Although many of them were still impressive, their majestic structure radiating quality and beauty was apparent only to the sensitive soul.

For Oscar, 230 Anderson radiated life. As he stood before it, he could see the sports articles hanging from the walls on the top balcony, proof that the inhabitants were alive and well, and he could hear the sound of music, always present in the background. He couldn't put a finger on it, but there was definitely something appealing about this particular address. Climbing the stairs onto the porch would usually accelerate the pace of his heart, because he never knew what to expect when he walked in.

Oscar knocked once on the front door (this was out of habit since he knew through experience that nobody ever answered) and walked in. The stereo was blaring Bob Seger's "Hollywood Nights". He looked into the main living room on his right. The furniture had been placed along the walls to leave room for people to stand in or dance. A poster of a pretty young blond woman was taped to the wall. The picture had been taken from behind as she bent over to pick up a tennis ball. She was dressed in a T-shirt and a tennis skirt minus the underpants.

"Eddie!" Oscar called out. No answer. "Rod!" Still no answer. "Anybody home?"

"*The music's probably burying the sound of my voice,*" he thought.

Oscar walked into the next room, the TV room. For the party, all the furniture had been taken out and replaced by two huge containers placed end to end and full of ice-covered beer. Along the wall behind them, the cases of beer purchased that afternoon were neatly stacked, their contents ready to replace the beers pulled out of the cooling containers during the party. Oscar recognized one of the ice-filled tubs. It had been borrowed from the university engineering pub. The other container was a huge ancient bathtub. Oscar could hardly believe his eyes.

"Where did they get this big sucker?" He laughed, "Knowing these guys, there's probably somebody who won't be able to take a bath tonight."

The kitchen at the back of the house had been left intact, except for the kitchen table that had been moved out of the way.

"Yo!" He yelled out. Still no answer. He walked back down the corridor into the TV room. Stopping beside the old bathtub, he pulled out a beer.

"Ah, a good old brew. A party ain't much without it." Taking a drink out of the bottle, he continued down the hallway and up the staircase that led to the upper rooms. He could hear some laughter coming from the bathroom. When he got to the top of the stairs, he peeked into the first room to his right. It was Rodney's room. No one to be seen. He walked towards the bathroom.

The voices intensified but he still couldn't make out the conversation above the loudness of the music. With a swift kick, he opened the bathroom door. What he saw made him laugh. Rodney and his roommates, Edmond Bishop, Leo Theodore and Eugene Gallagher were all sitting in the bath together, their legs dangling over the side of an old tub similar to the one converted into a beer cooler downstairs.

"Hey Dude!" the four bathers exclaimed simultaneously.

"It's about time you got here," Edmond barked out. "Where'd you disappear to?"

"I went home to change. So, how are you ladies doing? I hope you're not all naked in there?" he asked, hoping they would say no.

The four guys looked at each other. Oscar could almost read the non-verbal communication that existed between them. All together they got up, showing their friend that there was no chance that any underwear of theirs would be fading in that bathtub.

"See? Circumcised, circumcised, circumcised and turtleneck," Leo pointed.

Startled by this exhibitionism, Oscar laughed, immediately joined by his by now quite inebriated friends.

"Hey turtleneck," he called out to Rodney.

"Hey, I've had no complaints!" Rodney protested. "I can grow into it."

"And when he does grow into it, the blood rushes away from his brain causing him to faint," Eugene added. More laughs.

"I'll drink to that," Leo toasted.

"You'll drink to anything," closed Eugene.

The four fellows sat back down in the tub, letting their legs hang over the side. Beside the bath was a big plastic garbage receptacle with a cover. Edmond removed the cover and reached into the container. He pulled out a beer and a small can of V-8 juice, then poured both liquids into a big beer stein. He reached beside the bathtub, pulled out another beer mug and threw it towards Oscar, who caught with his left hand.

"Mix yourself a drink," he commanded.

"Don't mind if I do," Oscar accepted. Taking the bottle of beer he had in his right hand, he poured the remaining contents into the stein.

"It seems to me that whenever I come to visit, you guys are in the john."

"Don't call it a john. That's vulgar. I prefer to call it a caucus room, where great minds meet and solve important matters," Leo said

"Caucus. Caucus. Hmm. Now, that's a Freudian slip if I've ever heard one," Edmond teased.

"Where great minds meet? Very poetic! What the hell are you doing here, Leo?" Rodney continued the tirade.

"Filling the void."

Oscar listened to the verbal sparring between his friends. He always got a kick out of the exchanges.

"By the way, where did you guys dig up that antique bathtub?" His question drew a blank expression from his friends. "The one being used as a cooler downstairs," he clarified.

"Oh, that one. Ah yes! I guess you could say we borrowed it from the University," Eugene replied. "Pretty neat, huh? It holds twelve cases of beer."

"Actually, Steve, our friendly neighbor, has volunteered to lend it to us," Leo explained.

"So, what time is the wife coming in, Dude?" asked Eddie.

Of the five boys, Oscar was the only one who had a steady girlfriend. She was a high-school sweetheart whom he'd been dating since he was sixteen years old.

"She's supposed to come in on the eight o'clock bus," he replied in a serious tone.

"Is she taking a cab over?" Leo asked.

"No I'm meeting her there."

"Oh, Mrs. Dude is not a big enough girl to come here on her own," Edmond commented in a sarcastic tone.

Oscar, a bit embarrassed, looked away from his friends. "Well, she wants to drop off her things at the apartment before coming over."

"I hope that your intentions are honorable," Eugene teased in a suggestive tone.

Oscar took a deep breath and changed the subject, "Real nice day out there isn't it?"

The bathers chuckled and drank some beer. There was an unwritten agreement between the boys that there would be no prying into Oscar's love-life since he'd made clear that it was just that - private. And after all, when you're six-foot-three and two hundred and twenty-five pounds, whatever you say usually goes.

The phone rang. Leo reached down beside the toilet and picked up a telephone for which an extension line had been passed through a small hole in the wall.

"Club 230," he answered. Then, "Hi Jane, how're you doin'?"

He looked at his friends motioning an imposing bosom with his hands, while the phone receiver rested between his cheek and shoulder.

Of the four roommates, Leo had the most active life in the girl department. The young co-eds seemed to melt under his charm. Leo always seemed to find the right word, the right compliment. Women always felt comfortable in his presence. The most amazing thing was that he usually dated many girls at the same time and rarely found himself in troubled waters.

"She's hot for my body," Eddie teased in the background.

"If you want my body and you think I'm sexy, come on, baby, let me know," he sang the words to the Rod Stewart tune.

Leo rolled his eyes and motioned to his friends to quiet down.

"Oh we're just having a few brewskies by the beach."

The comment generated some chuckles. Everyone in the room was listening in on the telephone conversation.

"The boys and I were just discussing tonight's planned activities." Leo paused. "That sounds great! So you'll be here tonight?" He paused again. "People should start coming in around eight." Pause. "That's great. See you then," Leo concluded as he hung up the phone.

"That was Jane. She's bringing her friend Cindy. Guys, I think we're in business!" he cheered as he got up in the bathtub and started doing the twist.

"If we don't get lucky tonight, we're all queer!" Eddie exclaimed.

His friends reacted to the comment by clinking their beer mugs together.

"Wall to wall girls!" Eugene toasted.

"I second the motion," supported Rodney.

"I've got to go and get Angie," Oscar told his friends. "I'll see you later."

"Hey dude, don't forget we have a party tonight," Eugene reminded. "Girls have a tendency to make one forgetful."

"Hey, have I ever let you guys down before?" Oscar tried to reassure his friends.

"If Angie was my girlfriend, I'd forget us!" Rodney replied.

"Did you ever notice the way she looks at me?" Edmond teased trying to raise a reaction.

"That's only because she's never seen such an ugly looking sap before," came the answer.

"Ooh! Low blow," Edmond chuckled at the scathing comment.

"Well, I've got to go. Ciao, boys!" Oscar closed the door.

The music had stopped and the sound of Oscar stepping down the old staircase replaced it, followed by the familiar screeching of the portico door closing behind him.

"Whose turn is it to go and put on a record?" Edmond asked.

"I got it last time," Eugene pointed out.

"I'll get it," Rodney volunteered.

He stepped out of the bath and grabbed a towel from a wall rack beside the tub. After drying himself quickly, he wrapped the towel around his waist and went out of the room and into his bedroom where the stereo controls had been installed temporarily. Rodney selected a record out of the plastic milk box on the floor and replaced the record that was already on the turntable.

From his bedroom window, which was adjacent and at right angle to the bathroom window, he could hear his friends' voices. The consumption of beer having perhaps already put his inhibitions to sleep, Rodney impulsively climbed onto the windowsill and grasped the ledge of the bathroom window (which was smaller and higher than his own). He swung himself towards the adjoining wall and, hanging by the arms, pulled himself up until his head was above the edge and let out a blood-curdling scream, catching the others by surprise and provoking a collective scream. Then everyone laughed. The three bathers all got up and bent through the window, where Rodney was hanging.

"I wonder what would happen if I hit his fingers with my mug?" Eugene wondered out loud, his mug positioned to substantiate his threat.

Leo reached through the window and started tickling Rodney's armpits.

"Do we feel a bit vulnerable? By the way, how are you going to get back into your room?" he asked.

In a blink of an eye, Rodney's facial colors turned from a bright red, to sheet white.

"I didn't think about that. Maybe you guys could move out of the way, and I'll pull myself through the window."

"Nah, we've got bad backs," replied Edmond. "Maybe you should go back the way you came," he teased.

"Thanks Eddie, but I can't reach the room's window from this position," Rodney explained. "Please guys, let me in."

"Maybe, you should have looked before you leaped," Edmond persisted, evidently amused by the literal application of the old saying.

Rodney was not amused. "Great choice of words. Now, could we be serious for one second, and let me in," Rodney pleaded his voice straining.

"Hey Rodney. Look behind you!" Eugene exclaimed pointing.

Rodney turned his head, as much as his position allowed, to find that he'd drawn some attention. Three Asian students were peering through the window of the neighboring house, evidently shocked by what they were witnessing. They were new tenants in the building and probably new to the country. The sight of a near-naked man hanging from a second floor window must have been, to say the least, unusual.

When he turned back, the window on which he hung was shut and he knew for a fact that no amount of yelling would cause his buddies to open it again. He was left with only two options. The first was to try to get back into his room, a feat which demanded a considerable amount of coordination and cool. The second was to let himself fall into the bushes below him and risk putting his dreams of being a proud father to rest forever. He of course opted for the first choice and with great difficulty, managed to clamber along the wall and to pull himself back into his room, with his pride, luckily, the only part of him bruised. He sat down on the chair by his bed, weakened from the physical exertion, but mostly shaken by the thought of the risk he'd just taken.

"Hey Rod!" a voice cried from the bathroom.

He saw Leo's head appearing through the bathroom window looking down towards the ground. Seeing that Rodney wasn't there, he turned towards his bedroom window and called out:

"You made it! Great! Now you can turn up the music, we can hardly hear it."

He disappeared for a few seconds and reappeared.

"Come on in, the water's great."

"Oh I'm doing fine. Thanks for your concern Leo," Rodney shouted back sarcastically.

He smiled and shook his head.

"At this pace, I won't live to be thirty," he muttered as he got up and walked towards the stereo, which had been temporarily set up on his desk, beside his personal computer, and complied with his roommate's request. As he turned up the volume, his attention was drawn to a framed poster that was leaning on his desk. He picked it up and looked at it. It was a commercial replica of Leonardo Da Vinci's self-portrait. A rustic-looking frame had been glued on top of the modern-day replica.

"Hey Leonardo! How's it going?" He pointed towards the washroom. "Those are my friends. Can you believe it?" He positioned the poster on top of his desk behind the turntable and leaned it against the wall.

"I hope you like your new frame, Leonardo. I made it myself. Tomorrow, I'll mount you on the wall."

Rodney pulled a record out of its jacket and replaced the one already on the turntable, positioning the stylus at the beginning. He reached for the bedroom door and closed it. The distinct sound of Moon Shadow from Cat Stevens resounded through the walls.

The young man took off the towel and reached for sweat pants and a T-shirt and put them on. He sat on his bed and pulled a book from under his pillow.

He looked at the poster of the Renaissance Master.

"Ah!" he sighed with contentment as he sat comfortably on the bed. "Let's find out a bit more about you, Leonardo."

He opened the book where he'd last left a bookmark.

Florence, Italy (A Sunday in April, 1478)

Life in Florence was regulated by the bell chimes. From daybreak to nightfall, the bells told its citizens, a hundred thousand plus, whether it was time to rise, time to congregate in church to pray, time to eat or time to go to sleep. For the most part illiterate, they depended on the bells to tell them of all the important events in the community: births, deaths, weddings, impending danger, executions.

On this beautiful April Sunday morning, the church bells invited all parishioners to the weekly celebration of mass. Lorenzo the Magnificent left his Palazzo Vecchio with his entourage - his brother Giuliano, Francesco Pazzi, Bernardo Bandini and Cardinal Riario. Giuliano had been injured during a jousting tournament and was walking with the assistance of Francesco Pazzi. The richness of the men's apparel, costumes in tints of red, purple and gold, with lace trimmings adding the finishing touches, was the symbol of their privileged status in Florentine society.

Lorenzo had taken the helm of the Florence government when his father, Pierre de Medicis, succumbed to a violent bout with the gout. Therefore, at the young age of twenty-eight Lorenzo could already draw from eight years of experience as head of state. A handsome man, with dark cascading hair and a strong square well-defined face, Lorenzo had come to grips with his responsibilities. At the age of five he had been put under the watchful eye of Gentile Becchi, an ecclesiastic, whose purpose was to teach the young Lorenzo Latin, introduce him to philosophy and rhetoric, all so important in his grooming as the successor to his father.

"Is this not a splendid day, my dear brother," Lorenzo exclaimed.

"One of divine inspiration, no doubt," responded Giuliano.

"Are they not all?" retorted Cardinal Riario.

As they climbed the stairs to the Santa Maria del Fiore Cathedral, Francesco Pazzi held Giuliano by the waist belt to assist him in his climb.

"Pardon me, Master Giuliano, but you seem to have forgotten your trusted sword," Francesco pointed out.

"So have I, my friend," interjected Lorenzo, "We have come to worship the Lord. My people have had faith in our family for many generations now. If I feel threatened amongst my friends and people, whom can I trust?"

"And he who points a menacing finger towards my brother, will have to deal with me first," supported Giuliano, beaming with confidence.

"My Lord," interrupted Bernardo Bandini. "Should we make room for your faithful guards during Mass?"

"I have left them at the Palazzo. There is no need for them within the house of God," he responded, visibly annoyed by his friend's insistence. "I must be accessible to my people."

They entered the Santa Maria del Fiore Cathedral and walked to their reserved places. As was the case every Sunday, all the members of the bourgeoisie were in attendance and the entrance of Lorenzo and his cohort always attracted their attention. After all, he was the leader of their community. The Monsignor would never dare start the church proceedings without having his most noble subjects present. The de Medicis family was the wealthiest family of bankers in Florence, if not all of Europe.

Once the de Medicis had found their regular place, the Monsignor celebrated Mass in Latin, a language taught exclusively to those of noble descent.   Lorenzo had memorized every prayer, every word, as was expected of a de Medicis.

Then, at Elevation, as the parishioners knelt, bowing their heads in a moment of silence, Pazzi and Bandini, taking advantage of that moment of calm, pounced simultaneously on Giuliano and in a savage attack, stabbed their unsuspecting victim in the back of the neck.

Lorenzo witnessed the attack on his brother and, as he moved to help him, noticed that two priests, Antonio Maffei and Stefano da Bagnone, were rushing in his direction with their daggers ready to strike. Lorenzo quickly took off his velour overcoat and in one swift motion rolled it around his arm to shield himself from his assailants. Having repelled this initial attack, he jumped over the balustrade separating the choir from the nave and escaped into the Sacristy. His heart beats had accelerated to a furious pace; never had he come so close to death. Politien, a supporter of Lorenzo, and some of his friends followed him and locked the door behind them, thereby thwarting Bandini who, having made sure that Giuliano was dead, had seen Lorenzo escape, and chased him to his refuge.

"My Lord, you have been wounded in the neck," remarked Politien to Lorenzo. "Perhaps you should sit."

"Where is Giuliano, my brother?" Lorenzo queried, short of breath.

None of Lorenzo's allies present in the Sacristy dared to answer their master. They had all witnessed what had happened. There was no doubt in their minds that Giuliano had perished at the hands of his assailants. They all bowed their heads to evade the desperate gaze of their noble friend. Looking around him, Lorenzo noticed the imposing pipe organ behind him, a massive instrument that acted as an outside wall to the sacristy. He climbed over the permanent fixture. Once on top he had an unobstructed view of the nave and choir. To his absolute horror, he could see the lifeless body of his brother lying in his own blood on the floor.

"Murderers!" he screamed, pounding his closed fist against the wooden frame of the organ. "Nooo!" he shrieked desperately, looking up to the ceiling as if he was trying to force an explanation from the heavens.

Politien climbed up beside him, placing his hands on his shoulders. Lorenzo offered no resistance to his subject's comforting grip. They descended off the organ. Politien led him to a chair in which he collapsed, grasping his head with both hands.

"My poor brother... has been murdered... by animals," he sobbed. "Why should he have perished by the sword which was destined to kill me?"

With a sudden surge of energy, Lorenzo pounced towards the door that led back into the nave, but he was quickly stopped by his faithful supporters.

"My Lord," Politien forcefully intervened. "It would be dangerous for you to go out there unarmed. We must remain in this place." Politien climbed up the organ so he could assess the current situation in the nave. He saw that a crowd of de Medicis supporters had gathered in the church.

In fact, as soon as they had realized what was happening, the de Medicis supporters had unanimously and promptly sought out the culprits in order to castigate them in a fashion they rightly deserved - death. The first one to die was cardinal Riario, who was executed behind the altar by the sword of one of the retaliators. However, the fatal attack on the cardinal's person had given the other assassins a chance to escape from the church, unscathed. Outside the church, they and other conspirators had gathered and promptly converged towards the Palazzo Vecchio. Among them was Archbishop Salviatti who, until this moment, had been a distant observer. As they walked towards the Palazzo, they shouted "Liberate the people", in an attempt to stimulate support among the citizens who had gathered along the way. But instead, the citizens of Florence shouted "Vive Les Tourteaux" (the motto of the de Medicis) and pursued the assassins throughout the streets in order to lynch them.

Although Salviatti and the remaining conspirators managed to reach and penetrate the Palazzo, once they had entered the fortress, they fell upon the city magistrates who were anticipating their arrival. Petruci, the gonfalon carrier, grabbed Salviatti and single-handedly hung him outside the ledge of one of the windows of the Council Room. From the street, the citizens could see the macabre sight of the archbishop's cadaver swinging at the end of the rope. This was the first hanging by the enraged citizens of Florence people who seized the opportunity to seek political and personal vengeance. Within one half-hour, twenty-seven victims had perished to the vengeful swords. Francesco Pazzi, who had sought refuge in his own home, was dragged back to the Palazzo Vecchio and hanged beside Salviatti.

Politien jumped off the organ and returned to Lorenzo's side. "The coast is clear. Your loyal people have chased Bandini and his conspirators out of the nave," he comforted. "We are with you, My Lord."

Lorenzo extended his arm towards his faithful supporter. "My friends," he expressed, nodding his head, waving the other people present to come to his side. "Florence is indeed blessed with good people."

"Let us escort you to the Palazzo," insisted Politien. "We have to take you to a secure place as soon as possible."

Lorenzo nodded his approval.

The corpulent man walking along the narrow cobblestone street had a certain noble air. His apparel, though modest, had a certain quality, tastefully combining colors and accessories.

Andrea di Cioni, known as Verrocchio, was one of Lorenzo the Magnificent's favorite artists. Lorenzo had placed many orders for Verrochio's works of art, making him the most sought-after artist of Florence. Verrocchio was considered to be Donatello's best student. After spending some time as a silversmith, then some time as an engraver, he had joined Donatello's studio where, under the watchful eye of the Master, he had learned and mastered the arts of painting and sculpture.

Verrocchio paused in front of the door of a stone frame home. It was one of many houses that were squeezed together on either side of the narrow passageway of the street, where direct sunlight was limited to a few hours around high noon. The unaccustomed visitor seemed bothered by the stench of the neighborhood. He knocked on the door.

"Who is it?" asked a voice from inside.

"Verrocchio."

The door opened onto the youthful, healthy figure of a young man in his mid-twenties.

"Master Verrocchio," acknowledged the young man, in a respectful manner. "To what do I owe the pleasure of your visit?"

"My dear Leonardo, I have come with good news. May I come in?"

"Do forgive me. Please, come in," Leonardo invited. "I am surprised by your visit. Please excuse my humble quarters. They are not worthy of your person." He walked across the room and brought an old wooden bench for his old master to sit on.

Leonardo Da Vinci was a robust man, blessed with a strong physique and elegant features. The people who crossed his path and witnessed his natural grace felt drawn to him. He had the gift of helping melancholic souls regain hope. As a speaker, he had been known to swerve people's opinions.

"We have not seen much of you, Leonardo. How have you been?" Verrocchio asked with concern. "Your departure has saddened some of your comrades."

"Master, you know I had to leave."

"Had to? Leonardo, you did not have to. You know that my door is wide open," Verrocchio protested. "You were my most promising student."

"My stay in prison was unjustified, but it has opened my eyes," Leonardo explained, as his eyes darkened with anger. "It has demonstrated to me that in life, when judgment comes, I stand alone." He paused and turned away from Verrocchio. "When I painted the God-child I was imprisoned. What am I to expect if I paint Him as an adult?"

"You must refrain from thinking in this fashion, Leonardo," his master suggested. "Yours is a divinely inspired talent. Do not let human judgment destroy you."

Leonardo turned towards his tutor. "You have brought good news?"

Verrocchio paused and stared at the floor as if to bring back to memory the purpose of his visit.

"Hmm yes."

He lifted his eyes to meet Leonardo's.

"As you know, the Pazzi conspiracy has taken its toll. The death of Giuliano, as well as the attempt on Lorenzo's life, has brought total chaos to our city. Now that calm has been restored the Florentine Seigniory has decided to take remedial action, in order to deter any other similar attempts."

"Forgive me, Master, but what incited this conspiracy?" Leonardo asked, knowing that Verrocchio, with his position and influence in the Seigniory, would be well informed.

"For many months, the Pazzi had prepared this conspiracy in Rome, and were apparently able to get support from Pope Sixte IV. As you know, cardinal Riario was the Pope's nephew and his role consisted in ridding Florence of the de Medicis hold. This would have been the first step towards a total enslavement of the Florentine Republic's Church."

Verrocchio paused. He pointed a finger at the table on which were set a wine bottle, some cheese and a bread.

"I trust that you have wine in that amphora?"

Leonardo smiled at his old mentor's straightforwardness. He walked over to the table and poured wine into a delicate pottery glass, which he handed to his guest. Verrocchio had followed his every move like a child anticipating a treat from his mother.

"To Florentine vineyards!" he toasted as he took a drink from the glass.

"Would you perhaps like some cheese?" Leonardo offered.

"I have just eaten." This answer, however, was not in accordance with the intense way with which Verrocchio stared at the food.

"Where was I?" He collected his thoughts, although his attention was still focused on the food.

"Ah yes, the Pazzi conspiracy. Apparently, the plan was to have the prelate head a group of conspirators in the invasion of the Palazzo Vecchio to massacre all the members of the Seigniory who would not surrender. This was to be followed a few hours later by the entrance into the city of the mercenaries of Niccolo da Tolentino and of Lorenzo Giustini, who were to put an end to the powers of the de Medicis and replace them with the Pazzi family."

Leonardo observed as Verrocchio reached out for the bread stick and broke off a piece, his eyes practically protruding from their orbit, as if the eyelids were not able to restrain them. With his right hand he grabbed a knife and cut himself a generous portion of cheese. Then, as if to defy all laws of elasticity, he forced both the piece of bread and the piece of cheese into his mouth. He clasped his hands just below his rotund stomach, his joined arms forming a cradle that seemed to act as some sort of support.

"What about Bernardo Bandini?" Leonardo interjected obviously curious to learn more about the events that were shaking his city.

"You mean the murderer of Giuliano de Medicis?" Verrocchio barked out in a ferocious tone. The mention of Bandini's name had angered the Master, a man Leonardo had, until then, always admired for his calm. "The traitor managed, by some miracle, to reach Constantinople by boat, where he requested protection from the Sultan. Fortunately, the Sultan did not take too kindly to Bandini's notoriety. He arrested the culprit and returned him to Florence, chained like an animal." Verrocchio was visibly excited by the mental image of Bandini being chained.

"So what will happen to him?"

"He will get what he deserves," Verrocchio responded, enunciating every syllable. "Tomorrow, at dawn, he will be taken to the Bargello where he will be executed."

The Master paused. He looked at his young apprentice, with tenderness usually manifested by a father to his son.

"You have the potential of being a great artist. You are gifted."

Leonardo felt somewhat embarrassed by the master's compliments, but also derived comfort from his kind words. Never before had Verrocchio verbally praised his efforts so openly.

"The Seigniory has given orders to a group of artists to make paintings of the conspirators condemned to the gallows, as a warning to those who would attempt to oust the present government."

Verrocchio got up, walked towards Leonardo and put his hands on the young man's shoulders.

"Tomorrow, Bandini will hang. I have suggested to the authorities that you do the painting."

Leonardo's face flushed as the words left Verrocchio's mouth.

"You are mistaken, Master," he protested, as he turned away. "I cannot bring myself to witness such a barbaric event. I cannot bear the sight of humans taking other humans' lives. Unlike other people, I do not find public executions entertaining."

The thought of the event unsettled Leonardo's stomach. He shuddered as he felt a chill travelling through his body.

"The Seigniory requires the portrayal of the corpse of the conspirator hanging from the gallows as a warning destined to anyone who would attempt another overthrow of the government. The last thing we want is another blood bath. They feel that paintings testifying to the punishments may act as a deterrent."

"How can you ask this of me?" Leonardo turned back and looked at the older man, his eyes defiant.

"Leonardo, you must think of this as an opportunity to build a reputation as an artist. You know how Lorenzo appreciates art. You must expose him to yours. Tomorrow's execution, no matter how barbaric you may think it to be, may help you to gain control on your destiny. You must take advantage of this opportunity. After all, what good is a talent if no one can experience the beauty of its fruit?"

Verrocchio paused again.

"You must seize this opportunity, Leonardo!" came the thunderous conclusion.

Verrocchio's argument had hit sensitive chords in the young artist.

"Your wisdom has no limit, Master Verrocchio."

Leonardo could hardly contain his smile. Verrocchio, the man he had looked up to for so many years, had in one sense, lifted him on the same pedestal.

"The confidence you are showing in my humble ability is most flattering. I hope I will find the inspiration to live up to such expectations."

"Ah!" Verrocchio exclaimed, as he got up from his chair, visibly happy. "Your decision is a wise one." He walked to Leonardo and took him in a warm fatherly embrace.

The clouds in the Florentine sky were dark and heavy, a befitting setting for the events that were to take place. The hollow-sounding toll of the church bells seemed appropriate. Threatening rain would dampen the main event of the day for the Florentine people. Executions were one of the most popular attractions. Early in life, Leonardo had realized that the people had an insatiable thirst for blood, as long, of course, as it was not their own. He thought of them as vultures on freshly killed prey. They feasted on seeing a being pass from life to death.

Executions always followed the same pattern. Droves of breathing bodies would gather and cheer the arrival of the hero of the day - the condemned - on whom they kept a watchful and unflinching eye, in anticipation of the moment when the hangman disengaged the trap on the gibbets' platform.

Leonardo did not share his fellow citizens' lust for this barbaric entertainment and felt very ill at ease to be present on this day. Ironically, the Seigniory had arranged that he be positioned in an area offering the best possible view of the event.

Accepting Verrocchio's proposal had fueled some internal conflicts which he had not managed to resolve even now, as he sat and pondered the frightful task at hand. He felt heartbroken that he would have to use painting, his first passion in life, to reproduce the macabre playing-out of what he considered man's most repulsive act, the killing of another human being.

"I must try to draw this scene without letting my emotions show through. I must try to be objective," he mumbled, reminding himself of the true purpose of the exercise as he prepared the charcoal and paper that he would use to make his sketches of the horrid display.

All around him, the citizens of Florence had gathered, their voices blending into a frightful morbid chant. The dreadful noise penetrated Leonardo to the core. It resembled the growl of a huge feline about to pounce on its suspecting but defenseless prey. The growling suddenly transformed into a roar as the spectators cheered the arrival of Bernardo di Bandini Baroncigli.

Despite the inevitable outcome of this day, the condemned man had still insisted on dressing elegantly. He wore a hat, a black satin doublet with an overcoat lined in fox fur and a red velour collar. Long black breeches complemented his apparel.

"Death to the conspirator!" shouted a man in the crowd as Bandini was being led to the gibbet.

"Death to the conspirator!" acknowledged the crowd as they thrust their fists in the air. The collective mood was festive.

Leonardo looked around him and saw that the spectators of the grisly event were people from all occupations: merchants and peddlers; noblemen and beggars - they had all come to the Bargello to witness the execution.

The roar of the crowd reached a new intensity as Bandini was led to the hangman on the platform.

"Death to the traitor!" came the single voice above the roar of the crowd. Again, the crowd repeated the condemnation.

Bandini remained emotionless, seemingly in a trance, not offering any resistance to his captors. He stood calmly, resigned to his violent fate as his executor placed the noose around his neck.

"Death to the Pazzi conspirators! May they burn in Hell!" cursed a voice.

"Death! Death! Death!" the crowd chanted.

Suddenly, the floor of the gibbet collapsed, severing the victim's link with life. The body bounced at the end of the rope, changing within moments from a vessel of life into a breathless cadaver.

The sight had an almost magnetic effect on the artist. For what seemed to him like an eternity, his eyes had been riveted on the victim's head. The expression on the lifeless face, as well as the swinging of the suspended body, was burning into his memory. The experience left him numb. He finally managed to wrench his head away from the gruesome sight but he could not erase the etched image from his mind.

Then, he felt a sudden surge of energy. As if an external force possessed his left arm, he drew the hanging inanimate object with precise and skilled strokes of the charcoal crayon. Within minutes, he had captured the contorted shape. A few more strokes and the gibbet appeared, followed by other structures essential to the setting of the event. In the margin of the drawing, he made notes on Bandini's apparel, describing all the elements that would help him reproduce faithfully with paints what he had sketched in charcoal.

Somehow, he had managed to master his emotions and to visualize the scene as a subject waiting for a canvas. Despite his personal revulsion, the artist in him had taken over and he had used charcoal sketches and later, paints and canvas, as mediums that would transform the grisly event into a work of art.

2

Hanging Out at Club 230

Anderson Avenue burst with life on this evening. No one over the age of thirty could be seen. This could be explained partly by the fact that the area was mostly inhabited by students, but also because any non-student resident of the area knew better than to stick around on the first back-to-school weekend, reputed for its incessant festivities all around campus.

Most residences looked tame in comparison to Club 230. The line-up in front of the house was a dead giveaway that something worth waiting for was going on. No one in the line seemed to mind waiting; bodies moved to the rhythm of the Powder Blues Band's "Doing it Right" song blaring through the open living room window.

Oscar walked down the street, hand in hand with Angie Percy. The petite radiant young lady was dwarfed by his imposing size, but her naturally wholesome beauty detracted all attention from her height. Many heads turned as the couple walked past. Of course, none of the young men who caught a glimpse of the stunning woman dared to show their approval in front of the strapping giant, but once the couple had passed, they could feast their eyes. Angie felt genuinely uncomfortable with the attention paid her. At least, in her hometown, the many hot-blooded young men who appreciated her also respected her because of who she was, but also for fear of the consequences if they didn't.

The din of the festive crowd lined up in front of Club 230 grew louder and louder as they approached.

"We'll never get in!" Angie exclaimed.

"Don't worry." Oscar reassured. He led her down the dark driveway to the back yard. "We'll get in through the kitchen door."

From the yard, they could see that the kitchen was already overcrowded.

"I'm not going in there. Look at all the people. They're like sardines," Angie complained.

"Come on, we've made it this far!" Oscar countered as he gently but firmly led her by the hand into the house.

"Hey dude!" Eugene greeted Oscar above the blaring music and the noisy crowd. "Where's the lady?"

"Behind me," Oscar pointed over his shoulder.

Angie raised her hand to confirm her presence.

Eugene and Leo were busy behind the makeshift bar serving the thirsty guests, putting money paid for the beers into a cardboard box that they'd lined with a garbage bag and put at their feet. They extended their hands over the bar to greet their friend.

Eugene glanced at Oscar while pouring a beer into a plastic glass and then said to Angie, who had made her way to Oscar's side:

"Could you tell me what the hell you see in the guy?" he asked, trying to look serious.

"He's got certain talents," Angie responded with a devilish smile.

"It's definitely a case of falling in love with the underdog," Edmond interrupted from behind Angie. "It's obvious she fell for the poor scrawny and defenseless bastard who can't fend for himself. Angie found this weakness quite attractive and exploited it. The rest is history."

Angie turned around and faced Edmond.

Eugene shrugged his shoulders.

"I'd hate to see giants where you come from Eddie," he responded to his friend's answer.

"Hi Angie. How are you?" Edmond greeted.

"Dangerously good and ready to party," she answered.

"Nice to see you too, Eddie," Oscar tried to remind his friend of his presence.

"Just excuse me one moment while I get rid of this guy and I'll be right back with you. This shouldn't take long," Edmond said in his characteristically deadpan humor. Angie laughed.

Edmond greeted Oscar with a high-five hand slap in the air.

"So nice to see you could make it," Oscar teased.

"Rumor has it that I live here."

Eugene walked over from behind the bar to join his friends.

"Did you see the women around here. It's enough to make a guy dizzy," he exclaimed.

"Or cock-eyed," Edmond teased referring to Eugene's wandering eye.

"Cute. Real cute, you big ape," Eugene fired back.

"My! Are we getting testy or what?" Leo teased from behind the bar, enjoying the bantering between his two roommates. "But I have to admit with my friend Trap, that the women are absolute knock-outs, and I get first pick." He glanced towards Angie who seemed amused by the conversation. "My first choice would be Angie of course, but since she's already taken, I'll settle for second best."

Angie directed a coy smile of appreciation at Leo for his diplomatic comeback.

"You make me sick, Leo!" Edmond responded to Leo's recovery. "You're a pig."

"You're just saying that to make me feel good."

"Here's to a great party," Oscar toasted.

Beer bottles met in approval. The participants then drank the contents of their beer in a chugging contest.

Rodney, the evening's DJ stood behind his work desk, which had been transformed into a makeshift disk jockey table. Rodney's body moved to the sound of The Steve Miller Band's Jungle Love, as he fingered through the record selection, picking out the music that would be heard during the evening.

"Do you take any requests?" Oscar asked trying to adopt a British accent.

"As a matter of fact, I do, but I never play them."

"Care for a little brewski?" Edmond asked as he handed Rodney a beer.

"Don't mind if I do. Hmmm, this is a bit warm."

"We made a few stops along the way. There's wall to wall people downstairs," Oscar explained.

Rodney turned around and opened the door to a small bar refrigerator located beside his bed.

"Good thing I stocked the fridge before the party," he said as he pulled a beer bottle out of the refrigerator and replaced it with the beer can his friends had brought him.

"Do you think you have enough?" Edmond asked sarcastically pointing at the numerous beers inside the refrigerator.

"Better be safe than sorry!" Rodney replied. "Would you gents like one?"

"Do bears shit in the bush?" Edmond answered.

"Help yourselves," Rodney commanded as he changed records on the second turntable. He phased down the volume of the song that was playing, flipped a switch which brought the second turntable into line. As the Rolling Stone's song "Satisfaction" started, the three fellows danced blending their voices to Mick Jagger's while thrusting their hips suggestively every time the word satisfaction was heard.

"Yo-oh", a familiar shout resounded, barely audible over the loud music coming from the hallway. Charles entered into the room, his tall athletic body clad in a tapered peach shirt and beige cotton pants, quite a contrast to his friends' jeans and hockey jerseys.

"Charlie baby!" his three friends exclaimed.

"Look at the threads he's wearing," Edmond pointed out. "What did you do, mug Calvin Klein and steal his clothes?"

"I sure didn't get these in your closet."

"Glad to see you could make it," Rodney greeted extending his hand to his friend, Oscar and Edmond following suit.

"Did you bring the ladies?"

"They'll be here, don't worry. I told you I'd come through," Charles reassured them in a calm, confident voice.

Edmond turned to the refrigerator, opened the door, pulled out a beer and handed it to Charles. "Here's a cold one."

"Mighty appreciated", Charles thanked imitating a Texas accent.

"What did you do this summer?" Oscar asked. "From the looks of it, you must have hit the jackpot."

"You know me, Dude, a little bit of this, a little bit of that."

"Probably selling his body," suggested Rodney jokingly.

"Are you kidding?" interrupted Edmond. "At a quarter a shot, he'd be worn out before he'd paid for his socks." The comment drew chuckles from the group.

"I bet you he's pushing," Edmond continued.

Rodney observed Charles. He seemed nervous and distracted, obviously uncomfortable with the attention he was getting.

"Guys, I've got to go and check out the ladies. I'll see you later," he excused himself and left the room.

As he stepped out, Charles stopped cold in his tracks and backed up a few steps as if to avoid being seen by someone. He stood still for a few seconds and then continued into the hallway.

Rodney was intrigued by his friend's uncharacteristic behavior.

"I've got to go for a pit stop. Can someone be the DJ while I'm gone?"

"Sure, no problem," agreed Oscar.

Rodney walked out of the room and headed towards the bathroom.

As he reached for the door handle he saw, from the corner of his eye, that

Charles was stepping into Edmond's room and closing the door behind him.

"Hey Charlie!" he yelled out. The music and the chatter of all the people gathered in the hallway buried his voice.

Someone grabbed Rodney's shoulder from behind. The unexpected action startled him and he pivoted abruptly in response.

"Hi Rod." The melodious voice greeted him as he turned. "I didn't mean to startle you."

"Debbie!" Rodney acknowledged, recovering from the surprise. "I'm sorry, my mind was elsewhere, and I... and I..." Rodney stopped short of uttering an explanation as he looked over his shoulder in the direction of Edmond's room.

"When are you going to ask me to dance?" Debbie asked, as she put her arms around his waist and pulled him towards her, determined to get his full attention.

Rodney couldn't help but look again in the direction of Edmond's room. He then looked the other way down the hallway. Charles was nowhere to be seen.

Turning to his attractive friend he replied, "I guess you've just made an offer I can't refuse. Just give me a minute and I'll be right with you. Nature calls."

As he stepped into the bathroom he felt Debbie's hand take a hold of the back pocket of his jeans and she entered into the room with him.

"Do you need any help?" she asked suggestively. She joined her hands behind his neck and pulled herself towards him as she planted her lips on his.

Rodney was dumbfounded. He'd always perceived Debbie as a shy young woman, a devout, serious, no nonsense student, not a live-for-the-moment free spirit.

"Hmmm," he approved. "Normally, I'd give you two hours to stop what you just started, but..."

Debbie leaned against him, moved her hands down his back and firmly squeezed his buttocks.

"Perhaps we can continue what we started somewhere with fewer people," she suggested coyly.

"That sounds good, but I'll have to take a rain check on that," the surprised young man declined with hesitation. "I don't think I'd be too popular with my roommates if I disappeared."

"Are you sure? Why don't we go down and dance? I'll change your mind yet," she challenged.

"I'll join you in a minute," Rodney agreed with a grin, pleasantly intrigued by the proposal. "Now if you don't mind, Nature calls." Rodney gently showed Debbie out of the washroom and closed the door.

The coolness of the night air had a soothing effect on Debbie's skin. For over an hour, she'd danced vigorously in a room where air competed with a dense haze of cigarette smoke. The pores of her skin felt as if they were opening up again, taking in the fresh air. She leaned on the front porch's guardrail, receptive to the multiple aromas of the late summer's night.

Rodney joined her and gently but firmly grasped her hips and pulled them towards him until their bodies met. His approach met no resistance. She pulled his hands around her waist to maximize the effect of his caresses. They stood, oblivious to the activities and the music emanating from the house.

Their tender moment was interrupted by sporadic red, blue and white lights invading the evening sky. The intruding rays traced a path along which a police cruiser traveled. Rodney had a strong suspicion that 230 Anderson was the vehicle's destination and that the motive of their visit was business and not pleasure. The cruiser came to a halt in front of the house. Eric Clapton's "I Shot the Sheriff" was blaring through the open window.

Ironically, the tempo of the rotating red lights blended with the festive beat of the music. Two policemen climbed out of the car simultaneously putting their hats on as they stood beside the vehicle, both stereotypical in their demeanor.

Rodney could not help but wonder how these guys, one of whom was barely older than he was, could put on such an act. As they approached the house, the officers could hardly contain their smiles, especially when three cuties showed up on the porch to see what the commotion was all about.

"Hi guys. Come on in and party," the tall brunette invited as her two friends giggled.

The younger of the two policemen seemed to momentarily forget the nature of the call, but was brought quickly back to reality by his colleague.

"Good evening officers," Rodney greeted politely.

The officers nodded in response. "Are you the resident of this house?" the senior officer asked.

"I'm one of them," Rodney answered. "What seems to be the problem?"

"We've had a complaint of a disturbance. Apparently someone has been disturbing the neighbors by constantly ringing their doorbells," the officer stated.

"I was unaware of this, sir. I've been in the house most of the evening," he explained. "But I promise we'll keep an eye on our guests from now on."

Behind Rodney, the adjoining duplex's door opened suddenly giving way to a man in his late twenties, clad in a bathrobe, his curly hair uncombed and messy.

"There you are!" the man greeted the officers, who looked at him amused at the sight of the bespectacled man before them.

"Great observation!" Rodney quipped sarcastically in answer to his neighbor Steve's statement of the obvious.

By this time, Edmond and Eugene had arrived at the scene, both of them holding a beer in each hand.

"Stevie Baby!" exclaimed Edmond when he saw his neighbor. "So glad to see you accepted our invitation! But you really didn't have to dress up."

"Love the hair," Eugene added, blowing a mock kiss in Steve's direction while winking at him.

The comments generated laughs from the crowd that had gathered on and around the porch area.

"Officers, you should arrest these animals. They should be caged," Steve yelled, enraged by the boys' boisterous behavior.

The two policemen smiled despite themselves. The senior officer looked at the three roommates and decided to address his instructions to Rodney, undoubtedly because he felt that he would better follow his recommendations, given the inebriated state of his sidekicks.

"Could you guys please turn the volume down. Also do me a favor. Please show your guests where the washroom is," he recommended pointing out to the people urinating on the side of a neighboring house.

"Have a good party, fellows!" he concluded with a smile.

Steve, flabbergasted by what he'd just witnessed, retreated to his apartment in a huff, slamming the door behind him. The bystanders who had witnessed the deliberations cheered the departure of the twit who had tried to put an end to their fun.

"Calm down and go and have a nice bath," Edmond prescribed to his neighbor as he left. "Oh, I forgot, we borrowed it. I guess you haven't noticed... yet," he muttered in a chuckle.

Eugene, his right eye straying slightly due to his temporary drunken state, struggled to lift himself to a standing position on the porch railing.

"I've got an announcement to make," he shouted to the crowd. "Will th...the people responsible for disturbing our fr...friendly neighbor Stevie b...baby, please raise their hands." Eugene looked for a sign of admission of guilt.

Everyone looked to see if anyone else would confess, and if so, what would happen to the poor louse. A hand rose in the middle of the crowd.

"I admit. I'm guilty as sin," a voice confessed.

"Please step forward," Eugene commanded. He managed, with some difficulty, to get down from his perch. When the culprit reached him, Eugene hugged him. "Good going! Now please report to ... to the bar. The next beer is on the house! The administration of Club 230 would like to thank you for a job well done." Eugene's slurred public speech was met with another cheer and some laughter from the crowd.

"My... my first public speech," he told his friends, beaming with pride.

"Good old Trap. You should think of becoming a politician," Edmond teased. "You...you...you... sure have a way with words," he said mocking his friend's stuttering.

Many of the people who had gathered outside went back into the house. Others moved on to other destinations.

Debbie, amused by the recent events, grabbed Rodney by the shoulders and kissed him softly.

"The offer is still on," she reminded him.

"Let me walk you to your car."

"Maybe I'll convince you on the way." They walked towards her car, pausing frequently to kiss. Rodney leaned on the car with Debbie facing him. They embraced passionately, awakening a deep natural desire within them. Debbie backed away pulling her friend to a straight stand. She pulled her keys out of her coat pocket and in one motion unlocked and opened the car door. She sat on the passenger side, and closed the door. She then rolled down the car window.

"Catch!" she said as she threw the keys toward Rodney and flashed him a daring smile. "Let's go for a ride."

"Where to?" asked Rodney his mind racing as he thought of the possibilities.

"Around," Debbie answered evasively, knowing that she had his attention.

Rodney threw his head back and laughed.

"I'm sorry Debbie. Nothing personal, but I really should stick around." He paused and shook his head "You're a terrific girl. I can't believe I'm saying no."

"You can change your mind," she persisted.

Rodney pressed the car keys gently into her hands, his smiling eyes looking directly into hers.

"That's too bad," Debbie sighed. "Rain check?"

"Rain check. Definitely." Rodney agreed.

He took a deep breath, inhaling as much of the sweet evening air as he could.

"I'll tell you what. Since this is such a lovely evening, let me walk you home. It'll do us both some good and it'll give me the opportunity to spend a bit more time with you," Rodney compromised.

"But, what about my car?"

"You're apartment is only a hop, skip and a jump away from here. You can come and get it in the morning."

Suddenly his face lit up. "Hey, I've got a better idea! I'll drive it home to you in the morning if..."

"If what?" Debbie enquired.

"If you invite me for a nice home-cooked breakfast."

"Hmmm. Let's walk to my place and it'll give me a chance to make up my mind about that. You're not home yet, you know," she challenged.

"Trap, you're pissed!" slurred Edmond to Eugene while he struggled to maintain his balance. Eugene sat on the chesterfield beside Mark, a weekend visitor. Mark's face was devoid of color, an indication of his advanced alcohol-influenced state. Eugene's right eye still strayed off center as he tried to respond to his friend's painful but accurate allegations.

"You sh.... sh.... should talk, Eddie. You're so dr.... dr.... drunk you pissed your pants," he charged as he pointed to Edmond's pants.

Edmond bent over to see if what he was told was true, but the motion was too much for his impaired equilibrium. His attempt to recover his lost balance propelled him four steps back and onto the floor. However, true to form, he managed to keep his bottle of beer upright, minimizing the spill.

"See?" he pointed to his drink, proud of his achievement. "I didn't spill a drop!"

Sergio Rochetta, another of their friends, sat in an old and worn easy chair observing their jester-like actions with amusement.

"Way to go Eddie! That was really smooth. 'Whatever you do, though, don't tell anyone that we're friends.'"

Sergio was an old hat at the Club 230 follies. He was often teased, sometimes because he aspired to be a famous artist (he was a Fine Arts student) but mostly because the guys felt that he was compatible and complementary to their group. Sergio always took in stride the non-malicious jokes aimed at him and more often than not, came back with subtle and successful repartees of his own. He'd visit his friends on an irregular basis, that is, whenever it pleased him. And he was always received with wide-open arms.

"Where the hell are the other guys," asked Eugene, suddenly concerned by their absence.

"Oscar's gone home with Angie, which proves that sometimes it pays to take your lunch to a smorgasbord. Leo has disappeared in his room with a dish ... I believe her name is Jane ... and Rodney ... hmm ... where is Rodney anyway?" enumerated Sergio with remarkable verbal agility. As was usual with him, alcohol's effects were barely discernible. He seemed to have a high threshold of tolerance to booze. His stocky body was very efficient in dissipating the effects.

"I lost sight of him halfway through the evening," he continued.

"Last time I saw him, he was on the porch, talking to the cops," Mark Masters uttered with his eyes closed.

"Yeah, that's when I gave my speech," reminisced Eugene, obviously happy with the experience.

His comment was followed by the sound of the front door opening and closing, and then successive thumps of footsteps.

"Speaking of the devil! Gentlemen I give you Beelzebub," Sergio announced after peeking in the hallway.

"Where were you?" asked Eugene.

"Around," responded Rodney, tickled by this opportunity to use Debbie's evasive answer on his friends.

Other footsteps resounded on the staircase. A tall, well-proportioned brunette walked into the living room. She was a woman in her thirties.

Her very pretty face was highlighted by large dark eyes that somehow gave the impression that she may have encountered more than her share of hardships and defied any person who might try to touch her soul. She paused and looked at the younger men in the room.

"Who would like a brew?" she offered.

"Go for it, Rhonda!" came Edmond's affirmative reply, followed by a cheer.

"Rhonda!" the others echoed.

The self-appointed waitress did a head count and walked away towards the kitchen.

Rodney looked at Sergio and pointed in Rhonda's direction, asking who the stranger was. He was surprised to see a woman her age attending a campus party and even more surprised by the fact that she seemed quite at ease among students.

With his finger, Sergio gestured that Rodney should wait a minute, as if his question would soon be answered.

"Rhonda! Rhonda! Rhonda!" the cheer intensified.

"You guys leave my woman alone," protested Edmond, half-dazed.

Rodney looked at Sergio again, questioningly.

Sergio nodded affirmatively, a devilish grin confirming Rodney's suspicion. They both laughed.

"You heard!" exclaimed Mark, who had grasped the gist of his friends' wordless communication.

"The best part is that in the morning he won't remember a thing," Rodney burst into laughter.

"Rod, did you meet my woman?" Edmond asked loudly enough to carry all the way to the kitchen.

"Not formally," he responded, thinking that any girl in her right mind would have disappeared after hearing such a chauvinistic comment.

"I'll introduce you to her."

He paused. Suddenly, he started chanting the chorus of the Beach Boys song. "Help me Rhonda. Help, help me, Rhonda..."

His friends laughed. "Give 'er Eddie!" they cheered.

"Here you go, fellas," Rhonda said as she walked into the living room, adroitly holding a tray covered with beer mugs collected from various unsuspecting local taverns and all filled with frothy brew.

"I thought you might appreciate your beer in a mug."

Rhonda offered Edmond a mug and kissed him on the forehead, provoking a collective "Woooooo!" from the other fellows. She then went on to serve his friends.

"Beer mugs served by big jugs," Edmond slurred his questionable rhyme, describing her obvious attributes.

"Oohh!!" the boys reacted, expecting some kind of retaliation from Rhonda. However, she merely turned and smiled at Edmond as though she'd been complimented by the coarse comment.

"What does he have that I don't?" Mark asked, in a fake naïve tone.

The self-appointed hostess smiled and raised her brow suggestively at Mark, which disarmed him and left him unable to utter any subsequent remark. He picked a mug of beer off the tray, his eyes fixed on the captivating waitress, seemingly hypnotized by her.

The front door opened and closed again. Charles entered the room, accompanied by Professor Collins, both men obviously impaired.

"Hey Rod, look who I brought!" Charles exclaimed pointing in Collins' direction, the expression on his face like that of a boy taking his idol to school to meet his friends.

Rodney was floored by this unexpected visit.

"What's the matter Rodney? You look like you've seen Elvis," Sergio observed his friend's surprise.

"Mr. Collins," acknowledged Rodney, trying to regain composure.

"People call my father Mr. Collins. You can call me Bill," William Collins responded. Like the young men gathered in the room, Bill looked somewhat pickled.

"I found h... him wandering on... on campus, so I asked him over," Charles explained, his body teetering. He placed his arm around the professor's neck. "Is that right, William?"

"You bet your booties?" acknowledged Collins in an uncharacteristic manner. He looked around the room and seemed to recognize Rodney. Then with an expression of puzzlement on his face he asked. "Excuse me, but, I know you, don't I?"

"I'm Rodney Blake, one of your students," Rodney answered, astonished that Collins' didn't recognize him.

Of course," Collins recovered. "Please forgive my memory lapse."

"Isn't that just wonderful!" Charles broke in. "He doesn't even remember who you are. Bill! Bill! Do you know who I am?"

"Don't be silly. You're my good friend Charles. My right-hand man in my brilliant work on the Sparo Spear project, the best damn plane ever built," Collins' voice cracked with emotion as he spoke, like a father proud of his child's accomplishments.

Charles and Collins locked into a fraternal hug.

"Give the man a drink. He needs one. He needs to get drunk," Sergio suggested.

"I think he's there already," Mark muttered through the side of his mouth.

"Okay! Then, let's get him drunker!"

"I'm an alcoholic," confided Collins out of the blue. "I'd been on the wagon for ... jeez, for over ten years. I've fallen under her spell once again," he explained, with a hint of disappointment in his voice.

"Whose spell are you under?" Sergio asked.

"The bottle, young man," Collins barked out.

"I never pictured him like this," Rodney confided to Charles, shocked by this revelation. It somewhat explained the professor's recent behavior in the classroom.

"Who is this guy?" Sergio wanted to know.

"My Aeronautical Physics professor," Rodney answered.

Sergio pulled a cigarette out of his pack and lit it all the while analyzing Collins, as was his habit. He inhaled the smoke and turned to Edmond.

"This is what we'll look like in thirty years," he predicted with irony.

"Right on," muttered Edmond oblivious to what was happening.

Charles crouched and sat on the floor, leaning his back against the wall. Collins, with surprising agility for someone in his state, not to mention his age, followed suit and sat beside him.

Rhonda walked towards them.

"Would you gentlemen like a beer?" she asked politely.

"Please, if it's not too much trouble," accepted Collins.   Charles nodded.

"By.... the way, Rhonda. Thanks for accepting the invite," Charles whispered.

"I wouldn't have missed it for the world, Chuck," Rhonda replied and walked out of the room.

"I bet you Jake will be pissed off," Collins said, his chin pivoting on his chest as he fought to keep it upright.

"Jake who?" Charles asked.

"Macintosh."

"You m … mean, him and Rhon …Rhonda are doing the mambo jumbo?" Charles was surprised at this revelation.

"I'm sur… surprised he lets her out of … of his sight. "

"She's a fox," Charles said, commenting on her appealing physical attributes.

"I'd … I'd say she's m… more like a hy… hyena," Bill Collins suggested.

Charles opened the door to Rodney's room. "Why are you hiding in here? You're knocked out?"

Rodney, stretched out flat on his bed, did not turn his head. "Just taking a short break. I'll be down for the extra innings."

Charles walked over to him. "Rod, this was a great party. I hope I remember it tomorrow." He looked up at the ceiling and let out a deep-felt sigh. Rodney, aware of the uncharacteristic on-edge-behavior of his buddy all evening, lifted himself up in a sitting position.

"Tell me about Collins."

"What... what about him?" Charles responded abruptly. Rodney had hit a sensitive chord.

"I'm surprised to see him here."

"He's a good man, you know. He's in trouble. I can't believe what they did to him. Something's wrong, Rod. Something stinks. I could tell you things that would make your skin crawl."

"What things?" Rodney prompted.

"It's complicated, man … right out of a spy novel..."

The door opened again. Eugene leaned against the doorframe.

"Mind if ... if I come in," he asked.

Charles turned to Rodney and commanded: "Forget what I said," and stormed out of the room.

"Was it something I said?" Eugene asked

"No, something I said, I guess," Rodney answered, more perplexed than ever by Charles' strange behavior.

"He's out for the count," Sergio proclaimed as he lifted Mark's arm. "Another victim has succumbed to excessive beer consumption at the festivities!"

Sergio placed an unlit cigarette between Mark's lips. The sight of Mark fast asleep, a cigarette hanging from his lower lip, generated some tired laughs from the few still awake.

"You guys are the best friends I have," mumbled Charles, the effects of the alcohol having taken its toll.

He sat on the floor next to Professor Collins who was leaning on the sofa, fast asleep.

"I really like being with you guys," he blubbered, tears streaming down his cheeks.

"You haven't seen the last of us yet," Sergio promised trying to comfort him. "Cheer up Charlie, we're having a party."

"I'm sorry guys," he continued, sniffing. "You don't understand ... you just don't understand ... I'm really sorry ... please ... please forgive me." Charles fell over against the sleeping professor and passed out.

Rhonda had quietly witnessed the conversation. She got up from the easy chair she'd occupied for the past hour and grabbed Edmond, who was still struggling to stay awake.

"Come on. It's time for us to go to bed," she commanded as she took his arm and pulled his one hundred and eighty pound body to its feet.

Sergio and Rodney observed the ease with which she handled her mate. They looked at each other, impressed by this demonstration of strength and balance.

"Good night fellows," she said over her shoulder.

"Do you need any help?" Sergio volunteered.

"I'll be just fine," she reassured.

"You should ask Eddie if he'll be okay," corrected Rodney. "I think he's biting off more than he can chew," he complimented.

Rhonda turned her head towards Rodney and blew him a kiss followed by a wink in appreciation of his comment.

"I'm just a pussycat," she added and led Edmond up the stairs.

"Wow. What a woman!" Sergio said to Rodney. "How did he manage to get her?"

Rodney shrugged. "She must be desperate."

"I'm all hers, whenever she wants," Sergio wished.

"Could it be that you're desperate... or maybe jealous?" Rodney tried to get a reaction.

"Both! Aren't you?" Sergio replied.

"Hey, I'm too buzzed to be jealous. And I'll leave the desperate part to you." Rodney paused and stretched out his arms.

"We're the only two still going," he pointed out as he muffled a yawn. "I'm beat." He sat back in his easy chair and observed Sergio puffing on a cigarette.

"Why don't you quit smoking?" he asked, concerned.

"I like it too much," came the reply. Sergio yawned loudly, mouth wide open. He stubbed his cigarette in an empty beer bottle and lay down on the chesterfield, his feet hanging over the end and his head resting on Eugene's lap.

"I'm so tired all of a sudden. It's hitting me, just... like..."

He didn't finish his sentence. Like his buddies before him, Sergio was out like a light.

The sight of his friends' motionless bodies made Rodney all the more conscious of his own fatigue whose grip became more like a stranglehold by the minute. His mind gradually dissociated itself from reality and began its nocturnal tour of dream world.

The early morning sun sent beams of intense light into the living room of Club 230. Eugene moved his right arm and tried to cover his eyes. His head pounded like never before, feeling as if his skull had somehow been wedged in a large vice. Unable to find a comfortable position, he shifted his thigh from under Sergio's head and rose from the chesterfield. Struggling to keep his body steady, he slowly shuffled out of the living room, laboring to keep his feet from dragging on the wood floors.

The stairs seemed steeper than usual, causing him to grip the banister in an attempt to find more leverage as he climbed. At the top, he turned towards Edmond's room. The half-opened door partly blocked sunrays streaming through the curtainless bedroom window. However, when he pushed the door to walk in, the blinding beam of light that suddenly lit the hallway forced Eugene to back up to the darker side of the hallway. After a few moments, he got his bearings and as he'd done many times before, he entered Edmond's room without knocking.

The room was in shambles. The dressers had all been stripped of their drawers, the contents thrown into one big heap in the middle of the floor. Eugene's heart started racing at the sight of the unusual mess. He turned towards the bed. On it laid Edmond's naked, motionless body, face down on top of the sheets. Eugene froze, dark thoughts frantically spinning through his mind.

"My God, can it be?" he wondered, fearing the worst.

His heart pounded loudly, resounding in his ear like a drum. He slowly approached the bed and leaned over, listening for any sound from the prostrate body on it. He couldn't hear any breathing. Desperately, he grabbed Edmond's shoulder.

"Eddie!"

The body reacted to the touch.

"Hey!!" Eddie slurred his protest. "Leave me alone."

"Phew!" he exhaled relief as he sat beside Edmond his back leaning against the headboard. He was immensely relieved.

"What the hell happened here?" Leo's voice thundered from the room entrance. "Did I miss a hurricane or what?"

The loud volume generated by Leo's voice, woke Edmond who pushed himself away from the mattress and dazedly looked around the room.

"What the fuck?"

The sound of his own voice was too much for his hangover. He fell back onto the bed and turned to his side, grasping his forehead with one hand and shielding his eyes from the light with the other.

"My head!" he complained.

Within moments, the others, awakened by the commotion, gathered in the bedroom.

"What tornado hit this place?!" Sergio exclaimed as he walked in with Mark.

"When did this happen?" Mark asked.

"I don't have a clue," Edmond answered as he lifted himself off the bed and started to sift through his belongings, trying to establish if anything was missing. "Where's my wallet? Ah there it is," he exclaimed happy to find it. "Nothing seems to be missing," he added, as he looked through its contents.

"Where's Rhonda?" Rodney asked.

"Who?" Edmond didn't remember her. His reaction prompted laughs of disbelief.

"She's the lucky woman who had you last night, remember? Your woman," mocked Sergio.

By the blank look on Edmond's face, it was clear that he didn't remember that part of the previous evening.

"You missed a good party last night, Eddie," Eugene teased.

"Where?"

"Here," retorted Rodney, chuckling.

"Do you see anything missing?" Leo asked.

"All I have in here is clothes. What would anyone want to do with my clothes?"

"Burn them, comes to mind," Leo suggested.

The image of Charles going into the room during the party flashed in Rodney's mind. *"Could it have anything to do with that,"* he thought. *"Should I mention it to the others?"*

Rodney chose not to bring the subject up, at least not until he'd had a chance of confronting Charles.

"I'm dry," complained Eugene. "I need something to drink. Who wants milk?"

Seeing that his friends were preoccupied by the situation, each one of them probably running through his mind his own personal theory to explain of the events, he didn't insist and made his way downstairs to the kitchen, knowing that the white medicine would be appreciated.

"This pisses me off," Leo shouted in anger. "We organize a frigging party and invite people and to thank us, some asshole decides to ransack through our stuff and rip us off."

"We'll give you a hand with this stuff," Rodney offered to Edmond.

He stopped in mid-movement as an alarming cry resounded from downstairs.

"Oh my God!! No!" Eugene's horror-filled voice reverberated on the old walls.

In answer to the blood-curdling cry, they all rushed out of the room and down the stairs.

Eugene was leaning against the kitchen doorframe, facing out, his hands clutching his head. As the others got closer to the kitchen, they could see feet dangling inside. Rodney walked in first.

Charles' lifeless body, belt around his neck, was hanging from a crossbeam on the ceiling. From the bluish, bloated face, the open eyes were staring blindly at Rodney.

"Nooooo!!"

Sobbing, he grabbed the dead man's legs and lifted him, in a desperate and futile attempt to help his friend.

3

The Bacon Casts Some Doubt

The rustic decor and lived-in look of the tavern conveyed a homey and warm atmosphere. Turn-of-the-century artifacts, testimony of the old ways of logging, were fastened to the barn-like wooden walls, contributing to the cozy ambiance of the draft-beer oasis. Judging by the few occupied tables, it was likely early afternoon, the only time other than after-closing hours that bodies were not filling practically all the available spaces. In the background, the Beatles' song, "Yesterday" blended its memorable lyrics and soothing melody to the quiet afternoon mood.

Rodney, trying to balance his pine chair on its hind legs, was absorbed in his thoughts, indifferent, if not oblivious, to his environment. The formal wear he'd donned for Charles' funeral clashed with the casual decor of the tavern, where jeans and sport shirts, rather than the sober two piece-suits, was the norm.

Rodney could not get used to the idea of his friend's death, nor could he agree with the conclusions of the police.

"It's probably suicide, but we can't confirm it yet," the officer had told him with his raspy voice, a few hours after the roommates had witnessed the macabre scene in the kitchen.

"We've been trying to get a hold of that professor of yours, Bill Collins, but we haven't located him yet. We know that over two months ago, he booked a flight for a NATO conference in Belgium he was supposed to attend. But he didn't get on the plane this morning, like he was supposed to. From what you tell me, he was pretty drunk last night, so chances are he probably crashed somewhere with some broad and didn't wake up in time."

The policeman placed an unlit cigarette between his lips with his tobacco-stained fingers. "He's wanted for questioning, but my guess is he's not a likely killer. He's got no record and everyone I talked to says he's not the killing type. But, we won't know for sure 'til we get a hold of him, now will we? Maybe he bit the bullet too, kid," the man said with intended sarcasm.

The stocky policeman paused as he lit the cigarette.

"Nah, not a chance. We'll find him, you'll see," he waved the smoke away from between them with his hand.

"I'm not a betting man, but my guess is that your buddy turned his own lights out. There's no trace of a struggle. Of course, we'll have to wait for the coroner's report, but I've seen this shit many times before, kid. Everything points to suicide."

Rodney refused to believe that Charles had committed suicide. After all, he'd known Charles since childhood. If there was someone who was up on life all of the time, Charles was the one. When his parents had died in a car accident earlier that year, Charles had still managed to keep a positive outlook on life. He knew that no matter how painful it was, he had to carry on and assume the responsibilities of taking care of his two younger sisters. He would never duck from his moral obligations or not keep the promise he made to his sisters. He had been taught solid family values and he was committed to them.

Rodney also remembered his last conversation with Charles on the night of the party. His behavior had been strange, more like someone who feared for his life than someone who had given up on life.

"We've seen these cases lots of times," Rodney remembered the investigating policeman's cold and insensitive words.

"The kid feels pressure in school. He gets loaded, takes a bit of crack cocaine, and then, pow! he hangs up his skates. It's usually an open-and-shut case."

"It's an open-and-shut case...it's an open-and-shut case..." The words were going round and round in Rodney's mind, echoing the policeman's edict.

Exasperated, Rodney slammed his fist on the table, causing the pitcher of draft to bounce and the half-empty beer mug to fall over and spill its contents off the table and onto his pants. Embarrassed, he saw that all eyes were looking in his direction.

"Where the hell are you, guys?" he growled through his teeth, regretting his burst of anger. He didn't even bother to wipe the beer off his pants. Instead, he lifted his mug off its side and poured in more draft.

"Here Rod, use this to wipe yourself," suggested Mike, one of the waiters on duty.

"I'm really sorry about Charlie. I mean that," he sympathized as he put his hand on Rodney's shoulder.

Rodney turned to the waiter and looked at him nodding his appreciation, his eyes red from all the times he'd cried since the tragic incident.

"Hey Rod!"

Edmond was walking towards him, accompanied by Eugene, Oscar and Leo. The four men, also dressed in suits, joined Rodney at the table. Edmond raised his right arm and with two fingers, indicated his order to Mike who responded with his customary nod, knowing, from the friends' frequent visits to the pub, exactly what he meant. He filled up two pitchers that he held by the handles with his right hand. With his left hand, he opened the freezer door and pulled out five chilled beer mugs and brought everything over to the table.

"I'll take this round," Oscar offered.

"That's all right. This one's on me," Mike covered.

The five boys looked up at him and smiled.

"Thanks Mike," they said, appreciatively.

Eugene got up from his chair, raised his glass and, looking at his friends around the table, toasted:

"To the memory of our buddy Charles. May the memories of our good times together remain forever."

The others got up and raised their beer mugs to meet Eugene's.

"To Charles." They all drank to their friend and sat, observing a moment of silence as if it had been pre-agreed. Each one was absorbed in his thoughts, remembering something dear he'd shared with Charles, trying to understand what had happened, wanting to know why.

Oscar jumped up from his chair and walked to an adjoining table, brought out a chair and set it between his and Rodney's. He then walked towards the bar and proceeded nonchalantly to the freezer where the beer mugs were stored, opened the door, took one out and brought it back to the table.

Leo picked up on Oscar's idea, filled up the mug with draft and placed it on the table before the empty chair.

"Godammit! We're honoring the guy and we didn't even have a chair for him to sit in," Oscar barked out, his voice straining with emotion. Then, pointing his glass towards the chair, he said:

"Here's to you, Chucky baby."

There was not a dry eye around the table. For what seemed like a long time, they stared at the empty chair, as if they hoped that Charles would appear, look at his friends, pick up the glass of beer and join them in a toast. The energy generated by the common wish was of such intensity that they suddenly felt as if, strangely, their friend was among them for a last farewell.

Edmond sat back in his chair and looked around the table at the empty expressions on his friends' faces.

"You guys look like a bunch of veges who've just given their last pint of blood. Wake up, for God's sake! Christ! If one of you guys had croaked, Charlie would be the first one to live it up and party. He knows that that's the way we'd want it. He deserves the same treatment."

"Charlie died because of booze and drugs, man," objected Eugene. "Didn't any of you guys get the message? He was high on crack when he hung himself because..."

"Bullshit!" Rodney interrupted vehemently. The rumble of voices inside the tavern came to a stop and once again all attention was focused on Rodney.

"Take it easy, Rod," Edmond said trying to calm his friend.

"You guys know damned well that Charlie was no quitter. And you know fucking well, Eugene, that Charlie didn't do cocaine. He was high on life, not on drugs," he defended.

"But the cops..." Eugene tried to substantiate.

"The cops don't know dick-all. Caldwell's finest took the easy way out. That means less paperwork, that's all," Rodney growled angrily.

"Cool it, guys!" Edmond intervened with a downward motion of his hands. "The fact is, Charlie is dead, whether we want it or not. We can't bring him back. Give him a break! Who are we to pass judgment?" He paused. "Are we going to get loaded or are we going to jerk around all night? As his friends, we owe him a celebration."

Edmond's rhetoric had the desired effect.

"I'm sorry, Rod," apologized Eugene.

"Forget it. We're all a bit on edge," he accepted.

"Let's get pissed!" suggested Oscar, as he clinked his glass to the one he'd poured for Charlie.

"Let's indulge in Charlie's favorite pastime," toasted Edmond.

"Now, there's an idea!" approved Leo. "Let's find ourselves some ladies."

In times of sadness or sorrow, Rodney usually found solace in late-night walks. Nothing soothed him like the midnight strolls through the city streets, alone with his thoughts when most other people were sleeping soundly in the comfort of their bedroom. The walks usually followed the same pattern. At first, there was the brisk pace, with deep breaths and the infrequent pounding together of the hands. This was the phase of mild depression and self-pity. After a few miles, he usually gained a positive outlook on the problem at hand and came up with possible solutions and self-motivation. Finally, by the time he reached home, he felt ready to tackle any situation.

Rodney had parted ways with his friends when they decided to try their luck with the young women from the next table. During the past few days, tension had invaded his body and had kept him in a grip like that of a champion Sumo wrestler whose title was on the line. The eight-mile stroll from the tavern located in Pratt, over the bridge, along the downtown streets of Caldwell and then across the bridge to the campus, had worked its wonders. After two miles, the impaired walk had given way to a more balanced stride until it reached, near the last quarter, a normal, purposed pace. During the long walk, Rodney had achieved the same clearness of mind that he sometimes found during an intense workout in the gym or during a physical hockey game.

The cool night wind had colored his cheeks a healthy red. The fresh country air that had replaced the city's noxious day gazes supplied the necessary oxygen to rid his mind of all polluting thoughts.

Although he knew that he could not bring his friend back to life, Rodney had decided that he would clear Charles' name. Suicide after all, was considered the coward's way out. Charles' death and the so-called facts surrounding it had given him that reputation and cast a doubt on his character. Rodney had a nagging feeling that Charles had perished by someone else's hands. As his friend, he had to follow his intuition and get to the bottom of it all. He owed it to Charles. He owed it to Charles' two young sisters, who had been devastated by the event.   Moreover, he owed it to himself.

Rodney considered mornings exciting.   Although some awakenings were harder than others, mostly due to previous-night excesses, he always woke up eager to take on the day.   Perhaps it was the fact that his life as a student seldom had any surprises.   The trick was to show up for classes, take good notes, hand in homework and wait until the last minute before cramming all the information gathered for a test or an exam.   Perhaps the idea that the student was accountable only to himself offered some sort of comfort: the only one who benefited from his actions or suffered from the lack of them was Rodney himself.   While summer work had the pressures of a boss telling you that you have to do this by tomorrow and do it well, or else, as a student, Rodney was not accountable to anyone: boss, co-workers, not even to his parents, for that matter.   The responsibility of success or failure was his and only his.

Rodney felt well.   He stretched as he lay in bed.   He noticed that he was still dressed in his suit, which was now quite wrinkled.   Lifting his right leg, he saw that he was still wearing his shoes.

"Hmm. All I have to do now is wash my face, brush my teeth, and go straight to class," he mused. "I must have been really tired," he whispered to himself.

In an energetic hop, he jumped out of bed, walked over to his stereo and turned on the radio.   The morning peace was now broken by the voice of the announcer reading the morning news.

" ...the fatal crash of the combat plane, Sparo Spear M40, during a test flight at the Sparo test air strip.   Prospective buyers of the new revolutionary plane who witnessed the accident were shocked by the event..."

The newscast caught Rodney's attention.   He remembered how the Sparo Spear project had been the subject of many conversations he'd had with Charles. Charles lived and breathed for the day where he could get involved in the project.

"...the pilot, Captain Michael Mazenkowski, was killed instantly. Officials at Sparo Aeronautics had no comments on the incident, but sources have confirmed that due to restrictions imposed by the Federal Government, the shutdown of the national aeronautic manufacturer is a definite possibility." Pause. "In Rome, Prime Minister..." the news continued.

"Damn! There goes our dream, Charles," Rodney muttered with disappointment.

"Fuck! That'll kill the project for sure." He paused. "First Charlie's death, now this. Charlie's dream has died with him."

The boys were in the kitchen, each one setting up to perform his assigned task: Eugene, to cook the food; Edmond to toast and butter the bread; Rodney to wash the dishes; and Oscar to set the cafeteria-type table with a mismatch of many incomplete sets of plates and cutlery.

"Where's the bacon?" Eugene asked.

"On the counter beside you," Edmond answered "Watch it, it might bite."

"I should've known. Who else has enough money to wrap his frozen food in tinfoil?" Eugene remarked, carefully unfolding the wrapper. Then turning to Edmond he said:

"Since when do you wrap your meat in white bond paper?"

"I use it to label my food, so I know what I'm eating," Edmond responded.

"You sure use strange language."

Eugene took the piece of bond paper that had been wrapped inside the tin foil with the bacon and waved it in front of his friend's eyes.

"Where did you find that?"

"Wrapped with your meat. I told you."

"I didn't put it there."

"If you didn't, who did?"

Edmond looked at the paper and read the letterhead: "Sparo Aeronautics. Hey. Isn't that where Charles worked during the summer?"

"Yeah," confirmed Rodney, puzzled by the discovery.

"What are all those numbers?" Oscar asked.

"Some sort of technical numbers, I suppose," Rodney guessed. "How did it find its way into Eddie's freezer?"

"Can I take a look?" Oscar took the sheet from Eugene's hand. "SACOL-OP / HOLD245 / SAM-MOD / SAM-DAD" he read out loud.

Rodney reached for the piece of paper.

"That's Charles' handwriting for sure. Look! He circled this one and wrote N.E.D. beside it and B.I.L. on the other one with a question mark beside it, then crossed it out. I wonder what this means?"

"Why would Charlie pull out specifications?" Oscar asked. "Wouldn't this be top-secret information?"

"We're assuming that they're specifications. But I'd be surprised that a student worker like Charles would have access to classified information. Maybe it's just a worthless piece of paper," Rodney tried to reason.

"Yeah, but why would it be wrapped with my bacon? I sure as hell didn't put it in there!" Edmond paused. "Somebody hid it and the only reasonable suspect is Charlie."

"Okay," Eugene interrupted. "What we have here is the evidence that will solve one of the world's most intriguing mysteries. We've always suspected that Charles was an international spy, right? Come on guys, let's get back to reality. Even if the paper was put there by Charles, on which we all seem to agree, and supposing that this is really classified information, there are still some questions to answer."

He started enumerating the unanswered questions, using his fingers as counters:

"One: Why would Charlie take that piece of paper out and take a chance of being caught? Two: What was he going to do with it? Three: When did he stash it in the freezer? And four, and this is really stretching the imagination, did it have something to do with him killing himself? Did he feel guilty? Or hey, maybe he was killed by someone who found out he had the information!" he mocked.

"To-roo-too-too, too-roo-too-too " Oscar tooted the theme from *The Twilight Zone*. "Something's cooking."

"Come on guys! Wake up and smell the coffee! Charles' death is affecting your brain and prompting you to see things that aren't there. James Bond is fiction!" Eugene reached for the cream pitcher, a ceramic Holstein cow, its tail broken.

"I don't care what you say Trap, but this is weird." Rodney broke in. "One thing for sure, the police were premature in closing this case. It appears to me that there are many stones left unturned."

"I agree," supported Edmond.

"*I may not be crazy after all,*" Rodney thought.

"The only reason I can see why anyone would take out information is to sell it," Oscar was saying. "Corporate espionage is a big thing, you know. They make movies about this stuff. There was even an article in the paper about it, recently."

"Ah, come on, Oscar! Do you really believe Charlie could've done something like that?" Rodney answered. "Charlie was one of us. I don't think any of us would be able to do such a thing."

"All I'm saying is that someone may have offered him good money, maybe so much that he couldn't resist. Or, maybe he was coerced into participating. Maybe someone was blackmailing him, I don't know!"

"What about being innocent until proven guilty," Rodney attacked. "Don't you believe in that?"

"You're right," Oscar conceded. "It's not fair for me to attack someone who's not here to defend himself. But you've got to admit that something's caused Charles' death, either directly or indirectly."

"You guys really believe that, don't you?" Eugene sighed. "Let's allow, for a minute, that it's true. What are you going to do about it?"

"Maybe we should approach the police with the new evidence. Who knows, maybe this'll be sufficient proof to make them ask more questions," Oscar suggested.

"I disagree. Maybe all it'll do is incriminate Charles. How can we explain the paper without making him look guilty? Knowing Charlie, I'm sure he pulled that document out for a good reason and I have difficulty believing that he wanted to sell the information to the highest bidder. I've got a feeling that there's something else behind it." Edmond again reviewed the mysterious wrapping document.

"I'm ready to bet that whoever turned Edmond's room upside down the night of the party was looking for this," Rodney pointed at the paper.

"What makes you so sure of that?" Eugene asked.

"During the party, I saw Charles walk into Edmond's room. He looked nervous. I'll bet he was seen by whoever ransacked the room."

"I'm surprised nobody heard anything that evening," Oscar remarked. "After all, they must've made a lot of noise, by the looks of things."

"Yeah, I'm surprised by that to," supported Eugene. "With all the people who slept here that night, it's strange that no one heard anything."

"Interesting point," Rodney added. "Maybe we should have reported the ransacking to the police."

"We didn't see the use at the time," defended Edmond. "Nothing had been stolen, and as you know, the events of that day sort of took our focus off that."

"They sure did!" Rodney agreed sadly.

"What are we going to do?" asked Oscar.

"I don't know. But for now I suggest we keep it quiet," recommended Edmond, "at least, until we can find some sort of explanation or more evidence."

Rodney could feel the tension building up inside him again. And it seemed that his friends were experiencing the same thing.

"Is anybody interested in an omelet," he offered, trying to change the subject and bring down the pressure.

They all nodded affirmatively. Eugene reached into the refrigerator and pulled out an egg carton and a milk jug, and concentrated on making breakfast. He separated the frozen bacon strands and lined them on a grill, which he then placed on the pre-heated stove.

"Breakfast should be ready in about twenty," he announced.

The telephone rang over the noise in the kitchen. Rodney walked to the living room to answer it.

"Hello?" Pause. "Speaking." Pause. Yeah, Sergeant. What? When?" The color drained from his face. "Yeah... Yeah, OK. I'll talk to you later." Rodney dropped the receiver and stopped it from hitting the ground by grabbing the wire.

Edmond walked in the room. "Who was that?"

"The cops."

"What's the problem," Edmond asked reluctantly.

"They've just found Bill Collins."

"That's good isn't it?" Edmond asked not knowing how to read Rodney's reaction. "Where did they find him?"

"At the morgue."

"What?"

"He got hit by a car, after the party. He had no I.D. on him. Someone just made a positive I.D. today."

Florence, Italy, 1504

As he walked near the Santa Trinita Church accompanied by his friend Giovanni de Gavina, the artist, Leonardo was invited to join some prominent people who had gathered in a group.

"We were discussing Dante's "Divina Comedia" and we were wondering what your impressions are regarding his view on the "Inferno", the "Purgatorio" and the "Paradiso"," asked one of the men.

Pointing in the direction of a small man who had appeared as the question was being asked, Leonardo responded:

"Why don't you ask Michelangelo? He should be able to respond to your question."

Everyone turned and looked in the direction in which Leonardo was pointing. Michelangelo, a slightly hunchbacked man was angered by Leonardo's comment. Thinking that he was making fun of him, he barked out:

"Answer them yourself, you who had set to cast a bronze life-size version of a horse, but abandoned it, so much were you ashamed of it." Michelangelo turned his back on the group and walked away at a brisk pace, his head nodding nervously, as he shook his tousled hair.

When he heard the sculptor's words, Leonardo blushed. He excused himself and walked away followed by Giovanni. *"How could he say such a thing?"* he thought. *"After all, I did complete the clay version of the equestrian monument of Francesco Sforza. Everyone knows the French destroyed it by using it as a practice target."*

"I believe you have something interesting to show me," Giovanni de Gavina said, as he compassionately tried to divert Leonardo's mind from the painful insult he had just received.

His friend's presence made Leonardo feel better. "You are right, my friend. I am sure that you will be impressed by what I have to show you." He stopped suddenly and looked back in the other direction where, in the distance, he still could see Michelangelo. To mock him, he assumed his hunched posture and imitated his gait. "Have you ever seen such grace?" he asked maliciously.

Giovanni knew that the antagonism that existed between the two geniuses stemmed from the pressures exerted on both men by the Florentine court. In public, they both ridiculed the other man's achievements. It was expected of them. However, Giovani knew that this behavior veiled a profound mutual respect.

"Master Leonardo," Salai called out as Leonardo and Giovanni entered the workshop. "We have completed the skeleton of the wing. We will be able to start fabricating the membrane tomorrow."

"Good work, Salai," Leonardo complimented his assistant, placing his hand on his shoulder. Then turning to his friend he asked: "What do you think, my dear Giovanni?"

In the middle of the room stood a huge structure that resembled a giant bat's skeleton.

"What in the name of God is this?"

"This, my dear friend, is the answer to one of man's dreams. It is the first step towards liberating him from the bonds that keep him so close to the earth, stopping him from soaring in the skies free like a bird."

"You cannot be serious, Leonardo!" Giovani exclaimed skeptically, believing that Leonardo was playing some sort of trick on him.

"Serious? Of course, I am serious! I am persuaded that man will be able to fly one day. It is a matter of working with and understanding all the laws of nature," Leonardo protested emphatically, his voice resounding through the room. He paused a few seconds and collected his thoughts.

"For many years now, I have studied the flight of birds, of insects, of bats, and I have forged an understanding of the rudimentary principles of flying. This understanding is the foundation on which I have based myself to design a flying machine."

Indeed, Leonardo had collected in a notebook all his observations, his thoughts and his plans and drawings for future projects. It was while he worked for Ludovic in Milan that he had sketched his first flying machine.

The machine, which looked like a gigantic bird with massive wings, had been suspended from a ceiling. Its inventor had also designed a special ladder that would allow one to climb to the top of the big bird. He also had, at that point, decided to write a four-part treatise on the flight of birds. The first part dealt with the flapping of their wings; the second analyzed their soaring and floating on air; the third compared their flight with that of bats and insects; and the last explained instrumental movement. He had established that human muscles were not sufficient to generate the required energy necessary to propel man into the air. He had therefore endeavored to find a means to convert one pound of human energy into twice or three times its power in order to allow flight.

"But Leonardo, how can man achieve unnaturally something that is inherent to birds?" Giovani asked.

"It would be naïve to think that man can achieve the full potentiality of a bird in flight. As you know, the mind and the body of the bird act as one, permitting it to achieve all the subtleties of flight, such as instantaneous adjustments of power and shifts of weight. Of course, since a flying machine cannot integrate the mind and the body of man into its structure, its reactions and movements will not be as quick nor as accurate as that of a bird."

"Therefore you are admitting that it will be impossible to fly like a bird," Giovanni concluded.

"That is true," confirmed the inventor.

"Then, why do you persist on continuing to find a way of flying?" the painter asked, seemingly confused by the contradiction.

"I agree that man will never be able to fly like a bird. But that does not mean that man cannot fly. You see, the power that a bird requires to simply keep itself aloft is much less than the power it uses for all the other functions necessary to its survival, which force it to do pure acrobatics. The purpose of my research is to find a way of keeping my flying machine in the air, which is the easiest of all flying functions."

Leonardo paused and looked at his friend, whose skeptical frown had changed to one of intrigue as he studied the machine in the middle of the room.

"Perhaps you could explain to me how that device enters into your plan," he said pointing at one of the parts of Leonardo's invention.

"That my friend, is a wing." Leonardo walked across the room and searched through his notebook. He returned to the painter's side. "I have calculated the ratio of wing-span to weight in birds." He pointed to some figures in his notebook.

"For instance, if we take a bat with a body weight of two ounces, it will have a wing-span of half a braccio. However, if we take an eagle weighing 240 ounces, its average wingspan would be of three braccia. From this information, it is safe to assume that the size of the wingspan is not necessarily proportional to the body weight. I have nevertheless been able to acquire some idea of the necessary wing-span to weight ratio."

"What about the wings? A bird's wings consist primarily of thin and light membranes covered with feathers. I fail to see any feathers on your wing," Giovanni pointed out.

"Good observation," Leonardo congratulated his friend, visibly happy that his theory was being challenged by intelligent questions.

"That is the most challenging aspect of constructing the wing. From my many hours of studying birds and bats, I have discovered that the feathery wings of birds require more power than the membranous wings of bats, and that this is mostly due to the permeability of the first, which probably explains why the armature on a bat's wing is much lighter than that of a bird. Therefore, I opted to use a membrane on a wing structure that is very similar to a bat's, as you can see. My next concern was to find materials that were light, resilient, flexible and strong enough to permit the construction of the membranous wing. After much thought and research, I have decided to build a skeleton of green fir branches and willow, with strong raw silk and wire to make the nerve-like chords, steel springs for return motion, strong leather treated with alum for the joints, greased oxhide for thongs and finally, taffeta and fustian for the membrane." Leonardo pointed out to the different materials as he named them.

"Impressive!" praised Giovanni. "However, now that you have given me all the background and the rationale behind your research, can you explain to me in what manner this experimental contraption will fly?"

"With pleasure." Leonardo was becoming more and more excited and voluble. "What I am attempting do is to show that the force deployed by a man on the handle in order to lift the wooden block, which is attached to the wing, will be less than the weight of the block. You see, the handle, which will balance over the fulcrum, is joined to the trunk, if you will, of the wing. Therefore, a downward pressure on the handle will be transferred into an upward motion at the other end of the handle, which will make the wing descend. The combined force of the wing descending with that of the handle going up will be sufficient to lift the block off the ground. This means that one hundred pounds of lift could be credited to the wing and one hundred pounds to the man. If my theory proves true, then two wings together should be able to achieve the force necessary to sustain a man in the air."

"Fascinating, simply fascinating. My dear Leonardo, I am impressed, once again, by your understanding of the laws of nature," Giovanni paid homage. "Tell me. When will you be ready to perform this test?"

"In due time, my friend. In due time!" came the enthusiastic response.

Soaring through the air on its powerful wings, a kite was moving up to a high orbit in order to expand its privileged view of the territory spread out below. From its lofty vantage point, the ruler of the sky kept a vigilant eye on the activities of its subjects, patiently seeking its next prey. Its attention was drawn to the movements of a young boy, strolling through the fields, unaware of the risk he was taking by trespassing on the territory of the king of flying predators.

The lad was absorbed by the whistling wind that rustled through the prairie, kissing every strand of golden grass and every flower stem on its path, making them dance under its gentle caress. Then, as if possessed by an exterior force, he looked above him and saw the kite. As he watched the graceful bird effortlessly suspended in the air, he became mesmerized by its use of the elements to maintain its altitude and its position. However, as the bird started to circle and descend, he was overcome by a familiar fear, as if he knew what the immediate future had in store for him, as if he had lived the same situation at some previous time. Hypnotized, gripped by fear, he watched the kite as it came down towards him. Dark clouds had gathered in a circle around it and the golden sun centered behind, caressed it with luminous strands, emphasizing the contours of its magnificent wings. But as it came closer, the boy could see that its clawed feet were now cocked and extended forward to grab its chosen prey.

Coming out of his stupor, he turned and scurried to escape. However, his feet felt like lead and despite the energy that he deployed, his attempt to flee became sluggish, all forward progression hampered by seemingly slow-motion gestures. He was unable to gain full control of his body's muscular activity. His mind had no control over his body. Uncontrollable panic, amplified by the deafening sound of his frenetic heartbeat, paralyzed his movements and impaired his hearing.

On the ground ahead of him, he could see his slow-moving shadow being progressively covered by that of the predator. Then, at the same moment that his was swallowed by the other's darkness, he felt the predator's claws grip his shoulders. His sense of panic intensified as he was carried higher and higher, helpless in his captor's grip. The child looked below him, and as a whole new perspective of the world unfolded before his young eyes, the fear subsided and was gradually replaced by a feeling of carefree abandon that opened his senses to the new stimuli. The feeling of the wind through his hair, like the caress of a loving mother, brought him to a high level of exhilaration. He felt invincible, superhuman. Pastures and forests were visible for as far as he could see. The altitude gave him a feeling of dominance. Where before, the grip of the predator had been merciless, it now gave him a sense of security, as if he had been lifted by a parent so that he could get a better view of the world.

Suddenly, the grip on his shoulders loosened and the sense of security was lost and replaced by one of foreboding. The talons then released him and as he plummeted at a breathtaking speed, he was enveloped by a sense of boundlessness, as if falling through infinity. Total darkness prevailed once again, and solitude, its customary ally, maintained the distorting effect on the illusion. Somewhere, the sound of an accelerated heartbeat could be heard again, amplifying as if it were approaching.

A clap of thunder resounded, followed immediately by a blinding light that illuminated the glassless window. In the flash of light, the young boy once again saw the dark form of the bird as it approached, its wings fully deployed, its open claws aimed directly at him as it flew through the window and hovered, its wings repeatedly hitting him as he lay paralyzed in his bed.

"Noooo!!" screamed Leonardo. "Please, please no more!" he shrieked as he opened his eyes.

The early morning sunlight was entering through the bedroom window and extended to the bed where Leonardo sat upright, his graying hair and long beard matted by the perspiration that the nightmare had caused.

"Master, are you all right?" inquired the young man who was lying beside and had been awakened by Leonardo's desperate cry. "Was it that dream?" He brushed some of the moisture off Leonardo's face.

Leonardo nodded affirmatively. He patted his bedfellow's covered leg.

"I'll be all right, Salai."

Since his childhood, Leonardo had been having this recurrent nightmare. But this time was the first that he had actually experienced the sensation of flying. "Perhaps this is due to all the energies I have concentrated on developing my flying machine," he tried to explain. He had tested the wings that he had built and had failed to make them fly. Perhaps the solution lay in the soaring. But he had no inspiration as to how he could achieve it.

He shook his head, got out of bed and walked to the bedroom window. He extended his arms over his head and stretched, in an attempt to relax his muscles still tense from the disturbing dream.

"It is truly a beautiful morning, my dear Salai," he said cheerfully, trying to dispel the effects of his nightmare. "It is a splendid day for traveling." He paused, looking out the window at the activities on the street. Then, turning to Salai, he said:

"Master Appiani, Lord of Piombino awaits me. It will likely be beneficial for me to be away for some time. It may allow me to gain some perspective." he said, taking his lover by the hand. "I will think of you." He affectionately stroked the younger man's hair.

It was All Saints' day when Leonardo arrived at Piombino, a small maritime town situated on a point of land jutting into the Tyrrhenian Sea. Its bay, besides being an ideal location for a port, had proven to be strategic and effective during frequent wars and conflicts. From the castle of Rocchetta, which had been erected at four hundred and fifty yards from Piombino as a fortress to defend the territory, it was possible to monitor the multitude of ships that passed through the port of Falesia with their metal cargo from Elbe Island.

As he walked towards the old fortress, Leonardo, wearing a black toque on his head and a pink cloak, symbol of nobility, that covered his shoulders and his pink dress, was well aware that he dressed conservatively in comparison to other gentlemen and lords who tried to outdo each other by donning the most intricate of laces, the rarest of feathers and the finest embroidered fabric. He wished to adopt a style that differentiated him from his contemporaries. He felt that in order to be successful, and therefore be noticed, one had to stand out.

Leonardo considered himself primarily an engineer and an architect. He was practical in nature, always wanting to learn through experience. He had difficulty understanding what motivated philosophers to try to define such intangibles as the soul and the meaning of life. Their definitions were subject to various and divergent interpretations of abstract concepts. There were so many essential and tangible things around him that could be experienced first hand and whose mysteries still remained whole. Therein lay his passion.

Leonardo entered the castle of Rocchetta and introduced himself to one of the magistrates.

"I am Leonardo Da Vinci, Military Engineer and Master Architect, sent by the government of Florence to offer my services to Lord Appiani."

"Ah yes. I am Lorenzo Pastriani, magistrate of Master Appiani's cabinet." responded the magistrate bowing his head, a gesture returned by Leonardo.

"You have come highly recommended by your compatriot Nicholas Machiavelli. Master Appiani has been awaiting your arrival." Gesturing towards a chair, he added: "If you will excuse me, I will announce your arrival to his Lordship."

The magistrate turned and walked towards the huge doors leading to the Lord's quarters.

In his quarters, Iacopo Appiani was occupied with his favorite pass-time. Wearing only black leather boots and the belt for his sheath and sword, he was standing by his bed and looking around him.

"Where are you, my little flower?" he said in a teasing voice. "You cannot hide from me forever." Noticing feet that showed at the bottom of one of the arras, he quietly tiptoed towards it, and with one swift motion, uncovered his playmate.

The young brunette, clad only from the waist down, her beautiful perky breasts exposed to the eyes of her master, smiled, obviously enjoying the little diversion. Giggling, she ran away from the visibly excited Lord, who gave pursuit.

"Halt! In the name of the Pope, I order you to surrender!" the knight in shineless armor ordered, adopting his most authoritarian voice as he pulled his sword from its sheath. Although there was pounding on the door, neither the Lord nor his mistress paid any attention, so enthralled were they by their little chase.

Outside the room, Lorenzo knocked repeatedly, trying vainly to get his master's attention. After some time, giving way to impatience, he entered the room to announce the arrival of the visitor. He was greeted by the fleeing beauty who, surprised by the appearance of Lorenzo, stopped in her tracks. In a moment of exhibitionism, she flaunted her imposing bosom, lifting her arms and shaking her torso from side to side. The eyes of her obviously surprised and involuntary spectator were riveted to her breasts. Behind the tantalizing beauty stood the Lord, in all his excited glory, his facial expression frozen into a shocked grimace, eyes and mouth fully opened.

Lorenzo, undoubtedly regretting his initiative, backed out of the room without uttering a word, gently pulling the doors shut to avoid disturbing anything more than it had already been. For a few seconds, he stood facing the doors, his head bowed and shaking. He returned to the awaiting guest.

"Lo...Lord...Lord Appiani, was ... uh ... momentarily ... incapacitated," he said, struggling to cover the true nature of what he had seen within the chambers. "I will try again in a few moments, if you will bear with me," he added, flashing an embarrassed smile.

Observing the magistrate's discolored face and demeanor, Leonardo, though he had not witnessed the events that had led to his embarrassment, was able to make a fairly accurate assessment of the situation. He turned his back on his host and muffled a laugh.

The doors to the chambers opened and gave way to the young damsel who had caused the Lord to be caught with breeches off and pride exposed. For the sake of appearances, she carried a basket of fruits, but this did not fool anyone. In fact, under the circumstances, it made the situation even more comical. Leonardo contained his smile with great difficulty and in his habitual gentlemanly fashion, bowed his head in respect to the young woman as she passed in front of him. The magistrate, having noticed Leonardo's amusement, wiped the cold sweat from his brow with a chiffon, regretting his actions more and more by the minute. Leonardo directed a sympathetic smile towards the poor man in an effort to relieve him of some of his misery. Indeed, the poor Lorenzo was provided some comfort by this show of support from his distinguished and charismatic guest. In a sudden burst of courage, the magistrate straightened and walked once again towards the massive doors. He knocked. From the other side, a voice invited. Lorenzo entered the room. Iacopo Appiani had donned black breeches and an embroidered purple tunic decorated with white lace.

"How dare you enter uninvited into my quarters?" he barked out to his subordinate. "Speak, before I do away with your tongue!"

Lorenzo swallowed with difficulty.

"My Lord." He paused, nervously clearing his throat. "I knocked several times. Failing to receive any response, I was afraid that something might have happened to your Lordship, so I thought it better to investigate. I beg your forgiveness," he pleaded, bowing his head in repent.

Iacopo's eyes softened as he listened to his faithful servant's explanation. "What is so important that it makes you act so stupidly?" he asked.

"The long-awaited arrival of the Florentine engineer, my Lord," Lorenzo answered, hoping that this would bring his master's clemency.

"Please let the man in. And Lorenzo, I want to speak to you after my meeting with the engineer," he commanded, his raised eyebrow suggesting the possibility of punishment.

Lorenzo bowed his head in response to his master's warning and walked towards the room where Leonardo was waiting.

"Lord Appiani will see you now," he said and bid him to follow.

"Leonardo Da Vinci, engineer from Florence to see you, my Lord," Lorenzo announced and left the room, closing the doors behind him.

"My Lord," Leonardo courteously bowed.

"I am so sorry to have kept you waiting Master Leonardo, but as you know, the responsibilities of governing the people of Piombino are never-ending," he tried to convince Leonardo. "However, enough about my responsibilities; we must tend to the reason you have been convened."

The Lord paused as if trying to recollect the purpose of Leonardo's visit. "I have heard many good things about you from your compatriot Machiavelli," Lord Appiani complimented. "I hear you have served as a military engineer under Cesar Borgia."

Seeing that his statement had brought an expression of total surprise to Leonardo's face he added: "Do not worry. I have no quarrel with you. The conflicts with Borgia's army are now a thing of the past. After all, we have regained Piombino, haven't we?" he said with a laugh, which to Leonardo's ear, sounded more like a growl.

"I have also had the opportunity to work for Ludovic Sforza for the better of seventeen years." Leonardo pressed. "I have the knowledge to serve you well, my Lord."

"The Florentine government will also benefit from your work, my dear Leonardo. As you know, Piombino is strategically located for the defense of the Republic of Florence. And I need Florence to help me rebuild the Palazzo Rocchetta in order to make it the magnificent and impenetrable citadel it once was."

"Other than the age of the fortification, what are the major problems you are faced with in the instance of an enemy attack?" Leonardo asked, trying to get as much information as he could about the work to be done.

Iacopo started pacing around the room, his right hand pulling on his facial hair, his left hand crooked behind his back.

"As you know, the location of the fortification is ideal for observing the approach of any enemy ships; it gives us a chance to ready ourselves for attacks. Unfortunately, as you have probably noticed, the hills facing the fort can and have played in the favor of our enemies who have been able to find refuge behind the trees and rocks, making them virtually invulnerable to any fire from our soldiers." He paused for a few seconds.

"And then there is the problem of trying to protect the residents of Piombino. Should there be a surprise enemy attack, it is almost impossible for any of the citizens to find shelter within the walls of the fortification, mostly due to the distance that separates the village from the fort. And of course, there is the problem of the existing structure itself: the many assaults that it has resisted have weakened it to a point where sometimes we feel that it may not be able to repel any future attacks, especially from canons."

As his new employer spoke, Leonardo was recording his comments in his notebook. He did this in the fashion of left-handed writers, writing his notes from right to left, which meant that to decipher the scribbling, one would have to use a mirror. He paused, looking at his notes to make sure he had all the necessary information.

"My Lord, in order to give you an accurate assessment of what can be done to restore the Rocchetta castle, I will need authority to go about the castle and within Piombino as I please, without any restriction whatsoever," he requested firmly.

"You have my full authorization, as the Lord of Piombino. I will advise Lorenzo of my decision."

"My Lord, I would also require the assistance of your faithful servant Lorenzo. I believe that his knowledge could be instrumental." He hoped that this request would spare Lorenzo from being punished for a minor error in judgment.

"Possibly...Perhaps a little change will do him good. Why not?"

"Very well. I will start immediately." Leonardo turned and walked towards the door.

"Just one moment," interjected Iacopo, surprised by the Leonardo's promptness to get into action.

"Lorenzo!" he opened the door and beckoned to his servant. "Please show Master Leonardo to his quarters."

"Yes my Lord."

"Oh yes, and by the way. Until further notice, I will not be needing your services any more," he informed his magistrate.

Lorenzo felt the breath escape his body, as if pierced by a volley of arrows.

"You will assist Master Leonardo until he no longer requires your services." He paused. "Only then will you resume your responsibility as the magistrate of my court."

Lorenzo felt blood flow through his veins, again.

"Thank you my Lord," he said, relieved by the leniency of his usually unmerciful master. He turned to Leonardo.

"May I escort you to your quarters, Sir," he offered.

As they walked out of the room, Lorenzo turned to the visitor and smiled at him knowingly, aware that his magnanimous nature had saved him.

"Thank you, Master Leonardo. I hope I will be worthy of serving you."

Leonardo smiled back at him. "We have much work ahead of us. You may wish that you had received punishment instead," he warned, laughing. "I will introduce you to the world of science. But first things first. Here is my bag," he ordered jokingly, handing it to Lorenzo.

In early spring, Leonardo, accompanied by Lorenzo, returned to the chambers of Lord Appiani, carrying long sheets of rolled paper fastened by a red ribbon.

"Ah, I have been looking forward to hearing from you on this matter," acknowledged Iacopo as he crossed the room to Leonardo. "My people have been keeping me informed of your research and your questioning. I hear that you have been very thorough in your analysis." He seemed excited by the arrival of Leonardo, like a child waiting to unwrap a gift. "Let me wait no longer. Come and tell me what you have found."

Leonardo looked around the room.

"I will need a table on which I can lay my drawings. Ah, this one will be perfect," he pointed to a table near a window. "The lighting is perfect." He unrolled his drawings and used four artifacts, one on each corner, to keep the paper from rolling up again.

"My Lord, if you will," he gestured to the visibly eager Iacopo to approach the table.

Lorenzo remained in the background, trying to draw as little attention to himself as possible. His master's memory was excellent and he did not wish to remind him of the secret he unfortunately shared with him.

"I have taken into consideration your main concerns, and I have also physically studied the castle's structure, as well as the external factors such as Piombino and the natural physical features surrounding the castle and the village," Leonardo took charge with his usual eloquence. On the drawing, Leonardo had accurately reproduced the Palazzo Rocchetta, the outer limit of Piombino, as well as their surrounding topography. To the existing structures, he had added the features that he wanted to propose to Lord Appiani.

Iacopo was impressed by the accuracy of Leonardo's plans.

Leonardo continued: "My Lord, I recommend four different projects. The first would consist of digging a trench measuring six-hundred and forty cubits, which would link Piombino to the castle." He pointed to the map: "As you can see, with its width of ten cubits and its depth of four cubits, this trench would act as a first barrier for the enemy in the instance of a surprise battle. The trench would run along the southern wall of Piombino and would continue westward to the castle's southern wall, acting as a border between the castle and the land to the south." Leonardo paused. "Do you have any questions?"

Iacopo, dazzled by the genial display, could only nod his answer.

Leonardo returned to his drawings, and pointed to a planned addition to the fortification.

"The second project would consist of expanding the citadel by erecting a reinforced tower inside the southern courtyard of the castle. This tower of twenty cubits in height and of fifteen cubits in depth and width would permit your arquebusiers to have a better vantage point on activity in the hills." Again, Leonardo paused and looked at Iacopo.

"Carry on. This is fascinating," Lord Appiani encouraged.

"The third project, will be an extension of the second. It would consist of cutting all vegetation on the hills facing the castle and leveling the ground in order to give the arquebusiers posted on the new tower an uncovered front on which they can aim." Leonardo picked the underlying paper and covered the top one.

"The fourth and final project would consist in digging an underground tunnel which would connect Piombino to the Palazzo. I suggest this for the same reasons you mentioned during our first encounter. This tunnel would measure approximately seven hundred cubits in length, with a width of approximately five cubits and a height of approximately four cubits. "Pointing to the third option he continued: "The trees that will be cut during the clearing of the hills can be used to make the structure that will support the tunnel." He paused, and then turned again to Iacopo.

"My Lord, I have presented to you the four projects that will make the Palazzo Rocchetta a solid fortification that will help defend the Republic of Florence."

Iacopo Appiani turned and paced the room, absorbed in his thoughts, all the while fingering his dark beard.

"Tell me, Leonardo. Why is it that you have not mentioned the existing structure and the condition of the outside walls."

"My Lord, I have looked at the existing structure. It is in need of some masonry work, but this can be completed by one of the many capable masons of Piombino. My studies have brought me to conclude that there is not much use in trying to reinforce the walls of the castle, unless your wish was to change them entirely. The walls, in fact, should be able to withstand many more battles to come, as long of course, as the additional measures I have presented to you are accepted and implemented." Leonardo paused, looking at his host for some sort of commitment.

"In your opinion Leonardo, which of these projects is the most vital to our defense," Lord Appiani inquired. "You must understand that the recent wars have practically dried up our coffers, and although the government of Florence is willing to lend money at favorable terms, we cannot allow ourselves onerous outlays. Your suggestions are very impressive and you have lived up to your reputation, but I am obligated to work with the resources that I have."

"My Lord, I appreciate your situation," Leonardo sympathized. "That is why all the different projects I have proposed can be executed within the constraints that bind you." Leonardo pointed to his drawings once again. "I have determined an order of completion that would minimize the costs of these operations. As you can see, the earth that will be dug out of the trench can be used to level the terrain on the hills. As I mentioned before, the trees that will be cut off the hill can be used to make support beams for the tunnel." He paused, trying to use time to his advantage. "All the natural resources necessary to complete the work are within reach. Piombino, on the other hand, has all the human resources to complete the work."

"Master Leonardo, now you have stated your case, I must take some time for thought." Iacopo concluded. Night brings guidance," he stated philosophically. "I will inform you of my decision tomorrow."

"My Lord, I have completed the task for which you have hired me." Leonardo informed. "I must now return to Florence, where other obligations await me."

"But what about the projects? Who will supervise their completion if we decide to adopt your suggestions?" interrupted Iacopo, surprised by the announcement.

"Your faithful servant Lorenzo, who has assisted me during my stay, would be quite capable of accomplishing this task. Barring myself, I can think of no one else who would be more adept to bring this project to successful term," he recommended, thereby giving the ex-magistrate the certainty of regaining the favor of his Lord.

Leonardo bowed to Iacopo. "It has been an honor to serve you, my Lord. I shall be leaving in the morning."

The F-18 model airplane suspended from the bedroom ceiling reminded Rodney of the thrill of flying. He had always been fascinated by the fact that an airplane could fly and had spent many afternoons near the airport watching passenger airplanes take to the sky, loaded with their precious cargo - human lives.

Rodney admired the men who spent their lives understanding and defying the laws of gravity. The inventions that were the fruit of their imagination fed his obsession with modern aviation. Since the beginnings of time, Man had spent much time and energy trying to accomplish one of Nature's most wonderful and captivating feats - flying. Throughout history, a great number of people had, at one point or another in their life, been mesmerized by the flight of birds. Finally, some of these people's observations of flight had been successfully applied to the construction of the amazing flying machines that had become a widespread means of transportation.

Rodney looked at the poster replica of Leonardo Da Vinci's self-portrait that he'd framed and hung on the wall. Leonardo, his idol, had often been a source of inspiration to him. He had spent many hours reading about the Master, as he called him. He wanted to learn from Leonardo's life as an artist, an architect and an engineer. Da Vinci had proven to be a man centuries ahead of his time. Many of his designs and drawings had inspired technological breakthroughs in the centuries that followed. In fact, many of the observations that Leonardo made on the flight of birds during the fifteenth century influenced the construction of the first airplanes at the turn of the twentieth century.

The poster of Leonardo had become an icon to which he turned in moments when the challenges seemed impossible, as he did now.

"What next?" he asked. There were never any audible answers, but oddly enough, the mere presence of the poster had inspired him and under Leonardo's watchful eye, what had been challenges became solutions in waiting.

Images of Charles came back to mind. Rodney remembered the many hours that he'd spent discussing airplanes in all shapes and forms with him. They both shared the same love for flight and had compared notes on many occasions. However, during the past summer, Charles had reached a new milestone. He had found a summer job at Sparo Aeronautics on the Spear M40 project. He and Rodney had both filled out applications for one of the few jobs given to engineering students. Rodney remembered Charles' elation when he'd been accepted.

"I've got the world by the tail. You are now speaking to an employee of Sparo Aeronautics."

He relived the discussion they'd had when he too had been accepted. However, Rodney had said that he'd prefer to spend his summer back home, in the sun.

"You're crazy!" Charles had protested. "This is a chance of a lifetime! You and I working side by side. Who knows? Maybe we'll play a leading role in the Sparo Spear's future."

The next day, when Rodney had announced his final decision to Charles, he'd been touched by the disappointment he'd read on his friend's face.

"Man, this is what we've been studying for. What's with you? You can't recognize a great opportunity when it looks you in the face?" Angry, he'd tried to insult him.

But that hadn't changed Rodney's mind. He had been looking forward to summer, away from any responsibilities, back to good home cooking, back to the secure routine of cutting grass and soaking up the sun. "I have plenty of years of work ahead of me. I have to take advantage of my summers while I can," he'd reasoned. In retrospect, his arguments sounded pretty lame and he now wondered if he'd really refused to accept the challenge for fear of failing. For the first time, Rodney felt remorse for not accepting the position.

"Maybe Charles would have confided in me," he thought. *"Maybe I could have helped him. Maybe, he'd still be alive today. If I hadn't been so damned stupid..."* he blamed himself.

Suddenly, it dawned on him. He had been so miserable since his friend's death because he felt responsible for it, subconsciously, at least. The real reason behind his anger had finally surfaced. But it didn't make him feel any better. He couldn't live with the loss any better than he could before. In fact, if anything, he felt worse.

The house was quiet. To change his negative train of thoughts, Rodney pulled out his book on Leonardo Da Vinci's life and opened it. As he was reading a thought kept crossing his mind: what would Leonardo do if he were here? He felt as if he were floating, lost between his Anderson Avenue reality and the world of his Renaissance mentor.

"What next Leonardo?" he asked out loud.

As he lay in a dream-like state, echoing the question in his mind, Rodney noticed that a dark, perfect circle had formed on the ceiling above him. He felt hypnotized by the total darkness of the circle and by its perfect shape. In his dazed, somnolent state, he felt his body levitating toward the ceiling, as if drawn by the dark shadow. A strange force possessed his mind. Then initial grip of fear was however overcome by curiosity. His hands were drawn toward the darkness. Simultaneously, thunder clapped and a bolt of lightning flashed through the bedroom window. He felt his body disappear inside the black hole, as if it had been drawn into the eye of a tornado.

Walking freely in the fields, close to nature, was Leonardo's favorite pastime. It allowed him to admire the wonderful interaction of nature's players. Nowhere else would his senses be so pleasantly and subtly aroused. The beauty of the countryside mixed with the pleasantly intoxicating aroma of fertile earth, the grass and the wild flowers, the comforting caress of the wind brushing against his face and stroking his free-flowing beard, soothed his heart and invigorated him.

On this day, as Leonardo leaned against a mature oak on mount Ceseri, a rocky outcrop dominating the plain leading to nearby Florence, he once more looked at the beauty around him, as far as his gaze would allow. He had completed honorably and to his satisfaction the work that he had set out to do at the castle of Master Appiani. Although he was happy to return to Florence after a long absence, he had chosen to come back by the road that would allow him to revisit this spot near the small village of Fiesole, where he had often found peace.

"So much of this beautiful world has yet to be understood, he mused. *"So much has been taken for granted. Man learns by associating things he has learned and experienced to new objects or life forms that he sees for the first time. I have followed that principle in trying to create the flying machine. But, the knowledge that I have gathered through my readings, my experiences and my observations have not been sufficient to make my mechanical bird fly. It is true that some of my friends and supporters consider me to be a genius. On what grounds do they come to such conclusions? How can I accept such recognition when I have nothing to show but the drawings that reproduce on paper the flights of my imagination? These must be brought to fruition. Once successful, then I will be worthy of the accolades and the glory. I now know that my machine will not fly by the flapping of its wings. I must find means for it to soar like a magnificent kite. "*

At that moment, an acorn fell from an oak tree on which he was leaning. During its trajectory towards the ground, the speed at which it rotated in the wind seemed to create a braking effect on the speed of its descent. This natural phenomenon attracted Leonardo's attention, prompting him to make note of it in his notebook. He then picked the acorn up from the ground and weighed it in the palm of his hand.

"The weight is relatively high," he muttered. He threw the acorn up in the air once again and observed its activity and trajectory. "How does it manage to break the pull of gravity?" he asked himself. He wrote down a few more notes. He then gathered as many fallen acorns as he could and placed them carefully between the pages of his notebook.

"Is there a link between the flight of the kite and that of the acorn?" he wondered. "Perhaps there is. Perhaps…"

Leonardo was exhausted from his traveling and needed to give his mind some rest. He turned his attention to the various shapes and movements around him. Looking at the sky, he amused himself by describing out loud the different objects that he saw in each billowing cloud.

"A sleeping dog. Hmm. A proud rooster displaying his cockscomb. A corpulent matron sitting on a bench. A kite in full flight."

In a dream-like state, he observed once again the flight of the raptor gliding through the sky, as though suspended by an invisible thread. Looking at the bird, he pictured himself flying freely in the sky as he had recently dreamt, but this time doing so under his own power, controlling his own destiny.

"I must fly," Leonardo muttered, as the fatigue accumulated throughout his long voyage made any further thought almost impossible.

The kite maintained its position in the skies, effortlessly suspended. Dark clouds were gathering in a circle around it. A thunderous bolt of lightning flashed, emphasizing the contours of its magnificent wings. Yet now, the darkness of its form filled the circle in the clouds as it descended, clawed feet cocked and extended forward to grab its chosen prey.

The clear, blue sky was showing little contrast apart from a few white cottony clouds floating on the atmospheric canvas, resembling the background of a Renaissance masterpiece. From his resting point by the river, Rodney was gazing in the distance at an oddly shaped object traveling in his direction. At first, he thought it was a hang-glider supported by the warm summer breeze, responding to the deft control directives of its daring flyer. However, as it came closer, he saw that the flying object was powered by immense wings flapping to maintain its course. The young man's eyes and attention became fully focused on the flying vision.

He observed in awe as a giant kite, clutching an old man by the shoulders with its powerful claws, flew towards him. The white-bearded passenger seemed quite at ease in this precarious position. His light red embroidered tunic and fuchsia cloak fluttered gracefully in the wind, as did his white beard, which was expanded in volume, exposing every hair follicle to the fresh exhilarating air. When the bird reached the youth, it hovered with its precious cargo a few feet above him. Mesmerized by the sight, the young witness raised himself on one elbow and asked:

"What next, Leonardo?"

4

Pleased To Meet You Bo!

Thunder rumbled and a flash of lightning shot across the bedroom. Rodney sprung into a sitting position, his heart pounding. He shook his head, unsure of what had awakened him.

"...it's a sunny but chilly morning on this Saturday. For those of you who are planning on going out today, don't forget your umbrella. The weatherman is forecasting some scattered showers this afternoon. We will return to you with some music from the Boss, Eurythmics and Billy Joel's latest, after this brief commercial."

"*Funny, I don't remember setting the radio to go on,*" Rodney thought.

"... where shopping is fun." "It's seven thirty three." The announcer was back. "This is Roger T. Sawyer, wishing you a good morning. We now have Bruce Springsteen and Born to Run on your favorite station B.E.A.T, 97.9 on your FM dial."

"Where am I? What is this chatter?" came a voice from below.

Rodney's heart stopped at the sound of the unfamiliar voice.

"Who's that?" he yelled.

He pulled himself to the side of his bed, and looked towards the floor, in the direction of the voice. An old, not unfamiliar-looking bearded man wearing a peculiar, but not *unfamiliar*-looking outfit sat, looking around him wide-eyed and manifestly perplexed. His hands were nervously fumbling with a canvas bag on his lap.

"Who the hell are you?" drilled Rodney, frantically searching for some sort of weapon he could use to defend himself.

"Hell? I am not a demon," came the reply.

"Who are you?" Rodney persisted.

"I am Leonardo, engineer and architect at the court of Florence," the strange man replied.

"Yeah, and I'm Bo Derek!"

"I am pleased to meet you, Bo," the man responded sincerely, as he stood up and bowed.

"Quit the charade or I'll call the cops."

"Cops? I do not know "cops"," was the response. "Where am I? What is this place?"

"You're in my house, without being invited, and if you don't tell me who the hell you are and what you're doing in my home, right this minute, I'll call the cops," Rodney barked angrily.

"I have told you. I am Leonardo Da Vinci," the man persisted in a choked up voice. "Please tell me where I am." He pointed at the clock radio. "What is this?"

"That's a clock...grrrr..what am I saying?" He took a deep breath. "Okay, Moses. Stop the comedy and tell me who the hell you really are."

"I do not understand why you persist in asking me who I am. As I have already told you, I am Leonardo, engineer and architect in the state of Florence." He paused. "Where am I?"

With his right hand, Rodney looked for the book on the life of Leonardo Da Vinci that had kept him awake until the end of his conscious hours. He couldn't find it. He turned and looked around to where it might have fallen when he fell asleep. No sign. He looked under the pillow. No book. He reached for the side of the mattress and felt the hard cover of a book. He pulled it out and jumped off the bed.

He looked at the intruder and brandished the book in his direction: "Listen Bud…"

"I am Leonardo," the man insisted.

"Okay, Leonardo, or whatever your name is. You know what this is?" He pointed his index to the name on the book cover. "This is a book about the life of Leonardo Da Vinci who died close to five hundred years ago. And you know something else? Leonardo was Italian, and…"

"And I do speak Latin and some French," the old man clarified.

"…and he didn't speak English," Rodney continued. "I don't know if you've noticed, old man, but you and I have been speaking English, which you not only seem to understand quite clearly but also speak quite fluently. Now try to explain that to me." he insisted, certain that his argument would provoke the intruder's disclaimer to fame.

The impostor seemed puzzled as he listened to Rodney's reasoning. His brow contracted into a series of parallel waves.

"That is strange, is it not?" he admitted. "How could I have learned a language without even studying it or being exposed to it? Before this moment, I did not even know that this language that we are speaking is English."

Rodney was impressed by the man's performance. *"This old man is good,"* he thought.

"You may be able to convince some naïve people with some Cinderella story, but you won't fool me. No way, old man. You might as well face the music and be straight."

Proud of his statement, Rodney looked defiantly at the intruder until his attention was caught by something on the cover of the book. It looked different from the one he'd been reading. He read the title: *Those Amazing Flying Machines*. Something strange was going on, here. He remembered reading that book, all right, but he'd returned it to the University library just before returning to his hometown for the summer holidays.

The bearded man was calmly looking at his young would-be prosecutor, his expression again showing bafflement.

"Cinderella...No way...Face the music...Be straight..." he repeated. "I do not understand these terms."

Rodney ran his hand through his hair. His cheeks expanded outward as he blew out some air in frustration.

"Listen. We're not getting anywhere." He walked to the window and looked outside. None of the trees had leaves. In the back of the yard, on the south side of the cedar hedge, he noticed a strip of crystallized snow that had not yet melted. He suddenly felt like he'd been hit by a sledgehammer. He felt the blood draining from his face and a strange numbness take over his whole body. A chill ran down his spine.

"What the.." he exclaimed as he dashed out of the room and fled down the stairs in two hops. He opened the portico door and ran onto the porch, wearing only his underwear. The newspaper had been delivered at its usual time. He picked it up and looked at the date. "Saturday, April 16, 1988," he read. "April 16, 1988," he repeated out loud. "No! This is September. This can't be! I must be dreaming. This can't be," he babbled, shocked. "I must be going out of my mind." He leaned against the doorframe, feeling faint.

"Time in a Bottle", Jim Croce's song played on the radio.

In a second outburst of energy, he sprung back into the house and up the stairs, running to the end of the corridor to Leo's room. It was empty. He came back and entered Eugene's room. No life. He ran to the other end of the corridor, past the washroom, along the banister at the top of the stairs, past his own room and into Edmond's room. No Edmond. "My Daytimer," he uttered, as he ran back to his room and past the intruder to his desk. Rodney pulled his Daytimer from his school bag and fumbled through the pages: "March 19......March 30.....April 9.......here it is, April 16," he said. He read the notes he had written in his book.

"Boys in Springer until next weekend" was written at the top and circled. Below it, he had noted: "Sparo Aeronautics - Yes or No? Must give answer by next Friday."

Rodney remembered. Their exams had finished on April 15 and his roommates had gone to Springer. They had all accepted work in Caldwell for the summer, so they'd wanted to spend some time in their hometown before reporting to their respective summer jobs. He also recalled that the fact that his friends were staying in Caldwell had also tempted him to stay and accept the job with Sparo Aeronautics.

"My God!" he exclaimed.

The old man seemed oblivious to Rodney's dismay and pushed on the nose of a model jet fighter airplane that was suspended by a transparent fishing line. He observed with fascination as the plane swung back and forth in the air.

"Is that a flying machine?" he asked.

"Wha...what?" grumbled Rodney, whose racing thoughts were interrupted by the question.

"Is this a flying machine?" repeated the man.

"It's a model airplane, a scaled-down version, made from a kit," Rodney answered as he rested his head in his open hands. He walked to the wall beside the doorway, where he flipped one of the light switches to give his uninvited guest a better view of the plane. A spotlight came on, aimed in the direction of the model.

"Magic."

"What?" Rodney asked, not understanding the old man's reaction.

"How did you do that?" asked the man, obviously impressed.

"Do what?"

Rodney picked up the sweat pants and hockey jersey that were hanging over the back of his chair and fumbled as he tried to dress. His efforts were mechanical and lacked purpose. He looked dazedly in front of him. He slipped his feet into his running shoes; but did not tie the laces.

The old man watched him dress as if he had never witnessed such a thing before. He walked towards the spotlight and touched the bulb with his index finger. He quickly pulled his hand back.

"It is hot," he noted in amazement.

The phone rang, causing the elderly man to turn quickly in the direction of the sound.

Rodney slowly walked out of the room, shaking his head. *"That old bird is weird,"* he thought. *"He probably escaped from an asylum or something."* He could picture the hallways of the hospital, packed with two Napoleons, five Einsteins, three Julius Caesars, all of them convinced that they're the true McCoys.

The phone rang again. Rodney picked up the receiver.

"Hello?"

"Hello?" the old man in the room echoed.

"He's... he's away until next weekend. Who is this?"

"I am Leonardo," the man in Rodney's room answered.

"How are you?" Rodney asked.

"I am well. How are you?" the visitor returned the greeting.

"I'm fine," Rodney answered. "I haven't seen you in a long time."

"We have just met, this morning," the old man said perplexed. "How can you say such a thing!"

Rodney could hear his uninvited visitor speaking in the background, but was unaware that he was answering Rodney's part of the telephone conversation. He turned around and waved his hand at him to indicate that he shouldn't speak while he was on the phone. The old man gazed at Rodney with the look of a Basset Hound that doesn't understand why his master is reprimanding him.

"That's right, I did see you the day before last," Rodney continued, now confused by the old man's expression.

"I tell you, I have never met you before," the old man barked out. "I would remember you if I had." He paused and said wryly. "One does not meet every day persons who dress as oddly as you do. I definitely would not forget."

He turned and looked at the refrigerator located under the frame of the raised bed. Curious, he walked towards it, pulled on the handle and opened the door. When the light inside it turned on, he was taken aback.

"I'll tell him you called. Good-bye," Rodney concluded his phone conversation.

"Where are you going?" asked the interloper.

"I'm not going anywhere, " replied Rodney. "What makes you think I'm going somewhere?" Then, pointing towards the bulging canvas-like bag on the floor. "Hey, what's in the bag?"

"You said good-bye," reminded the old man, almost simultaneously to Rodney's question. Nevertheless, he reached for the bag, and looked inside. "This is strange," he noted. "Someone has taken the trouble of gathering all my notes and putting them in this bag. This truly is odd. For what purpose?" He paused. Then with a lift of his eyebrows, he resumed his questioning. "You said good-bye did you not?"

"I said good-bye to the person on the telephone," Rodney clarified, the nagging thought in the back of his mind becoming more and more pressing.

"Telephone," the old man repeated with some hesitation. "What is a telephone? Where is the person? I see no one." He again reached into the refrigerator. His eyes lit up. "It is cold," he observed.

"Of course it's cold," Rodney said sarcastically. "Refrigerators are cold. What do you expect?"

Then, hearing a familiar name on the radio playing in the background, Rodney's blood quickened and he diverted his attention to the newscast.

"...more from Don Goodchild in London." The news correspondent from London adopted a serious tone: "In the past twenty-four hours, various notebooks of inestimable value written by Leonardo Da Vinci, the great Italian Renaissance artist, engineer and architect, have mysteriously vanished from collections in various locations throughout the world. All documents were stolen without any trace of forcible entry and the different chapters of the more than seven thousand pages of documents seem to all have disappeared simultaneously. One of the locations where some of the stolen notebooks had been kept was Windsor Castle. Officials at the castle are at a loss to explain the baffling circumstances of..."

"This is a refrigerator? the old visitor asked, pointing at the appliance.

Rodney nodded slowly, his mouth half open, his mind racing.

"Show me your telephone," the old man demanded.

The young man pointed to the device, not able to utter a word, his jaw frozen in by the conclusions that he was drawing.

The old man walked towards it and picked it up gently, as if he were handling a fragile, valuable artifact.

"I fail to see anyone on the telephone," he pointed out. "In fact, I doubt that this could support a person's weight," he added, visibly annoyed that Rodney had lied to him.

"I don't understand," a confused Rodney said.

"You have told me that you said good-bye to someone on the telephone," the old man recalled. "There is no one on the telephone."

Rodney felt his calm disappear and anxiety take over. *"I must be dreaming,"* he thought. *"This is too absurd."*

He was frightened. If his hunch was right, and more and more evidence seemed to indicate that he was, through circumstances that he couldn't explain, he'd been brought to meet a man who'd been dead for close to five hundred years. He pinched his arm. He could see the redness replace the whiteness caused by the pressure. *"What's going on?"* he asked himself. *"What's the meaning of this?"*

"Bo," asked the man. "Are you all right?"

Rodney smiled lamely.

"My name is Rodney." He paused, then asked the obvious.

"You're really Leonardo Da Vinci, aren't you?"

"I am," answered Leonardo, happy to be believed at last.

"Who sent you, Leonardo?" Rodney asked, trying to find out if Leonardo knew how he had managed to travel through time.

"Sent me. What do you mean?"

"Do you know what year this is?" he asked the Master.

Leonardo looked around the room. He had never, before this day, seen any of the objects that surrounded him.   He knew that something extraordinary had happened to him, but he did not know what or why.

"I have no idea," he responded sadly.

"This is the year nineteen hundred and eighty-eight," Rodney informed the artist. "You have traveled close to five hundred years ahead in time."

Leonardo remained calm as he assimilated this information. "This is a miracle," he finally said. His expression was one of wonder.

Rodney agreed. Something or someone had brought them together. Who or what? He had no answer.

Rodney looked at Leonardo's canvas bag. He recognized one of Leonardo's famous notebooks. They had returned to their rightful owner. Rodney was overwhelmed.

Rodney turned on the water and plugged the drain hole in the bathtub. He returned to his room, where Leonardo was busy filling his notebook with sketches of some of the mysterious objects around him. He looked over the artist's shoulder and observed as he wrote from right to left with his left hand. Rodney, who was well versed on Leonardo, knew that he wrote backwards so that his hand wouldn't drag in the wet ink. This fact in itself eliminated the doubt in Rodney's mind. He was really in the presence of the Master. Who would believe it?

Leonardo paused frequently as he dipped the quill feather pen in the ink container, both objects having also mysteriously been transported with him through time. Rodney reached into the top drawer of his desk and pulled out a ball-point pen. "Why don't you try this?" he suggested to Leonardo, as he handed it to him.

Leonardo reached for the pen and silently examined it.

"It can be used to write," Rodney explained.

"What is this strange material?" Leonardo was pointing out to the casing of the pen.

"It's plastic," Rodney answered scratching his head. "Hmm. It's a synthetic fiber." Leonardo was absorbed by the instrument. "Why don't you try to write with it?"

Leonardo took a last close look at it, dipped the end in his ink container, and before Rodney had a chance to intervene, started a new sketch beside the one he had started. The tip of the pen, covered with ink, left ink stains that didn't meet with the artist's approval.

"I'm sorry, Leonardo. I should've told you. You don't have to dip the pen in ink anymore." Rodney grabbed the pen, wiped it clean with a Kleenex and pulled out the plastic filter. "The ink is stored inside this tube and it flows down by gravity to the point of the pen." He gave it back to Leonardo.

"Interesting," Leonardo said as he tested the novel writing object. Suddenly, his attention was caught by the sound of running water. "Water." he identified. "Is there a waterfall in proximity?"

"Come, I'll show you," Rodney suggested, smiling as he invited Leonardo to follow him.

The old bathtub was now half-filled.

"This is a bathtub," Rodney pointed out.

"Of course", Leonardo said. "But, where is the water coming from?"

"The water comes from a central water reservoir in the city and is drawn into each house through an underground aqueduct system."

Leonardo was awed. "All these amazing inventions within your own home. You must be one of high means and wealth," Leonardo complimented.

"No, I am not a Lord and I am also very far from being wealthy," he admitted. "You see, Leonardo, most homes in our city are equipped with these facilities. They have become essential parts of our everyday life. You may not believe this, but to most, the fixtures you see in this bathroom are old and almost obsolete."

Leonardo frowned as he assimilated this new information. Then, turning to the toilet, he asked sardonically. "And what, may I ask, is this old thing?"

"That is a throne," Rodney quipped.

Leonardo caught on to Rodney's game. "And when may I ask, do you reign on such a throne?"

"When you have a lot on your mind and you want to get rid of it."

He paused, seeing that Leonardo hadn't flinched at all at the answer. "Seriously it's used to... well you know... for the evacuation of sh... body residues," he tried to be proper.

"This is strange. I have always attributed the mind's functions to the brain," Leonardo noted sarcastically. "I must then deduce that, with time, not all things evolve," he dead-panned, giving Rodney a first-hand experience of his quick wit.

The blinds were closed, isolating the living room from all daylight. Rodney had scurried from window to window and closed out the outside world, hoping to thereby minimize the "future shock" of the time traveler.

Leonardo was discovering the comfort of the old Lazy-Boy chair. Trying to appreciate its total comfort, he leaned back. The action released the mechanism of the chair, which opened to its full, restful length. Other than the grip that tightened on the arms and the eyes that widened in an expression of amazement, there was no evidence of surprise. As a matter of fact, the inventor took the whole matter in stride. Using his legs, he pushed to regain the upright position. One could see his mind working and dissecting the components of the chair and its movement. He had evidently come to terms with the knowledge that he was now part of a new world, a wold full of surprises, and that to be shocked or perplexed by the various new stimuli would only hinder his sense of appreciation.

He kept a watchful eye on the young man's efforts to seclude them. "You are attempting to protect me," he said.

"Yes I am," confirmed Rodney.

"Of what, may I ask?"

"Leonardo I have the highest respect for you. I've read a lot about you. God, that's strange. I'm still not used to the idea," he digressed. He paused. "I'm convinced that you're Leonardo Da Vinci. But, some people would put me in a straightjacket if they heard me say such a thing."

"What is a...straightjacket?"

"It's a restraining vest used to control people who are nuts, uh...out of their minds, mad," he answered patiently to satisfy Leonardo's curiosity. "But that's not important." He sat back and tried to formulate what he wanted to say. "You see, Leonardo, there's a world outside of these windows, outside of this house, that's totally unknown to you. Not only are we on a different continent, but we're also in a different era, as you know."

"But that does not explain why you are keeping me in this room," Leonardo argued.

"I don't want to confine you in here for too long. As a matter of fact, I don't even know how long you'll be around. For all I know, you may just disappear and go back to the sixteenth century ten seconds from now. But then again, you may be around for a while." He got up and started pacing around the room. "Who knows? Maybe, we're victims of some sort of freak of nature that has sent you four hundred and fifty years ahead in time." He threw his hands up.

"I still do not understand", Leonardo insisted.

"What I want to do is inform you as well as I can about the world out there before you step out. I'm sure, of all people, you can adapt. But there's a bunch of suspicious and crazy people out there who'd put us behind bars if we tried to explain to them who you really are. Nobody would believe it."

He walked to the other side of the room and pointed to a series of identically bound books that were piled on a table.

"I've pulled out these encyclopedias that I'd like you to read. They've got pictures of things from our century and other centuries, with written descriptions." He paused again. "You can read English, can you?"

"I do not know; I have never tried. Perhaps since I have somehow been inspired with the gift of speaking this language, I will also have the ability to read it," Leonardo deduced.

Rodney pulled out one of the encyclopedias and opening it at random, pointed to a word.

"Can you read this?" he asked.

"Landau n..."

"That's "landau". The "n" means that the word is a noun. "

"Four-wheeled carriage with top of which front and back halves can be... This is not a manuscript. What is this?" Leonardo held up the book, his eyes flashing with interest.

"It is an encyclopedia and it is printed. In it you'll find the description and definition of many objects, cities, people, animals, inventions, like printing, for instance. The names are all listed in alphabetical order. If you look at these books..." He paused and picked up another encyclopedia: "... this one has all the words starting with the letters L-E to M-I," he said pointing at the letters.

Leonardo had already started to devour the information before his eyes and was totally absorbed.

"What I suggest is that you go through the books and try to familiarize yourself with as many things as you can so that..." Rodney noticed that his last comments were not being heard. He smiled at Leonardo's expression, which was somewhat like that of a miser not willing to be diverted from the addictive treasure before him.

"Leonardo," he called. There was no response, nor even a hint of acknowledgment. Putting his hand on the page before Leonardo, he managed to distract the reader. "There is one thing we have to agree on."

Leonardo looked up. "What is that?" he asked impatiently.

When the time comes that you meet someone, you have to make sure not to give them your real name. For the time being, you're not Leonardo Da Vinci. We'll call you... hmm... let's say... Leonard... Yeah, that's it! Leonard Vincent."

"My name is Leonardo," the Master reminded, adamant.

"I know that," Rodney sighed.

"I will use my best judgment," Leonardo assured. "I understand the predicament in which we are placed. I plan to use my time for research and be the least conspicuous possible."

The Master's eloquence impressed Rodney and reassured him that things would be just fine.

"By the way, we'll have to find you some new clothes," Rodney decided.

"Why?" Leonardo protested feeling the cloth of his garments. "These are made of the best fabrics in Florence and are notorious for their quality."

"I've no doubt about the fine quality of the material," Rodney tried to be diplomatic. "But you will find that people in this century don't dress in the same manner. Please trust me on this one."

Leonardo didn't answer, leaving Rodney with the nagging feeling that the artist might not be willing to concede so easily. *"I'll deal with that later,"* he thought.

Meanwhile, Leonardo had resumed his reading of the encyclopedia.

Leonardo sat on the Lazy-Boy chair with encyclopedia volumes stacked on the coffee table beside him. The concept of the encyclopedia fascinated him with its consistent lettering format, the images provided for explanation purpose, the alphabetizing of the subject matter and the neatness of the pages making it so easy to read. *"No more mirror reading is required,"* he thought.

As he leafed through one volume, his eyes were drawn on a write-up about Michelangelo. He was somewhat surprised to find written matter about his younger contemporary and he read with interest.

"Michelangelo Di Lodovico Buonarroti Simoni. Born March 6, 1475. Hmmm! He looks much older than he really is," he read out loud grinning with contentment at his finding. Leonardo read with renewed interest.

Leonardo's curiosity was triggered once again. He placed the volume face down on his lap and reached for the pile of volumes beside him scanning the spine of each one. "Since they wrote about him, maybe ......" he muttered. He swiftly pulled one of the volumes out of the pile, opened it and leafed through it until he reached the desired page.

"Leonardo Da Vinci. Born in the year 1452 ......died May 2, 1519 ...." He sighed. The reality of his own mortality shook him. He looked into empty space trying to come to grips with the information. *"This is the year nineteen hundred and eighty-eight. You have traveled close to five hundred years ahead in time."* Rodney's words played back through his mind. A smile suddenly emerged on his face. "Leonardo Da Vinci. Born in the year 1452 and still living in 1988," he rectified with a smile of contentment.

Leonardo placed the encyclopedias side by side on his lap. A frown formed on his face as he noticed an injustice. He ran his fingers beside each article.

"Fifty lines compared to thirty-seven. How dare they write more about that hunchbacked poor excuse of an artist?" he fumed.

The whiz of the hair blower filled the bathroom. Rodney expected that Leonardo would appear at any moment, trying to identify the source of the unusual noise. In fact, from the corner of his eye, Rodney saw that the door was opening slowly. He imagined the Master behind the door, sliding it open, ever so gently, prepared for any eventuality, including an unsolicited attack from a strange object. Rodney tried to keep from looking right at the door, even though he could feel his feet moving with the flexing of the hardwood floors straining under the weight of the intruder. Despite himself, he turned to face the door, already grinning in anticipation.

"Leonardo..."

He stopped short and gasped. In the door stood Charles. Rodney looked at the blue-gray tint of his facial skin and the blood-shot eyes bulging out of their orbit. Like those of a zombie, his teeth were parted and threatening to pierce the skin in search of a jugular. The stench in the room was nauseating. Rodney was petrified. His heart seemed to stop. Panicked, he threw his hair dryer at the ghoulish apparition and backed up to escape, but bumped into the bathtub and fell into it instead.

"What the hell is the matter with you? You look like you saw a ghost!" Charles said in a definitely non-ghostly manner.

"Ch...Charles," Rodney mumbled tentatively. "You scared me. What are you doing here?" he asked trying to figure what was going on.

"What kind of question is that?"

"You look terrible." The words escaped Rodney's mouth, his voice perceptibly shaking.

"Oh thank you," Charles responded. "I can always count on you for support. What's this, pick on Chuck day?"

Thoughts were rushing through Rodney's mind. This day's date suddenly flashed: April 16, 1988. He reminded himself that he had been taken four months back to a time where school was ending, not starting, a time when his friend was among the living, not the dead.

Charles had opened the old medicine cabinet on the wall. "Where's the Eno?" he was asking as he belched and let his fingers fumble through the cabinet's content.

"There should be some in Trap's room, "Rodney managed to answer, though he was still shaken. He knew that Charles practically lived on the citrus extract because they brought him relief from most stomach pain. Charles went out of the room. Rodney heard him walking down the hall, toward Eugene's room.   There was a pause, and silence reigned momentarily. Steps resumed, once again resonating in the hallway.

"I'll never drink again," Charles complained when he came back into the room. He looked at Rodney and added: "For a guy who was near death last night, you sure look pretty damned lively."

Rodney remembered. He and Charles had tied one on the night before, or should he say four months ago. Nevertheless, he remembered how sore his head had been the day after. At least his time travels hadn't rekindled his drunken stupor.

"Well you know me. I've got the constitution of a horse." He was regaining some of his cool. "Speaking of horse, it sure smells like a barnyard in here. When's the last time you had a bath?" he asked Charles sarcastically.

Charles looked under his shoes.   The memory of dog droppings sticking to the back of his friend's pants flashed into Rodney's mind.

"Look on the seat of your pants," he suggested, anxious to see if the same thing had happened again.

Charles looked over his shoulder. "Ah shit!" he exclaimed, as he turned around to show some reddish-brown dung on the seat of his pants.

"Oh, you've got that right. What happened to you? Wait, I bet that on your way here, you slipped while walking through the park and you fell on dog dirt."

"Are you psychic or what?!" Charles was amazed at the accuracy of his friend's guess.

"Those damned dog owners should be shot for letting their dogs shit in the park," he said understandably angered.

Rodney, goggled-eyed, was having the frightful experience of being able to lip-synch the words as Charles said them. The sheer amazement that he felt, combined with the comical nature of his friend's predicament, brought out his natural sense of humor and he laughed heartily.

"I guess we'll have to call you pooper-scooper from now on," he bantered.

"You tell anyone about this and you're dog meat," Charles threatened.

"Yeah, and then I can haunt you again during your next stroll in the park," Rodney continued, tears of laughter rolling down his cheeks. He stood up and stepped out of the bathtub to make way for Charles. Charles got in and removed his pants and shoes. Leaving them in the tub, he got out and turned the hot water tap to its fullest and positioned his pants under the flow in order to remove the caked dirt.

"It's good to see you, Charlie," Rodney said sincerely. For the first time in this crazy day, he was happy of his fate. Just a few hours ago, he'd thought of Charles as a dead man who lived only in his memory. The return in time had reunited them. However, he was saddened by the knowledge of what the future had in store for his friend. That chilled the warm feeling of rekindled friendship.

"You're talking as if you've found a long-lost friend," Charles remarked, still bent over the tub trying to clean his pants. "Believe me, I feel just as bad as I look. But I've got a feeling that I'll be hanging around for a while yet. I'll be there to haunt you."

The combination of words made Rodney feel somewhat uncomfortable. You would have thought that Charles knew unconsciously what fate had in store for him.

"We never know what lies ahead," he philosophized lamely. *"How can something out of our past suddenly become something in our future?"* he thought to himself.

Suddenly it dawned on him that the events he had been reliving since he had awakened were not exactly the same as they'd been the first time. Charles' arrival, for one, was totally different. He remembered that the first time he had lived this day, Charles had come into the bedroom to find him sleeping soundly, still under the effects of the previous evening's excesses. He also remembered, though, that Charles had looked as bad the first time as he did this time around, without, however, provoking the panicked attack of this day. Actually, Rodney had found it, as he recalled, quite hilarious. Of course, at that time, Charles hadn't died yet. Other details, such as the soiled pants and some of the words, hadn't changed.

"Now let's get down to business," Charles said, as he rolled up his sleeves. "I believe you've got something to tell me," he reminded his friend.

"I do?" Rodney asked, not knowing what his friend was referring to.

"You told me that you'd give me an answer today on whether or not you'd accept the summer job with Sparo," he refreshed his memory. "And that's why I came all the way over here. I really want to know. Of course, I think you should accept. Hey, we'd be able to work together. We could even make history!"

Charles paused.

"Now that I'm officially an employee of Sparo Aeronautics I feel like I've got the world by the tail! You really should join too. This is a chance of a lifetime. You and me working side by side, who knows? We may revolutionize the industry with an invention," he predicted enthusiastically.

Rodney's pulse had accelerated as he relived the situation. This was more than déjà vu: this was déjà lived. *"Whoa! This is scary,"* he thought. He suddenly felt sympathetic towards the main characters in the Twilight Zone episodes that he had seen on TV. To think he used to make fun of them! What seemed farfetched and unrealistic to him then had an all too realistic edge now. And though it occurred to him that he could change the outcome of his friend's future, he was afraid of the impact that any interference on his part could have.

"I haven't been able to decide yet," Rodney answered, trying to brush off some of the pressure he was feeling from his friend and from the peculiar situation in which he found himself.

"Man, this is what we've been studying for. What's with you? You can't recognize a great opportunity when it looks you in the face," Charles tried to insult him, in anger. But I guess a maybe is better than a definite no," Charles reasoned. "I hope that by next Friday, you'll see the light, and give me a positive answer."

"Well, I still have a week to decide, and I do want to make the right decision." Rodney answered, now very disturbed by the dilemma with which he was faced.

Charles looked at his soiled garments in the bathtub. "Hey. I really have to get out of here. I've got some research to do at the library before my hot date tonight. Can I borrow some clothes from you?" he asked. "Maybe your blue..."

"...sweat pants with my gray-hooded sweat shirt," Rodney completed the request.

"My, we can read minds, too!" Charles didn't quite know what to make of his friend's evident ESP.

Rodney didn't answer.

Once Charles had charged out of the house, Rodney opened the door to the living room where he found Leonardo avidly reading. He sat down in an easy chair across the room from him and tingled at the realization that he was in the presence of the Master. After all, not many people got the opportunity to meet their idol, much less an idol who'd lived almost five centuries before. Unfortunately, he couldn't share the excitement of his experience with anyone. Who'd believe him? In any case, this was much better than looking at the self-portrait poster in his room. Leonardo resembled, but was not exactly the same as he had drawn himself. To Rodney's eye, he was more handsome in the flesh than in the self-portrait. "That's probably why I didn't spot him right off," Rodney thought. But the resemblance had been close enough that it had nagged him through the harrowing events of that morning. After hearing about the disappearance of the notebooks, the step to full recognition of the intruder had been a very short one.

"By the way, where is that poster?" he asked himself. He hadn't seen it on the wall since he'd returned to his past. "Ah yes, I purchased that poster just before starting fall trimester. Or, should I say, I'll be buying it just before starting school…"

"Wow!" he muttered. His mind started reeling again at the thought of his travel in time. To have recollection of one's future was something hard to fathom. How could he explain this to his friends? *"I remember what'll happen in your future,"* he'd say. *"They'd put me in a padded room and throw away the key."*

Rodney observed the nearly motionless person before him. "Maybe he's a ghost. Maybe I'm the only one who can see him. Maybe he's a figment of my imagination."

This thought jolted him. This possibility hadn't occurred to him. Leonardo was absorbed in his reading.

"Ahem!," Rodney tried unsuccessfully to make the famous painter aware of his presence. "Leonardo, " he called out. Still no answer.

Without giving it much thought, the young man got up, walked over to Leonardo, reached for his arm and pinched his skin.

Leonardo quickly pulled his arm away from his assailant, but not before Rodney had seen the pinch mark on the master's arm.

The old man looked straight into Rodney's eyes.

"I am real," he said. He returned to his reading without any further comment. Rodney shook his head in disbelief.

"I just pinched you. Aren't you going to react?"

Leonardo didn't reply. Rodney, flustered by this lack of acknowledgment, turned the light switch off and on to attract the reader's attention.

"It is unnecessary to act this way if what you want is to speak to me," Leonardo warned.

"I've been trying to get your attention for the last minute, but you don't answer," Rodney protested. "I need to talk to you Leonardo. I have a problem." He stopped, seeing that the Master was still absorbed in his reading. Exasperated, he sighed.

"Continue. I am listening," insisted Leonardo, his eyes still focused on the book before him.

Rodney was relieved to finally be able to speak and be listened to. "You've probably accepted the fact that you've traveled in time and that you're now close to five centuries in the future."

"Hmm-hmm," acknowledged Leonardo.

"Well, I've also traveled in time, but not as drastically as you did. I've somehow returned four months behind into my past."

"I suspected something of the sort."

"How could you?" Rodney asked.

"The mere fact that you have accepted my plight and my story proves it. I do not believe that anyone in his right mind would accept such a story unless he had experienced something similar," Leonardo reasoned.

The comment hurt Rodney. He felt that he was being judged wrongly. *"Who does he think I am? Thomas the disciple, who has to stick his finger in the wound to believe?"* he thought.

"Thank you for giving me the benefit of the doubt," Rodney said sarcastically.

For the first time Leonardo diverted his attention to Rodney.

"I did not mean to offend you, young man. I have based my judgment on the nature of man, and I do include myself as one of the skepticals. If placed in your situation, I would react in the same fashion, perhaps even more drastically. I have always had much difficulty tolerating philosophers who spend their days trying to understand the meaning of life and of the soul. I am more pragmatic in my approach, therefore I have devoted my life to understanding the things that stimulate the senses. However, this experience is making me realize that there are many things that I have yet to learn about what we cannot see and cannot touch." He looked at Rodney with empathy.

These words comforted Rodney. He felt as if the Master had reached into his mind and had rearranged everything into a more comprehensible order.

"This afternoon, I had the visit of a friend of mine. It was a very strange experience," Rodney continued.

"What made it so strange?" Leonardo asked, still giving Rodney his full attention.

"Two things. First of all, I was reliving an experience from four months ago. Secondly, the friend who visited me today died a few days ago."

"I do not understand."

"My friend Charles is dead. But this death will occur in the future, as we stand today. You see, if things don't change between now and then, Charles will die next September," Rodney tried to explain. He paused. "When I saw him today, I was really scared. I felt as if he didn't belong, when in fact, I'm the one who's out of place. My four months of experience into the future make me the freak of nature. It's a weird feeling to know what someone's future holds for him," he said sadly.

"Yes I can imagine," Leonardo sympathized.

"What are we supposed to do? Why are we both here, together in the past? There must be an explanation," Rodney desperately wanted to know.

"I am unable to understand the object of our meeting," Leonardo admitted. "Perhaps time will tell. I also believe that there is a purpose for our meeting. I can see no other explanation for this phenomenon."

"In the meantime, what am I supposed to do? Am I to return to my hometown and spend my summer over there like I did before? Why was I brought back to this city, at this precise time?"

"I think you have answered some of your questions," Leonardo observed. "Our common predicaments seem to indicate that we are to remain in this city. Perhaps the experience you have lived in the future is to be used in the more immediate future."

"But where do you come in?" Rodney asked. "What's the purpose of your presence?"

"Time will tell," Leonardo repeated in his usual calm tone.

"It's funny," Rodney remarked. "Between the two of us, you're the one who should feel the least at ease, but in fact, you're the one who's showing the most calm and who's adapting best."

Leonardo acknowledged Rodney's compliment with a reassuring glance as he picked up his book. Moments later, he was once again captivated by his reading.

Rodney was still looking at him. While he'd listened to his reasoning, another one of his questions had been answered. There was now no doubt in his mind that to serve its purpose, fate's twisted scenario had chosen Leonardo for his analytical brilliance and notorious intellectual capacity, a logical choice that had already been validated by his ability to adapt to a totally different environment. But Rodney had difficulty understanding his own involvement. If he'd been brought back to do something, as they both seemed to agree, what was his mission? The possible answers brought some doubt to his mind. He felt pompous to think that he was a determinant factor, that he'd been selected by some outside being or force to do some sort of work that could have bearing on events. He had difficulty believing that. His meeting with Leonardo was most likely the result of some unexplainable mix-up of the time and space continuum.

Leonardo now seemed oblivious to his presence, but Rodney was itching to ask the famous man a million questions about his thoughts, his drawings, his era. However, the inventor seemed so captivated by the encyclopedias that Rodney felt it best not to disturb him at this time.

Rodney decided to stay at home, even though this was a Saturday. Saturday nights were usually spent at the tavern with all the boys, drinking draft beer as if it was going out of style.

In the few days since he had come into Rodney's life, Leonardo had hardly budged. His eyes and brain worked in tandem to assimilate as much information as possible. His only physical activity had consisted in the flicking of the wrist to turn a page. He also slept, if indeed he did sleep, in the living room. Rodney had offered to prepare meals, but there was rarely any response. So Rodney placed some of whatever food he prepared for himself beside the Master, and later picked up the often barely touched plate. "He's going to get hungry at some point," he told himself. But the Master's mind was hungrier for knowledge than his body for food.

"Leonardo," Rodney called. No answer.

"Leonardo," Rodney attempted to get the Masters attention again.

"Ah, Rodney," Leonardo turned his head. "It is a pleasure to see you again." He pointed at the book in front of him. "I have learned so many fascinating things through my readings. It is a wonderful world in which you are living."

"I'm happy that you're pleased with the written information you've read," Rodney responded. "But I think that what I'll show you today will stimulate your interest even more."

"What have you for me today?"

"Today you experience the new world," Rodney announced. "You and I are going outside today and you will get a chance to see some of the things that you've read about. How does that grab you?"

"Grab me?

"Hmm, I mean, how would you like to do that?" Rodney clarified.

"I look forward to it," Leonardo accepted with some anticipation. Rodney was starting to identify some of the Master's tones. Although his temperament was fairly uniform, Leonardo's interest or his indifference could be identified by the barely perceivable variations in tones.

"First of all we'll have to find you some new clothes. Follow me and we'll get you some new duds," Rodney suggested unaware that he was using more jargon.

"Duds," Leonardo repeated, his brow retracted in puzzlement. He followed Rodney to his room.

"I will not wear such ridiculous clothing," Leonardo protested with indignation. "I have never, in all my time, seen such tasteless apparel."

"You can't go out there dressed as you are."

"And why not?"

"People don't dress that way any more. I'm sorry, but times have changed. If you go out dressed like that, you'll draw a lot of attention. Attention will bring questioning which will put us in a precarious position." Rodney held out a pair of dress pants and a shirt.

Leonardo reluctantly took the clothes. "All right, I will wear this," he said. He rolled the fabrics between his fingers. The feeling of the material brought an expression of disdain to his face. "What is this... this fabric?"

"Polyester and wool, I think," Rodney answered.

"Polyester? What plant or animal does polyester come from?"

Rodney chuckled. "Polyester is a man-made fiber. It's commonly used in the manufacturing of clothing. Unlike wool, it's made from petroleum extracts."

"What is petroleum? I have not yet reached the P's in my readings."

Rodney paused before answering, well aware of the vicious circle this could lead him into. "Petroleum is a sort of liquid mineral...hmm...an inflammable mineral oil which has many uses." He paused once again trying to find an accurate explanation to which Leonardo could relate, but nothing came to mind. "I'm sorry, I guess the best way for you to understand would be to see some of the things that are made out of petroleum. We'll talk about that when the time comes," he suggested.

Leonardo seemed to understand Rodney's situation and didn't insist. "Now if you will excuse me, I will change into these garments."

Rodney walked over to his dresser and opened the top drawer from which he pulled out a pair of underwear and a pair of socks. He threw the undergarments in Leonardo's direction.

"Here, you'll have to wear these under your clothes." He left the room, offering the artist some privacy.

Leonardo sighed in protest.

"This is the first time someone has dictated how I should dress. And to make matters more unnerving, I have to wear apparel unworthy of a noble man," he mumbled.

The door opened and the contemporarily clad, obviously uncomfortable Leonardo came out. Rodney was impressed at how Leonardo had observed and adopted the way of tucking his shirt into his pants and how he had grasped the mechanism and correct use of the belt. As Rodney's attention moved down, he saw that the Master was still wearing his own footwear and that he was holding the socks in his right hand. Leonardo was satisfied that he had been able to retain part of his old garments, thereby minimizing the impact of the imposed changes.

"That's great!" Rodney commented, satisfied that the pants and shirt fit Leonardo as if they were made-to-measure. "You'll blend in perfectly with the people on campus."

"Blend," exclaimed Leonardo. "You speak of me as if I was a color to be used in a painting."

"You could describe it as that," agreed Rodney. "You wouldn't want to use a color that didn't fit with what you were attempting to paint, now would you?" He paused and looked at Leonardo's feet. "Now, all we need are some shoes and a jacket." He walked back into his room and returned with a black pair of loafers. "Try these on," he suggested and went to the hall closet to find a suitable jacket.

When they had first come out of the house Leonardo's attention had been caught up in the discomfort of the confining shoes that squeezed his widened feet. *"Some sort of vice,"* he thought.

However, a car parked in front of the house soon caught Leonardo's eye and Rodney noticed the magnetic effect that it had on his companion. "I see you like the car," he said.

Leonardo frowned and looked at Rodney: "Is this not an automobile?" he asked.

Rodney laughed again, impressed by Leonardo's quick assimilation of his recent readings. "You're right," he admitted. "But it's also known as a "car". It's the usual name for it."

Leonardo reached for the car door handle and pulled on it. The action triggered the high-decibel screech of the anti-theft alarm system. The Master recoiled and placed his hands over his ears.

"They are very noisy machines. One could be deafened from using them," Leonardo noted loudly.

"Cars don't usually make that kind of noise," Rodney yelled back.

"What, then, is this infernal noise?"

"A car alarm," Rodney shouted as he grabbed Leonardo by the hand and pulled him away from the car.

"I have read about fire alarms in the encyclopedia. I suspect that the purpose of an automobile alarm is not to warn of a fire but more to discourage unwanted intruders," Leonardo concluded when they were away from the disturbance.

"You got it! Now I'd suggest that you ask me before you touch anything else. Let's walk away before someone comes and asks us questions."

"I now understand why they call it an alarm. I have never before heard anything quite so deafening. It is a fitting name," Leonardo said shaking his head as if to readjust his hearing.

As they started walking up the hill, Leonardo looked, wide-eyed, at the new world around him and his sore feet were soon forgotten. The architecture of the homes, the concrete sidewalks below his feet, the pavement on the roads as well as the wide green spaces around the properties, each momentarily grasped his attention. By the time he focused his attention on a particular object, something else caught his eye. Of course, many of the new things that he saw he had already read about in the encyclopedias. But there, they had been separated from other objects and he had then been able to concentrate on each one for as long as he pleased. Now, he was experiencing many of them almost simultaneously, and although the effect was unsettling, he observed everything along the way, stopping now and then, executing full three hundred and sixty degree pivots to get different perspectives of his new discoveries.

Some time after they'd started, they crossed a group of men wearing peach and white robes, their head shaven, except for a tiny wisp of hair tied at the back. Leonardo looked at Rodney with annoyance.

"You have asked me to dress in these clothes so that I would not attract attention. I think that my own garments are in better taste than those of these people."

Rodney laughed. "The people we've just met are members of a sect called Hare Krishna and they're far from being mainstream. Believe me, they do attract a lot of attention with their costumes. Even you noticed," he justified.

"Oh, even I," Leonardo repeated with lots of sarcasm.

"You know what I mean," defended Rodney. " Even though life in the twentieth century is new to you, you still were able to notice that they were not dressed like most people."

They walked for quite a while. However, Rodney was careful to choose quiet streets in order to allow Leonardo some time for adaptation. Also, quieter streets had less people around who could see Leonardo's strange behavior.

As they walked along a street by the river, Leonardo's attention was suddenly diverted to a construction site where various types of heavy machinery were being operated. He observed a mechanical shovel as it broke the ground and extracted the earth to load it into the box of a heavy-duty truck. The Master took out a conventional notepad and pencil that Rodney had given him and that he carried in his pant pocket, and drew a few sketches of what he witnessed. Rodney observed with what precision and ease Leonardo reproduced the construction site, as well as the equipment operating around it.

In the background, behind the building, Leonardo noticed the metal structure of a Derrick crane's boom.   Intrigued, he walked along the sidewalk towards the construction crane to get a closer look and sketched the crane with its boom at an angle, hoisting structural steel to the third floor of the building.   He started walking again alongside the barricade erected to keep observers off the construction site.   His eyes stayed focused on the crane as he went around in order to see it from several different angles.

Rodney followed Leonardo, attentive to the intensity in Leonardo's observing of the crane.

"Pretty impressive isn't it?" the young man said.

"Hmm!" Leonardo replied.

Rodney frowned at Leonardo's reaction.

"What is the name of the structure that protrudes at an angle?"

"I think it's called a jib," Rodney answered.

"Who is the architect and engineer for this construction?" Leonardo inquired.

"Chances are that, unlike you, the engineer and the architect are two different people," Rodney clarified trying to be as tactful as possible. He pointed to a man wearing a white hard hat speaking to two other men with yellow hard hats.

"You see that all the people working on the construction site are wearing hard hats."

"Why?"

"Because it's required by law to protect the workers."

"I am not surprised that they need protective hats given the imminent danger," Leonard observed.

"What do you mean?"

"Who is the person of authority here?" Leonardo asked.

"That would be most probably the guy wearing the white construction hat. But why do you want to know?"

Leonardo walked to an open gate and entered the construction site, with Rodney in tow.

"You're not allowed in here!" Rodney's protest didn't deter the architect and engineer from Florence.

The man wearing the white hard hat noticed the two men walking in his direction.

"Gentlemen, you're in an area restricted to construction personnel."

"May I ask who you are?" Leonardo asked.

"I should be asking you that question. But if you really want to know I'm the project manager for this project."

"I would like a word with you," Leonardo told him.

"What about?"

"The angle of your jib is not right, if you put too much weight on it, the whole machine will topple." Leonardo volunteered his opinion.

"Who is this joker? Einstein?" the now angered project manager wanted to know.

"I am Leonardo, architect and engineer in the court of Florence, and…"

"Ahem!" Rodney interrupted.

"Listen Leonardo, Mr. Architect and Engineer. Out here, I'm the engineer and the boss of this fuckin' project and I don't need an old geezer like you to come and show me my business. Now, you're not supposed to be on this site without a hat so I suggest you get the hell outa here or else I'll get your sorry ass kicked out!" the man's face had turned beet red.

"Consider yourself warned, Sir," Leonardo replied in a very calm tone.

"Why don't you warn this!" the man gave Leonardo the finger.

"Let's get out of here," Rodney said taking Leonardo's arm and leading him off the construction site. "What are you trying to do? Get us killed?"

"I should consider that gesture with his finger as a provocation, should I not?" Leonardo asked his young friend. "My only wish was to warn the man and prevent any harm being done. I do not think that my words warranted such rudeness."

"You were out of line, Leonardo."

"Out of line? What is that?"

"This man is an engineer, he's supposed to know what he's doing."

"I am sorry, but I do not share your opinion. The angle of the jib is wrong. I suspect that the machine is not level. Something will most definitely happen unless someone takes corrective measures."

"Don't worry Leonardo. These are the eighties. We're talking about state-of-the-art equipment, operated by professionals. Things have changed you know."

"The laws of physics remain and they have to be taken into account," Leonardo concluded gruffly, irritated by Rodney's defense of the new technology.

Leonardo was fascinated by cars.

"Why do we see all these automobiles that are empty along our path? Have they been abandoned because they are no longer useful? he asked Rodney.

"They're not broken and they're definitely not abandoned. They're parked."

"And what does parked mean?"

"Well, the owners of the cars park their cars whenever they don't need to use them. People use their cars to travel to and from work. As you've noticed, lots of car owners park along streets."

When finally they reached Anderson Avenue, Rodney increased his pace and walked over to a red car parked not too far from Club 230 and leaned against it.

Leonardo reacted by bringing his hands to his ears, and turning around to walk in the other direction.   After a few moments, hearing no noisy alarm, he turned towards Rodney, though he still kept his hands over his ears.

Rodney laughed at his reaction.

"Relax Leonardo. This car has no alarm on it."

"How can you be so certain?"

"Well, for one, it's an inexpensive car and I happen to know the owner.

"Is it yours?" Leonardo's eyes were shining with excitement.

"No. It belongs to my brother Anthony," Rodney chuckled. So feel free to touch it. I borrowed it from him to take you for a ride, if you like.

Leonardo had not heard that last comment. His attention was centered on the impressive invention as he moved around it and felt the shiny metal.

Rodney, remembering that he'd forgotten to pick up the car keys from the living room table, walked the short distance to the house.

During this time, Leonardo was moving his hands along all the curves of the hood as he walked toward the passenger door. He reached for the door handle and pulled. The unlocked door opened, to Leonardo's delight, and while he still held on to the handle, he swung the door open and shut, gently, as he analyzed the mechanism of the hinges. He got in the car and sat on the passenger side. He remembered that the description he had read explained that the automobile could propel itself by the means of a motor. He examined the dashboard with all its gauges and indicators. He looked at the steering column on the driver's side. As he placed his hand beside his left thigh, he accidentally brushed the gearshift. Intrigued by its appearance, he pushed it up and down and felt some sort of mechanical click with each motion. His attention was then diverted to an angled lever with a small button at the end of it.   He grabbed the handle and was impressed by the indentation that permitted a comfortable handle for the fingers. Instinctively, he let his thumb depress the button at the end of the lever, which prompted it to fold downwards.

Leonardo studied the series of buttons in front of him. He pressed them one by one to see if they initiated any action. He suddenly experienced a feeling of motion. He looked outside the window and noticed that he was moving, and that the speed of his vehicle was increasing progressively. A sudden feeling of helplessness set in as he recognized the potential danger of his situation. Knowing that one of his actions had set the automobile into motion, he reacted by pressing on the last mechanisms he had touched before he felt the car move, hoping that one of them would stop it in its tracks. He pressed the buttons one by one, in combination, and then for lack of results, simultaneously, but to no avail.

Meanwhile, Rodney, who'd just stepped out of the house, looked on helplessly as his brother's car rolled downhill past him. "Oh shit," he exclaimed. He jumped off the porch and started to run after the rollaway car, yelling at the top of his lungs: "Press on the brakes, Leonardo! Press on the damned brakes!"

He noticed, with horror, that another car had come to a stop at the intersection one hundred yards away. The runaway car, which was accelerating at an alarming rate, was headed directly into the path of the stopped car.

"Runaway car! Runaway car! Get out of the way! Get out of the goddamn way!" he yelled waving his arms in a frenzy.

The driver of the other car, hearing the cries that were directed at him, looked in the direction of their origin, his defiant look soon changing into an expression of horror when he saw that a motor vehicle, with a passenger but no driver, was coming straight at him. In a last-second reflex, he backed his car out of the path of the oncoming vehicle, which missed the front bumper by a hair.

Rodney, in pursuit, was gaining ground. The car finally slowed down when it reached a flatter section of the road. Rodney ran to the side of the driver's door, reached for the handle and in one motion, opened it. Using the open door for leverage, he stood up on the doorframe and tried to reach the brake with his right foot in a last-resort attempt to bring the car to a complete stop.

A loud noise resonated and the car's front end was jolted upwards. The vehicle had come to an abrupt and sudden stop. A cloud of dust surrounded the car and floated away on the breeze.

"Oh shit!" Rodney exclaimed.

"This is one of your preferred expressions, is it not?" remarked Leonardo, seemingly unscathed by the whole experience.

Less than twenty feet away, a flabbergasted policeman, standing beside a car that he had stopped for a traffic violation, witnessed the whole incident. Through his windshield, Rodney could see the officer approaching the scene of the accident, slowly flapping his ticket pad in his open-gloved hand.

"Oh shit!" repeated Rodney, shaking his head.

"Who is that odd-looking man?"

"He's a cop, Leonardo. Whatever you do, don't say a word. Please. Please, let me do the talking."

5

My Dad's Friend

"Anybody home?" Edmond called as he opened the door. Eugene, Oscar and Leo, carrying their luggage, followed him into the house and continued up the stairs. However, Edmond, noticing the unusual darkness in the house, was drawn to the closed living-room door. *"This was odd,"* he thought. It was agreed to leave it open at all times because the hallway was too dark when the door was shut. They'd even secured it open with a concrete block that supported a planter. Edmond opened the living room door and saw an older, bearded man sitting on the sofa, absorbed in his reading and oblivious to Edmond's presence, no doubt because of the stereo headphones on his ears.

"Excuse me," Edmond tried unsuccessfully to get the man's attention.

"I'll turn down the volume," he said to himself out loud as he walked towards the stereo amplifier.

To his surprise he noticed that the volume control was at zero. Bending over, he saw that the power button was at off.

"Hmm, strange," he said.

He looked again at the man sitting in the chair. He thought there was something vaguely familiar about him.

"I guess Santa Claus came to pay us a visit," he mumbled. He turned and as he walked towards the stairway, he started to sing: *"Oh you better watch out, you better not cry, you better not pout, I'm tellin' you why, Santa Claus has come to the Club"*.

He walked up the stairs calling out in a singing tone: "Oh Rodney, where are you?"

"Over here," Rodney's sleepy voice came from his room.

"Ah, there you are!"

"That's very perceptive of you." Rodney sat up in his bed and yawned. "So tell me, how was your week in Springerland?"

"It must've been great, I don't remember a thing. But let's not talk about me. Let's talk about you. I don't know if you've noticed, but there's an old geezer downstairs in the living room who's got headphones on and I'm sure you know something about him."

"What makes you so sure of that?"

"He's reading your encyclopedias and I know firsthand that that requires your full consent."

Rodney sighed, "Eddie, I admit. I'm the one who did it. Your private eye skills are too good for me."

"Quit the crap and tell me who the old fogy downstairs is."

"An old friend of my dad's," Rodney answered calmly, having often rehearsed the scenario. "I've invited him to spend some time over here while he completes his research at the University library. I hope you don't mind."

"I don't see any inconvenience, I guess, unless the other guys disapprove," Edmond answered, sounding somewhat confused. He paused. "You know that any friend of your dad's is welcome here."

"Thank you." Rodney knew that Edmond and the other roommates were fond of his dad and that by using him as an excuse, he'd have better chances of getting Leonardo's acceptance from the group.

"Is he a bit weird?" asked Edmond.

"What do you mean?" Rodney was not really surprised by his friend's question.

"Well, he's sitting in the living room with the headphones on, without the music. That's not something you'd normally see..."

Rodney scrambled for an answer:

"He's absent minded...uh...you know those brainy people. They often start something without finishing it. But don't worry, he's a very nice guy."

"I hope he won't mind our strange habits. You know how we are sometimes. Let's hope there's not too much of a generation gap."

"Don't worry about strange habits. We may be the ones who find him strange." Rodney warned.

"Why do you say that?"

"He's artistically inclined. You know how eccentric artists can be sometimes," he said.

"Time will tell," Edmond conceded. Then, noticing the traffic ticket lying on Rodney's desk. "What's this?" he asked with a smirk.

"Do you want to buy a ticket?"

"To win what?" Edmond asked.

"My eternal gratitude. I've had a little bad luck," he said evasively.

"Oh and what is this infraction you've committed?" Edmond continued his questioning, trying to hold back his laughter.

"Nothing much. Do you want to meet your new roommate?" he asked trying to change the subject.

"What happened?" Edmond persisted, delighting in watching his friend squirm.

"Well I sort of had an accident. My brother's car ran over a... well... a motorcycle."

"Are you serious? And you were in the car?"

"In a way."

"What do you mean, in a way?"

"The car started down the hill without me in it. I ran after it and managed to get in, but it was too late. Before I had a chance to jam on the brake, the car had run over a motorcycle."

"Hm-hm! Now that's what you call an interesting story!" Edmond said, shaking with laughter.

"Yeah. But that's not the worst part."

"Hm-mm. This is getting better and better. What's the worst part?"

"It was a police motorcycle. The main thing is that the car miraculously has no damage. So I got lucky in a way," Rodney sighed, satisfied with the slightly modified version of the story.

"But, please promise that you won't tell anyone else," he pleaded with Edmond, regretting that he'd left the ticket in plain sight.

"How much is it worth to you?" Edmond asked still laughing.

Rodney jumped off his bed, grabbed his sweat pants from the back of his chair and put them on. He changed the subject.

"I guess it's time for me to introduce you to our new roommate."

"Sure," Edmond agreed. "That poor guy doesn't know what he's getting himself into." He paused and then yelled out to the other boys:

"Yo."

"Yo," came the response from three different directions.

"Come on down. Rod would like us to meet someone."

From the room at the end of the hallway Leo answered: "She better have breasts or else I ain't coming down."

Rodney and Edmond walked down the stairs and into the living room. The successive footsteps of the other four followed. Once they'd all convened and after he'd successfully gotten Leonardo's attention by placing his hand on the pages in front of him, Rodney announced:

"Gentleman I'd like you to meet Leonard Vincent, my father's friend. He will be visiting with us for a short while."

He turned to Leonardo and presented his friends to him:

"This is Edmond, this is Eugene, this is Leo and this is Oscar."

All four boys shook hands with Club 230's new resident.

Leonardo gripped each of their hands successively and bowed in acknowledgment to each one's "Pleased to meet you" greeting.

Eugene stepped back, and whispered to Edmond, "Who's the weirdo? He'd look less out of place beside a pile of wood, building an arc."

Edmond laughed at his friend's descriptive comment.

"He's not quite that old." Rodney downplayed after hearing the gist of their conversation.

"Where are you from?" asked Leo.

"Florence," responded Leonardo without any hesitation.

"Hm-mm, yes... well, Leonard has a villa in Florence, but he was born here... uh... he's been living in Florence for twenty years," Rodney quickly interjected, trying to quash any doubts. "Isn't that right, Leonard?"

Leonardo nodded affirmatively, not wanting to contradict his host.

"And, what brings you to Caldwell?" continued Eugene.

"Uh..." uttered Rodney.

"Research," Leonardo answered, obviously in control of the situation.

Rodney could feel the adrenaline pumping through his bloodstream. He knew that Leonardo would have to pass this crucial test to avoid any suspicions from his friends.

"What kind of research?" Leo asked, intrigued.

"I came to study your new advanced technology in engineering and architecture."

"Rodney told me that you were an artist," Edmond asked, perplexed by the man's answer.

Rodney felt beads of sweat forming on his forehead. He rubbed his hands on his sweat pants to dry off the moisture accumulating there.

"I am an artist," Leonardo responded without flinching. "But as you know, painting is a science and to be able to master it, one must be able to understand the scientific laws underlying it. The same applies to architecture and engineering. I strive to create solid structures and buildings that are also artistic and pleasant to the eye."

Rodney admired the ease and the calmness of Leonardo's reply. He knew that he'd charmed his friends. He sighed in relief. *"Here endeth the first test,"* he thought.

The phone manifested itself with its sharp ring and continued ringing at regular intervals.

"Can someone get that," Eugene's voice called out from the kitchen.

The telephone rang again.

Eugene burst into the living room, angered by the lack of response from Leonardo, who was sitting by the telephone, reading and showing no sign of wanting to answer.

"It's okay Leonard, I'll get it," Eugene snarled. He picked up the receiver.

"Hello... Hi, Leo. What? You're not serious! Okay, I'll come and pick you up... I should be there in about a half-hour. See you then," he concluded and hung up the phone. He turned to Leonardo.

"That was Leo. He called me from the hospital. Apparently, he stepped on some glass and had to get it removed surgically. I'm going to pick him up."

To his dismay, Leonardo didn't even seem aware of his presence.

"You smell like rotting fish," he said trying to provoke some reaction from the totally absorbed reader. Nothing. He made a masturbation motion, but that had no effect either. After many similar attempts, he gave up and finding the situation quite hilarious, finally left to go pick up Leo at the hospital. The figure in the living room did not react and restricted his movements to the turning of the pages.

With undivided attention, Leonardo followed Rodney's every activity as he cooked dinner on the stove.

"What are you preparing?" he asked.

"Tonight, my dear Master, you will taste Salisbury steak with broccoli and mashed potatoes."

Leonardo was captivated by the red-hot elements under the frying pan. He thought the concept of cooking without an exposed flame quite revolutionary and he marveled at its efficiency.

"Do you know where Eugene's gone?" Rodney asked.

"He told me that he had to pick up your friend Leo at the hospital. Apparently, he injured his foot when he stepped on a piece of glass," Leonardo specified.

"I hope it's not too serious," Rodney expressed with concern.

"From what I gathered, everything was fine," Leonardo reassured.

Rodney was happy to hear that Eugene had managed to communicate with Leonardo while he read. *"I'll have to ask how he does it,"* he made a mental note.

The vibration of the footsteps on the porch was felt in the kitchen.

"Perhaps your friends Eugene and Leo have returned," Leonardo predicted.

But as the footsteps came closer to the kitchen, Leonardo gathered that there was only one person. His observation was justified when Charles entered the kitchen.

"Rodney, my man," he exclaimed. "I heard the good news!"

"What good news?"

"I've heard through the grapevine that you've accepted the position with Sparo Aeronautics."

"Good news travel fast, I guess. I'm sorry you didn't hear it from me first. I would've liked to tell you the news myself," Rodney explained.

Charles walked over to his friend and gave him a hug. "I'm just happy that you've changed your mind."

Rodney felt strange knowing that someone who would die in the near future was hugging him. The vision of his friend dangling from a rope flashed through his mind, causing him to shudder.

Charles noticed the sweat on his friend's forehead. "Jesus Christ, Rod! Are you feeling alright?"

"Of course. I'm okay," Rodney said, awkwardly trying to conceal his emotions.

Charles looked at him with solicitude. Then seeing Leonardo, he extended his hand.

"I don't think I've had the pleasure."

"The pleasure of what?" Leonardo asked candidly.

Rodney tried to intervene. He walked over to Leonardo and grabbed him by the shoulders.

"This man likes to joke around. Charles, I'd like you to meet Leonard, our new roommate for the summer."

"Pleased to meet you," Charles greeted.

Leonardo replied with his characteristic nod.

"I've got to go, me boy. I've got m'self a date with a mighty fine lady, t'night. I just wanted to stop by and congratulate you on your fine choice. I'll talk to you later. Hey, by the way, did you guys hear about that crane that crashed on a construction site by the river? Apparently the fuckin' asses overloaded the jib and it came crashing on the building. The guys were saying that apparently the machine was not level or something."

Rodney's lower jaw fell open as he heard the news. He turned towards Leonardo who had a "See, I told you so" look in his eye and a chill went down his spine.

"There you go again Rodney, me lad. You're going pale again. Don't worry nobody got hurt."

"The laws of physics are constant through time," Leonardo reminded Rodney.

"Yeah. Hm! Well … Charlie, drop by any time. But next time don't stay so long," Rodney stammered.

Sounds coming from the entrance interrupted the discussion. This time, footsteps were accompanied by the sound of someone hopping.

Edmond called out from upstairs:

"Hey, Peg Leg, what happened to you?"

Leo's voice replied:

"A little accident, nothing too serious, honey. I just need a few days' rest and then I'll be good as new. Thanks for caring."

The hopping sound came nearer. Leo, assisted by Eugene who was chuckling at his friend's predicament, hobbled into the kitchen. Edmond's footsteps could be heard on the stairs.

"I'm sorry I didn't leave a message, but I had to go and pick up Leo at the emergency room," Eugene explained apologetic.

"I heard," Rodney acknowledged.

"How did you know? Did Leo call you from the hospital?"

"No, Leonard told me. Apparently you informed him."

The blood drained from Eugene's face and he sat down on the chair beside Leonardo as if he'd lost the strength in his legs. He looked at Leonardo, who looked back at him with a knowing smile.

"Jesus Murphy!" Eugene was now beet red.

"What's the matter, did you see a ghost?" Edmond asked.

"Boy do I ever feel stupid!"

"Trap, are you okay?" Leo seemed concerned.

"I don't want to talk about it," Eugene's tone was definite. He was remembering, and regretting, his foolish actions of the afternoon.

Leonardo just sat there, serene, vindicated.

"Leo, what happened to your foot?" Rodney asked.

"I stepped on broken glass from a cologne bottle that broke in the University showers. The doctor cleaned it all up and told me not to walk on my left foot and to use crutches for a week," he said as he pointed at the crutches that Eugene had placed against the kitchen doorframe.

"Poor Leo," Edmond said in his best imitation of a doting mother as he patted the top of his head. "You poor baby."

"So what else is new?" Eugene asked.

"Well, I'm not sure if I should say this," Edmond said, knowing full well that he shouldn't say it, "but I know that one of the people present in this room had a little accident recently."

Rodney glared at his friend for letting the cat out of the bag and breaking his promise.

Edmond continued: "Apparently our roommate Rod scrapped a police motorcycle with his brother's car."

"Thanks for your silence, Eddie. I knew I could count on you." Rodney was really angry.

"Don't mention it. It was my pleasure."

"Tell us more about this, Rod," Eugene prompted. He walked over and placed his hand on Rodney's shoulder. "Now, tell old Trap all about your adventures of the weekend," he insisted.

"Your dinner is ready Leonard," Rodney evaded the prodding from his friend. The others all chuckled and nudged each other behind Rodney's back.

"I'd like to hear the whole story Rod, but I'm really tired. Leo was now showing some signs of fatigue. I guess I'm still feeling the effects of the local anesthesia." He pulled himself up, and hopped over to the door and grabbed his wooden crutches. "Good night guys," he bid his friends, and slowly proceeded to his room.

Since the return of the three roommates, peace and quiet were not operative words at Club 230. Leonardo now made the living room his quarters, using mainly the sofa bed and the big armchair. He was growing accustomed to the constant hullabaloo. Also, things had quieted down somewhat now that the clement weather had arrived and the boys were spending more time in the open area on the balcony above.

"Leonard!" Rodney called out.

Leonardo kept his eyes riveted to the encyclopedia and as usual, showed no acknowledgment.

Rodney smiled, walked over to the artist and pulled the book away from him.

"Let's stop the games," he said.

"What game?" Leonardo asked.

"The make-believe-that-you-are-too-absorbed-by-your-reading-to-hear-or-see-anything-else game."

Leonardo sat back in his chair and smiled.

"My dear Rodney, what you have observed in my behavior is not an act but a character trait," Leonardo expressed.

"Is that right?"

Leonardo joined his hands behind his head. "When I am concentrating on something, I try to give it my undivided attention. But that does not mean that I am not aware of other things that happen around me. I am aware of them, but I do not usually respond to them, since the most important thing for me is the task at hand. That explains why I do not usually answer you when I am reading, unless..."

"Unless I do something to obstruct your ability to see or feel what you're doing," Rodney interjected.

"That is correct. I am truly sorry if I seem rude, but that is the way I am."

"But what makes you work that way?" Rodney asked, not fully sure of what Leonardo was trying to explain.

"I suppose that the best explanation would be nature."

Leonardo paused. "Since childhood, I have had the ability to do many things at the same time. As I progressed in years, I unconsciously conditioned myself to focus most of my energies on the primary concern of the moment, while still assimilating other events or things around me."

"You're telling me! When we speak to you while you're reading, you don't even acknowledge our presence or react to what we tell you. How do you explain that?" Rodney asked.

Leonardo paused and collected his thoughts. "Perhaps the best way I can explain it is as follows. As you know, man is gifted with five senses that permit him to experience his environment. To me the most important of these senses is the ability to see things. It is difficult for me to determine which of my senses is in second place. As you would say, it would be a toss-up between the sense of touch and that of hearing. In all my readings since I have come to this time, I have learned much about the processes of the senses and in this way have come to understand myself better. In ordinary times, all senses have the same probability of being stimulated, depending on the environment and the activity. But when I am reading, I see the letters unfold into words before my eyes and my cerebrum decodes and makes sense of these words so that I understand them. That is quite demanding in itself. So what probably happens is that I condition myself to give priority to my sense of sight while I am reading so that I may understand what is written. Therefore, all other senses become secondary to the first. In the meantime, if something is said to me, it is most probably registered in my mind or memory until it can be recalled later when I have brought my five senses back to equal levels."

Rodney was quiet for a moment. The Master's reasoning proved that logic transcended time and experience. He was actually able to corroborate everything that he'd read on Leonardo's character. He relished the extraordinary opportunity that was his. The shock of having traveled back in time now seemed worthwhile.

"It's true, I have traveled back in time," he reminded himself. Oddly, he'd forgotten about that during the past few hours. "What made me forget?" he asked himself. Suddenly it dawned on him that what he'd experienced since the return of his friends was all new. In his previous past, he'd left the morning of their return and hadn't seen them again until the end of the summer. Everything seemed so normal that it made him forget that he'd gone back four months in time. Also, it had been more important to spend energy hiding Leonardo's true identity than trying to hide the incongruity of his own presence. He was an intruder who, in his prior past, hadn't experienced what he was living now. He suddenly felt like an impostor.

"...seems that I have lost you my friend," Leonardo observed.

Seeing that the haze was disappearing from Rodney's eyes, he felt confident that he'd regained his full attention.

"So tell me what has brought about this conversation?" he asked.

"Hm?" Rodney returned from his daydream. "Conversation..." he recollected. "Oh! Eugene came to see me earlier on and told me about his jester-like behavior with you yesterday afternoon. He couldn't believe that you'd clearly heard the so-called monologue he had with you."

Rodney turned and walked to the sofa where he sat down. "He regrets some of his words and actions."

"And so he should," approved Leonardo, "I can describe his behavior in one word: insolence."

"Don't judge him too harshly," Rodney defended, "After all, you must admit that to them, your behavior is a bit odd. I must confess that I've been pretty frustrated too, when I needed to talk to you and wasn't able to get your attention. On a few occasions, I've come awfully close to resorting to what you call insolence."

Leonardo smiled, touched by Rodney's loyalty to his friend.

"You are right. My behavior must seem rude at times. I apologize. But alas, it is a character trait from which I will never part, for it is an integral part of my being," he explained philosophically. I will pass no further judgment on our friend Trap, as you all like to call him," Leonardo promised.

Leonardo pointed to a big white bag that Rodney had brought into the room and placed beside the easy chair.

"What is that?" he asked.

Rodney smiled: "That's a bag full of surprises." He reached for the bag and put it on his lap.

"I thought you might want to be creative." He pulled out paint tubes of various colors. "So, I've bought some oil paints, some brushes and all sorts of neat little things that you can use for painting. And I've got some canvases upstairs in my room that you can use."

Leonardo reached for the paint tubes and examined the unfamiliar format closely.

"Neat," he repeated the young man's jargon.

From where he sat in the living room, Leonardo saw Eugene pass by on his way upstairs, carrying a big drum-like container. Edmond was close behind toting plastic bags full of small, opaque blocs that Leonardo now knew were called ice. Rodney completed the pack with a case of beer. They wore shorts and no T-shirts, a clear indication of the warm weather outside. After spending the early afternoon hours soaking up the spring rays with their bare torsos, they were thirsty.

The stairs cracking under the weight of the trio was a familiar sound to Leonardo's ears. He was able to identify each one of his younger roommates by the sound and rhythm of his footsteps on the staircase. For the first time, he felt a certain fellowship with the other tenants of the household, something that he had not experienced until then. *"I am starting to feel like one of them,"* he thought.

"Leonard, feel free to join us for a drink if you want," Rodney called from upstairs.

"There's lots of brew for everyone," Leo added.

"Thank you but I have some more reading to do," Leonardo declined.

Hearing the sound of water running in the bathtub, he was intrigued. However, he had witnessed so many surprising things since he had arrived that he decided it was best to remain downstairs. He smiled at the thought of the young men sharing the bathroom in the morning. Never had he experienced such openness. However, he was a bit unnerved by the lack of privacy that prevailed in the household. Yet, he found their camaraderie fascinating, despite the non-stop pranks that they played on one another.

Meanwhile, in the bathroom, the boys had emptied the bags of ice into the plastic garbage container already full of beer bottles. Eugene drew the bath and checked the temperature of the running water every few seconds to make sure that it was just right. Leo had removed his shorts and was sitting on the toilet seat, waiting patiently for the bath to fill. In the meantime, Edmond placed as much beer as possible under ice to accelerate the cooling effect. All operations were being performed in silence.

"How's the bath coming along, Trapo?" Edmond asked.

Eugene taking off his clothes was his answer. Leo raised himself from his sitting position and tried to negotiate an entry into the bath.

"I'm ready for a cold one," he said.

Rodney, who had left the bathroom for a moment, returned with the traditional cans of V-8 and Mott's Clamato juices and placed them in the makeshift cooler. He gave each person one of the beer mugs that were hanging in his hands and then placed the one left over on the toilet tank.

"Who's the other glass for?" Eugene asked.

"It's for Leonard, in case he changes his mind and joins us for a beer," he answered.

"This is going to be great," Edmond anticipated as he too removed his underwear.

"Hm, somebody got a sunburn and will hate himself in the morning," Eugene pointed out.

"I'll be okay," Edmond shrugged. "Men like me can take it," he jokingly bragged.

He retrieved four beers from the bucket and handed them out to his friends, who accepted the cold refreshment quite heartily.

"Anyone for some Clamato or V-8?" he asked.

"Clamato. Clamato. V-8," came the successive responses.

Edmond opened the cans of cocktail juices and handed them to his friends.

"My, my! You'd make a great bartender, Eddie my man," complimented Rodney.

"He should with all the practice he's had making his own drinks," Eugene agreed with a touch of irony.

"I think that's quite a polite way of saying that he's a lush," remarked Leo with a big grin.

"Thanks guys. It's so nice to be appreciated," Edmond retorted.

"Ah, we're so sorry," Eugene said, in mock sympathy.

"Come and sit beside Uncle Leo," Leo said as he patted the water beside him. The action caused a certain amount of splash.

"Hey, cut that out," protested Rodney.

From the living room, Leonardo could overhear the conversation in the bathroom and he felt compelled to go and see what all the action and discussion was all about. The reunions in the bathroom were usually a thing of the morning. But recently, there had also been some in late afternoon. Motivated by his curiosity, he climbed the stairs and walked to the bathroom where he was greeted by the boys sitting side by side in the tub, their legs hanging over the side, their hands holding their respective mugs of beer.

"Hey, Lenny baby," Leo called out with unprecedented familiarity. "Come on in and have a little brewski."

"Brewski?" Leonardo asked confused.

"Yeah, a beer," Leo continued, "Haven't you ever had one before?"

"No," Leonardo paused, and then reconsidered. "It has been so long since I have tasted one that it seems that I never did," he fibbed calmly.

From his position, Rodney reached out and pulled out a beer from the container. "Who's got the church key?" he asked, looking around him for the bottle opener.

"Who needs one? The caps are twist tops. They have been for years." Edmond reminded.

"Would you hand me the glass, please?" Rodney asked Leonardo, pointing to the mug on the toilet tank.

Leonardo complied. He watched Rodney's motion as he opened the bottle and poured it into the beer mug, inclining the glass to minimize the head. So many questions were going through his head, but he thought it better not to ask them, lest they underline his naiveté in front of Rodney's unsuspecting friends. He grabbed the now full mug that Rodney handed to him.

"To our new roommate," Eugene toasted, pointing his glass in Leonardo's direction.

Leonardo observed the other boys' reactions and imitated them in meeting the toast.

His first sip of the potion surprised him with the bubbly effect that it had in his mouth. Then he was taken by the strong, bitter taste. His grimace didn't go unnoticed and generated some laughs.

"It has been a long time," he tried to explain.

The second sip had very much the same effect, and the boys relished his reaction.

"Believe me, before the summer's ended, you'll have acquired a taste for the stuff," Edmond promised.

"Here's to beer," Eugene toasted raising his glass.

"Hear! Hear!" came the collective response.

A second case of beer was now stacked in the corner over the first one. It was the receptacle for empty bottles. The four bathers, who were showing the creeping effects of their drinking, were singing along with an old Rolling Stones tune that emanated from Rodney's room.

"...*You can't always get what you wa-ant...But if you try sometimes...You get what you need...*"

Leaning against the doorframe, Leonardo, notepad in hand, was intently sketching the bathers. At first, his face had been emotionless and passive, so hard looking that one might have thought he had been chiseled out of stone. His eyes traveled from side to side, trying to capture every form, every curve of the strong youthful bodies before him.

"...*You can't always get what you want...*" the offbeat chant continued.

The drunken roommates were oblivious to the artist's presence. They swung their beer mugs from side to side, spilling some of it as they did. The beer no longer had the reddish Clamato-enhanced tint; it was just traditional blond beer.

"Guys we've got to think about going out and finding some women," Leo suggested.

"Babes!" Eugene cried out. "Prrrr...prrrr".

"You see, Miss, I'm studying to be a doctor. I will major in gynecology." Leo acted out the sleazy pick-up lines.

"Why don't we go to your place for a full physical," Eugene continued the obscene clichés.

"I don't think we'd stand a chance if a girl heard us now," Rodney said, "My feeling is that they'd probably turn around and walk as quickly as they can in the opposite direction."

"After kneeing us in the balls," Leo added.

"I guess we could say that these are pretty chauvinistic remarks," Edmond expressed.

"You guys are so damned perceptive," Leo said with sarcasm.

"We're just the average, sensible and sensitive university students," Eugene added.

The sound of bubbles coming up in the bathtub water caused a sudden silence among the bathers.

"Speak again, oh toothless wonder," Leo wisecracked.

"You stink!" Eugene yelled out to Leo with an air of disgust. He gulped down the rest of his beer, hoping that it would help to make the stench disappear.

"I think you died, but you don't know about it yet," Edmond cried out at the culprit.

"It's a sign of good health," Leo protested, "My mother always told me that you could always determine the health of a person by the stench he left behind after a good crap."

"If that's true, you're the healthiest guy in town," Rodney concluded laughing.

"Thank you," Leo said chuckling.

"Well, if you let another one of those go, you won't live to benefit from your good health," Eugene warned.

"None of us will," Edmond concluded. "We'll all be dead."

The comments generated belly laughs from the group.

Rodney observed Leonardo, who worked seemingly undisturbed by the boisterous mood in the room. *"Either his theory on senses is true or he has a problem with his sense of smell,"* he thought remembering their earlier conversation.

But, in truth, Leonardo was feeling the lust building up inside him at the sight of Edmond's strong chest, Leo's powerful arms, Rodney's muscular stomach. A picture of Salai ran through his mind. How he had enjoyed the strong physique and the well-defined facial features of his young protégé. How he longed for him. His craving, whetted by the memories, became overpowering. The images of his lover became superimposed on the young bathers and he longed to join him. As his desire overpowered him, he forcibly tugged at his clothes, shedding them piece by piece.

Rodney noticed the dramatic change in Leonardo. He saw the hunger in his eyes and he knew what had put it there. He could see that his friends had also seen their new roommate's strange behavior. Within seconds, Leonardo had stripped down to his breeches, which were obviously strained by his excitement.

"Leonard! What the fuck are you doing?" an angry Rodney yelled out.

Rodney's angry voice brought Leonardo back to reality. He shook his head and realized that he was not in the presence of the tantalizing Salai but of his hosts. He was now painfully aware of his state of undress. Embarrassed and ashamed, he picked up his clothes and backed up until the wall stopped him from going any further. He felt his way along the wall to the door and escaped from the scene with surprising swiftness for a man of his age. Having found refuge downstairs in the living room, he closed and barricaded the door behind him.

Since the water festivities had given way to a tragic freak show, silence reigned in the bathroom. The four boys remained in the bath, wordless, motionless, trying to understand what they'd just experienced.

"I don't want any goddamn faggot living in this house," Leo protested emphatically. They convened in Edmond's room to discuss Leonardo. Leo sat on the bed, his back against the wall. Eugene had found some space beside him and lay on his side, his head supported by his hand. Edmond was sitting on a reversed chair, his forearms crossed over the backrest and Rodney remained standing, leaning against the doorframe to the hallway, his arms folded on his chest.

"I agree," Eugene supported. "We don't need to have a fairy living in this place. Maybe he has AIDS and all; we don't need that kind of crap."

"There's no proof that he's gay," Rodney tried to defend.

"For Chrissake, what other proof do you need?" Leo growled, put off by Rodney's weak defense. "The guy was wearing those pansy pants and had a hard-on big enough to hang a dozen donuts."

"I want the cock sucker out of here," Eugene was emphatic.

Edmond remained silent and listened to the deliberations, the way he usually did when a serious issue was being discussed. Rodney looked at him for support, but his friend had obviously decided to remain impartial.

"You guys are prosecuting the poor bugger as if he was a criminal," Rodney pleaded.

"He's in my book," Eugene said, not willing to bend.

"I think that he probably learned his lesson today when he saw our reactions," Rodney continued his defense. "He won't try it again, I guarantee it."

"What makes you so damned sure he won't?" Leo was now quite worked up." Has he been porking you on the side? Is that why you're so intent on defending him? I bet he gives good head."

Rodney's control had now lost its bout with his anger. He moved menacingly towards Leo. Edmond got up from his chair and placed himself between the two friends.

"Smarten up guys. You dick-heads won't get anywhere by fighting", he said.

"I don't want to fight with a queer," Leo continued his provocation. "He might bite me and give me AIDS."

Rodney, livid from the scathing comments, screamed and pounced towards Leo, pushing Edmond off to the side. "It's a fight you want, you've got it," he said.

There was a flurry of punches, but Edmond's strong intervention soon put an end to them.

"If you guys want to fight, you'll have to deal with me first," he said firmly. The two infuriated fighters backed off.

"I'm gettin' the hell out of here," Leo growled and left in a huff.

"I'm not sticking around faggots," Eugene supported as he followed Leo out the door.

Rodney was devastated by his friends' feelings. He let himself fall onto the chair and took his head in both his hands.

"What the hell have I gotten myself into?" he asked himself.

He knew that trying to explain the real situation to Leo and Eugene would have been fruitless. They'd never believe the time-travel story. "*I'm damned if I do, and I'm damned if I don't*", he thought.

"Do you want to talk about it?" Edmond offered.

"What is there to talk about? You've heard them. I'm a homosexual. I've just been convicted."

"That's not what I'm talking about. You're hiding something about this Leonard Vincent guy. I can tell. There's something bizarre about that man that you're not telling. Why don't you spill your guts?"

For a moment, Rodney had the eerie feeling that Edmond could read right through him, that the cards he was so desperately trying to hold from him were transparent.

"I don't understand," he said trying to act confused.

"Think about it. If you want to talk, my door is open. If you don't, well, I understand. It must be something pretty important if you're going through so much trouble to hide it. Your reputation is the price you're paying, though."

He paused and looked directly into Rodney's eyes.

"By the way, if you're queer, I'm a ballet dancer," he testified.

"I appreciate your trust," Rodney thanked. "I'm sorry about the trouble Leonardo's caused."

"Leonardo?" Edmond repeated.

Rodney didn't even try to rectify the slip of the tongue, for fear of giving more away.

"Your friend can stay."

"What about the other guys?"

"Leave it to me. They'll see my way."

Rodney got up and firmly shook his ally's hand. A hug was somehow out of the question.

"Thanks Ed, I really appreciate your support."

"Just try to control our friend Leonardo," he recommended, with a little knowing spark in his eye.

"I will."

Rodney had often found solace in the comfort of his bed. He lay on his back, his hands folded behind his head, pondering his adventure back in time. He felt as if nature had put him in the pillory, exposed and vulnerable to ridicule because of his extraordinary situation. His problems seemed dwarfed, however, when he thought of Leonardo's plight. *"He should be the one feeling sorry for himself,"* he thought.

He felt even worse because despite the fact that Leonardo's homosexuality had been intimated in some of his biographies, he'd recklessly exposed Leonardo to the temptation. He couldn't forgive himself for making such a mistake.

His mind wandered. He thought of the heart-warming and confidence-boosting support he'd received from Edmond. He was amazed by his friend's rationale, by his way of analyzing a situation objectively without letting his personal biases or feelings get the better of his judgment.

The question remained. Should he be told the secret? Should he be made aware of nature's manipulation of time? *"Perhaps he won't believe my story,"* he thought. Somehow that seemed unlikely. He had a feeling that if anyone was to believe him, Edmond and perhaps Oscar, were the people who would. But was it fair to implicate them? Rodney couldn't see any advantage to their knowing. He didn't want to subject them to the humiliation he'd just lived. Perhaps the best thing was to keep them out of the whole matter. In any case, what could he tell them?

"Hey guys, guess what? I've seen our future. You know our good friend Charlie? Well beware. Be nice to him. Because come September, he'll be history."

"No, they don't need that burden," he thought. *"After all, Leonardo may disappear as quickly and as unexpectedly as he came, to return to his past. I may return back to the future where I belong."* Still, the feeling that his reunion with Leonardo through time travel had a purpose kept haunting him. What purpose? He still had no answer.

Someone knocked on his bedroom door.

"Come in," Rodney called out.

The door opened, and Edmond's head appeared. "Do you have a minute?" he asked.

"Sure. As you can see I'm not too busy."

Edmond walked in and sat on the bed.

"Have you spoken to Leonard since...since the incident?"

"No, I haven't. He's barricaded himself in the living room and hasn't come out since. I've tried to get his attention by knocking on the door and by calling, but so far, I've been unsuccessful," Rodney explained, troubled by the Master's behavior. "I guess he wants to spend some time alone." Rodney sat up in his bed. "Why do you ask?

"I just walked by and heard some pretty strange noises," Edmond said.

"What kind of noise?"

"It sounds like he's moving furniture all over the place."

"Maybe that's his way of getting rid of his frustrations," Rodney assumed with a shrug. "I'm sure we'll see what he's up to soon. He'll have to come out of there for food sometime, or to go to the john."

"I have a question," Debbie said, her arms wrapped around Rodney's waist.

"Go ahead, I'm listening."

"What made you so sure that I'd say yes, when you asked to come over to my place?" she asked still shocked by Rodney's boldness.

"I gambled."

Having lived in the future had its advantages. Rodney had needed to get out of the house and put some distance between himself and the recent events. He'd remembered the good time he and Debbie had had on the night of the future party. He'd enjoyed her company, her straightforwardness, her sensuality. He wanted to relive those pleasures. *"How interesting,"* he thought. *"I have the advantage of knowing her most intimate secrets without her having any idea of mine."*

"I had a terrific evening," she thanked. "You're quite a gentleman."

"I enjoy your company." His arm around her shoulder gently tightened and he smiled down at her pretty face.

She kissed him, appreciative of his comment. "You know, I've been dreaming of going out with you," she confided. "Since I first set my eyes on you at school, I've thought of you as a pretty special guy. And now, look at us."

With her hands, she reached for his head and pulled it softly towards her so that she could kiss him once more. They locked into an embrace that made time meaningless.

"Will you excuse me for a moment?" she said as she pulled herself away from him.

Debbie walked to her room and closed the door behind her. A few moments later she left the bedroom and entered the bathroom with a small fabric bag under her arm.

Rodney kept his eyes fixed on her every movement. His heartbeat accelerated with the sudden flow of adrenaline as he anticipated what was to follow. More than anything, he wanted to relive the passion and the tenderness they'd shared.

Trying to calm himself, he looked around the room. Now that he was able to give it his full attention, the quality and the beauty of the decor impressed him. The furniture and the artifacts, as well as the sumptuous apartment, were not what one would expect to find in a young student's apartment. Rodney assumed that Debbie came from a well-to-do family. He imagined her as the daughter of Mr. Big Shot, the company executive. He pictured a silver-haired, well-dressed man sitting in front of Debbie telling her:

"Now that you've reached adulthood, you must learn to fend for yourself. You must learn to survive. That's the only way you'll build your character and become self-sufficient. Therefore, I suggest that you live on your own during your University studies so that you can learn all about roughing it. No more luxuries for you, young lady. I know this may sound harsh, but you will thank me for it later."

The imaginary man then walked over to Debbie and gave her a fatherly embrace. He reached into his breast pocket, pulled out an envelope full of money and handed it to her.

"Here you go, my dear. Don't spend it all at the same place," he warned. "Until you graduate, you will have to drive your own car. No more chauffeur for you, young lady."

Rodney walked over to the Louis XIV loveseat beside a brass- legged table supporting a Tiffany lamp. Rodney admired the plush, colorful Persian rug that gave him the impression of walking on a cloud.

For the first time in days, Rodney felt really good about himself, about where he was and about the circumstances. The experience he was living with Leonardo was a fascinating one, but it left a heavy cloud of anxiety over him. Debbie's company alleviated the pressure, for now, and supplied him with a temporary couldn't-give-a-damn feeling. She was now the center of his attention and of his desires. He wanted to open up all his senses to her. He wanted to fall prey to her will and enjoy a night without inhibitions.

The bathroom door swung open to give way to Debbie's seductively clad figure. The lace and silk lingerie defined her upper body's voluptuous forms, clinging to her curves, the patterned fabrics concealing very little. One of its spaghetti straps had slipped down one arm as if to show the way. The short length of the apparel highlighted the firm buttocks and shapely legs rising above high-heeled pumps. She posed for Rodney, letting the bathroom light in the background accentuate her curves.

Rodney's heart raced with excitement. Never had he felt so out of control. His swallowing became labored.

"So. What do you think? Do you approve?" she asked in a seductive tone, looking suggestively in his direction.

"Yeah...uh...I mean, you look fantastic," he fumbled for words.

Never had a woman made him feel so awkward. His young body was bursting with desire, but his mind made him feel like a bumbling novice. The women he'd met before had always been reserved and somehow more compliant than what he'd experienced with Debbie.

She moved closer to him and planted a soft kiss on his half-opened mouth.

"Let's see what you have to offer," she said as she slowly undid the top button of his shirt, placing her warm hand on his muscular chest.

She unbuttoned and opened the shirt, exposing his torso, and traced circles with her moist probing tongue on the exposed skin. Her hands wandered all over his exposed abdomen, seeking out every curve, every muscle.

Rodney was motionless, his breath activated by the ecstasy of her touch. His body soaked in the caresses from the talented hands. His eyes closed, he savored the seduction.

Debbie walked behind him and continued the sultry massage with her hands as she kissed the back of his neck and his strong shoulders. With precise dexterity, she brought Rodney's pants down to his knees, careful to leave the tight fitting underwear on.

"Tonight, you're mine," she ordered with a whisper. "I have you under my spell."

Rodney experienced the hypnotic effect of her love dance. He felt the devious curse she'd cast. He felt his body fall under the control of her whim. Powerless, he gave in to her imagination and her fantasies.

The moonlight that had found its way into the room stimulated Rodney's imagination. The shadows it helped define were ever changing due to the unknown quarters in which he found himself. He remembered being led into the room by his insatiable lover. There, they'd chosen the bed as the next nest of their intensive lovemaking.

For the first time in his twenty-two years, he was feeling something that was beyond description. It was like pain, but not a sharp pain like from a bump or a cramp. The feeling was more generalized. It was pleasant unceasing pain, an addictive sensation of tolerable restlessness.

Rodney looked at the sleeping beauty beside him. *"She looks so angelic,"* he thought. *"But now, I know better, don't I?"*

He smiled satisfied and proud of being in the presence of such a person. He felt compelled to get up, walk to the window and yell out to the world how he felt.

"But, how do I feel? Am I in love? Is this love?"

If it was, he wanted it to stay. Thoughts raced through his mind. Again, the trip back in time seemed almost worth it. Perhaps nature had used a peculiar route for him to meet the woman of his dreams. His imagination created a whole scenario that justified the situation. However, one factor remained unsettled. No matter how creative his scenario became, the mere presence of Leonardo brought him back to reality. He was the one piece in the puzzle that never fit. In fact, its shape was so peculiar that the piece seemed meant for another game altogether.

"One thing's for certain. Debbie and I are meant for each other," he concluded, trying not to dampen that part of his fantasy.

He cuddled against her barely covered body as if he was trying to transfer his feelings to her through osmosis. He kissed her neck as he wrapped his arm around her, molding his body to hers. The enchantress responded with a sleepy moan of approval.

The ringing of the telephone broke the peace of the moment.

Debbie jumped from her sleep and groped around on the night table to locate the disturbing machine.   Rodney heard the answering machine kicking in to take the message.

"Hello," she answered, her voice coarse from sleep.

She turned on the light beside the telephone.

"It's okay, I don't mind," she said, her voice slowly losing its sleepiness.

"I'll be there in half an hour." She paused. "I will. Good-bye."

As she hung up the telephone, she looked at Rodney with an expression that said: "Whatever you do, don't ask me what this is about!"

"Rod, I have to leave for a few hours. I'll be back before you know it. I don't have time to explain.   We'll talk when I come back, okay?" she pleaded with him.

She picked up the phone and dialed.   She paced the room waiting for an answer.   "Could you send a cab to twenty-five twenty five Steeple...Apartment eighteen-fifteen...In ten minutes.   The destination is 245 Holditch.   Thank you."

Debbie walked to the bathroom and closed the door behind her. Rodney heard the bath water start to run, followed by the sizzling sound of the water shooting out of the showerhead.   He sat there wondering what was happening.   What seemed like a dream a few moments before had suddenly turned into a strange nightmare, one that his mind would not have dared create.   The feeling of elation he'd experienced earlier on was now being replaced by one of confusion.

"What the hell is going on here?" he asked as if he was expecting an answer.

The shower stopped.   Within a few seconds, Debbie stepped out of the bathroom, a towel wrapped around her body.   She walked towards a chest of drawers topped with a three-faced mirror.   She turned the mirror lights on and started to apply some make-up, showing remarkable adroitness and speed.   She followed with the brushing of her hair.   Within moments she'd entered the walk-in closet from which she came out within a bat of an eye, wearing a black satin pantsuit that enhanced her figure.

"My! Do we always dress up like this at this time of night?" Rodney asked sarcastically. "Whoever you're meeting must be pretty special for you to rush out to him in the middle of the night."

"You're right."

Debbie offered no other reply. She continued her preparation and pulled out black high-heeled shoes from the closet.

Rodney felt the cloud of anxiety forming over his head once again. His whole body tensed with anger and annoyance. He walked over to the living room, turned on the light and picked his clothes up off the floor. An image of the distinguished gentleman ran through his mind once again. He was dressed in fine clothes. But this time, he was not her father. The caresses he was receiving from Debbie were not incestuous. The physical traits Rodney's mind attributed to him suddenly looked so different now that there was no possibility of blood relation.

The man reached into his breast pocket and pulled out an envelope with money.

"Here you are, my dear. Don't spend it all at the same place...like I just did," he was now saying, not without some irony. "My chauffeur will come back and give you a lift home if you so desire."

"Rodney," Debbie's voice called him back from his self-inflicted nightmare.

She laughed when she saw him standing naked in the middle of the living room, daydreaming. He noticed how classy she looked as she approached him. Her hand reached for his chin.

"I hope you'll be here when I get back," she said using the seductive voice that had worked wonders on him previously.

She kissed him, but he didn't return the kiss with the same warmth. He stood before her, looking through her, his usually expressive face almost lifeless.

"Please stay," she asked with apparent sincerity, "I'll be back as soon as I can."

Rodney didn't respond. The buzzer resounded, announcing the arrival of the cab.

"I've got to go," she said as she walked towards the door. "Bye," she said sadly, as she looked back.

Rodney couldn't answer. He stood, as if immobilized by some intruding force. The pain of heartbreak was creeping in.

He got dressed. Then, his mind reeling from the rude awakening, tortured by the let-down and curious about the person on the other end of the telephone conversation, Rodney rewound the tape on the recording machine. He pressed on the play button and sat on the edge of the bed.

"Hello," Debbie's voice answered.

"Debbie," the man's voice responded, "I'm sorry to wake you."

"It's okay, I don't mind," she responded.

"You'd make someone really happy if you came now. When can you get here?"

"I'll be there in half an hour."

"Dress nice. It's always a hit," the man requested.

"Good bye," she replied.

"Click," the phone echoed.

Rodney lay back on the bed, his arms spread-eagle above his head, his legs hanging off the side, feeling like a jerk.

"This must be love," he uttered with sad irony.

6

Four Students Bathing

Rodney was staring at the middle-aged waitress, who looked like she'd risen on the wrong side of the bed. He even got the impression that no matter from what side she got up, it would be the wrong one. Her unfriendly attitude would probably be the same throughout her shift - that of a bulldog that hasn't yet taken its unwilling master for its daily walk.

"What wouldya like?" she asked in a dry, hurried voice.

"I'm not sure," Charles responded.

"Well I'll come back later. I've got other people waiting and they've probably made up their mind by now," she snapped in a make-a choice-now-or-maybe-never tone and then walked away from the table in a huff.

"What's her problem?"

"She didn't get any last night," Charles joked.

"Jeez, judging from her remarkable humor, she probably never got any."

The laughter had a positive effect on Rodney who'd been feeling rather strung out since he got up that morning. His eyelids were finally regaining their strength and elasticity. His body was struggling to adjust to the sudden change in habit.

"Why did you insist on waking me up so early?" he asked his wide-awake friend.

"Hey, this is our first day in dream land. D'you know how long I've been dreaming about this? We have to start the day with a good breakfast so that we can benefit from our experience to the fullest," Charles cheered, like a coach trying to explain the purpose of winning.

Rodney didn't share Charles' enthusiasm. His subdued attitude may have resulted from the early-hour rising which was playing havoc with organs that were usually shut down at such an ungodly hour. It may have originated in the half-hour bus ride on roads that had been damaged by spring thaw, a ride that had left his stomach in knots. It may also have been because he knew what lay ahead for his friend. He didn't want to relive that. And not helping either was the knowledge he had of Sparo Aeronautics' unavoidable fate, which no one, especially not two greenhorns on summer assignments, could change.

Rodney was certain of one thing. He'd monitor his friend's activities as closely as possible and try to cheat fate. He'd been powerless on one occasion and it seemed now that God or some supernatural force had given him a chance to rectify an injustice.

The female ogre came back to the table for a second try.

"Have you made up your mind?" she asked in her drill sergeant, unpleasant tone.

"Yes, I'd like a number one with sausages, a coffee, and an orange juice," Charles ordered.

"I'll have the same, but I'd like a milk instead of a coffee," Rodney acted quickly for fear that if he didn't, the lady might take him outside for a few rounds.

He noticed that she hadn't taken too kindly to his special request for milk. The waitress noted both orders on her pad and walked away as quickly and as rigidly as she had the first time.

"Damn! She obviously loves her job," Rodney commented.

"How dare you ask for special treatment?" Charles teased. "It means more time yelling out the two orders. Now the poor lady is faced with the unpleasant task of asking for two number ones, two juices, a coffee for one guy and a glass of milk for the other. It would have been much less stressful to order two number ones, period.   No special requests. Everything exactly the same.   Some customers are so inconsiderate. Shame on you Rod!"

"Some professional football teams would pay a fortune to have her as a linebacker," Rodney added laughing. "But she'd probably chew up the coach."

"Literally." Charles savored the moment. "I'm sure happy that you've accepted the job, Rod. You and I can do wonders. We'll help put the Spear right up there where it belongs: the best damned jetfighter in the world."

Rodney shared Charles' feelings for the Sparo Spear project. Test pilots from around the world had taken the fighter for test flights and they all came to the conclusion that it was, bar none, the best fighter airplane in operation. It was the pride and joy of the Sparo engineers. It was a technological wonder. But it had been very well documented that the newly elected Federal Government, which had adopted the policy of eliminating any subsidies to what it assessed to be a weak aeronautical industry, had threatened to withdraw the financial support that had been promised by the previous government. Unfortunately, the decision to put an end to subsidies stemmed from a political ideology that believed that an enterprise should be able to survive with minimum state intervention.

Rodney couldn't understand politics. During the past ten years, his country had witnessed the growth of an industry and had contributed a lot of money to see it through. And suddenly, when there was finally some hope of a breakthrough, a possibility of making money, the new government threatened to prematurely withdraw its support and jeopardize the project. There was hope for the project, though; Sparo Aeronautics had identified serious buyers for the Spear M40 and these orders would permit the company to fly solo, without governmental aid.

Two plates with eggs and sausages were dropped before the two young men.

"Such finesse should be rewarded," Charles said with apparent annoyance at the waitress' unrefined serving skills.

"You're right, my friend, but let me take care of this," Rodney insisted.

He reached into his pocket and pulled out three pennies that he placed between their plates.

"You don't have to do it now. Wait until we've finished breakfast. You should eat your breakfast while it's still warm."

"Warm!" Rodney laughed, "These eggs have never seen a skillet." He pointed at the three pennies on the table:

"For the service and the quality of food, this is more than enough."

Charles smiled and nodded.

"Shall we eat," he suggested with a grin.

"I don't know," Rodney replied. "These eggs look more unstable than my stomach and that ain't good. They seem to have had more success with these," he said pointing at the barely browned bread. "I hope you don't mind if I pass on the eggs."

"Raw eggs are good for you," Charles fibbed

"Look at these people. Don't they have any taste? How can they eat in this joint?"

"Most of them are still asleep and they don't realize what they're eating," Charles joked.

Rodney's face brightened suddenly. "Hey, I've got a surprise for you," he announced as he pulled a business card out of his wallet and threw it on the table so that Charles could read it.

"James P. Knoll, Engineer - Flight Simulator Division, DBF Ltd. Charles read the card out loud. "What's this about?"

"This guy Knoll is a friend of my brother's. He invited him to try the flight simulator of one of the jets they work on. You and me have been invited," Rodney explained.

"Wow! Which simulator are we going to try? Isn't DBF the company that built the M40 simulator?" Charles asked.

"Could be," Rodney answered. He looked at an old clock on the wall.

"Hey we'd better get a move on," he warned. "We have to be at the office in fifteen minutes. It wouldn't look too good if we came in late on our first day of work."

The Sparo Aeronautic plant was far from being as impressive as its offspring, the Sparo Spear supersonic jet fighter. But to Charles and Rodney, it was like walking into the temple of aviation. Throughout their adolescence, they'd attentively followed the media coverage on the development of the supersonic. With the kind of attention it was getting, the jet fighter had taken even greater dimensions in their imagination and its high-tech appearance led them to believe that all combat planes were built in ultra modern futuristic-looking development and manufacturing facilities. This was certainly not the case with the Sparo plant. It consisted of hundreds of thousands of square feet inside rectangular warehouses around an airfield. The complex was located at the outskirts of the city and it conveyed everything but hi-tech appearance.

From the moment that it was first presented on a drawing board, the fighter plane's design had raised quite a few eyebrows. At first, it was met with the skepticism of scientists who argued that what often looked good on paper was very disappointing in trial tests. Moreover, the research and development costs of such a plane were almost prohibitive. Since Sparo Aeronautics required substantial financial backing, the government had eventually agreed to offer it some assistance in an attempt to make aviation a national industry and bring the Sparo Spear Project to the forefront.

It had also become a matter of public knowledge and well documented that the Sparo Spear had experienced some difficulties in its initial flights.

Newspapers had covered the events quite recklessly, causing some second thoughts among potential investors and buyers. In fact, engineers had encountered some problems that didn't affect the jet during the first years of its life, but would have proven bothersome and costly to Sparo in the long run. To rectify the problem, Sparo decided to keep the whole affair secret until a proper solution had been found and thus avoided any further negative coverage. Unfortunately, at some point, someone had leaked the information to the press and the whole affair had been blown out of proportion. To satisfy public curiosity and prove its viability, the company management had been forced to extend its initial timetable until it had found a solution to the problem in the M40 series. These changes were to be presented to the public at the end of the summer, fifteen months behind schedule. This delay also implied cost overruns, which entailed supplementary financial assistance from the state and thus the taxpayers.

This had given political fodder to the opposition in government who used it as an election platform, saying that the private and the public sector should not work towards the same goal, that business was business and better left exclusively to the private sector. Now that it had been elected, the new government meant to keep its promise and stop funding to the Sparo project. The down side of the new government's stand was the potential loss of many jobs in advanced technology for specialized manpower that would now be forced to seek employment in foreign countries. Because of this exodus the technology developed at Sparo Aeronautics would be transferred in foreign companies.

The message was clear. Sparo Aeronautics had one last chance. Like many state-owned corporations that had been sold to private interests, no matter how profitable they were, it had to get orders from potential users and use these orders as proof of the health of the project. This was the reason behind the test flight in front of representatives from various countries in September and the subsequent testing of the available prototypes by pilots from the different Western forces during the weeks that followed.

In preparation for this event, a special program had been devised by Sparo to hire young engineers from local universities as low-tech help to the company. It was a long-term program to train the next generation of Sparo employees. It was purported that only students showing great potential had been hired for this internship, and Rodney and Charles were two of them.

The young men entered the building through the main entrance, in the section where the offices were located. Charles, with Rodney in tow, walked over to the receptionist's desk and proudly introduced himself.

"Hello. My name is Charles Durkin and this is Rodney Blake. We've been hired as summer students. We're here to see Miss Scott."

"Please take a seat. Miss Scott will be with you in a few minutes," the receptionist said in a very polite and cheerful tone.

When the two friends turned in the direction that had been shown to them, they were surprised to find three more students, who'd apparently been hired for the same purpose. Within the next few minutes, several more students showed up and sat down in the available chairs. Fifteen minutes later, there were no remaining sitting space and several students standing.

Rodney found the situation quite comical. In Charles' very convincing interpretation, they'd been very fortunate indeed to have been selected for this project, the number of positions being limited to a few of the top engineering students. The "few" students were steadily increasing. Four more students walked in, all using essentially the same lines of introduction, and all receiving the same cheerful directions from the receptionist.

He looked at Charles. Although they'd been on the premises for only a few moments, Charles had already experienced his first letdown; he looked as if he'd been hit in the solar plexus by a boxer's powerful right jab. And by the looks of the other aspiring engineers in the room, Charles' was not the only ego that had been deflated. In fact, Rodney could have sworn that he saw some tears of disappointment on some disillusioned colleagues.

After a while, a stunning dark-haired woman in her early thirties entered the room and walked to the receptionist's desk. She projected the grace and confidence that Rodney associated to more mature women. After getting a confirmation from the receptionist, she walked to the center of the room.

Rodney nudged Charles in the ribs with his elbow.

"Hey that's Rhonda!" he exclaimed.

"Who?" Charles asked.

Rodney realized that Rhonda was part of his future not his past.

"Oh, just… hmm… a girl I've seen before."

"Well, she obviously doesn't remember you," Charles teased.

"Everyone has arrived, and on time, I might add," the woman said. "I'd like to welcome all of you to Sparo Aeronautics. I would also like to congratulate all of you for having been selected to participate on our summer project. I'm sure you will find your experience exciting and fascinating."

The hostess paused, turned and faced different people. "My name is Miranda Scott, but most people call me Rhonda, and I've been asked to take you on a plant tour. The tour itself should last approximately two hours, after which you will be taken into the conference room where each one of you will be assigned to a specific engineering group." She paused and pointed to a corner where three big boxes were resting.

"You will find safety hats, goggles and ear muffs in these boxes. I would ask you to note the numbers of the equipment you take beside your name on the form located on the table. You will be responsible for those items for the duration of your stay with us. They must be worn at all times when you're inside the manufacturing facilities." She paused.

"Does anybody have any questions?" she asked as she glanced at everyone present. "The bathrooms are on your right. You have five minutes before the tour starts."

Charles looked at Rodney and smiled.

"Did you see the legs and the tits on her?" he asked. "I'm in love."

"That's something new, for you," Rodney said with a touch of sarcasm. "But you did notice the engagement ring on her finger. That usually means that someone has agreed to be faithful to someone else. And you ain't the man," he said. However, this observation had hit a chord. *"If she's engaged, what the hell was she doing at the party with Eddie?"* he asked himself.

"Hey, a guy's gotta have dreams. And today she's it," Charles said adopting a confident air.

One of the full-height mahogany doors leading to the executive suite, flung open. Rodney and Charles recognized Professor Collins who was walking at a brisk pace towards the main entrance. A tall and elegantly dressed man in his fifties gave pursuit.

"...you know I had no choice, Bill," the man said as he reached for Professor Collins' arm.

Bill Collins tried to pull his arm away from the man's grip. As he did so, he turned and noticed the students gathered in the reception, witnessing the scene. The other man, seeing Professor Collins' reaction, turned towards the source of his diverted attention. When he saw the students, he took his hand off the professor.

"Let's discuss this matter in my office, shall we? " he suggested.

The professor reluctantly complied.

"That's Jake MacIntosh, the President," Charles whispered the unknown man's identity to Rodney.

Rhonda positioned herself between the doors leading to the executive suite and the students.

"We have less than one and a half hours left for the tour. Please follow me. "

Inside the manufacturing facilities, the structural steel covered with metal sheeting walls amplified the deafening noises made by the various assembly line activities. In the center of the seemingly endless building, an assembly line stretching from the receiving area of materials to the point where the finished product was inspected bore a number of fighter planes at different stages of completion. Rows of workstations with specialized machinery were strewn on each side of the path of travel of the fabulous machines. Unlike the car assembly lines, the equipment was not in continuous motion. As Rhonda would explain later, each plane would rest at the same station for days at a time. Technicians and machinists worked laboriously at each stage of production, all striving to complete their part of the technological marvel within schedule.

The group of visitors came to a stop at the sides of a nearly completed aircraft.

"Can everybody hear me?" Rhonda asked.

"Well, this is where it all happens," she said. "Ladies and gentlemen, I would like to introduce you to the Sparo Spear M40!" she said pointing to the imposing airplane. She paused and looked at the young students, who all seemed awestruck by the big mechanical bird. Since they'd entered the building, they'd hardly noticed anything else but the fighters. The hostess smiled. The Spear, with its aerodynamic lines and its imposing size stunned everyone who set their eyes on it for the first time.

Rodney felt the same amazement as his new colleagues. Like most of the people present, he'd never seen the Sparo Spear from up close. His sightings had been limited to magazine covers and to televised reports. He turned to look at Charles. He was staring intently in front of him, a smile of excitement etched on his face.

"The Sparo Spear is a two engine, two crew fighter that measures eighty feet, two and one half inches in length (that's including the probe) or seventy-seven feet one and one quarter inches without the probe, and has a wing span of forty nine feet, eight and one half inches. It requires two crewmembers due to the complexity of the fire control systems during combat. In the event of an automatic system failure, the pilot would be required to perform a manually-controlled attack, which would make it nearly impossible for him to operate the fire control systems." Rhonda paused and looked around her.

"By the way, if you have any questions, feel free to interrupt me as I go," she suggested.

"There are two reasons why the aircraft was designed with two engines. The first is due to the large weapon payload and fuel load that the craft would have to carry on a long-range mission, which would make the aircraft too heavy for a single engine. Secondly, it offers dual engine safety. If one engine fails, the other engine will generate sufficient thrust to bring the plane to a safe landing."

A young man at the front of the group, raised his hand and asked:

"In the news coverage that we see on television and in newspapers, they usually refer to the Delta Wing configuration of the plane. What is the advantage to this?" he asked.

"As you probably all know, the Delta denomination represents the triangular swept-back shape of the wing of the aircraft. In order to achieve supersonic speeds, the fighter requires thin wings. To achieve thin wings you require a low thickness to cord ratio. The structural and aerostatics efficiency of the Delta wing offers these properties and more. On this fighter, the large area of the Delta wing, which is approximately twelve hundred and fifty square feet counting the area above the fuselage, increases the fuel capacity of the aircraft, since, as you know, the fuel for the aircraft is stored in its wings. It also offers more room for the undercarriage." Rhonda paused again and then pointed to the wing.

"You will notice that the fighter's wing is located at the top of the fuselage and is known as a "High Wing". It permits the achievement of the lowest structural weight. This is due to the fact that the wing structure goes straight through the fuselage, permitting a simple wing and fin attachment. The High Wing also allows better access to engines and armament, for installation and maintenance."

"Excuse me," a woman's voice interrupted. "The aircraft seems slanted. It looks as if the front is higher than the rear. What is the reason for this? Does it have anything to do with aerodynamics?"

"Ah yes. The front of the plane is higher than the back. There is an inclination of four degrees. The reason for this is simple. It shortens the length of the back landing gear, which can thereby retract inside the wing. However, it has no aerodynamic advantages." She stopped and looked at the group before her to see if there were any more questions. "Notice that there is a wing notch and a leading edge extension on the..."

Charles turned to Rodney.

"I'm in love," he said in a low sigh.

"It's the first time I've seen someone get a hard-on over a plane," Rodney wisecracked.

"The plane is great," Charles responded. "But I prefer Rhonda's lines."

"She can't keep her eyes off me," Rodney quoted Edmond's favorite line.

"Not a chance. Once she's met me, she'll forget she's engaged."

"I've got five bucks that say that you'll fall flat on your face," Rodney wagered.

"I hate taking your money."

"...breakaway at high angle of attack," she continued. "The fighter is powered by two Orenda Iroquois OR100-IR-229 turbojet engines that generate twenty-one thousand one hundred and fifty pounds of dry static thrust, and twenty-eight thousand pounds of static thrust with after-burners. What does this mean in simple terms, you may ask? That means that the Sparo Spear should be able to attain an altitude up to 60,000 feet at Mach speeds, which is impressive by any standards," she boasted proudly, like a mother speaking of her child. "That also means that the Spear should be able to maneuver at 5G's at an altitude of 50,000 feet and at a speed of 2.5 Mach without losing altitude or speed."

Her comments generated a collective rumble of amazement from the young crowd. She turned to the aircraft once again, looking for the next feature to describe:

"Excuse me, Rhonda. You spoke earlier on about "automatic system failure. Could you explain what that automatic system is?" the voice of a young man broke through the mumbles.

"It means that the Spear can fly itself and that the pilot, when the system is activated, is just there in case of emergencies. Everything is controlled from an onboard computer that makes its calculations based on preprogrammed data. In extreme circumstances, all the pilot has to do is start the engines, taxi the aircraft to the take-off point and let the plane literally fly itself. And once the plane has landed, the pilot would only have to taxi the fighter back to the hangar," she explained. "Does that answer your question?"

"Amazing," came the reply.

"What's the use of having a pilot?" someone asked.

"During air combat, the fighter pilot flies the plane. The speeds of dueling planes is so great, that maneuvering the aircraft at those speeds has been compared to riding a bicycle in a phone booth. Just imagine. Two airplanes flying towards each other at 400 knots is like flying in one direction at 800 knots. Now imagine dodging enemy fire at those speeds."

She continued her presentation:

"You will notice that the fuselage configuration consists of..."

A few minutes after noon, the plant cafeteria had filled up. People with bagged lunches and others with trays circulated along the aisles trying to find a place to sit. Even at lunchtime, the employees could not escape the assembly line concept. After choosing from a limited menu, they had to wait in line for someone across the counter to complete their order and then follow the queue in an orderly fashion until they'd paid the cashier sitting at the end of the line.

Rodney and Charles, being rookies in the worker's lunch hour world, found no adjoining seats available in the room. Since they wanted to compare notes, they decided to have their lunch standing up.

"You won't guess who I'll be working with," Charles said. He didn't give Rodney a chance to reply:

"Collins himself," he said laughing.

"You're not serious." Rodney feigned surprise. "Did he quit his job at the University?"

"No. Apparently he's one of the experts when it comes to the Sparo Spear. He's showing me how they use titanium in the construction of the jet engines. Apparently using titanium instead of an aluminum alloy can achieve substantial weight savings. I was told by the other engineers in the group that Collins is one of the world's leading experts in that field," he said, his eyes dancing with excitement.

"I'm happy to know that he's good at something," Rodney said, "He sure can't teach worth a damn."

"I don't know. They seem to think quite highly of him, over here," Charles pointed out. "Apparently he was involved in other projects before that, too. I don't know what they were, though."

"I'm impressed," Rodney admitted.

"Who are you working with?" Charles asked.

"His name is Roger Simpson. He's the chief Aerodynamics Engineer. He's a pretty funny guy who seems to have a wise crack for every situation," he announced. "I'm pretty excited about the whole thing since I'll be able to see some of the wind tunnel testing that they'll perform." He paused. "I guess some of our work will be related."

"It's too bad we aren't with the same group. But I'm sure we'll get to see each other often enough."

"Too often, I'm afraid." Rodney grinned. He had to perform some acrobatics to pick up the submarine sandwich from the tray that was balanced on one arm. Carefully he raised the sandwich to his mouth and took a bite.

"Thank God," he commented after swallowing his first bite. "It's edible. I was afraid that we'd be stuck with the same kind of food we had for breakfast."

It's going to be great," Charles said excitedly. "I'll be working on the computer, inputting the coordinates required for the design of the different components. The computers they have in here are just bloody amazing. They give a view from every angle you can imagine. And if there's any problems, they list the problems down on the side of the design. When you finally find the right solution, all you have to do is print it and voilà, the laser printer gives you a copy of the design."

"It sure beats our PCs at home doesn't it?" Rodney said.

"We're talking a different budget here, Rod baby. And don't knock our machines, we haven't used them to their limit yet."

"I guess you're right."

"Anyway, I wish I had the opportunity to be involved in the programming of such a project. Those computer programmers must have had a ball," he wished out loud.

Rodney respected his friend's talents as a programmer. When his parents had died, Charles had retrieved two computers from the computer consulting firm that his father had operated very successfully from the comfort of his home. His father had hoped that his son would take over the reins of the business one day and Charles had spent a lot of time with him learning his way around computers. When it came to computer programming, he was like a fish in water. Most of his free time was spent reading about computers or working on them, and there was no doubt in his mind that he'd be up to the task and comply with his father's wishes. However, he'd always planned to get some experience at Sparo Aeronautics before getting into the family business.

"You can't do everything. We're here to learn, remember," Rodney reminded him.

"I know, I know," Charles agreed. "By the way, what will you be doing?"

"Pretty much the same thing as you, but I haven't had a chance to see how the computer works yet," he explained. "I'm looking forward to it. By the way, did you get a chance to find out what department Rhonda works in?"

"Yep. She's the assistant to Bob Wringley, the chief engineer. Apparently, her job is to help coordinate all the various engineering groups' efforts and make sure that everyone is going in the same direction. I guess that explains her impressive knowledge of the Spear. And that means that I'll get to work with her sometimes," he said with a twinkle in his eye that implied that she wouldn't be able to resist his charms.

"That means that I'll also get a chance to work with her," Rodney said. "Maybe I'll win the bet."

"This will be the best summer of our life," Charles predicted, ignoring his friend's comment. "Some people would give their lives to do what we'll be doing."

Edmond sat in Rodney's chair, by his desk.

"A girl called this afternoon and left a message," he informed Rodney, "I think her name is Debbie. I told her that you'd call back."

Rodney was expecting that call. He wasn't really looking forward to hearing from her, but somehow he believed that she was sincere when she said that she liked him. However, the secret profession that he suspected she practiced, had served quite a blow to his feelings and his ego. He wanted to keep away from her.

"If she calls again, tell her I'm away for the summer," he said.

Edmond observed his friend's reaction and felt it best to change the subject.

"He's been locked up in that room for almost six days now," Edmond said, referring to Leonardo. "I haven't seen him come out of there at all since that incident."

"I'm sure he's been out to the bathroom on a few occasions when no one's around," Rodney assured. "The thing that worries me is that I don't think he's eaten anything since then. No one has complained of any food missing."

"He's a strange animal, isn't he?" Edmond expressed.

"Where are Trap and Leo?"

"They're in the TV room downstairs, watching the news. I guess they're following that mysterious disappearance of the Da Vinci papers. Shit, there's been a hell of a lot of coverage about that lately, hasn't there? They still haven't got a clue as to what happened to them. It's like they vanished into thin air, or something.

Rodney smiled at his friend's interpretation of the event. It was as good an explanation as any. Rodney knew where they were, but couldn't explain how they'd ended up in his house, nor why. He'd lent his filing cabinet to Leonardo so that he could store his documents and lock them up away from curious eyes. The last thing he wanted was to be arrested and questioned for the unlawful possession of those documents. He found it ironic that if Leonardo was found in possession of the famous papers, no one would ever believe his true identity. He could serve time for holding something that really belonged to him.

They heard the sound of the living room door opening followed by the sound of footsteps climbing the stairs.

"Speak of the devil," Edmond exclaimed.

Leonardo walked into the room. His complexion was gray and his traits were drawn like those of someone who'd had little sleep.

"Leonard," Edmond greeted in a cheerful tone. "How the hell are you?"

Leonardo nodded his acknowledgment. He looked at Rodney and said:

"Please gather your friends in my quarters, I have something to show you," he invited in a feeble tone.

"You look awful," Rodney remarked undiplomatically. "Are you all right?"

Leonardo didn't respond. He turned and went back downstairs.

Edmond and Rodney looked at each other questioningly. Rodney followed Leonardo downstairs, while Edmond summoned Leo and Eugene. Everyone gathered in the living room, where a sheet now hung on the wall over the poster of the young bare-bottomed woman. Leonardo spoke.

"My dear friends. I know that during these past days, you have questioned my self-imposed seclusion. I also know that I have lost some of your respect and confidence due to a regrettable incident. I wish to apologize to all of you and I swear that it will not happen again." He paused to let his words reach their intended receptors.

"In recognition of your tolerance, I have a small, modest gift for you." He turned and pulled the sheet away from the wall. Silence reigned for a few moments as the four boys, their mouths open in surprise, took in the breathtaking painting that now covered the wall.

"Gentlemen, I call it "Four students bathing," he introduced his painting.

Leonardo had reproduced the four roommates in the bath. The detail and accuracy of the painting was beyond description. It looked like a photograph that had been enlarged and pasted to the wall. But there was dimension and warmth rarely found in photography. Not only had he captured the likeness of the models, but also he'd given them an aura of life that left the onlooker feeling that he or she could touch the flesh. Each person in the painting looked as if he was about to move, making anyone watching feel as if he or she was witnessing a live event.

"Holy shit!" Leo exclaimed in total amazement.

"You don't like?" Leonardo asked, giving the word its pejorative sense.

"Like it! It's awesome!" Edmond expressed with excitement.

"Un-fucking believable," Eugene said in astonishment.

Leonardo, confused by the profane expressions, scratched his head, thinking that he had failed.

"I thought you would have liked it," Leonardo expressed with disappointment. He had wanted to please them.

Leonardo was expressing some signs of doubt in his talent, in his art. He was showing definite signs of fear of rejection. Rodney picked up on it.

"Leonard, we think this is absolutely beautiful. It's a masterpiece," he said with sincerity.

"That's the most beautiful thing that I've ever seen," Edmond supported. Of course, how could it be otherwise when one of the subjects is me," he deadpanned.

"You're absolutely right," Leo teased. "That homely face of yours makes us all look good."

Leonardo's face, which had been strained from the fatigue due to hard work and the lack of sleep, lit up. Contentment resulting from his young friends' appreciation set in and he felt invigorated and fulfilled something he had not felt for the past week. The young men's bantering indicated reconciliation and acceptance.

"Thank you," Eugene said appreciatively. "But really, I think that we're the ones who owe you an apology. But we wouldn't ever be able to offer you anything as beautiful as this."

"You have something better and more precious than what I offer you. And that is friendship. Many people, myself included, have never experienced anything quite like what you lads share. Never lose sight of that," Leonardo said with conviction.

"Leonard, consider yourself a lifetime member of Club 230, where to become a member, you must be a true friend," Edmond declared.

"Hear! Hear!" the other boys cheered.

"Rodney, could you please run these numbers in the program for me?" Roger Simpson, the project leader, asked.

Roger Simpson was a tall slim man in his late forties, whose slightly graying sideburns were the only signs indicating his age. He had a boyish look about him.

"Sure, no problem," Rodney agreed.

"I'd like you to pay specific attention to the drag coefficient requirements for this one. These are the parameters you can work with," Roger explained as he pointed to the data on the sheet.

"Okay, Boss."

"So how are you getting along with Mavis?" Roger asked. Mavis was the nickname affectionately given to the computer.

"She's doing fine. She's quite user friendly."

"You can thank your Professor Collins for that. He's the mastermind behind the system," he said giving credit to Rodney's teacher.

"I thought Professor Collins was a specialist in aerodynamics and metallurgy, " Rodney said.

"Bill Collins is a very versatile man. He has an incredible knack for learning. When the project was in its infancy, we needed to use more advanced computer technology to help us in the design and construction of the fighter. The big problem was that we didn't know how to go about it. Collins was then working with us as a consultant. When he heard about our computer needs, he offered his services. As the program progressed, Bill became more and more instrumental to the success of the project. He became involved in all aspects of the business. In fact, I don't think there's anyone around who knows more about the M40.

The versatility and ingenuity of his old professor impressed Rodney more and more. He'd always perceived him as the straight professor who played everything by the book, because the book was all he knew. So far, his perception had been proven wrong. A new image of the professor had evolved in the past few weeks: that of a highly respected man, with a love for challenging work and tight deadlines.

Even though most of his work consisted of data entry, Rodney recognized its importance, no matter how tedious it became. He'd also been given the opportunity to see first hand how powerful the computer was and he was impressed with the complexity and performance of the computer program with which he worked. The whole engineering department swore by the system. No one even dared to think of what they'd do without it. It permitted them to approach problems and designs from various angles and come up with the best possible solution in a fraction of the time that it would take otherwise.

Rodney was also happy for Charles. He could now see the many similarities between his friend and Professor Collins. They were both versatile people, who both enjoyed turning stones and trying to understand everything. Rodney got a flashback to his future. He could remember how receptive Charles had been to Collins when they'd returned to school. *"That's probably what he wanted to explain,"* he thought. His positive and respectful demeanor towards Collins was now logical. He'd come to respect the genius of the man. After all, Collins was recognized and respected by some of his colleagues as the cornerstone of the Spear M40. Charles had known all that. Everything suddenly made sense.

Rodney focused his attention on the computer in front of him once again and started entering the information that Roger had given him. The kind of work that he'd been assigned was far from challenging. All it required were some basic typing skills, a limited knowledge of aeronautics and an understanding of PCs. But the job did allow him to witness all the operations within his engineering group. The purpose of every study, of every test, of every analysis result was explained to him in detail, as if he was an integral part of the team. The patience that the permanent members of the team showed towards him made him feel right at home. They encouraged him to ask questions whenever he felt the need. Rodney marveled at how much he understood of what was presented to him. Somehow, he'd imagined it to be much more complex. But what he was learning was the application of theories and laws that had been taught to him. The real world is not so frightening after all.

He regretted that in his previous past, he'd passed up the opportunity of working with Sparo. *"If I hadn't been such a chicken, perhaps Charlie would still be alive,"* he thought. *"But he is!"* his mind argued. *"He's part of this world, in flesh and blood."* Suddenly, his mind started playing a strange game that made time inconsequential in his reasoning. Charles' death, which was part of his past experience, was only a possibility of his future, given that he was still alive. This confused him. His mind raced trying to make sense of his whole experience, of his role in his second future. For the first time, he identified a constant factor: Charles. Perhaps the purpose of the extraordinary circumstances that had brought him to a second reliving of his recent past was to change something and give Charles a long and prosperous life. It became clear to Rodney that he had to do everything in his power to save Charles from his terrible fate.

James Knolls led his guests into a brightly-lit, high-tech room at the end of a hangar.

"Rod, your brother told me that you work on the Sparo Spear project and I thought you might enjoy this baby," James announced.

Charles walked towards the cockpit of the simulator that dominated the room.

"Woo. You're cruel. The presence of this machine makes my mouth water." Charles said. "Which of the simulators are we going to try?"

"This one," the host replied.

A man wearing a white service jacket entered the room.

"Gentlemen, I'd like you to meet Fred Masters. Fred will be the engineer at the control board and he will be setting the flight scenarios for us."

"But I thought this was restricted stuff," Rodney said.

"Yeah, restricted to people privy to the program. You and Charles work on the project don't you?" James replied. "I guess we can chance it with you." He entered an adjacent locker room and returned with a pair of helmets that he set carefully on two work chairs.

"Okay guys. First of all, I'll give you very basic information. This will take forty-five minutes to an hour and then I'll let you try to fly...and believe me when I say try."

"Flying this machine must be a breeze. The computer handles everything. The pilot's a mere passenger," Charles declared.

"Well in automatic flying mode, you're right. But you mustn't forget that pilots are in complete control when faced with an enemy. Some pilots have compared flying a jet fighter in air combat to getting laid on a high wire. In the Sparo Spear, computers will help the pilot assess the situation and react better under pressure, but the pilots are very much in control of the plane during those circumstances. "

"During this simulation there will be a computer failure. When the computer shuts down your mission will be to land the plane manually using instruments."

"That sounds like a smash-up derby to me," Anthony predicted.

James smiled. He put on a helmet and detached the oxygen mask. "We'll forget about the oxygen for today. I'm sure we'll have enough to worry about, other than this."   He paused momentarily to collect his thoughts. "I'll go on first and, from the cockpit, I'll explain to you what the main controls are and what they do and try and teach you the basics of flight. I must warn you. Your chances of success are almost nil. Most pilots go through long, intensive training before even sitting in the simulator."

"I hope we don't damage anything," Anthony cautioned.

"Don't worry. Let's go through a crash course, pardon the pun, and then you can try it out. We'll see what you guys are made of."

The pilot looked at the simulated horizon through the canopy of the plane. He listened to the A.T.I.S. on VHF for airport weather info and runway news.

"Center, this is Flight zero-zero-seven requesting descent back to airport." The pilot asked the tower for descent clearance.

"Flight zero-zero-seven you're cleared to descend eight-zero." The tower responded.

The pilot descended to 10,000 feet and reduced his speed to 250 knots. As the plane lost altitude, he reduced the fighter's speed. At 6,000 feet he could see the runway in the distance. He brought out the flaps, which reduced his air speed to 220 knots.

"Flight zero-zero-seven, you're clear for the approach on Runway one-eight. Call tower on two-three-two-point-seven-five."

The pilot adjusted his radio to the prescribed frequency.

"Tower, Flight zero-zero-seven on the approach, runway one-eight." The pilot informed the tower of its descent.

"Flight zero-zero-seven you're clear to land on one-eight. Altimeter setting twenty-nine-point-eight-three. Winds one-eight-zero at fifteen knots."

"Flight zero-zero-seven is clear to land," the pilot acknowledged. He brought out the landing gear as he completed his before-landing checklist. "V-ref speed at 180 knots," he said as he concentrated on his approach. He looked at the digitized runway he was approaching. He felt one hind wheel touch down, followed quickly by the other. The nose wheel dropped violently on the tarmac. He pulled the thrust into idle position, spoilers up, as he activated the chute and felt its drag as he slowed the plane using the pedals for brakes.

The pilot sighed with relief and thrust his fist in the air as he felt the adrenaline rush through his bloodstream. He'd landed safely. Applause could be heard through the canopy.

"Are you sure you've never flown before?" the voice in the headgear asked.

"In another life!" Rodney responded half-truthfully. He opened the canopy, unsnapped his oxygen mask and removed his helmet. His friends cheered him on, impressed by a most surprising performance.

Charles reached for the chilled pitcher of beer and poured the contents into two cold and frosted beer mugs.

"Ah, the mugs have just been pulled out of the freezer," Charles said.

"There's nothing like a frosty," Rodney agreed.

They were sitting alone at the table, enjoying their favorite refreshment.

"It's good to hear you say something, Charles. You've barely said a word since the simulator test."

"Jesus, I still can' t figure it out."

"What's that?"

"How did you manage to do it?"

"Do what?"

"Duh...I don't know, Rod. Maybe the fact that you pulled the plane out of a fatal dive and landed it, not once, but both times you tried." He paused. "I hate to admit it, Pal, but when it comes to flying, you're a natural. You should take flying lessons. Maybe you've missed your calling."

"It was just luck, I guess." Rodney felt ill at ease with the comments.

"It's...it's as if you've flown in a prior life."

Charles' words hit like lightning. Rodney felt a jolt run through his nervous system as his entire skin reacted with goose bumps. A noticeable convulsion exploded through him. *"There is another life,"* he thought. That life was happening simultaneously in Springer, where he was indeed taking flying lessons. He had the full-fledged knowledge and skills of a certified pilot, without having the permit. How could he explain this to Charles? Who would believe this?

The central P.A. system convened all non-essential personnel to leave their work post and witness the Spear M40's maiden flight. Management was showing its appreciation for the energy and devotion of its employees in meeting the deadlines. In fact, work had gone so well in the past few months that the initial flight was four days ahead of schedule, which gave the company a little more than ten weeks to perform its testing and adjustments before the big day.

The weather cooperated with its clear skies and moderate winds, ideal conditions for testing and viewing. Workers were now evacuating the building as if in a fire drill. All the employees felt they had a part in the success of the project and shared the excitement of seeing before them the result of a collective effort. To the last one, they hoped that the initial flight would take place without any major incident.

Michael Mazenkowski climbed the tall boarding ladder, the crowd watching his every move intently. As the company's senior test pilot, he'd grown accustomed to the pressure and responsibility created by a test flight. No matter how confident he was about the skills of the personnel who'd built the plane, he knew that he was at the mercy of the thousands of parts that constituted the aircraft. He was also aware that since many of these parts had been designed specifically for the Spear, they never before been put to the test.

He handed his flight bag to the ground crew and eased himself into the plane. He adjusted his seat and pedals to achieve the optimum position for his flight. He then fastened his shoulder harness. The ground crew pulled the pilot's helmet out of the flight bag and handed it to him. He put the headgear on and connected the oxygen mask to the supply. He pushed the oxygen mask to his face and alternately toggled the emergency flow switch and the one hundred percent flow switch.

"Oxygen okay," he called out as he started the before-start checklist.

He verified to make sure that the Ground Power Unit, which supplies the electricity to the plane until the engines are started, was live. He turned the master switch on. The flight instruments on the dashboard lit up. He completed the flight-instruments check followed by the drag-chute and the ejectable-seat checks.

He pressed the oxygen mask towards his face once more.

"Ground, Flight one-zero-two requesting clearance for Flight zero- zero-two."

Ground control assigned the flight parameters. "Flight one-zero-two, you're clear for Flight Test zero-zero-two. Runway one-eight, flight level three-five-zero and four-three-zero. Altimeter setting two-nine-eight-three."

Captain Mazenkowski set the altimeter and the COM/NAV instruments. He signaled two thumbs up to the ground crew. He then activated a switch that closed the canopy. He locked it. When he noticed the ground crew ahead of the plane, he signaled that he was prepared to start the engines by turning two fingers in the air.

The ground crew removed the wheel chocks and made sure that the area behind the engines was clear for engine start-up. Thumbs up, one of them signaled to the pilot that all was clear.

Engine start. Oil pressure check and temp check. Generator check. The pilot completed the after-start check. Once satisfied with the readings, he signaled to the ground crew with two thumbs up.

"Ground, Flight one-zero-two ready for taxi to Runway one-zero-eight," he advised ground control.

"Flight one-zero-two, you're clear to taxi Runway one-zero-eight, winds one-seven-zero at ten knots."

As he taxied the plane, Mazenkowski completed the before-take-off checklist. The plane was now approaching the runway. Once he'd reached the take-off hold position, the pilot called the control tower.

"Sparo tower, Flight one-zero-two ready for take-off."

"Flight one-zero-two clear for take-off, Runway one-eight, winds one-seven-zero, five to ten knots. Contact departure three-two-five-point-six-five."

The pilot positioned the plane on the runway for take-off. He was totally concentrated now and his mind directed the succession of actions and checks required to become airborne. His right hand pushed the thrust lever to generate the necessary take-off momentum. The fighter started to roll. The impressive acceleration brought a smile to the pilot's face. Step by step he ran every detail of the checklist. Check N1 's, the tack percentage for turbines to monitor and adjust the take-off power. Check EGT. Check oil pressure and temperature. The plane is rolling. Maintain a straight line on the runway using the rudders. V1, wait decision speed.

"I've reached rotation speed," he thought. He pulled on the stick. The nose rose and the fighter broke contact with the runway and took to the skies. The pilot aimed for the take-off rotation angle and waited for the positive rate.

"The gear's up," he said as he heard the mechanical clunk below him. The landing gear light turned off simultaneously. Using the climb thrust, he propelled his high-tech bird to the climbing speed.

"Spear M-four-zero has taken off at ten fifty-nine a.m. and cleared to company tower," the controller's voice resounded in his earphones.

The crowd on the ground broke out into a thunderous cheer as it witnessed the successful takeoff. The aircraft climbed to 18,000 feet at a speed of 500 knots. The pilot reset the altimeter at twenty-nine-point-nine-two, activated the after-burners propelling the plane into a steep climb. At 35,000 feet, Michael leveled the craft and maintained altitude until the two chase planes that had been dispatched as observing planes reached him.

"Everything normal from starboard", a voice resounded in his phones.

"Chase plane number two checking in at eight o'clock. Situation normal," said the pilot of the second chase plane. "Roger," Mazenkowski responded. "All information on panels indicates normal operation. I'm now activating fly-by-wire mode and taking fighter into four G's turn, at one-point-nine Mach," he informed.

"Roger, all systems clear, you have clearance for maneuver."

Mazenkowski activated the A.F.C.S. control and the plane accelerated leaving the two chase planes behind. He felt his body sink deep into his seat as the fighter's after-burners kicked in. The crossing of the sonic barrier was without incident. At one-point-nine Mach the fighter banked into a sharp turn to starboard, the pilot acting as a mere passenger. He experienced the gravity forces of the turn without interfering with the controls.   The fighter remained steady and stable. Its passenger experienced exhilaration that not even the gravitational pull exerted on his body through the turn could dampen.

"Wowie!!" he exulted. "Unbelievable machine!!   The baby is maintaining altitude and speed as required.   Piece of cake!!"

"That's a Roger. Way to go Michael," control tower cheered.

"You guys on the ground did a hell of a job! Work well done! Returning to home base," the voice echoed over the P.A. system.

It was received with a resounding cheer from the jubilating and proud employees.

The two chase fighters soon rejoined the aircraft and the trio descended in the clear skies on their way back towards the launching airport. At that moment, a nuisance light flickered on the control panel of the Spear M40 aircraft. The pilot, after a quick evaluation, brushed it off as a minor problem in the air-conditioning system. The Spear, with the two chase fighters in its wake, made a spectacular pass over the airport. Near the end of the runway, the two chase fighters peeled away and assumed position for landing, while the Spear went for a last and final rolling climb before coming down for a landing.

Sparo's workers proudly witnessed the aircraft's impressive aerobatics as the pilot gave them a show of the technological marvel for which they'd all striven. Within a few minutes the aircraft returned and aimed itself at the runway, coming in for a soft and controlled landing. The final approach was met with a collective roar from the crowd.

The six o'clock news anchorman was wearing a seasonal light-colored sports jacket.

"...and that the Minister would respond to the matter in the next few days. In local news, the initial flight of the Spear M40 was marred with problems today. An official at Sparo Aeronautics has confirmed that the air conditioning system of the aircraft failed to operate, cutting the trials and tests short. The Spear fighter aircraft and its predecessors have been renown for snags in their maiden flights. The development of the aircraft is the initiative of a joint venture between Sparo Aeronautics and the Federal Government, the latter subsidizing the research and development costs of the project... In England today, the Queen Mother...'"

"Can you believe that?" Rodney exclaimed in anger. "Where the hell do they get their information?"

Leonardo entered the room, seemingly concerned by Rodney's comments.

"What seems to be the problem?" Leonardo asked. Rodney was sitting on the chesterfield, his arms crossed in front of him. He looked up at Leonardo and answered, "The damned media, that's the problem".

Leonardo looked at his young friend with an expression that showed his lack of understanding of the matter. "Media, which media?"

"The television," Rodney said.

"Television: simultaneous visual reproduction of scenes, objects, performances, etc. at a distance by means of a camera which converts the image into electrical impulses which are transmitted by radio to a receiver, which converts them by means of a cathode/ray tube, into a corresponding image on a screen," Leonardo recited.

"You probably won't believe this, but I've never looked at its definition before," Rodney admitted.

"The definition is quite elaborate", he said. "It is a very impressive invention that is discussed at length in many of the books that I have been reading. However, I would be interested in studying it from a more practical standpoint."

He looked at the newscaster on the screen. "Where is that man located?"

"At the TV station. It's a building from which all the television signals originate. The man is filmed with a camera that transforms the picture into signals that are transmitted through the cable until they get to the television." Rodney paused. "You know what? You should speak to

Eugene. He's some sort of technical director with the local television station. He could probably explain this much better than me. In fact he's involved in the newscast that we're seeing right now. "

"He does that as a student?"

"No, actually he studied broadcasting in college and worked for a few years as a technician after he graduated. Then he decided to come back to school although he kept his job and tries to balance school and work at the same time. "

Leonardo changed the subject. "You were uttering some comment concerning the television media."

"I'm upset by the bullshit newscast on the Sparo Spear's test flight today. I witnessed the test. It went without any major problems."

"This seems to trouble you," Leonardo remarked.

"It does. It's just that we've developed one of the most sophisticated and technologically advanced fighter planes in the world, but somebody, somewhere, wants to make sure that the project fails. The present Federal Government disapproves wholeheartedly of the project and the media seems determined to paint the darkest picture they can of the whole project."

"Why has the government taken this position?" Leonardo asked.

"The present government has the obligation to support something that had been set by the previously-elected government and since governmental aid to industry goes against the party policy, to condone such a project is, in their eyes, a sure way to political suicide."

"Why is this?"

"While in the opposition, this political party swore that if it was elected, it would abolish most government subsidies. The party platform maintains that healthy and competitive companies don't need government subsidies to survive.

Leonardo looked very confused by Rodney's explanation of the events.

"Political parties. Policy. Platform. I have read of these things, but this is the first time that I hear of them in context," he commented. "This all seems very complicated...illogical."

"It's too long a story for me to explain. Rodney paused. "But to make a long story short, there seems to be some sort of conspiracy. Someone is leaking secret information to the press. And this is what's been causing all the negative coverage that the project has been getting. I can't understand why people who are involved in such a great thing, such an important project, do something that can jeopardize its livelihood. In fact, the success of the Spear M40 can only have a positive impact on our country as a whole."

"Greed," Leonardo muttered.

"What do you mean?" Rodney asked.

"You spoke of a conspiracy", Leonardo pointed out, "and this reminds me of the Pazzi conspiracy in Florence. In fact, you remind me of a bright young man I've had the opportunity to serve. You look very much like him and you have a very similar temperament."

"Oh really? Who's that?"

"Lorenzo de Medicis. People of his own entourage, whom he trusted, from whom he never expected any harm, conspired with the help of high-placed clergymen to take away his power hold, renowned as the strongest in Europe. The motivation was quite simple: greed. They wanted more power and the wealth of the Florentine government. Lorenzo was a victim of others' greed and this caused him a great loss, one that can never be replaced: the life of his brother Giuliano."

"Maybe these guys were mistreated."

"This is unlikely. They all had prominent positions in the court of the Medicis and Lorenzo saw to their wellbeing and fortune. However, after some time, this was not sufficient. They wanted more."

"I don't quite see the similarities", Rodney said.

"In time, you will understand," Leonardo predicted.

"You seem sure of this."

"Greed has been a common ailment throughout time, at least in mine. And like engineering principles, human nature never changes," Leonardo added with a twinkle in his eye.

The familiar beep woke Rodney from a sound sleep. He looked towards the desk where the sound had come from. Leonardo sat there, completely absorbed in the operation of the computer. As Rodney observed Leonardo, he was surprised by the apparent knowledge that he demonstrated as he operated the machine.

"Leonardo", Rodney called out.

Leonardo continued consulting the computer manuals opened beside him as if he hadn't heard Rodney.

"Leonardo!" The Master turned and Rodney caught the smile that the pride in his achievement had formed on his usually calm face.

"Who taught you how to use the machine?" he asked.

"The book. It is quite explicit." He turned towards the machine. "This is child's play. I find the operation and the writing with this device quite interesting", he said as he pointed at the keyboard. "The left-handed writer is not disadvantaged anymore. There is no more need for mirror-inverted writing."

Rodney shook his head in disbelief. In the month since Leonardo had dropped into his life, Rodney had daily been given the occasion to observe the old time-traveler's ability to adapt to a totally new environment. His awkwardness in the New World was vanishing with every day of exposure to it. Leonardo had managed to transcend the mindset of his era and now projected a sense of belonging. He'd experienced an unconscious metamorphosis that now made him a man of the Twentieth Century. Rodney was sure that most people of Leonardo's physiological age in this time didn't appreciate the changes in technology as Leonardo did. There too, his true genius prevailed.

"I wish I had worked with this type of machine before", he was saying. "I really believe that the invention of the micro-chip has expanded the possibilities of learning and achievement for man," he said, obviously knowledgeable of the essence of the new technology.

In fact, Leonardo had very early on been attracted by the computer in Rodney's room and had naturally started to study the manuals that lay beside it. In the daytime, while Rodney had been working at Sparo Aeronautics, he had initiated himself to the wondrous machine and had by now reached a point where his knowledge of computers surpassed that of most people.

Rodney started to see that the mental adaptability of a person was not necessarily limited to the era in which he lived. Leonardo's intellect was timeless. He witnessed with awe and delight the intensity of Leonardo's quest for knowledge. His assimilation of knowledge was all consuming, generating an energy that fueled his ever-active mind.

Since Leonardo now devoted much of his energy to understanding and exploiting the potential of the computer, it was natural that the P.C. be moved into Leonardo's quarters downstairs. Rodney agreed to the move without any hesitation because he didn't really have any use for it at this time, but mostly because he was fascinated by Leonardo's affinity for the machine. In the past few weeks, Leonardo had become a computer whiz. He sat at the terminal day in, day out, without a sign of fatigue. And Rodney took every opportunity to learn from the Master. He'd return from work, prepare two sandwiches, pour two glasses of milk and share them with the computer fanatic.

Rodney stood behind Leonardo to see what his friend was up to. He placed the sandwich plate and the glass of milk on the left-hand side of the keyboard. To his great surprise, he saw the configuration of a jet engine on the screen. The computer wizard displayed views from different angles with the press of a few buttons.

"How did you get this?" Rodney exclaimed, baffled by the display, undoubtedly the reproduction of the Mohawk engine used to power the Sparo Spear M40.

Leonardo turned to him. "Oh, Rodney, you startled me."

"Where did you get the information to make that drawing?" Rodney asked emphatically. "That's the Mohawk engine. It's classified information."

Leonardo picked up a sheet from the desk and showed it to Rodney. "I got the information from this sheet. I found it in your desk."

Rodney looked at the very familiar sheet. It was the sheet of paper that he'd found in Edmond's freezer, before he'd come back in time. On it there was the logo of Sparo Aeronautics with a series of odd numbers and coordinates. On the back were the same handwritten notes that looked like part numbers or perhaps codes. Somehow, the sheet of paper had traveled with him through time and been placed in his desk drawer. In the same way that Leonardo's notes had been gathered and brought back with him.

"I recognize the sheet," Rodney told Leonardo and explained to him the circumstances surrounding its discovery after Charles' future death. "But I can't make out the importance of the data," he added.

Leonardo looked at Rodney and pointed to the chair beside him, so that the young man would sit.

"The numbers, as you see them are coordinates used to make the various diagrams on the screen. Each series of numbers identifies one particular segment of the drawing, its angle, length and direction. So the numbers as such, gathered together, make the design in itself. All I did was write a simple designing program that constructs the diagram using the numbers from this sheet. I input the numbers and this is the result."

"I don't understand". Rodney was puzzled. "I'm involved in the inputting of data, but I've never seen a data input sheet as simple as this one. Usually, in order to get a design, I must enter many coordinates based on the questions presented to me by the computer."

"You must understand that this program is just for testing the graphic design abilities of the computer", Leonardo clarified. "It is some sort of way to verify the accuracy of the design. Let me show you."

Leonardo cleared the screen and entered a code into his program.

"You see, if I take only a few of these numbers and input them into my system, this is what comes out," he said as he punched in the numbers. The computer monitor suddenly displayed two intercepting lines.

"I can see", Rodney said, understanding Leonardo's presentation. "But I don't see the reason why Charles went through so much trouble to hide this piece of paper if its sole purpose was for testing."

"Perhaps, there is a flaw in the design that is indicated on this sheet."

"What is it?" Rodney asked.

"The only way to find out is to enter the memory bank of the source computer from which this information originates," Leonardo answered.

Caldwell (UP) - Today the Federal Government announced that it would stop subsidizing the Sparo Spear Research and Development Project on December 31, 1988. The future of the project now depends on the success of the public test flight scheduled for September 6th, 1988 at the Sparo Aeronautics airstrip. Although some sources remain doubtful that the Sparo Spear, which has been marred with problems in past tests, will succeed the test flight, company officials are confident that it will not only be successful, but it will generate orders from national and foreign air forces. John (Jake) MacIntosh, President of Sparo Aeronautic says that they've been in close negotiation with three major NATO countries, which have shown interest in the Spear. "Representatives from these nations and other Western Nations will be present during the demonstration. Following the test flight, pilots from NATO countries will be given an opportunity to study and try out the Spear for evaluation purposes. We are confident that this will generate some orders." Inside sources have confirmed to us that Belgium and Japan were among the interested nations.

Rodney walked down the corridor towards where Charles worked with the engineering group responsible for the work on the Mohawk engine. As he approached the office, Dr. Collins, seeming somewhat perturbed, walked out of the room.

"Good morning Dr. Collins," he greeted.

The professor, absorbed in his own thoughts, didn't respond.

Rodney entered the office where he was greeted by Charles, who'd remained alone.

"How are you doing, Charlie?"

"Hi Rodney. What are you doing here?" he asked, sounding almost annoyed by his presence.

Rodney paused, surprised by his friend's mood. "I just dropped by to see how things were. Where are the other fellows?" he asked.

"They're in a meeting", Charles responded. "I had to stay. I've fallen behind in my work".

"You look pissed off. What's bugging you?"

"Nothing", Charles said dryly. "It's just that I'm very busy and I don't have much time to talk."

"Hey, its me you're talking to! Don't give me that bullshit."

Charles leaned back in his chair and ran his fingers through his hair, tugging at it in frustration. He apologized to his friend.

"Hey, I'm sorry, I just don't know what got into me. Things have been kind of strange in here lately, there's something going on". He paused again and sat in his chair. He leaned both elbows on his work desk and clasped his hands together, leaving white marks on his knuckles from the pressure exerted by his fingers. "There's something going on in here that stinks," he said in an angry, but controlled tone.

"What?"

"I just don't know, but I definitely feel that there's something rotten. Collins has been out of his mind for the last week. It's just not like him. It's as if he's in some sort of trouble."

"Hey, the guy's under a lot of pressure. You know that," Rodney tried to justify. "You know that this project means a lot. There's pressure on everybody right now."

"Nah! I don't believe that! Collins has the reputation of being cool as a cucumber when under incredible pressure. I think there's something else".

"What?"

"All I know is there's been some tough talks between Collins and the big honcho."

"Who?"

"Jake MacIntosh. He stormed in here the other day and barged his way into Collins' office. They had quite a run-in. It was behind closed doors, but we could hear them howling like banshees."

"What about?"

"I couldn't make it out. All I know is that it's serious enough. Collins is considering dropping out of the project." Charles confided in a low voice.

He got up and turned off his computer and monitor.

"I'm outta here." He grabbed his jacket and left the room. Rodney followed.

7

Compromising Talent

The hot and humid weather of the past days was taking its toll on the citizens of Caldwell. Many employees worked longer hours to take advantage of their cooler working environment and waited for the heat to subside somewhat before attempting to return to their homes.

Rodney started his journey back home on the city bus at a later hour than usual, hoping to avoid the evening rush hour. He stared through the bus window, his eyes wandering vaguely over the monotonous scenery along the bus route. His thoughts wandered back to the peculiar events of the past hours, particularly the mysterious resignation of William Collins, who'd left the company in a glowering rage. Since no official version had yet been given, his departure created a lot of speculation, especially among the engineering personnel, who were left with a feeling of insecurity since so much of the project's success depended on Collins' expertise. Granted, there was a little less than a month before the big test. Most of the remaining work consisted of minor corrections of snags experienced during the trial flights. But it was strange to see someone who'd been so involved in the project leave so close to the moment of truth. Some people had interpreted the action as Collins' lack of confidence in the success of the final test.

Nevertheless, Rodney found it somewhat odd that a man who'd overcome so many obstacles during the infancy of the project should suddenly decide to leave. *"Something's not right. There has to be something else,"* he thought. Unfortunately, he had no idea what it might be and was left with a nagging feeling.

"Check this out, Eddie," Eugene said as he pointed to the long painting that took up most of the space above the urinals. "Did you see the name on this?"

Edmond looked up and peered at the artist's signature. "Why, that's our friend Sergio. And he's exposed himself in the University washroom." The friends chuckled at the *double entente*.

Edmond walked away towards the vanity to wash his hands, all the while looking at the painting in the mirror. It was an abstract on canvas, composed mainly of fleeting lines. Eugene turned around and looked at Edmond's reflection. They grinned at each other. Without speaking, they each took an end of the painting and brought it down. Eugene opened the washroom door to make sure that they had a clear path and turned off the bathroom light.

The only person in the hallway was an old security guard walking along at a slow pace, absorbed by the pastry he was devouring as he completed his evening check looking for any students who might still be in the building. He bypassed the washroom, continued to the elevator and pressed on the call button. As he waited, the floor indicator changed to the descending arrow, followed by a countdown of numbers from the upper floors. The elevator doors opened and the guard got into the empty cab. The doors closed behind him.

"The coast is clear," Eugene said as he motioned with his arm. The nocturnal pranksters picked up the painting and slipped out the door.

"And we're off like a dirty shirt," Eugene recited in a chuckle.

"I don't know why I get into these things with you", Edmond moaned.

"Hey, you like adventure. Besides it's dark out there, and you don't like to walk alone at night."

They walked towards the fire exit, opened the door by pressing on the latch, and carrying their prize, went out of the building.

The heavy pounding of boots reverberated through Club 230 as the early morning visitor climbed the stairs to the upper floor. From his raised bed, Rodney saw Sergio appear at the top landing. He seemed very agitated.

"Sergio. What's goin' on?"

"Man, this is a great day. I can't believe this has happened to me. This is fantastic". He was restlessly walking in erratic circles around the room, his stocky figure emphasized by his baggy pants with the cuffs rolled inside high cowboy boots.

"What's fantastic?"

Edmond, then Eugene, then Leo, all ragged and half-asleep, came into the room.

"What the hell is going on in here?" Leo asked annoyed at having been awakened so rudely and so early.

"Guys, you won't believe this. The most incredible thing has happened to me." Sergio was nearly gasping for breath, barely able to contain his excitement. "I got called by the University security, this morning..."

"That's reason for excitement?" Leo interrupted.

"No, wait. The security called this morning to tell me that someone has stolen one of my paintings. Isn't that great?"

"Stealing is usually a criminal offense. I usually get upset when someone steals from me," Edmond noted, tongue in cheek.

"You don't understand," Sergio protested, "Somebody appreciated my painting. He liked it so much that he took the risk of being caught just to steal one of my paintings. That's the biggest compliment an artist can get!" he rejoiced.

"I guess congratulations are in order," Rodney expressed. In reality though, he was somewhat confused by his friend's peculiar logic.

"I've advised the school newspaper and the city newspaper. There was even some mention of the robbery on the school radio this morning," Sergio said in one breath, tickled pink by the coverage the whole matter was receiving.

"I told you that this guy was going somewhere," Eugene said to Edmond, maintaining a serious expression.

"Just think. This'll probably increase the demand for your artwork, which means that you'll be able to get more money. Some people get all the breaks!" Edmond laid it on thick.

"I'm so excited," Sergio exclaimed. He paused for a moment, as if remembering something. "Well, guys, I've got to go. I've got so many things to do. I just had to share this with you."

"Hey, we're touched," Eugene said innocently.

"Thanks guys. I appreciate your support. I have to go now." Sergio turned away and was down the stairs and out the door in two hops, ready to announce the news to the world.

"Hey that's pretty neat, isn't it?" Rodney said.

Eugene and Edmond looked at each other and smiled.

"Guys, Eddie and I would like to show you something. Follow me," Eugene said as he headed down the stairs.

Leonardo sat before the computer, ever so absorbed, oblivious to anything going on around him. The wall painting of *Four Students Bathing*, as the occupants liked to call it, animated the room with its great colors and its lifelike projection. From his kneeling position on the chesterfield that had been backed up against the wall, Eugene looked out of the living room window.

"He's here!" Eugene yelled as he rushed away from the window and towards the TV room.

A platter with a bottle of bubbly wine, disparate wineglasses and a plate containing neat rows of assorted cheeses and crackers had been placed on the coffee table. Leo, Edmond and Rodney were sitting near it, eagerly awaiting their friend's arrival.

When they heard the sound of the portico door opening and closing, Eugene got up and walked over to meet the guest.

"Sergio, my man, how are you?" he greeted enthusiastically.

"I'm doing great!" Sergio responded with exuberance. He was wearing a white silk dress shirt topped with a predominantly burgundy-colored paisley ascot.

"We're glad you could come," Eugene said. "As you know, we've decided to honor you today with a little wine and cheese, in appreciation of your talent and of the extraordinary events of the day," he explained in a formal tone.

Sergio's face radiated with pride and satisfaction. To be recognized by his friends was a great honor for him. *"These guys finally appreciate me for the artist I really am,"* he thought.

In the meantime, Rodney had poured the sparkling wine into the glasses. "Serve yourself, boys," he said. "Help yourself to some cheese and crackers, Sergio."

Everyone in the room gathered around the table to partake in the food and drink. Then, the four resident boys sat down, leaving a chair that had been positioned in front of them with its back to the far wall, on which now hung Sergio's painting. The young artist walked over to the chair and sat down, not noticing anything out of the ordinary. From the other boys' vantage point, Sergio had now become an integral part of the painting behind him.

"This has been such a hectic day," he said emphatically, conveying the impression that he thought the newfound fame to be bothersome.

His devoted listeners looked at him, all smiles, which Sergio attributed to their happiness for his success.

"Tell us more about your day," Eugene prompted.

"What is there to tell? I've spent half my day with policemen and the other half with reporters or friends who wanted to know more about what had happened. I've even had some people who've asked to see some of my work, perhaps in a private viewing. I tell you, this whole affair should increase the value of my paintings," he predicted with confidence.

"If they exhibit your work, make sure you invite us," Leo suggested.

"You guys are the first on my list." Sergio promised. "You were also the first guys I informed this morning, remember?"

"We know," Leo grumbled, remembering the rude awakening.

Sergio got up from his chair and walked over to the coffee table where he helped himself to more cheese and crackers, filling his hands to the maximum in order to delay subsequent trips.

"I appreciate the trouble you guys have gone through to organize this little celebration," he said. "Thank you."

"No trouble. Actually we were looking forward to seeing your reaction," Edmond said.

"I'm still the same!"

"We're going to the old tavern for some food and drink tonight. Would you care to join us?" Leo asked.

"Sure, I'd like that," Sergio answered as he straightened up and turned to face the wall behind him. His body froze and remained motionless for a few seconds.

The four hosts, who could only see his back, noticed the flush of red on his ears. They struggled to contain their laughter, as they scrutinized their friend's back.

"Bastards!" Sergio growled, keeping his back to his friends. His head fell forward and shook from side to side in disappointment.

"We like the painting," Eugene affirmed. "That's why we took it. We felt that it would look much better in our house than in a public washroom."

"Yes, but what about the coverage I'm getting?"

"I don't think you'd ever have received as much coverage as you have today if we hadn't taken the painting," Eugene said matter-of-factly.

"You guys will stop at nothing to get a laugh."

"Hey, we won't tell anyone if you don't," Leo said. "You may even get your exposition yet. "

"Yes, but now that I know the truth, I feel foolish," Sergio admitted.

"Don't you always?" Edmond teased.

"I knew I could count on you for sympathy," Sergio said, unable to hold back a smile. He knew that his friends intended no malice. In fact, he did recognize the promotional value of their actions for his art.

"Let's go and eat," Rodney suggested.

"And drink," Edmond added.

"Before we do that, I'd like Sergio to give me his impressions on something," Eugene said. "Follow me," he said to Sergio and led him out of the room.

Sergio and the three roommates followed Eugene down the corridor and entered Leonardo's room.

Pointing to the wall painting, Eugene asked: "What do you think of this?"

Sergio's eyes darkened and his lower jaw dropped. His face flushed with excitement as he examined the masterpiece before him.

"My God, who did this?" he asked his voice squeaking with emotion.

"Leonard painted it," Eugene answered. "It's pretty nice isn't it?"

"Nice is not a word that can define this. "This is brilliant. It's...it's divine." Sergio corrected. "Who is this Leonard?"

"Leonard," Eugene called out. "Leonard!"

Leonardo turned his head in the direction of the voice. "Yes?"

"I would like you to meet a good friend of ours, Sergio," he introduced. "Sergio this is Leonard Vincent, a friend of Rodney's dad."

Leonardo bowed. Sergio returned the courtesy.

"I admire your talents, Sir," Sergio complimented. "I don't know of anyone in our era who uses this type of stroke or color mixture. It's a style usually attributed to the Renaissance."

Sergio's comment disturbed Rodney. His neck muscles tightened and he felt that perhaps too much attention was being channeled Leonardo's way.

"It is," Leonardo agreed.

"Where did you learn to paint like that?"

"I studied under the great Ver..." Leonardo started to explain, almost giving himself away.

"The great Vercheres," Rodney interrupted, picking a name out of the blue.

"I've never heard that artist's name."

"He lived in Milano," Leonardo said, picking up on Rodney's efforts to conceal his identity.

"I'm a great lover of everything that touches the Renaissance," Sergio said. "Florence especially. It was the bastion of Renaissance art, with great figures such as Boticelli, Donatello..." Sergio enumerated.

"Verrocchio..." Leonardo interjected.

"Leonardo, Michelangelo..." Sergio continued.

"Michelangelo... pfft. That hunchback is a poor excuse for a sculptor and is nothing but a person who has concentrated his efforts on his only talent, that of an artist." Leonardo's face was now tense with disdain.

"But a great artist he was," Sergio insisted.

"I'm sure Leonard agrees with you," Rodney interrupted trying to take the sting out of Leonardo's comments.

"Will you be coming with us for dinner?" Sergio asked. "We have so much to talk about."

"No, I think that Leonard has some pressing things..." Rodney interjected.

"I have just made myself available," Leonardo accepted Sergio's proposition.

"Let's go, guys," Eugene prompted.

From across the table, Rodney was looking at the two artists discussing animatedly. To his dismay and great frustration, the loud music in the bar made it impossible for him to overhear the conversation. He was angry with himself for not taking the chair beside Leonardo when they'd entered the tavern. He'd been so absorbed in his thoughts about all the dangers that Leonardo might face if he was found out, that everyone had sat down leaving him the seat at the far end of the table.

Rodney motioned to Leo, who was sitting beside Leonardo. "You want to switch chairs with me?"

"Sure," agreed Leo. He got up, pulled up his chair and handed it to Rodney.

Rodney looked at Leo, with a blank expression.

"Well what? You asked me to change seats."

"You know what I meant." The relief he'd experienced from his friend's answer had been killed by his action.

"Take a break, Rod. You don't have to always act like you're his mother, you know. After all, he's a grown-up now."

"I just want to listen to what they have to say. It seems to be interesting," Rodney said, desperately grasping at straws.

"Thanks a lot," snapped Eugene, who'd been listening. "Are we unable to communicate at your level, Genius?"

Edmond had been watching Rodney's behavior since they'd left the house. He'd noticed that he seemed uncomfortable since Sergio had met

Leonardo. He got up and walked around the table, bringing his chair with him, and placed it between Sergio's and Leonardo's. He winked at Rodney who was grateful for his intervention. Once again, his friend had come through in a pinch.

"Are you gentlemen ready to order?" The waiter's voice came from behind Rodney. He received affirmative nods from everyone except Sergio and Leonardo. They had hardly noticed Edmond when he sat between them and unconsciously, had leaned forward to continue their discussion.

"We are," Leo said as he pointed to his three friends. "You'll have to ask those other two directly," he suggested, pointing to the two artists.

The crowd in the tavern had warmed up to the musicians' interpretation of the Beatle's *Nowhere Man*. As usually happened on every Saturday, those in the tavern milled into a big, happy, somewhat drunken family.

Leonardo looked around him. He had not taken any alcoholic beverage all evening and he was not impressed by the behavior of the people swaying and dancing around him. He was amazed, however, by the knowledge that Sergio had shown. The young man had managed, even in his inebriated state, to carry on a conversation that the citizen of the Renaissance found captivating.

"One thing I find a bit disturbing about the Renaissance in Florence and Milan is how violently people settled their differences," Sergio was saying. "People were always challenging each other to duels and the winner was the only survivor." He downed the remaining beer in his glass. He reached for the pitcher of draft and filled it up again. "I mean, from what I read, murder was common. Then there were all the wars, like the Florentine war against the Pope, the Pazzi conspiracy, all the internal conflicts. Then, when France became a threat, they all fought side by side."

"I must agree that this period," Leonardo paused before using its historical designation, "the Renaissance, is one of common conflicts, and this is unfortunate." He pulled gently on his beard. "I, for one, believe that matters can be settled in more civilized manners."

"It's strange, isn't it, that an era that had so many great artists, engineers and architects was so full of hate and conflict?" Sergio mused. "I'm glad that we live in a much more peaceful time."

"I think that the key factor is emotion. Emotion can enhance the creative genius of man, but at the same time it can lead him to destroy the end product of this creativity," Leonardo explained. This is as true now as it was then."

Leonardo paused. There was so much that could be said about life in his time, about Florence, about himself and his contemporaries. In all his readings, he had paid little attention to what had been written about him. He thought of his voyage to the future as a fortunate experience and an extraordinary opportunity. After all, there was so much to be learned. Why dwell on himself? Therefore he had concentrated on assimilating as much as he could about what had happened since his time. He also believed that he had been brought into the twentieth century for a reason, and that once his mission had been completed, the same forces would most likely return him to his own time. He thought it best this way. In the meantime, he enjoyed being the outsider experiencing a new world. But now, he was starting to feel some strain from the conversation. Not because of the content, but mostly because he had to weigh his words in order not to reveal his true identity and origin. He was aware of Rodney's preoccupation that his identity remain unknown, although he felt a bit annoyed by the young man's surveillance of his every gesture which he felt was a lack of faith in his judgment. However, he realized that the pressures exerted on his young friend by their common experience were greater. He understood that knowing what the immediate future had in store for Charles was a burden for Rodney.

"I am impressed with the accuracy of the knowledge that you have of the Renaissance period," Leonardo complimented Sergio.

"Thank you," Sergio responded with a slur. "I feel that the only way that I can really understand art and its evolution, if we can call it that, is through knowing and understanding the history of the era in which artists lived," Sergio explained. "But like you, I've gotten all my knowledge from history books, and who knows if what they say is the way it really happened?" He paused and looked at Leonardo with a stern look.

"Did anyone ever tell you that you look a lot like Leonardo Da Vinci?" he asked.

"I thank you for the compliment, but I have no reason to believe that I am his descendant," Leonardo said calmly and smiled. "Indeed, I find the comparison to be quite amusing."

For the first time, Leonardo felt that his freedom could be compromised and paranoia set in. *"Perhaps Sergio suspects my true identity and the sole purpose of this evening's intense discussions has been to substantiate his suspicions,"* he thought. From now on, he would have to be more careful. He became conscious that he had been carefree, almost glib, over the course of the evening and had enjoyed himself, but perhaps by doing so he had set a trap for himself. The last thing that he wanted was to jeopardize Rodney's trust. If he did, there would probably be no way of redeeming himself.

"It seems to me that I'm in the presence of a great man who's more than what he admits," Sergio was saying. "Is it possible that you have something to hide?"

"What man does not?" Leonardo answered.

Sergio smiled. "That's true. You've got a point." he conceded.

"Would it not be extraordinary if I were indeed the one and only Leonardo? " Leonardo said, taking the offensive. "I would be a five hundred year old man, a medical wonder," he added, laughing.

"That would be amazing wouldn't it? But even with today's medicine, it wouldn't be possible."

Meanwhile, across the table, Rodney had reached the state of semi-consciousness, due to the countless ounces of draft that he'd ingested. Sometimes the sounds, sometimes his surroundings, sometimes both simultaneously, seemed to temporarily fade away. Then in a tremor, they would return and he could see through a haze and hear distorted noises. Every so often, in sporadic bursts, everything came back into focus but just as soon, was lost again under the dulling influence of alcohol. At some point, he looked up and saw Charles' silhouette zooming in and out of focus. In his drunken stupor, he had the impression that he perceived some sort of vision, a ghost. The distorted body extended an arm and touched Rodney's shoulder.

"Get away from me!" Rodney screamed, sliding his chair into the table behind him. "You're supposed to be dead. Don't...bother me, don't touch...me. You're a ghost! You understand?"

He turned around and inadvertently spilled a pitcher of beer over the lap of a young man sitting at the table. Angered, the young man pounced and swung his fist at Rodney's head. Fortunately, at the same moment, Rodney lost his balance, allowing him to duck the punch which, failing to hit its target, propelled the aggressor to the ground. Rodney, still oblivious of the attack, got up and walked towards the exit, struggling to maintain a direct course. The would-be assailant, his pride and reputation shattered, pursued him, accompanied by three of his friends.

Leonardo, Edmond, Charles and Sergio all witnessed the series of events and, after assessing the imminent danger that Rodney was in, decided to give him a hand. When they got to the parking lot, Rodney was surrounded. Unafraid due to the excessive alcohol that hampered his judgment, Rodney readied himself to face the four fighters.

"Rodney are you okay?" Edmond called out.

"Of course I am. I'm just about to teach these little faggots a lesson," Rodney responded in a slurred speech.

"Who're you calling a faggot?" the flustered young man cried as he grabbed Rodney by the shirt.

"You look limp-wristed to me, buddy."

His comment attracted a punch to his stomach, causing him to double over in pain.

Charles ran to his friend's rescue, Leonardo and Sergio in tow. As Rodney's adversary turned to assess the situation, he was caught off guard by an upper cut to the genitals from Rodney, who'd evidently recovered his wind. His aggressor fell to the ground and remained there, in obvious pain. Feeling cocky, Rodney sat on the injured attacker and watched his friends take care of the other attackers.

After a few minutes, Leonardo left his sparring partner lying on the ground clutching his arm and grimacing in pain and walked over to Rodney. Sergio and Edmond were still involved in their respective scuffles with Charles making sure that they had the upper hand. In a desperate attempt, Sergio's opponent picked up a piece of structural lumber that lay on the ground near a garbage container and before Charles could react, swung it at Sergio, forcing him to retreat in a corner. In a swift motion, Leonardo grabbed the assailant's wrist and blocked what could have been a devastating blow. The master's grip tightened on the victim and in an amazing demonstration of strength, he hoisted the young man with one hand and flipped him to the ground. The exhibition of sheer power had the desired effect. The fighting stopped almost immediately and the four strangers scurried away and disappeared in the darkness of the unlit parking lot.

Leonardo turned to Sergio and smiling, said with irony: "I love the peaceful life of the twentieth century. Don't you?"

Leonardo was awakened by the sound of footsteps on the porch then heard the sound of voices behind the closed door. The squeaking noise of the door opening followed, giving way to clearer sounds. He could distinguish Sergio's voice but did not recognize the other.

"I guess they're not awake," Sergio was saying. "I don't hear anybody moving."

"Are you sure he won't mind?" the stranger's voice asked.

"Don't worry, we're good friends," Sergio said in a confident tone.

The door to Leonardo's quarters opened to make way for Sergio and a man of approximately Leonardo's age. Sergio saw that Leonardo had lifted himself on his elbows in order to get a better view of the early morning intruders, the sunlight streaming through the fabric of the blind behind him highlighting the contours of his body.

"Ah, Leonard. I'm glad to see you're still here."

"Where do you expect me to be at this time of the morning?" Leonardo asked dryly.

"Perhaps we should come later," Sergio's companion suggested.

"I'm sure he doesn't mind," Sergio said. He walked to the wall and switched the light on.

The stranger, a man with a thick mane of gray hair and a dense unmanaged crop of beard stained by a yellow streak on the side where he held a pipe in his closed lips, followed him in. He peered at Leonardo, puffs of white smoke escaping from the corner of his mouth.

"Leonard I'd like you to meet my teacher, Professor Nick Holmes. Nick this is Leonard, the man I told you about," an ecstatic Sergio made the introductions.

"It's a pleasure," Professor Holmes said in an unemotional tone, as he continued his rhythmic inhaling of the pipe smoke.

Leonardo, upset by the intrusion, failed to show his usual good nature and did not acknowledge the introduction.

"This is it," Sergio said, beaming, as he pointed at the mural. "What do you think?"

Nick Holmes turned away from Leonardo and set his eyes on the painting. His face remained emotionless. However, the cadence of the smoke escaping from the side of his mouth accelerated. Footsteps were heard coming down the stairs. Rodney appeared, his face glistening with sweat and marked from the metallic wrist watch on which it had rested.

"What the hell are you doing here?" Rodney asked Sergio, his voice trembling from the previous night's excesses and the annoyance at having been awakened so early. "Don't you ever knock before entering other people's homes?"

"Did you notice the incredible precision in reproducing the facial traits?" Sergio asked Professor Holmes, keeping his back turned and ignoring Rodney's comment.

"For crying out loud! Who the hell do you think you are to barge in like this?" Rodney grabbed Sergio's arm. "Do you know what time it is? It's seven-thirty in the bloody morning. We've been in bed for exactly two hours now."

"I'm sorry Rod, but I had to show this beautiful piece of work to Nick."

"There's such a thing as asking permission first."

Leonardo lay on the bed reliving the fears of the night before. Sergio's presence made him nervous and he felt that he could lose his anonymity. *"Perhaps I was not so clever,"* he thought.

Nick Holmes hadn't moved. The pungent aroma of pipe tobacco filled the air and literally clouded the early-morning events. He turned to Leonardo and asked:

"Who are you?"

"My name is Leonard."

"Listen. I've studied art for close to half a century and I'm quite familiar with the work of most of the good painters, dead and alive. Anyone with your talent would have been noticed and talked about by now."

"I have only painted as a hobby," Leonardo said, remembering the word he had read. "I have never sold any of my work. Perhaps that explains why you have never heard of me."

"Perhaps, but I'm very surprised. I would like to get to know you better. Maybe we could get together and talk."

"Maybe during my next visit," responded Leonardo. "I am leaving tomorrow."

Nick looked at Leonardo with a stern expression, his eyes trying to see what could not be seen. Leonardo knew that his encounter with Sergio's professor was not to be taken lightly.

"You'll find Professor Holmes' knowledge pretty impressive, Leonard. Please let me know when you come back so I can set up a meeting," Sergio said naïvely.

"I will," Leonardo lied.

"It's been a pleasure," Nick Holmes said in a dry tone, extending his hand to Leonardo, who obliged the more conventional way of exchanging salutations, trying to be as contemporary and as unnoticeable as possible.

The professor eyed the room, making sure that he'd seen everything, trying to find anything that could substantiate his suspicions.

"Goodbye," Sergio said as he left, escorted by his professor.

Rodney and Leonardo looked at each other. They both knew that Professor Nick Holmes could jeopardize their secret. His inquisitive and prying visit made them feel uneasy and they both felt responsible for the problems that could result from it. Trouble was no longer just a possibility, it was imminent. It was now a question of time and they had to act fast.

"Can't anybody get a decent night's sleep around here?" Leo complained as he entered the television room, every one of his hairs pointing in a different direction. He squinted from the premature awakening. Edmond and Eugene, feeling the toll of the previous night's heavy drinking, were already sitting side by side on the chesterfield. Leonardo and Rodney were also showing obvious signs of fatigue and strain, but mostly, they looked worried.

"Yeah, what's this all about?" Edmond yawned. "Whatever it is, let's get it over with so I can go back to bed."

Rodney looked at Leonardo, seeming a bit hesitant, as if he wasn't quite sure where to start. "Uh...guys, I'm sorry I dragged you out of bed like this, but I really needed to talk to you. Leonardo, I mean Leonard, and

I have a very important secret that we have to share with you," he started to explain.

"You guys want to tell us that you're now going steady," Eugene replied. The comment generated some laughs and helped alleviate the tension.

"I wish it was that simple," Rodney said. He paused trying to find a right way to say what he wanted. "All of you have either read or heard about Leonardo Da Vinci, right?" he asked.

"Right," came the response.

"We've also read and seen on television some reports about the mysterious disappearance of the famous Da Vinci notebooks."

"Why don't you get to the point?" Leo prompted.

Rodney walked over to a folding bridge table that he'd set up temporarily and pulled off the big brown bath towel that had been covering four neat stacks of parchment paper.

"What's this?" Edmond asked.

"These are the famous Da Vinci notebooks," Rodney admitted.

"Yeah and I've got Julius Caesar's laurels upstairs in my bedroom," Leo replied. The comment generated more laughter.

"I was expecting skepticism. But if you look closely, you'll notice three things. One, you can't find parchment like this anymore. Two, the writing is inverted, which means that the author wrote from right to left and backwards, so that the notes could then be read using a mirror. Leonardo was left-handed, and it's a well-documented fact that he wrote in that fashion. And three, you'll notice that the language used is Italian."

"How many pages are there, approximately?" Eugene asked.

"Over ten thousand," Rodney responded.

"Yeah, right! If you'd listened to the news, you'd know that there were approximately seven thousand stolen pages. That's the number of pages that've been recovered out of the thirteen thousand or so pages that he's said to have written. That sure shoots some holes in your story," Eugene argued.

"Please bear with me. The notes that we have here go up to the year 1505, which means that they don't include all of the notes," Rodney defended.

Leo picked up a few of the pages. "How do you explain the good condition of some of these pages. They're supposed to be over five hundred years old. Doesn't parchment turn a yellowish color after a decade or so?" he challenged.

"Yeah, and how can you be so sure that these notes stop in 1505?" Eugene asked in a defiant tone.

"Obviously somebody's gone through a lot of pain to forge all these documents," Eugene said.

"Does that make any sense to you?" Rodney asked. "Who in his right mind would try to forge ten thousand pages of notes, writing backwards?"

"I must agree it's a crazy idea." Edmond agreed. "But that still doesn't explain anything."

Rodney breathed deeply, as if he was trying to find some sort of inspiration from the intake of oxygen.

"Guys, I know this may sound crazy, but I'm asking you to believe what I'm about to tell you." He paused once more and walked across the room and pointed to Leonardo. "Our friend Leonard is the one and only Leonardo Da Vinci," he announced.

After a moment of surprised silence, the boys burst out laughing.

"Yeah, and I'm Napoleon," Eugene said as he put his hand in the fold of his housecoat, imitating the fabled French Emperor's gesture.

"Ah yes, Napoleon Bonaparte. Born in France in the year 1769. Died in Saint-Helena in the year 1821. A brilliant military figure who proclaimed himself Emperor of France. Short in stature but big on ambitions." Leonardo muttered.

"What's the relic saying?" Eugene teased.

Leo and Edmond shrugged. Rodney exhaled heavily, trying to relieve some of the pressure.

"Listen. The notes stop in 1505 because that's the year that Leonardo left his time and came into ours." Seeing the shocked expressions on his friends' faces, he took a deep breath. "Please hear me out and I'll try to explain everything," Rodney pleaded. He looked at Leonardo, who'd agreed to remain silent. "I was hoping that you guys would believe me right off. But I can't say I'm surprised by your reaction. This is pretty unbelievable stuff. I had trouble believing it myself. I wouldn't have if I hadn't traveled in time myself."

"Ah, quit the bullshit!" Eugene yelled out. "We've known you since you were a kid, for Chrissake! Don't try that story on us."

Rodney tried to remain calm. "Guys, I know it's hard to believe, but I've traveled backwards in time. No guff! I know what the future has in store for us. That's why I felt the need to let you in on our secret."

There was a stunned, unbelieving silence. Edmond looked around the room at his friends. He then looked at Leonardo's masterpiece on the wall and evaluated Rodney's strange claim. This would explain a lot of the odd things that had been going on and Rodney's recent strange behavior. Not to mention that Leonardo was really different. He was more than an eccentric by any standard.

"I've got a suggestion," Edmond finally said. "Rod, you have to admit that what you're asking us to believe is extraordinary, to say the least. But I think that there's a way to establish if your claim is true or not. Would you be willing to try it out?" he asked.

"I don't see why not," Rodney answered in a leap of faith, trusting his friend's judgment. "What is it I should try?"

"It's not for you," Edmond responded. "It's for Leonardo."

They all looked at the older man. His face remained impassive as he fingered his beard and nodded his approval.

Some time later, Edmond came back to the house carrying a large book under his right arm. He cleared the television room table and placed the book in the center. His companions came in one by one, intrigued by Edmond's test whose contents he'd been careful not to reveal in order to keep from compromising the results.

"I'm curious to see how you're gonna prove or disprove Leonardo's identity," Eugene said.

"If you guys would give me a few more moments, I'll explain," Edmond answered as he pulled photographs out of a brown envelope and opened the book, displaying a full-page color reproduction of the "Mona Lisa" painting.

Leonardo was sitting on a chair away from the table and looked down the hallway, seemingly absorbed in his thoughts.

"That should do it!" Edmond said as he straightened up from his crouching position. "My friends, as I told you earlier, I believe I have a way of proving without a doubt if this man is truly who he and Rodney claim he is." He took the photographs in his hands and sifted through them, selecting one. He then placed the other ones back into the envelope.

"Leonard, could you come over here, please?"

The Master got up and walked towards the table where Edmond had laid the book.

"Could you tell me if you recognize this?" he asked pointing to the photograph.

Leonardo looked closely at the color photo.

"Hmmm, the face and traits look right, but the colors are much too dark. I would have to say that it is a reproduction of a painting of mine. The lady you see is the wife of Franceso del Gioconda, Mona Lisa." He paused. Then, reminiscing, he continued: "Mona Lisa is one of the few portraits I have painted. There was a fascinating look about her that inspired me. I must admit that I quite enjoyed doing her portrait."

Leo and Eugene exchanged a look, satisfied that Leonardo's testimony had proved him to be an impostor. Rodney seemed totally confused that

Leonardo had declared that a painting classified as genuine by contemporary experts was a fake.

Edmond pursued his questioning: "You said something interesting. You say that you didn't paint that portrait."

"Not this one. However, I did paint a very similar portrait."

"Could you explain to us the major differences," Edmond asked.

"Hmmm. As I said before, the face, the hair, the silhouette, the hands and the shapes in the background are identical. But the colors, well...hmmm...they are much too dark. My painting had livelier colors. Look at the background, the colors are much too somber. They should be much brighter."

"I know that I may seem a bit pushy and persistent, but can you give me more accurate details? Do you remember the colors?" Edmond asked.

"Of course I do!" Leonardo said. "After all, it has not been so long since I painted this," he said. He paused. "However it is true that what seems to be like months to me, represents centuries in history books," he added, remembering his travel through time.

"Please proceed," Edmond urged.

"I have here photocopies of the results of an analysis that was made on the Mona Lisa earlier this year by European experts," Edmond announced once Leonardo had concluded his detailed reconstitution of his original painting. "The analysis was performed in order to establish what the original colors of the painting were, since they've somewhat changed over the past five centuries. I have copies for every one of you and I would like you to come to your own conclusions."

He handed the documents to his friends. All of them had been intrigued by Edmond's persistence in testing Leonardo and looked eagerly at what was written on the sheets that he handed to them. Rodney saw that the text had the format of technical specifications that he'd often seen in his engineering courses. A computer reproduction of the Mona Lisa had been done on the attached sheet and numbers had been used to identify the colors of the various features in the painting. The covering page explained the various colors according to the numbers identified on the computer printout. As he read the data, Rodney felt relief replace the tension that had, until then, been building up. Edmond had come through once more. His customary logic and his systematic approach to the problem had brought credibility to Leonardo's claim. The scientific description on paper echoed Leonardo's descriptions of the colors and left no doubt as to his true identity. He looked up at Edmond who sat on the chesterfield, his face expressionless as he waited for the verdict. Noticing Rodney's stare, he winked, reassuring his friend that he had no doubt that the older man was who he claimed to be.

Leo's and Eugene's faces were blank. They were shocked by what they were reading. They turned towards each other and exchanged puzzled looks.

Eugene whistled imitating the Star Trek communication whistle. "Beam me up, Scotty."

"Pretty scary isn't it," Edmond said with amazement.

Silence ruled for a few moments as everyone in the room assimilated the information. Eugene left the room and walked to Leonardo's quarters. As if they were on the same wavelength, Leo and Edmond followed. Leonardo and Rodney, curious about their friends' intentions, joined them. They found the three boys looking at the painting on the wall.

"Who'd have thought. We're rich!" Leo said. "From now on, we lock our doors."

"I'll buy a better lock," Eugene volunteered.

"Today!" Leo emphasized.

The walk downtown had helped Eugene put the events and the findings of the past hours into perspective. He, as well as his roommates, had pledged to keep the whole matter under wraps. *"Who'd believe me anyway?"* he thought. He hadn't yet found a style of straightjacket he liked. He'd maintained an unusually brisk pace throughout his walk. The situation dictated urgency. The once accessible home was now to become a fortress, restricted to the present tenants and a few selected friends. The locks Eugene had just purchased were to keep the unwanted people out. He and his roommates had a secret that they didn't want discovered.

As he came down the hill and approached the house on Anderson Street, he heard the sound of splashing water, then saw that water was flowing from a hose hanging out of Leo's second-story window and onto the gravel driveway.

"What the hell!"

He bounced up the porch stairs and entered the house. He could hear the sound of an electric drill emanating from upstairs. He continued up the stairs and walked towards Leo's room where he found Edmond holding the drill that had been adapted to a pump used to siphon the water out of Leo's water bed.

"What are you doing?" he asked.

"What does it look like?"

"Poor question," Eugene conceded. "Why are you taking the water out of the bed?"

"I think you'd better ask Rod. He's got one of his crazy plans in mind. He's sealed Leonardo's papers in plastic bags and he wants to put them in the water bed mattress afterwards."

"Won't they get wet?"

"You know Rod. He's tested his contraption in the bath and it seems to work okay."

"Does Leo know anything about this?"

"Of course not," Edmond answered, stating the obvious. "Apparently that's the purpose of the whole exercise."

"What is that supposed to mean?"

"I'm screwed if I know. Ask Rodney."

Eugene shook his head, and laughed. "I'm living with lunatics."

"Yeah but we're great-looking lunatics. Don't forget that," Edmond added with a grin.

"I believe I have locks to install," Eugene said with a sigh as he walked out of the room. "Conceited lunatics, to boot," he mumbled to himself.

8

Caffeine Could Be Fatal to Fighters

"*Where were you?*" Rodney asked.

"What do you mean, where was I?" Charles replied.

"I tried to reach you all weekend, but there was no answer."

"I was away all weekend, for Chrissake! What's your problem?"

"What the hell happened to Collins?"

"I wish I knew," Charles answered. "I told you before that something fishy was going on. Now you have the proof."

"That's no proof. A guy leaving a company is not what amounts to proof. There's a reason for it."

"What is it? I'd really like to know."

"Follow me. I've got something to show you," Rodney motioned his friend towards his office. He closed the door behind him to ensure privacy. He reached in his school bag and pulled out a sheet of paper. It was a photocopy of the printed side of the document that he and his roommates had found rolled up with the bacon.

"Do you recognize this?" he asked.

"How the hell did you get your hands on this? They're coordinates used for our graphics in the design of engines. This is classified information."

"Never mind where I got it. Who handles this data in your department?"

"Ned Richards and Collins are the only two guys who have the access codes to this data. Ned is the one who keeps tabs on it since Collins developed the program."

"Is there any way you can find out the access code to the data?" Rodney continued.

"Why would you want to access this. For God's sake! We could be put behind bars for tampering with that kind of information. You know as well as I do that this is classified information." Charles protested.

Rodney walked towards Charles.

"Answer my question. Can you get me the access code?"

"Are you out of your freaking mind? Why would you want me to take such a stupid risk?"

"Because, I think Collins' resignation has something to do with what is in that program. I don't know what, but I've got a feeling that it's something pretty bad."

"And because you have a hunch, you want me to put my ass on the line, is that right?"

"Believe me, if you don't, you'll put more than your butt on the line,"

"Is that a threat?"

"No, my friend, it isn't. I'd do it myself if I could, but that would be impossible for me to do without raising suspicion. Only you can help me."

"You managed to get that report before, why can't you do it now?" Charles asked.

"I'm not the one who got this report, and I can't tell you where I got it. You wouldn't believe me anyway, so you have to trust me on this one. I know what I'm asking you to do is risky, but it's necessary. Besides, I'm quite convinced that you want to get to the bottom of this just as much as I do." Rodney paused and took a deep breath. "Please Charles will you get me access to the system?"

Charles paced around the room, grabbing the back of his neck to bring some relief from the tension building up there.

"If you have suspicions, why don't you talk to the authorities?" Charles asked.

"I need proof before I can make any allegations. Please trust me on this. It's the only way we can find out."

"Okay I'll try, but you'd better be right, Rod." He paused, then added, "I don't know why I'm agreeing to this nonsense."

"It's my charm," Rodney answered.

No matter how much he tried, Charles had difficulty getting his work done. He reached for the Styrofoam cup on his desk. "How could I let him convince me to do this?" he asked himself. His heart beat erratically in his tense body.

He looked at his watch. Eight forty-two a.m. *"Ned should be going for coffee any minute now."* From his half-opened window he could see Ned Richards sitting at his desk. Charles knew Ned's routine by heart. At 8:20 a.m. he entered his office. After opening his filing cabinets he would key into the computer system. However, around this time, before he settled down in front of his computer, where he usually spent most of his day, he would go to the canteen for coffee. So far, this day had not been different and Charles hoped that he wouldn't deviate from his routine

"Come on, Ned. Coffee time. You need your morning fix, remember?" He muttered between his clenched teeth. "Any time now."

The previous day, he'd managed to enter into Ned's office without being seen. The few tense moments that he'd lived there reminded him of Einstein's theory of relativity. The thirty seconds or so he'd spent in the office sure did seem more like thirty minutes or even hours. Now, again, he had to find his way into the office without being seen. In a few seconds, Ned would leave to get his coffee.

"Hey Ned, I've got a little something for you." Charles recognized the voice of Roger Simpson, Rodney's immediate superior. He turned and saw Roger enter Ned's office, carrying a Styrofoam cup in each hand. He gave one to Ned.

"That's mighty nice of you. Thank you!" Ned greeted the visitor.

"I thought I'd take this opportunity to talk about a few things with you."

"I knew there was a reason behind this. You're too damn stingy to give something with no strings attached," Ned teased.

"Hey it's not that I'm stingy. It's just that I have short arms and deep pockets." Roger responded with a chuckle as he closed the office door behind him, reducing the voices of the two men within the room to an inaudible murmur.

"That's just great! Charles thought. Successive mini explosions had replaced his heartbeats. The temperature in the room became unbearable. He felt nauseous.

"I've got to get it out of there," he muttered to himself. "I'm in really deep shit. They're going to get my hide." The shaking of his hands amplified. "What if they find it?" he asked himself in a quasi-stupor.

Charles sat in the darkness of the TV room at Club 230, where he'd sought refuge and company. However, no one had been at home when he got there, so he'd let himself in, hoping someone would show up soon. He was clenching the fingers of his left hand with his other hand. His body couldn't find a comfortable position on the old sofa. He flinched every time he heard a noise. The shadows that danced through the window on the far wall of the room didn't help either. The lonely viewer interpreted each new projection as more frightening than the last one. However, the dangling figure of a hanging man was more than he could bear. He jumped towards the window and desperately struggled with the rope of the venetian blind in an effort to block out the shadow theater. In a loud clatter, the blind expanded and covered the window, leaving the room in total darkness.

Startled by the sudden noise, he backed away in horror and tripped over the coffee table. His legs failed to recover from the collision and he fell onto the cold hardwood floor. His strained breathing combined with the pounding of his heartbeats muffled all outside noises. Ironically though, it gave his mind some sort of reprieve from its self-inflicted madness. For the first time in days, he felt his tension subside somewhat, as if the fall had knocked it out of him. He curled up into the fetal position on the floor and slowly gave in to the fatigue of several nearly sleepless nights. His mind was now empty of all negative thoughts and nothing seemed more pressing than sleep.

The banging on the door and the rattling of the doorknob interrupted his sleep. Someone was trying to gain entry. Instinctively, he rolled over and pressed his body against the sofa beside him, his heart beating as intensely as the pounding on the door. Like an infantry soldier in a battle zone, he crawled towards the hallway, making sure to stay as close to the ground as possible. The infernal noise started up again.

"They know I'm here!" He muttered, breathing heavily as he continued to crawl towards the hallway. Through the window in the door, he could see the silhouette of a man highlighted by the light from the street but whose features were in shadow. The insistent knocking resumed.

"Goddamn it! Who took the bloody key?" a voice resounded through the door.

It was Leo. Charles sighed in relief and in a swift motion, came to his feet and rushed to open the door. He'd never been so happy to see Leo.

"Charles, my man. Thank God somebody's here," Leo greeted, visibly elated to have someone answer the door. "What took you so long to answer?" he asked.

"I ... I was asleep."

"Are the other guys asleep too?

"How did you get in?"

"I used the key from the hiding place. I ... well ... well I guess I forgot to put it back. I'm sorry," Charles explained, feeling embarrassed. "Rodney told me where I could find it," he continued anticipating Leo's next question.

"So much for security." Leo growled. "I'm off to bed. Make yourself at home, Charles."

The toasts jumped out of the toaster, their movement catching Rodney's attention. He hurried to put them on his plate and swiftly buttered them, taking advantage of the escaping heat.

Charles' fingers rapped on top of the kitchen table as he watched Rodney prepare his breakfast.

"Are you sure I can't interest you in something?

"I'm never really hungry when I feel that it may be my last moment of life," Charles replied dryly.

The prophetic words had an ill effect on Rodney's appetite. He pushed his plate away.

"Hey, don't lose your appetite over little ol' me, Rod. After all you don't have anything to worry about. You're not the one who's put his life on the line."

"I'm trying to save your life, Bucko!" Rodney thought, but said, "I really appreciate what you've done for me, Charles. I think we'll all benefit from this. You'll see." He paused. "You were able to get the access code number, weren't you?"

"I'm not sure."

"What do you mean you're not sure? You either have it or your don't!" Rodney snapped impatiently.

"Well, I think I have the whole thing on video tape. Ned would never access the computer when someone is around. As you know, that's against procedure. And, as you know, he'll never write his access code in any book. Like everybody else, he's memorized the code. That's standard procedure, right? So I hooked up a recorder to the security camera that's in his office. I got a wire to run from the camera to a recorder that I put under a nearby filing cabinet."

"Good going!" Rodney gave Charles an enthusiastic pat on the shoulder. "Where did you get the recorder?"

"I used the one from the audio-visual room at work, you know the one on a rollaway dolly. I had a great excuse. The guys had given me some footage they wanted me to look over. So I had a good reason to have it in our office."

"Wow! How'd you know the camera was focused on the keyboard?"

"The other day, when I went by the security desk, I noticed that the camera was pointed on Ned's terminal. Ned was sitting at the terminal at that time and the keyboard was in clear sight. And that's where there's a problem." Charles paused and stretched his arms behind him, joining both hands behind his head

"Why is there a problem?"

"As you know, they have that camera running twenty-four hours a day. They monitor all activities around that terminal. It's the computer that contains all the tricks of the trade and so, the problem is that while it's possible to observe whoever gets to work around the computer, I don't think that we have a clear enough view of the keyboard to see what keys are being pressed."

"I see what you mean."

"Plus, as much as I was careful to keep out of the line of the camera, I don't know if I got in the picture or not."

"There's only one way to find out. Let's play the tape!" Rodney suggested. "We'll have to find ourselves a video cassette player." He reached for a piece of toast, took a bite out of it and chased it down with a drink of milk. "Let's get to it!"

"If you don't mind I'd like to stay behind and rest," Charles said. "I think I've had enough excitement for a lifetime."

"As you wish, buddy. I shouldn't be gone too long. Feel free to take whatever you want to eat...from...from Eugene's fridge," Rodney offered with a grin.

"You're so generous. I see you're developing traits similar to your boss', deep pockets..."

"Deep pockets and short arms," Rodney completed the phrase. "I see you've met Roger Simpson," he chuckled.

"Yeah. He's notorious for his big heart."

Leonardo sat at his table, surrounded by an arsenal of electronic equipment, the computer monitor towering above all the other components, all units connected in a tangle of wires. Edmond watched in amazement as the Master confidently worked the keyboard. Since he'd been informed of Leonardo's true identity, he, like his roommates, spent a lot of time observing Leonardo, impressed by the ease and skill with which he manipulated the electronic and computer technology. Leonardo was certainly living up to his reputation of being a man five hundred years ahead of his time and Edmond was a first-hand witness.

Rodney walked into the room followed by Charles and Eugene.

"Are you ready Leonard?" he asked.

"Practically," Leonardo answered as he performed last minute adjustments.

"You'll see that Leonard is quite adept with computers," Rodney said to Charles.

"Have you worked much with computers?" Charles asked innocently.

"One could say that I have been spending considerable time working with them lately," Leonardo responded with cautious evasiveness.

"Leonard is an old hat when it comes to science and engineering," Eugene added, not missing the opportunity to play off Charles' not knowing of the Master's identity.

A sharp high-pitched noise interrupted the conversation. Eugene reached for his belt and put an end to the electronic signal.

"I see you're on call tonight, Trap," Rodney remarked.

"Yeah. Rain or shine, the news must come on. We're following a hot story. I guess this must be the call."

"What about?" Edmond asked.

"Watch the eleven o'clock news and you'll see." He winked at Edmond. "If you'll excuse me, I've got a phone call to make."

"That little device is fascinating," Leonardo noted.

"What device?" Rodney asked.

"The pager. I can find many good applications for it," Leonardo said as if he was speaking to himself.

"Well guys, can we start what we came here to do?" Charles suggested trying to bring his friends back on track.

"So Leonard, where do we stand?" Rodney asked.

Leonardo responded by turning on a few switches. An image came on a black and white television screen that had been placed on a shelf beside the desk.

"As you can see, the camera is focused on the workstation where the computer is located. At the bottom right of the screen you can read that the taping started at eight-thirty in the morning." Leonardo pressed on the fast forward button of the videocassette. "By fast-forwarding the tape we can come to the point of interest. Here we are. As we had observed during the first viewing, it was very difficult for us to identify what Mr. Richard's code is. This is mainly due to the bad quality of the camera and also to its distance from the computer."

Leonardo pressed the pause button, freezing the picture with Ned Richards sitting at his desk. He turned to the keyboard of the computer and entered a few commands.

"Now if you look at the computer monitor, you will notice that we have been able to magnify and focus on Mr. Richard's right hand."

The screen showed the hand poised over the keyboard.

"Wow, that's pretty amazing!" Charles exclaimed. "How did you manage that?"

"That's incredible," Rodney supported.

Leonardo did not answer. He reached for the slow motion button on the recorder. The original and the magnified pictures moved simultaneously in slow motion on the television screen and on the computer screen.

"I should like to bring your attention to the computer monitor. As you can see, the magnified picture shows the details of the keyboard as the fingers press on the keys one by one."

"Why are you only focusing on the right hand?" Rodney asked.

"Quite simply because Mr. Richards uses his right hand almost exclusively. The only time that he uses his left hand is to press on the space bar and the control and shift keys," Leonardo explained. He handed a piece of paper to Rodney. "I have written on this piece of paper the commands that Mr. Richards has used to access the computer."

"Caffeine! That figures!" Charles exclaimed.

"That's his password?" Rodney was surprised.

"It's ironic." Charles remarked. "I nearly wasn't able to retrieve the tape because of coffee. Can you believe it?"

"What do you mean?" Leonardo asked.

"I'll explain later."

"Now, all we have to do is access the computer and get the information we need," Rodney concluded.

"Easier said than done," Charles warned. "How can we manage to get to the computer terminal without being caught by the camera? And even if we're able to do that, we don't even know what we're looking for."

"Charles may have a point there," Rodney said. "I've got a feeling we may be looking for a needle in a hay stack."

"Or a contact lens in an Olympic swimming pool," Charles added with a grin.

"I may have a solution to our problems, but I shall need a day or two to prepare myself." Leonardo reached for books on top of the desk. "With Eugene's electronics books and some creativity, we may be able to concoct something."

"Come off it!" Charles exclaimed obviously doubtful of Leonardo's abilities. "How the hell are you going to get into a high-security area and find conclusive evidence?"

"This is where I shall require your help." Leonardo explained. "I will need both of you to assist me in finding a solution. I am certain that by pooling our talents we will be able to overcome any obstacle," he assured. "Rodney told me that you are quite knowledgeable about the Sparo project. If we combine this with your and Rodney's computer expertise and my modest scientific knowledge and "savoir faire", you may be surprised by the outcome."

"After seeing what you've been able to do with computers, I don't know if I can be of that much help," Charles conceded.

"Let us begin, then," Leonardo continued as if he had not heard the flattering comment. "Both of you have to tell me everything you know about your work, the computers you use or anything you feel may be helpful to our little project."

"Well, to start, our company builds airplanes," Charles joked.

"You don't say!" Rodney answered as he picked up a note pad. In block letters he wrote at the top of the pad: "PROJECT INFILTRATION".

"I hope you have a damned good reason for pushing this," Charles warned Rodney. "You know what will happen to us if we get caught."

"Yeah, I know. But the survival of the Sparo Spear may be at stake. I thought you cared about that project?" Rodney pressed knowing that he was touching a sensitive chord.

"What makes you so sure?"

"Hey, come on Charles. Who's the one who was telling me just a few days ago that he thought that something was going wrong. And remember how skeptical you were about Collins' departure."

"I just hope that your hunch is right and that you're not just crazy."

"Okay. Let's put it this way. I promise that if we don't find anything, we'll drop the whole thing."

"We'll have to anyway if we get caught."

"Ahem! Gentlemen. Shall we start?" Leonardo interrupted.

"He must be going out of his mind." Leo said as he pressed his ear to the closed living room door. "I swear, Trap. He's been talking to himself. He even changes his voice."

Eugene walked over to the door and joined his roommate in his eavesdropping. "I can't hear anything."

A muffled and high-pitched voice could be heard through the door. "Data reception almost complete."

"He sounds like ET for Pete's sake," Leo whispered.

"That's all we need! A man from Mars has moved in with our time traveler. And some people think that I'm not leading a normal life!"

"Shh! Listen!" Leo motioned.

"To think that I'm letting him use some equipment from work," Eugene worried.

"Are you serious? You're crazier than he is!"

The door off the portico swung open. Rodney and Charles walked in, carrying plastic shopping bags.

"Are we curious?" Rodney asked, guessing what his two friends were up to.

"He's gone nuts," Leo testified as he pointed to the other side of the door. "He's been talking to himself all afternoon."

"That's a very harsh accusation," Charles commented. "Can you substantiate it?"

"Go ahead and listen for yourself," Leo challenged.

"We will," Rodney agreed as he opened the door. He and Charles walked in, making sure not to let anyone else enter.

"What's going on in there?" Eugene asked the door. Leo could only shrug.

Edmond came down the stairs. "Hey guys, what are you doing? You look like a bunch of kids in line at a peep show."

"Eddie, do you know what's happening in there?" Leo asked.

"I think the guys are fooling around with computers or something. You know how technical these guys can get," he answered. "Why are you guys so curious anyway?"

"Curious? Us? We were just passing by and wondered..." Eugene fibbed.

Edmond walked towards the kitchen. The others followed him until they reached the TV room. They sat down and for a few moments, they were silent.

"I guess I'll turn on the old boob tube," Eugene suggested.

"That's a good idea," Leo approved.

"I wonder what they're doing in there?" Eugene wondered out loud.

As if on cue, they looked towards the kitchen entrance at the same time to see if Edmond was observing them.

"Let's go listen," Leo suggested as he got up and quietly ran towards the living room.

"Yeah," his fellow snoop agreed.

"A few more adjustments and we should be able to test it," Leonardo declared as he screwed a component onto his much-modified computer. The once unobstructed desk had been transformed into a maze of wires, computers, monitors and keyboards.

"You're costing me a fortune Leonard. It seems I use up my whole salary to buy all these components," Rodney complained as he pulled out packaged electronic parts from the bags with which he and Charles had walked in.

Leonardo turned towards Rodney and started sifting through the electronic components. His eyes sparkled with satisfaction. "Fantastic! I think we have all we need." He placed the components on the sofa beside the desk.

"Hey! I thought you said it was absolutely necessary that I get you all this stuff today," Charles protested.

"Keep your pants on, Chuck. We'll be using these in the second phase of our project. Right Leonard?"

Leonardo showed no sign of acknowledgment or support for the last remark.

Charles sat down amidst the electronic gadgetry, in awe of all the things that surrounded him.

"Tell me Leonard. Where did you get all these components? The compact disk player, the video camera and all that stuff? That's expensive equipment. It must have cost you thousands of dollars," he said.

"I sold some of my paintings." Leonardo admitted.

"You what?" Rodney's face had turned beet red. "What paintings? To whom?"

"Your friend Sergio's professor, Nick Holmes," Leonardo said in a calm tone.

"What paintings? When did you do that?" Rodney interrogated, as if Leonardo had committed a crime.

"What's the problem?" Charles asked, not understanding what the whole commotion was about.

"I went to the University Department of Fine Arts at Sergio's insistence. He had been pestering me for days. So in order to - how would you express it - get him off my back, yes I believe that's the expression, I obliged and went. I painted a tableau for them, and Holmes' wife liked it so much that she bought it from me."

"How could you?" Rodney asked, devastated by the news.

"Why are you making such a big fuss out of this? Why can't the guy sell one of his paintings, for crying out loud?" Charles demanded trying to understand the problem.

"You needn't worry, Rodney. I did a modern art painting, basically a group of colors in juxtaposition. People in this era seem to find it appealing. I myself think that it is...so...inartistic," Leonardo tried to explain.

"I thought we had an understanding." Rodney said through clenched teeth. "Do you realize how careless that was?"

"Yes, but it generated necessary funds for this project," Leonardo argued. "It is unfair you should have to finance the whole project."

"Are you going to fill me in on this?" Charles asked.

"See? Even Charles is suspicious!" Rodney tried to justify.

"I believe that you are the one who has raised his suspicions, not I," Leonardo defended calmly.

"Suspicions? What the hell are you guys talking about?" Charles cried out, exasperated.

"Let's forget it for now," Rodney suggested, turning to Charles. "I'll explain everything to you later."

Leonardo seemed relieved. He made some final adjustments to his super computer. "I think we can start testing it," he announced. He reached over and activated a series of switches, all located on the same panel. There was a familiar beep and the sound of the computer fan. A light blue background filled the screen of the color monitor.

"Okay. What do you want to show us?" Charles asked, not impressed so far.

Leonardo motioned his friend to be silent. "Plato, engage. Whenever addressed, you may answer whomever is speaking to you," Leonardo commanded.

"Plato engaged," a synthetic voice responded as the monitor turned to face Leonardo. A small red light on top of the video camera flickered.

"Plato, I would like you to meet my two friends, Rodney and Charles," Leonardo introduced as he pointed to the two men. The computer acknowledged by turning quite fluidly in the direction of the people introduced. As the camera focused on a subject, the image was reproduced digitally on screen with impressive resolution.

Rodney and Charles were agog.

"This is a joke, right?" Charles asked.

"Plato, who am I?"

"You are Leonardo," the computer responded.

"Nice Italian touch, Leonardo," Charles chuckled, unsuspecting. "But you could have programmed the whole thing. Voice synthesizers have been around for a while now," he concluded, still unimpressed.

"Plato, identify this man," Leonardo commanded as he pointed in Charles' direction.

The monitor turned towards Charles. "Your name is Charles. You are Leonardo's friend."

"Plato, describe Charles' appearance and physiology."

"Unable to fully assess the subject," Plato replied.

"What's the matter with your machine? I guess it can't do everything you ask," Charles said in a testy tone, thinking that the computer had failed.

Leonardo walked towards Charles and pulling him by the arm, moved him back, away from the computer.

"Please stand here," he asked in his usual calm voice. "Plato, reassess last command."

The computer camera zeroed in on Charles who could now see his full figure on the monitor. He observed a vertical red line that appeared beside the colored reproduction of his body and adjusted to his exact height. There was a series of quick successive beeps. The image on the screen showed the interior of Charles' form in various shades of green, then changed back to the original form.

"Subject Charles is six feet one and three quarter inches in height and weighs approximately one hundred and ninety-eight pounds. He has light brown curly hair and blue eyes. His fat to body weight ratio is of 16.3% which is higher than average for a man of his age, early twenties. He should try to reduce his fat ratio to a level between fourteen and fifteen percent," the computer evaluated.

"I'm six feet two inches and I'm not fat," Charles protested, flustered by Plato's comments.

"Plato, please evaluate apparent character traits," Leonardo continued.

"Subject is easily irritable, especially when unfavorable comments are made on his person. Harraps would define him as vain."

"Ho-ho! He sure has you pegged," Rodney chuckled, amused by the computer's description.

"He still has a few bugs when it comes to accuracy," Charles faulted.

"Plato is simply amazing, Leonard," Rodney complimented.

"I am quite proud of him, though I still have some work to do."

"I have to admit that I've never seen or read of anything quite like it," Charles conceded. "You're a real whiz, Leonard."

"How did you manage to get him to do all of this?" Rodney asked.

"Basically, I combined many existing technologies. First of all, I had to find a way to increase the memory of the computer, therefore I used the compact disk technology which increased it fifty-fold." Leonardo paused. "As you know, the problem with using laser disks is that any information which is etched on the disk will remain permanently. In order to maximize the efficiency of the system, I had to devise a processor that would classify any incoming information in either of two categories - permanent information or transitory information. In fact, I used the functions of the human mind as a model."

"Long-term and short-term memory," Rodney interjected.

"Precisely!" Leonardo paused and stared at Plato for a moment, as if in a trance. After a few seconds, he continued.

"After that, I had to give the computer a substantial data base to permit it to process information very much like a human. Finally, I wanted to give Plato the ability to interact with the outside world. The first phase was to develop its ability to speak and hear. The problem here was neither in hearing nor in speaking. No, the problem was to get the computer to think very much like you and I."

Leonardo paused, and paced the room. Charles and Rodney had sat down on the chesterfield as they listened, hanging on Leonardo's every word, every movement, not wanting to miss out on anything.

"You have likely heard of the research on synthetic intelligence that has been done recently. I have done considerable reading on the subject." He paused. "It is a fascinating concept." He stroked his beard with his left hand and crooked his right arm behind his back.

"How did you do it?" Rodney asked..

"It is impossible for me to explain at length in a few minutes something that has taken me weeks to achieve." Leonardo expressed. "Given the urgency of the task at hand, I think that there are more important issues to be discussed."

"But, Leonard why can't..." Rodney protested.

"Young man, please do not insist," Leonardo said firmly. He paused when he saw the expression of dismay on his young friend's face. "We are pressed for time. There are other features of which you must be apprised."

"How can the computer describe an object like it did earlier?" Charles asked, trying to alleviate the tension.

"Again I have combined different technologies," Leonardo explained. He pointed to the camera on the monitor. "First of all, the camera records the picture of the object. The image is then transformed into digital information that is then reproduced on the monitor screen. To establish the size and the dimension of the object, the computer uses radar to measure the distance between the computer and the object. From this reading, it calculates the proportions of the object on the screen taking, into consideration the distance, and from that, the size is determined."

"What about the physiological information?" Rodney asked.

Leonardo brought a chair in front of the two young students and sat astride on it.

"If you noticed, during the analysis, there was a time where Charles' features disappeared from the screen and were replaced by a variation of shades. Basically, what happened is that the computer used ultrasound to determine the density of the mass before it. Each part of the body has different densities. Therefore, the higher the density, the darker the shade reproduced on the screen will be."

There was a long silence, while each of the three men became absorbed in his thoughts. Leonardo got up and started pacing around the room slowly. Rodney sat back on the chesterfield, his arms folded behind his head. He looked at the ceiling in an attempt to assimilate everything that he'd witnessed and heard. Charles had reached for some of the components purchased that afternoon and played with the packaging, also absorbed in his thoughts.

"So, where do we go from here?" he asked.

"I believe that we are ready to launch into our operation," Leonardo concluded.

"How are we going to do that?" Rodney asked.

"By using the telephone," Leonardo answered.

Rodney shook his head, confused. Charles frowned.

"However, you will have a few things to do before we start." Leonardo picked up a small recorder. With his free hand he reached for a leather bag with a strap. "Our friend Eugene has borrowed a few of these from his employers." He handed the bag to Rodney.

"What's this?" Rodney asked.

"A portable cellular phone, I think," Charles guessed as he took the bag from Leonardo. He slid the zipper and opened it. "Hey! Where's the phone receiver?" he asked.

"I have modified the phone to suit our purposes," Leonardo replied.

"What are we supposed to do with this?" Rodney asked.

"Get the necessary information for our analysis," Leonardo replied as he took the bag from Charles. "You see, the sole purpose of this device is to transfer the information from the memory of the central computer to our computer. I have integrated a modem into the system which, if my estimates are right, will transfer the required information within eighteen minutes."

"Aren't you a bit optimistic about the time of transfer of information? That doesn't seem like much to me," Rodney cautioned the inventor.

"I have confidence in my estimate."

"Yeah, and then they can trace the whole operation to our phone number and we will then all be spending a nice long vacation at the expense of the State, and..." Charles predicted.

"That is assuming that we are using this telephone," Leonardo interrupted. He walked over to the chesterfield and knelt on it. He reached behind and pulled out a black leather bag identical to the first one. "We'll be using this telephone at this end. I planned on moving the necessary components into a car which will render us mobile during the operation."

"That's a great idea! That way they won't be able to trace any of the information to us," Rodney supported. A frown suddenly clouded his face. "Wait a minute. Who'll be billed for the air time used during the operation?" Rodney asked thinking that there might be a flaw in the operation.

"With Plato's assistance, I have been able to access the mainframe of a cellular phone company. I was able to activate a phone line."

"You did?" Charles was surprised.

"It was elementary really. I used the Internet."

"Internet. What's that?" Rodney asked.

"It is a newly-developed communication network shared by scientists around the world."

"If they ever trace this call, who will they trace it to?"

"The account has been opened for Sparo Aeronautics," Leonardo replied with a slight smile, reminiscent of the Mona Lisa.

"You're kidding!" Rodney howled.

"I am quite serious." Leonardo paused. "Incidentally, we shall need an automobile for this operation. Can we use your brother's?"

There's no problem. He's out of town on business. I've got the keys."

"I am looking forward to using it," Leonardo expressed, excited by the opportunity.

"If you don't mind, I'll get Eugene to drive you," Rodney suggested, remembering the first time he and Leonardo had sat in the same car. "So we're on for tomorrow night?" Rodney sought consensus.

Leonardo and Charles nodded.

None of the engineers looked up when Roger Simpson passed through the room where they were working to go to his office at the far end. Since everyone in the organization recognized the critical importance of the September test flight, not too much had to be said about it. After all, their jobs were at stake. There could be no last-minute changes to the design, which had needed many months of planning. They all understood that in the instance of a major failure during the official test flight, the Sparo Spear M40 project would most likely be terminated.

Rodney knew that they all shared the same love, the same dream for the Spear. There was no doubt in their minds that their fighter was the best and they were put off by the negative press that the plane had been receiving. Furthermore, they didn't understand the government's transparent plan to ditch the project.

Rodney, come September, would be back in school. But for the people who had generously shared their knowledge with him, the future was uncertain. Should the project fail, most of them would find themselves starting from scratch. Since there were very few positions in the aeronautics field in the country, many would have to relocate in foreign companies.

Everyone looked up when they heard a knock on the door. Jake MacIntosh came in, accompanied by a younger man.

"It's nice to see all of you hard at work," he said.

"Hi Jake," Roger Simpson welcomed the CEO and his assistant.

"I was just telling your staff how impressed I am by the devotion they're showing for their job," MacIntosh told Roger and then addressed the engineers. "It's people like you that make this project what it is today: the best damned fighter airplane there is. That's why our next test flight will be a success. Mark my words! When our fighter plane achieves speeds in excess of Mach four, those nosy vultures known as reporters will really have something to write about," Jake MacIntosh snarled. His face became expressionless, his eyes looking straight ahead as if he could see what the future had in store. "Well, carry on with your work."

He turned to Roger Simpson. "Roger I'd like you to meet my new assistant, Michael Keen. He'll be responsible for public relations."

"Pleased to meet you," Roger greeted.

"I guess I'll see you people at the meeting tomorrow," Roger said.

"Four o'clock sharp." Jake confirmed. "I'll see you then," he said as he and Michael Keen left the room.

Rodney was disappointed that he'd not been introduced to the president. Sam, one of the engineers, noticed his air of dejection.

"Hey Rod. I bet you feel bad for not being introduced to the big man. Don't worry, neither have we."

"Why is that?" Rodney asked surprised by his colleague's statement.

"We're not part of the brass, I guess," came the response. Rodney sat alone in the engineering room.

Roger Simpson and his crew had left. Rodney had managed to get some extra work sent his way in order to justify his staying late and was alone in the office.

The phone rang three times and stopped. Within seconds it ran again four times and stopped. Rodney recognized the signal that the coast was clear and that Charles was waiting for him. He walked to his locker, opened it and pulled out a black bag that he brought back with him to his desk. He sat down on his chair and placed the bag between his knees.

In the background, he could hear the rumble of one of the PC fans that had been left running. His heart although regular, beat loudly in his chest, giving some competition to the hum of the fan. Then, in the distance, he heard the sound of keys clinking together followed by the sound of footsteps that intensified as they got nearer. Rodney saw the figure of a young security guard, Walkman ear phones on, flicking the keys from hand to hand to the sound of the music blaring through his head set.

Rodney tried his best to look busy as the guard glanced in his direction. The sound of footsteps and keys diminished as the guard moved further down the hall. Rodney set the stopwatch on his wristwatch.

"I've got about thirty minutes before he comes back," he muttered to himself. "Lets get moving."

He walked out of his office and slipped on some thin plastic surgical gloves as he headed toward Charles' office, making sure that he stepped quietly in the brightly-lit, deserted hallway. After looking around him to make sure that no one had seen him, he slipped into the room where he found Charles sitting at a desk facing the plate-glass window overlooking the hallway. Without saying a word, Charles backed his chair away from the desk.

Rodney looked at his watch. Less than two minutes had elapsed. "Here's the key to the room," Charles said as he put a key in Rodney's gloved hand. "Remember, a flicking of the light means that someone's coming."

Rodney nodded. He gave Charles a charged look, stepped out of the room and crossed the hallway to Ned's office. He quietly unlocked the door, let himself in and closed the door behind him. He took a deep breath.

Making sure to stay out of the range of the security camera in the top right-hand corner, he crouched and approached it. He took the black bag off his shoulder and placed it at his feet. He unzipped the cover and peeked once again at his watch. Twenty-four minutes, fifty-six seconds.

From the bag, he pulled out a small camera and a small recorder that were already connected by a wire and activated the recorder. He lifted the camera and placed it under the security camera, pointing it in the same direction, to get as close a picture as the one taken by the security camera. There was a click as he pushed the button to start recording. He remained as motionless as possible so that the image would not blur.

"Thirteen, fourteen, fifteen, sixteen, seventeen, eighteen, nineteen, twenty," he counted. Click. The recorder turned itself off.

"That should do it. Leonardo wasn't fooling when he said that the loop would have twenty seconds," he muttered to himself, happy that the recorder had worked as intended. Rodney released the "on" button and peeked again at his watch. Time remaining, twenty-three minutes, thirty-three seconds.

In a swift motion, he disconnected the camera from the recorder and put it in his bag. He then placed the recorder on the floor and on one end of it, plugged a wire that he took from the bag. He connected the two clips on the other end of the wire to the security camera, thereby short-circuiting the live image and replacing it with the previously recorded image of an empty desk. He depressed the play button on the recorder.

Rodney glanced at his stopwatch. Twenty-one minutes, fifty-one seconds to go. With his right wrist, he brushed off the beads of perspiration forming on his forehead. "Less than twenty-two minutes," he counted silently as he picked up the black bag and walked to the computer terminal and deftly took the lid off the processing unit. From his bag, he pulled out a digital clock with two wires sticking out of it.

"First of all, change the clock time. Then set the time on the digital clock to eight twenty-five p.m.," he mentally ran through the operations as he did them. After pressing a button, he watched as the digital display went through a series of changes until it returned to the new set time.

"I have to remember to set back the time after," he made a mental note.

Rodney pulled more wiring out of the bag, unfolded it and connected it to the cellular phone unit inside the bag, taking the clips at the other end and connecting them inside the computer. As he finished the connection, the light flickered on the wall behind the terminal. He swiftly returned the lid to its position, making sure not to squeeze the wires, picked up the bag and brought it underneath the desk with him. The speed of his heartbeat intensified as he heard footsteps and saw a fleeting shadow go by. He mentally counted to ten, then quietly brought himself to his feet and made his way to the door. Through the window across the hall Charles was giving him the thumbs up sign. He looked at his stopwatch. Twenty minutes, twenty-two seconds remaining.

He went back to the computer terminal, sat in front of it and turned it on. The small spot of light that appeared at the center of the screen expanded to cover the whole screen. The white prompt gave way to the sky-blue corporate logo <<SPARO AERONAUTICS>> that immediately moved towards the top left corner of the screen. Then <<PROJECT SPEAR M40>> took its place briefly before following the company name to its corner..

<<ENTER ACCESS CODE>

Rodney typed in the code <<MAVIS>>. He pressed the return button. The computer accepted the code and flashed its second instruction.

<<ENTER USER ID NUMBER>>

Rodney looked at the inside of his left wrist on which he'd written the coded number 472389. "Add one for the first three digits and subtract two for the last two," he whispered to himself and typed in the numbers that he and Leonardo had identified from the first recording. "Five, eight, three, forget the fourth number, six, seven."

He pressed the return button once again.

<<ENTER PERSONAL PASSWORD>>

Rodney keyed in <<CAFFEINE>>.

Eight boxes showed up on the screen as he typed in the characters.

<<HI NED! HOW ARE YOU, TODAY? HAVE YOU HAD YOUR COFFEE YET?>>

The computer acknowledged that it had accepted the number as legitimate with its personalized greeting.

Rodney smiled at the greeting. "Hi Ned. Have you had your fix? Charles was right, he sure likes his coffee," he muttered in a mechanical tone.

<<WHAT DO YOU HAVE IN MIND FOR TODAY?>>

Rodney answered with a series of commands. He then grabbed his black bag and in a swift motion, knelt beside the terminal. Pulling himself under the desk he pulled the bag and the chair in front of him to form a barricade. He lit a penlight that he'd pulled out of the bag and pointed it on controls inside the bag. He first pressed on a red button. The action prompted the digital message <<System on>>. He dialed the mobile number to which the information was destined and heard its echo from the modem, then a soft ringing followed by a tone. As soon as two red lights started flashing, Rodney pressed on another button. This command was followed by the message: <<Data in transfer>>.

"Phhewww." Rodney sighed in relief. "Now all I have to do is wait. *"Nineteen minutes and eight seconds, with about one minute to spare,"* he thought. I'm playing it tight," he groaned referring to the estimated time it would take to transfer the information. *"This'll probably be the longest eighteen minutes of my life."*

He clutched his bag like a security blanket. *"I hope I'll live to laugh at this someday. Maybe this is all an exciting but very bad dream."*

Leonardo sat in the back seat of the car keeping an attentive eye on all the vital signs emanating from the electronic equipment he'd set up beside him.

"How much longer do you want me to drive like this?" Eugene asked, peering at Leonardo in the rear-view mirror. His query didn't receive any response. "If I had a meter running, you'd be deep in debt right now," he complained. "Over the past few hours, I've gained respect for taxi drivers."

A high level of humidity had intensified the heat of the day. *"Next time I see Rod's brother, I'll suggest he invest in an air conditioner for his car,"* he thought. Eugene found comfort in the fact that Leonardo hadn't given him any specific path to follow as long as he remained within the boundaries of the city. To drive in the downtown core for a few hours would have been intolerable and maybe even suicidal. The reluctant driver followed the main expressways of the big city. The breeze generated by the higher speeds brought some relief from the atmospheric conditions.

"This should do it," Leonardo exclaimed enthusiastically. "Mission accomplished!"

"What's this whole thing about?" Eugene asked one more time, hoping that this time Leonardo would give him a clear answer.

"Just a little test in electronic communication," Leonardo answered cryptically.

"Oh, is that all? That clears it up for me," Eugene retorted sarcastically, annoyed by Leonardo's useless explanation. "How silly of me!"

"Would you mind stopping somewhere alongside the road?"

"What, here?"

"Yes, here." Leonardo's tone was even.

"Do you realize that we're right in the middle of the freeway? I can't stop here!" Eugene protested.

"This will take but a moment."

Eugene sighed and brought the car to a stop on the paved shoulder. Leonardo opened the door and got out of the automobile.

Leonardo stretched. He was wearing his own garments, which he found much cooler and more comfortable in hot weather. He stroked the cloth of his clothing to remove some unwanted particles and approached the driver's door.

"I would like to drive, if you please," he told Eugene as he opened the door.

"But, Rodney asked me to drive while you were doing the testing," Eugene reminded the Master.

"Precisely. But all the testing is now complete. Rodney did not want me to drive because of the distracting nature of the tests. Now there is nothing to distract me."

"There is something you should know," Eugene tried to warn his elder friend. "We're getting low on fuel."

Leonardo did not acknowledge. There was determination in his eyes.

"I hope Rodney doesn't find out about this," Eugene warned as he moved to the passenger seat.

Leonardo sat in the driver's seat and buckled his seat belt. Eugene observed the Master's actions and felt some sort of comfort from the care that he seemed to put in setting up for his drive. His attention to detail almost made Eugene forget that Leonardo didn't have the same driving experience as most of his twentieth century contemporaries.

The engine revved to a mild roar under the master's initial activation of the throttle. Leonardo depressed the clutch as he moved the gearshift into first. The purr of the idling engine gave way to a mechanical growl as the car broke the inertia and advanced on the asphalt shoulder. The driver looked over his shoulder for any incoming traffic. With the coast clear, he directed the automobile onto the main road, his inexperience with the shifting of gears causing a jerking acceleration. The shaking leveled off as the car achieved the intended cruising speed.

Eugene admired Leonardo's resolve. Even though there was room for improvement, his driving skills were quite acceptable, given the circumstances. Eugene's confidence in Leonardo's abilities increased. In fact, he suddenly felt quite secure.

"Not bad for a beginner," he told the driver.

"If it is not bad, that means it is good," Leonardo replied.

The loud rumble of a speeding motorcycle broke the constant whistling of the wind through the open window. Eugene didn't pay too much attention to the fleeing two-wheel roadster, but when he looked at Leonardo's face, he recognized the expression that he saw there, and his heart sank. The screaming of the engine accelerating after being downshifted from overdrive gave away Leonardo's intention to give pursuit to the object of his curiosity.

"What are you doing?" You shouldn't do that, you know," he protested weakly, knowing that his words were being ignored.

As the motorcycle wove in and out of traffic, Leonardo and his machine kept pace. The tires screeched with the tight maneuvers and the engine whined with every gearshift.

Eugene gripped the side of his seat, his feet flat on the car floor, trying to find some sort of support in the event of an impact. His head bobbed, darted and dodged like that of a boxer at every obstacle along the way, as if this could have any incidence on the direction of the fast-moving car.

"I'm not enjoying this! Slow down!" he cried out.

Leonardo was handling the car quite adeptly and seemed very confident in his ability to keep the vehicle in control. The time traveler kept his eyes on the fast-moving two-wheel target in front of him.

Suddenly the car gave a light jolt.

"I knew this would happen. I knew it. I knew it!" Eugene complained, recognizing the symptoms.

The car coughed, rumbled and gagged as Leonardo directed it to the side of the road, where it came to a complete stop.

"What is happening?" Leonardo asked showing both concern and astonishment. "Have I broken something?"

"All you've broken is communication. I tried to tell you that the fuel level was low, but as usual, you didn't listen. Mr. Inventor was too clever to listen to old Trap. Well now, we're fifteen miles from nowhere, and we're out of gas!" he nagged.

"What do we do now?"

"Well, Mr. Leonardo smart-ass, you hitchhike to the nearest gas station," Eugene barked.

"Hitchhike? What does that mean?"

"That means that you go outside and stop a car and get a ride to the nearest gas station," Eugene responded, his patience diminishing by the second.

"And then what do I do?" Leonardo asked in his usual calm tone.

Eugene handed money to the Master. "Then you buy some gas and hitchhike back to the car," Eugene's voice was cracking with anger.

Without saying a word, Leonardo opened the car door and got out. He walked to the front of the automobile and positioned himself close to the highway. As the first car approached, Leonardo gesticulated frantically to try to stop it. The automobile slowed down, stopped and backed up toward the strange hitchhiker.

"We don't pick-up weirdoes in drag," the passenger of the automobile shouted through his lowered window before the car sped away. A second car acknowledged the unusual hitchhiker by honking its horn. After a while, Eugene stepped out of the car and in a comedic outburst, slammed the car door. He walked towards Leonardo, kicking stones and stomping his feet.

"I always get caught in Rod's shit. I don't know why I get involved in his schemes," he mumbled as he approached the older man. "Get back into the fuckin' car."

"If you insist. But tell me Eugene. Why must you young men always resort to obscenities whenever you are faced with adversity?"

Eugene turned away from the Master, and using the conventional thumb out signal, tried to flag a ride.

"Obscene this up your nose, you old natural freakish son-of ..." His words were drowned-out by a passing eighteen wheel tractor-trailer.

"The system is ready for analysis," the computer's synthesized voice informed.

"Plato, I want you to compare the following data banks," Leonardo commanded. "Cross-reference the jet engine specifications, the engineering graphics and technical drawings with the simulation results and conclusions from the wind tunnel tests..." Leonardo paced around the room, running his hand through his white beard. "...and the spec sheets for all the components of the engine. The objective is to find any discrepancies existing between the different data banks."

"Analysis and comparison initiated," the computer complied.

"What is the estimated duration of the analysis?" Leonardo asked.

"Approximately four-point-five minutes."

"Do you think it'll work?" Charles asked.

"I would not ask Plato to do this task if I was not confident in its ability to accomplish it."

"I'm sorry. It just seems like a tall order. I know for a fact that the computer at Sparo Aeronautics isn't able to perform such an analysis, and you know as well as I do how much memory and what capacity that system has."

"Plato is more than a computer. He operates more like the human mind than like a computer."

"Yes, perhaps. But it doesn't have the ability to reason like we do."

"Granted that in certain cases, the mind would be able to reason more rapidly than Plato. However, in the end, both would most likely reach the same conclusions," Leonardo explained.

"That's what I mean," Charles interrupted. "Our reasoning power is quicker than Plato's. You've just admitted it."

Leonardo exhaled forcefully in an uncharacteristic show of impatience. "I did. And this may be true if we wish to consider one isolated issue. However, if you wish to analyze many different problems simultaneously, Plato will prove to be much more efficient. Therein lies his superiority."

Rodney was sitting quietly on the chesterfield, listening to the debate. He was thinking that Leonardo might be an exception to his own side of the argument. He'd proven time after time that there were no problems that he could not solve, and often simultaneously, at that. In fact, Leonardo didn't seem to consider anything as a problem but more like a challenge. Besides, he was Plato's inventor and no matter how powerful, a computer is the sum of the data put in by the one who uses it. In this sense, Plato was a reflection of Leonardo's ingenuity, which so far, seemed to have no limits. He was definitely living up to his legendary reputation. On the other hand, Rodney couldn't help but notice how testy Charles was being with Leonardo. Perhaps he'd react differently if he were aware of the man's identity. He thought it best not to tell him, though, in part because of Charles's inquisitive and skeptical mind, but mostly because he was afraid that if he told him that part of the story, he'd have to tell him all of it, including his knowledge of what the future had in store for him.

"Guys, why don't we let the computer settle this matter," he suggested wisely. Rodney turned his attention to three sets of earphones located on the desk beside the computer.

"Jeez, Leonard. How many earphones do you need?"

"That's part of the latest project on which I have been working," Leonardo answered vaguely.

"Don't tell me you've invented a Walkman that talks back to you," Charles lampooned.

"Of sorts," Leonardo confirmed with a grin, not taking offense at Charles attitude.

"What is it exactly?" Rodney wanted to know more.

"In due time, my dear friend, in due time. I shall avoid giving skeptical minds any fuel before I can demonstrate its use and applications," he added pointedly.

"Okay, okay! I won't say another word," Charles promised with a smile. "I can take a hint!"

Rodney pretended to play a violin.

Eugene entered the room. "The car keys," he said handing them to Rodney.

"Thanks Trap. I really appreciate the help. By the way, I didn't get a chance to ask how your part of the operation went."

"Yeah, that's it. Thanks and everything is forgotten. Boy the nerve of some…" The end of the sentence was lost in the shuffle of his feet and the slamming of the door as he stormed out of the room.

"What's all that about?" Rodney asked Leonardo.

"We had a minor delay."

"And what, may I ask, was that delay?" Rodney asked, feeling that something unusual had happened and that Leonardo was most probably the cause, given Eugene's behavior and Leonardo's evasiveness.

"Nothing serious, by any means," Leonardo assured.

"Oh, really! If it's not serious, why don't you tell me?"

"There is very little to tell. You have my word."

The computer screen lit up once again.

"The analysis is complete," Plato announced much to Leonardo's relief.

"Plato, please give us the results of your analysis," Leonardo commanded.

"Ooohh, saved by Plato," Charles commented jokingly.

The computer monitor turned to face the Master.

"The analysis has found the following inconsistencies which can be divided into two categories. The first category identifies the differences that cause inefficiencies. The second category consists of flaws in the design that could cause serious problems under extreme conditions. Which area is of interest to you?"

"How presumptuous of that bucket of bolts and circuits to say that the greatest fighter plane is flawed," Charles protested.

"Can it!" Rodney shushed his friend.

"Plato, please concentrate on the second category," came the command.

"There is an integrated structural flaw in the design of the engine. The Danero T45P Mohawk's casing is made of titanium. The jet engine is placed within the casing and space is allocated between the casing wall and the engine for the free flow of air."

The computer monitor displayed a drawing of the jet engine. Within a few seconds, a front view of the engine appeared with light green shading the area that was being described.

"The spacing is adequate for the free flow of air at speeds inferior to Mach 2.5. However, at speeds of Mach 2.5 and more, and at altitudes exceeding thirty-three thousand feet, the high temperature causes the titanium to contract which results in the blockage of the required airflow through the engine. This could result in an explosion."

"What do you mean when you say that it is an integrated flaw in the design?" Rodney asked.

"Plato, answer the question," Leonardo ordered.

"Based on the specifications of the components of the engine and on the original design specifications, there should be no reason for this error."

There was a moment of stunned silence as Charles and Rodney let the full significance of Plato's revelation sink in.

"If what Plato says is right, then the design was modified after the fact," Rodney finally said, having absolutely no doubt on the integrity of the engineers with whom he worked.

"Sounds like sabotage to me," Charles concluded.

A chill ran down Rodney's spine. It dawned on him that the jet fighter for which he had so much respect was in fact a flying time bomb for whoever flew it. Up to that day, the trial flights had never achieved the Mach 2.5 speed. It had been tested at Mach 2.2 on many occasions, but due to the tight schedule, the higher speeds had been reserved for the final big test in front of thousands of people, in front of the government officials and potential buyers. The make it or break it test flight. It was now obvious that the second option was the likely one.

"Charles, can you explain how this kind of modification would come about?" Leonardo asked.

"Basically, whenever a change in design occurs, the drawings are approved by the head engineer. Then a work order is issued and sent with the new drawings to manufacturing, where the modifications are made."

"But how can there be a discrepancy between the specifications and the drawings on the computer?" Leonardo asked.

"In some instances, it's possible to override the computer and get the design made to new specs," Charles explained. "It's not a common thing, but it can happen as long as it's rubber-stamped by the head engineer. Once they're approved, the changes are implemented into the computer design program. A work order is then prepared and sent to the plant where it is fitted into a schedule by the planners, based on the rating of importance given by the head engineer."

Rodney nodded in agreement to Charles' explanations. "We operate in the same way in our division."

Leonardo resumed his pacing, all the while fingering his untrimmed beard.

"Plato, can you suggest remedial actions to the problem?"

The computer monitor turned towards the voice. As Leonardo was continuously moving the monitor rotated accordingly, following the Master's restless pacing. "Yes," came the synthesized response.

"How much space is required between the engine and the casing? Is it possible to make modifications without changing the casing?" Leonardo asked.

"The space between the jet engine and the casing will have to be increased by seventy-two millimeters. No, it is not possible to use the same casing," Plato responded.

Charles walked towards the desk. "Rodney, can you show me a copy of the sheet that you showed me before, the one about the engine."

Rodney looked at Leonardo.

"You will find it in the desk drawer," Leonardo answered his silent question.

Rodney walked to the desk and opened the drawer. He sifted through its contents until he found what he was looking for. He handed it to Charles.

Charles' face paled as he looked at the paper.

"What's the problem?" Rodney asked.

"I remember when they made this change. Yeah, Collins approved this. He was the only one who could make this kind of a decision, because of his expertise. Roger Simpson didn't even question the decision. I guess he had that much confidence in the man."

"When did they make this change?" Leonardo asked.

"Over a month ago, in the first few days I worked there," Charles said. "I remember because some of the designers got upset on account of the rush that was put on it. Yeah, that's it! They had to make the change before the last trial flight. All hell broke loose," he recalled.

"What did they do with the original engine casings?" Rodney asked.

"They must've stored them somewhere. Yes. I'm sure they stored them somewhere."

"It would be logical that they would modify the original casings to meet the new requirements," Leonardo supported

"The question is, have they made the changes yet?" Rodney wondered.

"I don't think so. Not with the government pressures and all. With all the cutbacks that we've seen so far, I'll bet nothing will be done to the casings before the verdict comes in on the viability of the project."

"Yeah, the Feds have been turning the screws on us." Rodney admitted. He paused. "We have to find a way to get the original casings re-installed, and..."

"Wait a minute! What's this "we" thing?" Charles protested. "All we're going to do is advise the authorities about our findings. We've stuck our necks out far enough as it is."

"Precisely!" Rodney supported. "That's why we have to take the initiative."

"No freaking way, man! I'm not putting my ass on the line any more!" Charles exclaimed as he brushed his hair back nervously. I'm going to talk to Simpson. He's cool. I'm sure he's the right man to talk to."

"Great idea, Charles. Excuse me, Mr. Simpson, but we've broken the code to the mainframe, accessed all the information, transferred it to our computer and found a little flaw in the design. Please overlook the fact that we've broken into and entered the facilities. The livelihood of the project is at stake." Rodney attacked. "Do you really think that he's going to like that? Did you also stop to think that maybe he's one of the guys behind this whole sabotage. For Chrissake, he may be tied into this with Collins for all we know."

"I think he's a good man," Charles defended, "and, we have no proof that Collins is guilty either."

"Right! You only admitted yourself that he's the one who ordered the change in the casing," Rodney derided.

Charles sighed. "I know, he looks suspicious as hell. But I just can't believe that he can do something like that, not in his right mind, anyway. You have to understand, Rod, the Sparo Spear project is his baby. The guys at the office told me that when Collins lost his wife about eight years ago he went absolutely ape shit and started drinking heavily. So much that he became suicidal. He tried to take his life on a few occasions. Somehow, he was able to kick the drinking habit. He replaced it with the Spear M40. He's eaten, drunk and breathed this project since then. It's the most important thing in his life right now."

Leonardo had stopped pacing and his arms crossed in front of him, was listening attentively to the conversation.

"I may have a solution to our little problem," he interrupted. "It will allow us to inform your Mr. Simpson without arousing any suspicions as to our involvement. It will also give us the opportunity to see if he is a trustworthy person."

"What do you have in mind?" Rodney asked.

"Good morning gentlemen!" Roger Simpson greeted his colleagues as he entered the room and walked directly into his unlocked office. He took off his sports jacket and hung it neatly on a hanger from the coat rack, brushing the shoulder of the jacket to remove some unwanted particle. He pulled his chair out from under the desk, placed his briefcase on the seat and opened it. He removed its contents and placed them on the desk. As he closed his empty briefcase, he noticed that there was another document on the desk. He picked it up and started to read it. He sat stiffly in his chair as he read. There was a stern look on his face.

From the drafting room, Rodney observed his every move. Roger Simpson's reaction to the document was definitely one of deep disturbance. Rodney was unable to look elsewhere. His throat became dry as the tension building up inside him shut down his saliva glands. Roger Simpson got up and rushed out of his office, his face livid.

"What the hell is going on?" Rodney muttered to himself. He looked around him and saw that Roger Simpson's hasty exit had not attracted any of his colleagues' attention.

Charles sat nervously sipping a beer in the tavern where he and Rodney had agreed to meet after work. Every minute or so, he looked at his watch. Then, Rodney strutted in.

"Hey, Rodney! So what's the scoop? What happened? Did he read it?"

"You bet he did!" Rodney was jubilant.

"So, what happened next?"

"He freaked out, that's what happened next! He stormed out of the room like a bat out of hell. When he came back about thirty minutes later, he issued a work order. The work order was to modify the casing to the original specifications. And Simpson was in a mother of a mood for the rest of the day."

"So Simpson's in on it." Charles concluded. He bowed his head and remained silent. "

"Heeeee-aaaa!" Rodney cheered. "Isn't this great? We did it! We did our job. And the Sparo Spear has been saved from a sure death. We're heroes!" he exclaimed as he gripped his friends cheeks and kissed him on the forehead.

"Yeah, I guess so...But why is it that I feel like shit?"

"Jeez, I sure don't know!"

"Did anybody see you place the report on the desk?" Charles worried.

"No."

"Does Simpson suspect that you're the one who brought the report in?"

"No!" Rodney was put off by Charles' reaction. "What are you so worried about? "

"I don't know. I feel like a sitting duck."

"Hey, buddy. Lighten up! I know. What you and I need, is a night out, my friend," Rodney suggested. "Tonight we go and have ourselves a night out with the rest of the boys."

Charles approved with a weak nod of the head.

The dark moon-less and overcast sky made the night more sinister than usual. In a car parked fifty yards away from 230 Anderson Avenue, a lone passenger had an unobstructed view of the house and of the dimly lit avenue. The only indication of a presence inside the vehicle was the glowing of a cigarette as the solitary occupant inhaled, waiting silently, eyes riveted on the activities at Club 230.

The lights on the top floor of the house went out first, then a few moments later the one in the kitchen, leaving the house temporarily in total darkness. Then the living room light came on, contrasting with the darkened silhouette of the house. The torsos of three men drinking beer could be seen at the bottom of the stairs. Soon, another one joined them.

The observer saw that the men were leaving the house, good humor prevailing as they exchanged pleasantries and laughter. As they closed the exterior door, the silent witness slid down on the car seat and put out the still-burning cigarette in the open ashtray.

The basement window flapped open. The intruder pointed a big flashlight inside the basement, lighting up the workbench under the window. Sliding his stocky body through the window, he used the workbench as an intermediate step to the floor. He aimed the flashlight up the stairs and followed the light beam. He entered the main floor area through the basement door and walked towards Leonardo's quarters. Reaching into his waist pouch, the night prowler pulled out a Polaroid camera. He opened the door and without entering the room, aimed the camera at Leonardo's wall painting. The camera flash lit up three successive times.

Suddenly, a cracking noise emanating from the kitchen caught his attention. After carefully placing the camera and the three Polaroid pictures in his pouch, he grabbed his flashlight and carefully walked towards the area where he'd heard the noise. He felt a sharp pain in the back of his neck and everything went black.

9

Hooked on Plato

The University tavern terrace buzzed with activity on this warm, late August evening. Beer pitchers and mugs covered the patio tables. Rodney, Charles, Edmond and Eugene were bantering as usual, enjoying each other's friendship and the success of their recent efforts. Stepenwolf's "Born to be Wild" blared from the strategically placed speakers.

"Great song!" Edmond exclaimed.

"That's us. The wild boys," Eugene said.

Edmond turned to Charles, who was looking rather glum. "Come on Charlie, get with it!" he prompted.

"There's Leonard," Rodney pointed to the entrance between the patio and the tavern. Leonardo had borrowed a pair of jeans and a cotton T-shirt from Rodney and looked like a Fine Arts professor.

"Our buddy is trying to blend in," Eugene remarked. "What's with the contraption?" He pointed to the receptionists' earphones and microphone that Leonardo was wearing on his head. The device was connected by means of a wire to a pager fastened to his belt.

"I don't know if you've noticed, but the earphones are not necessary if you want to hear the music," Charles joked when Leonardo reached him.

"I do not consider this to be music," Leonardo retorted. He took a chair from a neighboring table and placed it between Edmond and Rodney.

"Hey that's my pager!" protested Eugene.

"I will return it to you as soon as I have completed my experiment," Leonardo promised.

The table attendant walked over to greet the older gentleman. "Would you care for a drink, Leonard?" she asked.

"What's this?" Rodney asked, surprised by the familiarity between the two. "You two have met?"

"Yes we have."

"When?" Rodney persisted like a doting mother.

"If you must know, I came here with your friend Sergio and Professor Holmes," Leonardo responded dryly, irritated by Rodney's continuous prodding.

"Get off his case, for Heaven's sake! You're not his father," Charles said.

The expression on Leonardo's face changed suddenly from irritability to concern. He motioned to the younger men to be quiet. "Plato, please inform me of activity," came the remote command.

"Don't tell me he's plugged remotely to his computer!" Charles exclaimed in total amazement.

"Gentlemen, there are intruders in our house," Leonardo warned.

"Don't tell me. You also have ESP," Eugene responded.

Leonardo leaped from his chair and over the patio fence to the sidewalk. Rodney, Edmond and Charles, seeing the urgency in his action, followed.

"Trap, take care of the bill," Edmond commanded.

"If I pay the bill, I drink the rest of the beer," Eugene muttered to himself, not moving from his chair.

As he ran towards the house, Rodney noticed that most of the lights in the house were turned on. "Somebody's broken into our house," he yelled over his shoulder to the others.

"No guff; Sherlock, what was your first clue?" Edmond yelled back.

The door to the house was half-open, as was the door to Leonardo's quarters. All the computer equipment was gone, but nothing else seemed to have been touched.

"Hey guys, I need help over here," Charles' voice called out from the TV room.

The men rushed into the room to find Professor Holmes lying inert on the floor. Charles knelt beside him and held a hand to Holmes' neck, seeking vital signs.

"He's alive. Looks like somebody's knocked him out. Call the cops."

Rodney looked around the room and noticed that the old television had been disconnected from the cable and left unplugged on the floor. *"It looks like they had the intention to steal the TV but were interrupted or something,* he thought.

Professor Holmes raised his head from the floor. "Where am I?" he queried in a groggy voice as he slowly floated back into consciousness.

"The question should be, what the hell are you doing in our house?" Rodney said as he leaned down to grab the professor by the collar.

"Easy Rod. First ask the questions, then beat the daylight out of the bum," Edmond suggested.

Professor Holmes turned to his side and rubbed the back of his neck, wincing from the pain. His hands fumbled for his mid-section, feeling for the camera in his waist-pouch. Nothing. No camera. No pouch. He looked around him for his flashlight. No sign. All the elements that could incriminate him had disappeared.

"I came over to pay Leonard a visit and the door was half-open. I knocked but no one answered. So I walked in. Then someone hit me from behind. That's all I remember," he lied.

"Yes, I'd like to report a break-and-enter at 230 Anderson." Pause. "Yes that's right. How long will it take?" Pause. "We'll be waiting. Thank you." Charles hung up the receiver.

"Where's Leonard?" Rodney asked Edmond.

"I saw him go upstairs."

Rodney ran up the stairs to find him. As he reached the top landing, he looked into his room. Nothing was out of place. He continued to Edmond's room and entered. Everything seemed normal. He continued his search for Leonardo in Leo's room, where the Master stood near Leo's bed absorbed in his thoughts.

"Are you okay, Leonard?"

Leonardo didn't acknowledge his presence.

Rodney looked around the room to see if anything looked out of place. He then remembered Leonardo's notebooks, which had been placed in sealed bags inside the waterbed mattress. The waterbed was intact proving that they hadn't been moved from their temporary hiding place. Leonardo had probably come into the room to make sure that no one had taken his books, Rodney thought.

"I can't believe someone would break into this house. Whoever did seemed interested in the electronic equipment only. I wonder who did this?" he asked his mind spinning with questions. "I guess there's no more need for the head gear," Rodney said pointing to Leonardo's electronic communications device.

Leonardo remained motionless and unreceptive to Rodney's interventions. He stared across the bedroom, emotionless, quiet.

"The police!" Charles' voice called out from downstairs.

Rodney walked towards the stairs, leaving Leonardo in his near-zombie state. The timing of the break-in seemed suspicious. Perhaps their illicit activities had not gone unnoticed, he thought. There was a sense of danger. Rodney recognized that he and his friends were in over their heads, but whom could they turn to. The police? Unlikely. All the evidence they could provide would incriminate them. There would be no proof of what they were saying, since the changes to the fuselage had probably been done by now. The Sparo Spear had been saved. The coming test flight would be a success. So what would they say to the authorities?

"Rodney, I'd like you to meet Officers Stanley and MacTavish," Charles made the introductions.

Rodney smiled. He'd seen these two officers before. He greeted them with a handshake.

"We've already met, at the party."

Rodney suddenly realized that his memory of the meeting with the officers was something in the future and not in the past. They were the two policemen who had come to the party the night that Charles died. *"Or should it be the two officers that will come to the party the night that Charles will die,"* he thought.

"I don't recall meeting you," the senior officer responded perplexed by Rodney's statement.

"Hmm. I...I must be mistaken," Rodney retracted, a chill traveling down his spine.

"We've been notified of a break-in," officer MacTavish said, pulling out his notepad. "Has anything been stolen?"

"Yes, there has," Edmond answered. "Please follow me." Edmond led the officers to Leonardo's room.

"Guys, come see this," Edmond called out from the basement.

Rodney, Charles and the police officers walked down into the basement where they found Edmond standing over hockey equipment that had been dumped into a pile in the middle of the floor.

"I bet I know what the burglars used to carry the computer stuff out."

The single sixty-watt light bulb barely lit the somber room. The pungent aroma of humidity blended with the stale air was a give-away of its location in a stone foundation basement. There were no windows and the walls had been finished in gypsum panels, with only one coat of joint putty sparsely covering the sealing tape. The walls were unpainted and gave all indications that they'd been built haphazardly either by a novice or by someone in a hurry. The fir crossbeams were still exposed, as were the floor joists in the ceiling. Hot-air conduits spanned the room, the clean polished surface of the sheet metal the indication of a recent upgrade.

Open hockey bags filled with computer and other electronic equipment had been placed on a makeshift desktop, consisting of a ping-pong table pushed against the far wall, on which an old corkboard had been temporarily fastened. A Polaroid picture of Leonardo's computer set-up had been tacked to the board.

A young man, his shoulder-length hair tied in a ponytail, pulled the equipment out of the bag, one piece at a time, checking every piece to make sure that it had not been damaged in the move.

"Are you sure you know what you're doing, kid?" a voice called out from the nearby room.

"Not a clue. These are vacuum cleaner parts aren't they?" the young man replied in a condescending tone. Pause. "Are you sure these are all the parts? I've never seen computer equipment carried in hockey bags before."

"We took everything there was in there," the voice replied. "Are you looking for excuses or something?"

"No. I've got the picture as a starting point to base myself on," he said looking at the picture on the billboard. "If your gorillas moved this stuff without damaging it along the way, I'll have this gizmo working in no time.

"You need anything more than what you have here?"

"Yes, I'll need more light and a few power bars to connect all this equipment to. Make sure that the power bars are surge proof. Also, do you have a telephone jack nearby? This baby has got a modem and I'll need to connect it to see what it can do."

"There's a jack in this room. All we need to get you is an extension."

"By the way, where did you get this stuff?"

"Never mind," came the reply. "All I want is for you to put this equipment together so that it can work and to keep your mouth shut. Is that clear?"

"Don't worry about me, Sir," the young man replied. "My memory will go blank as soon as I get this job done. You can count on me." He pulled a portable video camera out of a bag, examined it, and deposited it carefully on the table. He turned toward the open door.

"Is there any way you can open a window down here? This room could stand some fresh air. I feel like mushrooms are going to grow on me."

"I'll see what I can do," the voice replied.

Leonardo sat at the kitchen table. It was a rare occasion when he joined his new friends for a meal. Until recently, his eating habits had been erratic at best, and usually consisted of a quick snack of fruits, vegetables and cheeses found in Rodney's refrigerator.

He had changed into his red embroidered tunic. For the first time since his journey through the centuries, he felt out-of-place and doubtful about what the future had in store for him. Would he see his beloved Florence ever again, and if he did, would it be the Florence that he knew, or a transfigured city? The discovery of the New World had given him very little time to ponder on the significance of his being here. In fact, all the information that was made available to him through encyclopedias, technical textbooks and computer magazines, or even through computer programs, had obscured reality.

The Renaissance Master had uttered very few words since the break-in and seemed to be in a trance-like state. He had refused to remove the communication device, which was camouflaged by the unkempt hair and beard.

"Maybe senility is setting in," Eugene offered in an unscientific diagnosis, referring to Leonardo's silence and to his insistence on wearing the electronic headgear at all times.

"He's sure been upset by the theft of the equipment," Edmond concurred.

"Rodney, you have to find a way to get him to return the pager to me. I need it for my work," Eugene pleaded.

"I'll see what I can do, Trap, but he hasn't spoken a word to me in close to twenty-four hours."

In fact, Rodney had tried on several occasions to get Leonardo to respond to his questions, but had been constantly faced with a blank expression. The only times that Leonardo had shown any emotion were on those occasions when Rodney had tried to convince him to return the electronic pager to Eugene. Leonardo would repel any attempt to touch the device, like a child desperately clutching to his favorite toy.

All of a sudden, Leonardo's eyes regained the brightness that had been missing since the break-in. His body stiffened and a grin spread across his face.

"Plato, engage main computer and deactivate monitor," he commanded with authority, as he sprung from his chair. Leonardo paced the kitchen floor frantically, animated by the communication.

"What's with him?" Eugene, like the others, was baffled by Leonardo's actions.

"Plato has been activated," Leonardo replied. He noticed that his friends did not understand the reason for his excitement. "When I designed this communication device, I ensured that in case of an intrusion into the system, Plato would go through an identification routine after the system had been booted. One of the routines was that it would dial via modem to Eugene's pager number if my voice had not activated the system within two minutes of start-up time."

"You can actually communicate with the computer using that gadget on your head and my beeper?"

"That is correct."

"So that's why you didn't want to part with the headgear," Rodney said, understanding Leonardo's insistence.

"I knew that the thieves wanted to access the data bank of the computer and by being vigilant, I ensured that they would not be able to activate the system. Only my voice and my password can activate Plato," Leonardo explained.

"So why were you so worried?" Edmond asked.

"First of all, I was not sure that Plato would react as programmed, since I had not yet tested this security feature, which I programmed less than forty-eight hours ago. I had a presentiment that it would prove useful. Secondly, I worried that if the thieves took the computer out of the city's area code, it would not be able to reach the pager number. You must understand that I designed this security measure to parry to any tampering with the computer. I had not envisioned a theft of the equipment."

"So the thieves are in this town somewhere," Edmond concluded.

"It also means that whoever stole the computer didn't steal it for the parts, but was interested in its contents since they went through the trouble of reassembling it as it was," Rodney said. "We're not talking 'bout punks, we're talking 'bout professionals."

"And that also means that if he's communicating with us, he's using a telephone line," Eugene deduced. "Can Plato give you the phone number of the line he's using?"

"Plato. Please advise of the phone number from which your communication originates." Leonardo commanded. There was a momentary pause, indicating that Plato was executing Leonardo's request.

"2, 3, 8, 9, 1, 7, 8," Leonardo repeated the numbers.

"Can't anyone hear him talk to you?" Rodney asked.

"No. The communication device overrides the speaker on the computer. This is another security feature that I designed."

"238, 238. That's the upper town exchange, I believe," Edmond said.

"Yeah, but there are thousands of numbers on that exchange," Eugene said. "How the hell are we going to find the right address?"

"I've got a cousin who sells real estate downtown, maybe he can help us. Let me phone him." Edmond proposed. He got up from the table and walked towards the living room.

'Holy shit, this is exciting!" Eugene exclaimed.

"Whoa, guys. I don't think we're dealing with just common criminals." Charles warned. He'd remained silent through most of the dinner, but felt that he had to intervene. "This is serious stuff."

"So what do you want to do? Just stop and think about it? Don't you think it's odd that all of a sudden someone has taken a serious interest in our activities? Did you ever stop and think about the possibility that the people who stole Plato are the same people who tried to sabotage the Sparo Spear project?" Rodney stood and pressed both of his arms against the back of Charles' seat. "I tell you buddy, if these guys find out what's on this computer, someone's going to want our hide. We'd better find some way to get that damned computer out of that hell hole before they get wise to us."

"Calm down, Rod," Eugene interrupted to diffuse his friend's anger.

"It may not be necessary to enter the premises to recover the equipment," Leonardo interjected.

"What do you mean?" Rodney asked.

"I have created Plato and I can create him again. I have back-ups of his programming and I can get him to operate just as he did before," Leonardo stated matter-of-factly.

"Yeah, but they have Plato in their hands. They're bound to find a way to access him," Rodney argued.

"Do not worry, my young friend. We can give him some instructions remotely and he can reformat his whole memory with a mere command if necessary. However, I would agree with you, Rodney, when you say that the theft of Plato is somehow related to the Sparo Spear project and I believe that we must get to the bottom of this. Plato can be instrumental in our quest for answers."

Edmond returned, waving a piece of paper over his head.

"Guys, I've got an address. My cousin was able to locate the number through a directory they use at work. The call originates from 245 Holditch. It's that area with all the big mansions in Upper Town, and that particular mansion belongs to – hold on to your wigs – Jake MacIntosh, president and CEO of SPARO Aeronautics!"

"Don't you think you're kind of old to be doing that?" Eugene asked Leonardo, who was climbing a large pine tree.

Leonardo hoisted himself on a branch that provided him the desired vantagepoint. From his sitting position he had a clear view through a neighborhood park, across a residential street and onto the mansion at 245 Holditch.

The Victorian-style mansion was strategically perched on the highest point of the property. Exterior floodlights enhanced the splendid structure and made it visible from across both streets that lined the property. The mature beach, oak and maple trees that dotted the lot offered all the desired shade and greenery as well as privacy from curious onlookers. The eight-foot high stone and cast iron fence was an effective first-line barrier against intruders and seemed impenetrable, especially when the gates were closed.

Taking advantage of the light of a nearby lamppost, Leonardo started sketching the mansion on a pad using charcoal crayons. From his perch, he could see the whole facade of the home, from the foundations to the peaks of the roof. He started by drawing the structure and shape of the building, reproducing the forms and angles. His keen eye captured all the components, the details and the textures and his skill allowed him to transcribe them faithfully onto the sketchbook without a trace of hesitation. In the margin he noted the colors and some other finer details.

Meanwhile Eugene walked on Holditch Street, one hand in each of his jeans back pockets, keeping an attentive eye on the nocturnal traffic and taking in the pleasant smell of freshly cut grass blended with the aroma of the park's flower beds. He saw a taxi approach and signal to turn into the driveway of the stakeout house. As the car passed by him, he thought he recognized the passenger. Eugene turned his head away and as he hurried towards Leonardo's perch, he heard the gate doors open and close. He quickly climbed the tree and found a place to sit on a branch beside Leonardo's. He reached into Leonardo's carrying bag and pulled out a set of binoculars that he pointed in the direction of the mansion.

His first impressions hadn't failed him. He'd seen the young woman before. "Well, well, well. I'll be damned."

"What is the matter?" Leonardo asked. "Do you know that young woman?"

"Not as well as Rodney does," Eugene replied. "Holy lizards, this is exciting!" The two men watched as the young woman entered the home and the taxicab left the property.

"Are you sure about this?" Rodney asked surprised by Eugene's findings. "How do you know her?"

"You introduced her to me on campus some time ago, said her name was Debbie, one of your classmates. I can't forget babes, Rod, and this one's a fox. And I'll bet my bottom dollar she's the same Debbie who called really often and that you refused to talk to." Eugene was convinced of the identity of the girl. "She was in that cab and she was dressed to kill."

"She was wearing a dress that hardly covered her. How can you say that she was hiding a weapon?" Leonardo protested, not understanding the expression.

"That means she was dressed very nicely," Rodney clarified.

"I thought Debbie had her own place," Edmond told Rodney.

"She does," Rodney replied quietly hoping to stop the discussion on the matter.

The group of friends was having a pow-wow in the TV room.

"Well now, what could a young woman be doing at such an hour, in such a place?" Leo asked pointedly.

"Maybe it's her folks' home," Rodney growled.

"Midnight.   Now, that's a nice time to visit your parents," Leo continued.   "So if her parents live there, she'd be a MacIntosh.   Debbie MacIntosh, that sounds right."

"This is bizarre," Charles stressed.   "First of all, the unexplained resignation and disappearance of my good old buddy, Professor Collins. Then we find out that there's been tampering with the design of the Spear M40 and that he's probably behind the mysterious flaw. After that, we risk our asses to save the Sparo project and we succeed.   We think that everything is fine and dandy, we pat each other on the back.   We're heroes, job well done.   However, we can't tell anyone for fear of punishment because we accessed the mainframe of the computer illegally to get the information.   Then someone breaks into your home and steals your computer equipment.   After that, through some technically dazzling feat, we trace the stolen goods to a huge mansion.   The owner of this palace, who is also the alleged thief is not just anybody, he's the President of Sparo Spear, Jake MacIntosh who in principle, should be doing everything possible to save the project.   Boy, do we lead a normal life or what?"   He paused.   "Guys, where will this end?   Someone's life may be in danger and I feel like mine is first on the line."

"What do you want us to do?" Rodney flared.   "Do you want me to go to the police?   And say what?   They'll ask for proof, but we have none." He was angry and shouting, knowing that Charles' life was in fact first on the line, but not knowing how to get through to him without having to divulge his and Leonardo's secret.

"There is no reason to shout," Leonardo intervened. "But if you will follow me to my room, I think that I may have a way of getting some evidence." Leonardo walked towards his quarters followed by Edmond, Rodney, Eugene, Leo and Charles. On the desk in the room, a computer monitor had been set on top of a stereo amplifier. On each side of the monitor, stereo speakers were positioned to face the audience. At the center of the setup, Leonardo's communication device was connected to a modem and to the amplifier. Leonardo donned the headgear.

"What did Boy Wonder dream up now," Leo queried shaking his head.

"I would first of all like to thank Edmond for his contribution to this project. It has permitted me to equip myself adequately."

"You're in on this?" Rodney asked Edmond, touched by his continuous support. Edmond nodded his head slightly to confirm.

"Plato, activate."

"Plato activated."

"Plato, send digital information for image through modem and keep local monitor deactivated."

A picture appeared on the computer screen showing a chair in front of a table.

"Plato, please help us to familiarize ourselves with your immediate environment," Leonardo commanded.

The image on the screen started moving as Plato showed the interior of the room on the monitor. The dimly lit room had no other furniture.

"The walls aren't even painted," Eugene remarked. "That's not much to go on."

"Plato, activate ultra-sound feature and give us a description of the building."

The picture on the monitor showed the structural trusses on the ceiling as well as the heating and ventilation ducts. Then, the image changed, making way for a grid of dark rectangles in various shades of gray as well as three red shapes, some of them fixed, others in motion.

"You will notice that Plato is using the ultrasound to show us the structure above him. I have established that Plato has been installed in the basement of the building. You will notice the thick, black lines. Those are the supporting walls. The gray lines represent partitioning walls. Over here, you will notice a winding staircase in the center of the building," Leonardo explained.

"What are the three red shades that we see on the screen?" Charles asked.

"People." Leonardo responded. "The displacement of this shade is a person walking in the house. This one, which is stationary, represents someone who is probably sitting."

"But what about the third red shade? It's smaller than the other one. Is it a child?" Leo asked.

"No. I would assume it is someone sleeping on one of the upper floors. Its smaller size is due to the greater distance from the ultrasound device," Leonardo paused.

"Plato, show image of the adjoining room."

The computer monitor image again showed the ceiling and turned towards the wall to its right. It transformed into the ultra-sound display showing a grid of dark and gray vertical lines and one horizontal line on which a red form lay.

"I would like you to focus your attention on the red shading. When I observed it yesterday, it was motionless and a much lighter shade of red. I suspect that it is the body of a person lying on a bed," Leonardo explained.

"You say a body. Is it dead?" Rodney queried.

"No. A dead person would not show in a shade of red on the computer monitor. The lighter shade can probably be explained by very low cardiovascular activity, like that of someone in a deep sleep. I have also seen another form entering the room and spending some time there, as if administering to a patient."

"It's weird that they'd have someone sleeping in the basement. Especially in a mansion with so many bedrooms," Eugene observed.

"Not weird if the person is held against his will," Rodney speculated.

"Look, there's some movement in the shading." Leo pointed to the movement on the screen. The red blob seemed to stir, as if the body was turning in the bed.

"I believe that the body's vital signs are stronger. He must be coming out of his sleep," Leonardo observed.

"This is really strange. Is there any way that we can get more information on the person in that room?" Rodney asked.

Leonardo nodded. "Plato, please give us some information on the person in the room beside you."

A rectangular box surrounded the red form and magnified to the size of the screen, the red shading increasing proportionally in size.

"Subject measures five feet, nine and one half inches and weighs approximately 165 pounds. The person in question is male and is aged in his late fifties or early sixties, based on the tone of the skeleton and the tissues," the computer evaluated.

"Could it be Collins? No one has seen him since his resignation," Charles asked as he walked towards the screen, excited by the prospect of confirming his suspicion that there may be foul play behind Collins' mysterious disappearance.

"Well, it matches Collins' description, but it's not proof." Rodney didn't want to jump to conclusions.

"Look guys, there's movement. It looks like someone is going down into the basement," Eugene observed pointing to the movement of a red shape on the computer monitor. All eyes focused on the red form.

"Plato activate external microphone and focus on the room beside you," Leonardo instructed the computer.

The distant sound of a metal door lock being opened, followed by the faint noise of door hinges that screeched under the shifting weight of a door, came out of the speakers. The computer monitor showed two red objects intersecting, one vertical and the other one horizontal.

"Are you awake?" Pause. "Still under the influence are we?" said a faint voice muffled by the gypsum wall that separated Plato from the occupants of the neighboring room. "Soon it'll be time for you to go back on the streets and mingle. A bit more of this intravenous stuff and you'll be ready to go back out into the real world."

No response came from the other person. The vertical shape moved away from the bed, towards the door. The sound of a door closing and locking followed.

"This is great. I feel like a fly on the wall, listening in on private conversations without being seen," Leo raved about his experience as an electronically assisted voyeur.

"You're right about one thing, Rod. Whoever is held in that room is being held against his will." Edmond supported his friend's suspicion. "Where do we go from here?"

"We still don't have evidence. We know someone is being detained in that house, we don't know who and we have no proof for the cops," Charles surmised.

"I have a way to get the necessary evidence!" Rodney exclaimed his eyes sparkling. "Eugene, I'll need your help."

"What do you have in mind?" Eugene asked doubtfully.

"Give me a bit of time, and I'll explain. First of all, there's somebody I have to talk to."

"Are you ready to order?" The young waitress asked as she set the paper place mat in front of Rodney.

"Not right away. I'm waiting for someone."

"No problem. Anything to drink in the meantime?"

"A draft. Whatever's on tap'll be fine."

Rodney set his hands on the table, fingers interlocked, absorbed in his thoughts, preparing the scenario for the meeting.

A hand gently grasped his shoulder and Rodney felt a warm kiss on his cheek.

"Sorry I'm late," Debbie apologized. She sat across from Rodney and reached out for his hands. "It's good to see you, Rod."

"Ditto," Rodney responded coolly. There was a momentary pause as they gazed into each other's eyes. Debbie had a disarming way about her. Her sparkling eyes and the dimples in her cheeks when she smiled made Rodney want to put his guards down.

"You didn't return my calls," Debbie said looking directly at him, anticipating an answer.

Rodney diverted his eyes. "I've been busy with stuff."

"Too busy to return my calls?"

Rodney kept silent.

"I really like you Rod. I think that you're a special person, someone I'd really like to get to know better. The night we spent together was really special to me and..."

"Yeah. So special that you got up in the middle of the night and split to go and meet somebody else. Boy, if that's the way you treat people you care for..."

"You don't understand. I had no choice," Debbie answered.

"Who's the mysterious man? Your sugar daddy?"

"Wow! Is that what you think I am? A cheap hooker?" Debbie reacted violently to Rodney's allegations.

"Oh, I don't think you're cheap," Rodney responded with seething sarcasm. "How is Mr. MacIntosh these days?"

The mention of the name had a daunting effect on Debbie as she realized that Rodney knew so much. She slumped back into the diner seat and looked down at her hands, sliding her keys nervously between them on the table.

"Who told you about this?" she asked in a low voice.

"So it's true." Her admission had knocked the wind out of him.

"First of all," Debbie hissed, "I'm not a whore." Her attitude was as defiant as Rodney's. "I've known Jake MacIntosh since I was a little girl. My father died when I was eight. Jake was a friend of the family and he provided for my mom and me after that. So when he asked my mom to marry him, she felt that it was the right thing to do. We followed him to Caldwell five years ago when Sparo Corporation hired him."

"He's family?" Rodney said, taken aback by the information. He paused for a moment feeling ashamed and remorseful for having been so blatantly stupid with Debbie. Still, his gut told him that he should be prudent. "Tell me about your mother."

"My mother? She's… she's not well." Debbie struggled to find the words. "She doesn't live at home any more. She's… hmm… she was committed to the psychiatric ward at the Royal Hospital a few years ago."

"I'm sorry." He paused. "Do you visit your step-dad often?"

"As little as possible. He and I don't get along so well, especially since my mother's been ill. I'm afraid he and I don't see eye-to-eye on anything. I usually come to the house on days when my mother is home. She gets weekend passes every once in a while and spends them at Jake's home. I usually visit late at night because it seems that my mother is most lucid at night. You see, she's heavily sedated," Debbie explained, tears welling up in her eyes.

Rodney reached for Debbie's hands and clutched them in his. "Hey, you don't have to say anymore."

"Jake pays for everything - my apartment, my car, my school, my credit cards. I guess I should be grateful to him for his help. But that doesn't make my mom feel any better. He can be so damned demanding sometimes. He doesn't call often, but when he does, the man expects me to come as soon as he phones. He treats my mother and me like his possessions and he can't stand it when someone doesn't do his bidding." Debbie stopped talking and looked in the distance, seeming to momentarily forget Rodney's presence. Tears rolled down her cheeks.

"Here take this." Rodney handed Debbie a napkin from the dispenser sitting on the table. "Have you seen Professor Collins lately?"

"I've seen him at Jake's a few times." She dabbed the tears from under her eyes, checking the napkin for mascara traces. "They used to be pretty close. Why do you want to know?"

Rodney grasped for a quick answer. "Hmm. The professor mentioned Jake's name on a few occasions at work. D'you know I found work at Sparo for the summer?"

"Yes. I heard through the grapevine. It's funny, when I phoned your place, they told me that you were gone to Springer for the summer."

"Yeah, I sort of told them to say that."

"Why?"

"I just figured it was best to cool it for a while."

"You got your wish." Debbie stared at Rodney. He met her stare. He could sense that he'd hurt her feelings.

"Jake seems preoccupied by his retirement these days. That's all he talks about. He's apparently expecting to receive a substantial amount of money, real soon. He calls it his retirement plan. I guess it has something to do with that new fighter airplane his company is building." Debbie stopped and sighed. She paused for a moment to regain her composure and thoughts.

"You know Rod, I get the feeling that Jake has stopped loving my mother. I'm convinced that he believes that she's the only thing that lies between him and a happy retirement."

"There seems to be no love lost between you and the guy."

"You know what? I hate his guts," she answered angrily. She paused and breathed out as if to expel all the toxins out of her lungs. "I'm sorry. I must be boring you with all this. Everybody has their problems," Debbie said, regretting her strong statements.

"You told me that Collins and Jake used to be good friends. What happened?"

"I can't tell you that."

"Goodness! Sounds serious. Why?"

"I just can't okay?" She rose quickly. "If you'll excuse me, I've got to go."

She said goodbye, kissed Rodney on the cheek and left the restaurant in a hurry, leaving him confused. Many of the things she said made sense. The phone call that memorable night he and Debbie had spent together, for example. But Rodney suspected that Debbie was holding back something. But what? The only possibly useful information that she'd given him was concerning Jake MacIntosh's upcoming retirement. This might start shedding some light on the Sparo Spear affair. There was little doubt that the Spear M40 project was still in danger. And judging from the way the engine casing was readjusted immediately after it had been 'leaked' that someone was aware of the scheme to reduce it, plus the fact that Plato had been stolen and was now in his mansion, it was likely that Jake MacIntosh had something to do with it.

"Now we have to find out what kind of danger the Spear is in and who's the big gun behind it," Rodney said to himself. "And I'll bet Collins knows."

Eugene walked into the newsroom with instruction papers.

"Well Mike, we've been assigned to the police patrol, to see how our friends in blue perform," Eugene instructed his colleague.

"Whose brilliant idea is this?" Mike Jefferson, the cameraman asked.

"Mine. I presented the idea to the news director and he loved it. But don't worry, my boy, we've been assigned to a very cozy area - Upper Town. We'll be reporting on the wave of break-ins in that district. And if you're nice with the officers, they may buy you an ice-cream cone at the end of the day."

"Wow. You sure know how to pick 'em, Eugene."

"If you'll excuse me, I've got one short phone call to make before we leave."

Eugene grabbed the telephone on a nearby desk. He dialed a number and held the receiver with his shoulder as he glanced at his watch.

"Yeah it's me, we'll be on the beat all night, starting in about an hour." Pause. "I'll find a way to be there. Count on me. Ciao!" He placed the receiver back in its cradle and started to walk out of the room, Mike following behind him.

"What was that all about," Mike asked.

Eugene turned to his partner. "I've got a feeling that we're going to have a very interesting evening, my friend."

"What have you failed to tell me?"

"Nothing. It's just a feeling I get."

Leonardo, Edmond, Rodney and Leo sat in Leonardo's room by the computer desk. A new computer had replaced the one that had been stolen. The desktop was less cluttered, however. Leonardo had designed a special rack on which he'd stacked various components of electronic equipment.

Edmond examined the new layout of electronic devices. "These units aren't connected together yet," he observed.

"They are," Leonardo responded as he completed his last minute preparations.

"I don't see any wires." Edmond continued.

"Trust me," came the answer.

"So Leo, are you ready for your part," Rodney inquired.

"As ready as I'll ever be." Leo banged three times with his fist on the doorframe. "Curtains please!" he exclaimed as he turned towards Leonardo.

"You find it dark?" Leonardo asked, not understanding Leo's expression.

"Curtains is a theatrical expression which means it's time to start the performance," Rodney explained.

Leonardo's eyes widened as he focused on the computer monitor.

"Plato, activate."

"Plato activated."

"Plato, please dial 9-1-1 and activate the remote microphone."

The speakers reproduced the sound of digital telephone dialing. Two rings followed as the telephone line transferred the call.

"9-1-1, may I help you?" the emergency attendant greeted.

"My name is Professor William Collins, and I need help. I'm being held against my will at 245 Holditch. I'm locked up in the basement of the home. Please, please send someone to free me," Leo pleaded in a low, raspy voice imitating an older gentleman in distress.

"Please remain calm, Sir. Are you at 245 Holditch Street?" The operator made sure she had the right information.

"That's right. Please hurry. I fear for my life," Leo improvised.

"Sir, there is help on its way. Try to stay calm."

Leonardo keyed in commands to cut the telephone communication.

"Plato, de-activate," he said, transmitting the signoff command through his headset.

"Well boys. Let's see what happens now!" Rodney said rubbing his hands in anticipation. "In the meantime, let's go take a look at Jake MacIntosh's place. We might be in for some entertainment."

The television camera was filming the driver as the police cruiser traveled along its assigned route.

"I hope you fellows have had plenty of coffee," the senior officer said to the two television employees, as he turned onto a residential street. "This could be a long and quiet night."

"My friend Eugene's got a hunch that something is going to happen tonight," Mike the cameraman said. "And you know what? I wouldn't bet against him. This guy's got a sixth sense."

"All we usually get on this beat is people who drive a little too fast, some drunk drivers occasionally, and once in a while, we'll get a burglar alarm," the younger of the two officers specified.

"But I thought there was a wave of burglaries going in this neck of the woods," Mike told the officers.

"Yeah, there's been. But the guys who break in are pros. The owners only discover they've been robbed the next day or later. It's the day patrol that usually gets the calls," the senior officer answered.

"So maybe we should be following the day beat," Mike told Eugene.

"We're here now," Eugene answered curtly.

The static sound of the car P.A. indicated that a message was coming through.

"Calling patrol car nine-one-four," the dispatcher's voice called out.

The young officer reached for the microphone on the CB unit.

"This is nine-one-four."

"Do you still have the television people with you?" she asked.

"Affirmative."

"Someone by the name of Grossman from the station asked that they return to the station A.S.A.P."

"Roger," the officer acknowledged as he hooked the microphone to the communication unit. "I guess you guys are wanted on another assignment."

"Fuck!" Eugene exclaimed, upset by the order.

"Why would Grossman call us back?"

"How the hell would I know?"

The driver brought the car to an ideal position and speed to complete a U-turn.

"Attention all units," the dispatcher summoned the officers' attention. "There's a possible ten ninety-six at 245 Holditch. Hostage name is William Collins. Is probably kept prisoner in the basement of the home."

The young officer jotted the information on a note pad and reached for the microphone once again.

"This is unit nine-one-four. We're on our way."

"This is unit nine-four-nine and that's an affirmative too," answered another voice through the speakers.

"That's a Roger, units nine-one-four and nine-four-nine. Please advance with caution and advise if backup is required," the dispatcher acknowledged.

The senior officer looked over his shoulder at his passengers. "I hope your boss will understand if you don't return to home base right away. This is an emergency."

"Go for it!" Eugene answered, relieved that the call had come just in time.

The car squealed into a tight turn and charged up the street with its red, white and blue caution lights and siren warning all people in their path of the urgency of their mission.

"The closest intersection to 245 Holditch would be Front Street," the young officer informed his partner.

The driver maneuvered between the cars that yielded to the emergency vehicle, slowing down at all intersections in order to assess the flow of cross traffic and gunning the engine when he was satisfied that the crossing was clear.

Mike sat in the middle of the back seat zeroing in on the action through the windshield. He was happy that the seat belt around his waist helped him to maintain balance as the car negotiated the high speed turns on the neighborhood streets. Eugene kept a vigilant eye on all the upcoming street signs. There's William Street, the next one is Queen Street and Front Street is after that, he went through the sequence of streets he'd memorized. "There's Front Street," he pointed out.

The police cruiser turned onto the street, causing the car weight to shift to the left, the passengers straining under the pull of the turn to maintain their positions on their respective seats. The tires screamed until the car regained its line, only to scream again at the following turn. Fifty yards away, car 9-49 had come to a full stop before the mansion located at 245 Holditch, manifesting its presence with flashing red, white and blue lights. Two police officers, an older gentleman and a young woman stood on either side of the cruiser in front of the property gate.

The senior officer walked over to the newly arrived police cruiser. "What's the scoop, Wally," the driver asked him.

"Hell if I know, Mack," he answered. "There seems to be no light in or around the house and the gate to the property is open. Let's drive in and go have a look." The officer paused and looked inside the cruiser. "I see you've still got the newsmen with you. I suggest you gentlemen step out of the car and remain on the outside of the property." He turned away and walked to his cruiser. Mack turned to his passengers. "This is where you step out gentlemen." Eugene and Mike reluctantly obeyed the orders. Then, the two police cars moved onto the property and went down the driveway to the main door.

Eugene was puzzled by the fact that there was no light inside or outside the house, contrasting with the night of the stakeout when the multiple floodlights surrounding it highlighted the mansion's magnificence.

"Come on, Mike. Let's follow them." Eugene ran towards the house motioning with his hand for Mike to follow.

"But they told us..." Mike started to protest as Eugene entered the property through the open gates. "But then again..." he caught up with his partner.

The two senior policemen stood side by side near the cruisers clutching their flashlights.

"Well Wally. What would you say if you and me went for a friendly visit? We'll be civilized and go by the front door, for old times' sake and we'll let our young friends cover the back."

"Sounds good to me Mack." Wally motioned the two young officers to move towards the back. He and his partner walked to the front door of the house.

Mack pressed on the bell button. He waited a moment, listening for any sign of movement inside the home. He rapped on the door using the doorknocker. Moments passed and still no answer.

"Look, the door's unlocked." Wally opened the door.

"That's strange. No lights, the front gate is open, the front door is unlocked. Some security!" Mack responded in disbelief. He drew his service gun out of its holster. Wally followed suit. Mack half-opened the door. "This is the police. Is there anybody home?" No answer. He entered the entrance hall and flicked on a light switch. The action had no effect. Wally looked behind him, towards the street, to verify that there was no general power failure.

"There's power all around the property but none here," Wally remarked. "There's something strange going on." Not knowing what to expect next, he felt a boost in his heart rate. The two policemen advanced cautiously into the home, their flashlights revealing bits and pieces of the surroundings. The only sound was the creaking of the wood floor under their footsteps.

A sudden surge of light from behind made them turn and crouch, aiming their service revolvers in its direction. The gunshot blast was followed by the sound of shattering glass. The light dimmed.

"Don't shoot! Don't shoot!" Eugene's voice pleaded.

Turn off that bloody light," Mack ordered. His command was obeyed. "We told you wise guys to stay the hell out of here."

"Damn! I pissed myself." Mike's voice squeaked. The service flashlights both pointed in the cameraman's direction.

The noise of fast-paced footsteps echoed through the house.

"Wally, Mack. Are you okay?" the young officer called out.

"You should ask these assholes. They almost got their heads shot off," Wally chastised as he flashed his light in Eugene's face.

Mack walked over to Mike and pulled the camera away from him. "Can this thing still light up?"

Mike reached to the camera and switched the light on.

"Well this is much brighter than our lights. We'll use it. Now get the hell outta here!" Mack commanded to the news people. "Jeff, I want you to go to the car and call for backup."

The young officer complied and walked out of the room.

"There's no power," the young policewoman told her colleagues.

"You figured that out all by yourself?" Wally retorted.

Mack, using the camera light, continued his search. "We've got to find the door to the basement," he suggested. The shadows cast by the furniture took on eerie shapes as he shone the light systematically from side to side. The three officers remained quiet, their ears attentive to any suspect noise. Nancy, the young policewoman, cautiously opened a door and pointed her light through the doorway.

"I've found the basement," she whispered.

Mack aimed the camera light at the door as he walked towards it, then without uttering a word, stepped down the stairs followed by his trusted companions. When he reached the landing, he stopped and flashed the light on the floor in front of him. On one side, there was a large open space that looked like an unfinished basement and on the other side was a partitioning wall and a corridor. He entered the corridor and stopped in front of the first door. He opened it and flashed the light inside the room. At the far end of the room, there was an elaborate computer set-up on a tennis table with a chair in front of it. Mack and Nancy entered into the room and flashed the light around. As the light beam panned a pad of paper that had been left beside the computer, the light in the room suddenly came on. Mack and Nancy both did a quick about-face towards the door drawing their firearms. Wally entered, surprised at the sight of his colleagues pointing their guns in his direction.

"Whoa, guys. Its' just me. Someone had turned off the main breaker to the house. No wonder the lights didn't work," he remarked, his face sporting a wry smile. "Have you found anything yet?"

"Not a thing," Mack answered as he turned off the camera light.

Nancy walked out of the room to continue her search.

"Some kidnapping," Wally remarked, as he took off his cap and wiped the sweat back into his hair.

"Yeah. Go figure," Mack replied. "It must have been a prank call."

Wally! Mack! Over here!" Nancy's agitated voice called out.

The two policemen rushed towards the source of the call. They entered the neighboring room and found the young woman standing over a folding bed on which the body of a man lay face down. Mack walked over to the side of the bed and placed his fingers on the man's neck.

"He's warm. There's a pulse. He's alive," he announced, relieved.

"What's this?" Nancy asked pointing to a cloth by the side of the bed.

Wally picked-up the rag and smelled it. By reflex, he pulled his head back quickly.

"Phooh. Chloroform," he said. "Someone put this guy to sleep."

Eugene and Mike burst into the room. Mike walked over to Mack and retrieved his camera. He stepped to one end of the room, behind the policemen gathered around the sedated body and started taking footage of the activities in the room. He filmed as Wally reached down to turn the body. He was able to zoom in on the face of the victim. However, when Nancy saw what he was up to, she yelled at him.

"Hey! Turn off the camera and get the heck out of here!"

Eugene was witnessing the spectacle with delight. The policemen had found the hostage. "Mission accomplished," he told himself.

"That's the hostage?" he asked to erase all doubts.

"What does it look like? Wally responded upset by Eugene's presence. "Now, will you please vacate the room, we have some work to do." He paused and looked at his partner. "You'd better call for an ambulance."

Meanwhile, Eugene had gone to the room that contained the computer equipment.

"Mike I'd like you to take some footage of this room," he called out to his cameraman who was now busily filming the corridor, making sure to get the detail of the entrance to the two rooms and of the closed door at the end of the hallway.

"I'll be right with you Eugene. But first, I want to get a good shot of that other door."

"What door?" Eugene stuck his head in the hallway and looked in the direction where Mike was filming. Intrigued, he went to it and tried to open it.

"It's locked. Looks like one of those two-way locks for which you need a key on both sides." Eugene banged on the door a few times. "That's a pretty solid one, too. Ah well, we've got what we came here for. Let's call it a night," he said to Mike, satisfied with the outcome of the evening.

Eugene walked into the TV room with two huge bowls of popcorn that he set on the large laminated cube in the middle of the room. He walked to the VCR and inserted a tape. Edmond, Rodney, Leo and Charles had all gathered as requested by the proud reporter. They all had a beer glass and the mood was festive.

"Well, my lads, I have the proof of our success on tape." He paused and looked around the room. "Where's Leonard?"

"Playing with computers as usual," Edmond replied.

"He was in this room a few minutes ago, looking for something," Leo said. "I saw him turning everything upside down, like he lost a contact lens or something."

"Well, I guess we'll have to savor the victory on our own," Eugene said, offended by Leonardo's failure to respond to his invitation. He grabbed the remote control unit.

"By the way, Trap, where did you get the VCR?" Leo asked Eugene.

"I borrowed it from the station for the night," he replied.

The TV replayed the footage in the police cruiser. Eugene pressed the fast forward button until he got to the beginning of the drive to the scene of the crime. Images of the patrol car maneuvering through the streets at break-neck speeds generated chuckles of excitement from the appreciative audience.

"Holy cow, Trap! This is better than the movies!" Charles exclaimed as he reached for the popcorn.

"You ain't seen nothin' yet, buddy," Eugene boasted with glee. At the end of the car ride, he fast-forwarded the video to the footage at the house. "Watch this!" he said with enthusiasm.

The image showed the police officers as they entered the house. Then, the TV screen went blank momentarily. The next image was of two policemen with their backs to the camera. The two men crouched and turned quickly and pointed their guns at the camera. A shot was heard and simultaneously, the image on the TV screen shook violently and swayed on all sides.

"Damn! Did they shoot at you, Trap?" Leo asked, shocked by what he'd just witnessed.

"Like I told you, we were in the line of fire," Eugene said as nonchalantly as he could.

The image on the screen went blank. The next scene again showed the backs of police officers. The legs of a man lying face down on a bed could be seen at the bottom of the screen. The image moved to the left as the cameraman sought a better shot. One of the officers reached down and turned the man around on his back. When the officer moved out of the camera's range, the picture zoomed in on the victim's face.

Rodney and Charles looked at each other, stone-faced.

"That's not Collins," Charles said.

"What do you mean, that's not Collins? Who the hell is it, then?" Eugene asked, feeling that his bubble had just burst.

"That's Jake MacIntosh," Charles answered.

"What?" Leo exclaimed.

Rodney bolted towards Leonardo's quarters.

"Leonard!" he yelled. He entered the room and found the Master in a crouching position looking for something underneath his desk.

"The police...," Rodney stopped short as Leonardo motioned to him to be silent. Leonardo got up and without saying anything, walked towards Rodney waving at him to follow. He went to the TV room where he quietly got the occupants' attention and led them out of the room, through the kitchen and into the back yard.

"What's going on?" Edmond inquired.

Leonardo waited until everyone had gathered around him.

"I know that the police did not get the right man," Leonardo told his friends.

"What do you mean, you know?" Rodney asked, surprised.

"This afternoon, I witnessed the moving of someone, Collins I suspect, back into the basement room of the mansion. Plato advised me of movement and I saw everything on the computer monitor."

"But what makes you so sure that it's Collins?" Charles asked.

"I believe that Mr. MacIntosh hid Professor Collins when he was apprised that the police were coming to his house. He turned off the power to the house knowing that he would gain time. As you know, strangers in a new surrounding, especially in darkness, feel very disoriented, all the more when there is imminent danger. Mr. MacIntosh, being a good student of human nature, understands this," Leonardo deducted.

"Wait a minute. The man we found in that room was sedated," Eugene protested.

"Agreed. Was there any substance found on the premises that could be used as a sedative?" Leonardo asked.

"Yeah. When I got into the room, one of the officers was holding a cloth and I think he mentioned something about chloroform," Eugene testified.

"Chloroform?" Charles exclaimed. "All MacIntosh had to do was pour some in a cloth and inhale and he'd be in la-la land."

"So it could be self-administered," Rodney concluded.

"Definitely," Charles supported.

"Well that's all very nice. But why did you bring us out here?" Leo asked.

"Mr. MacIntosh knew in advance that the police were coming. That would explain how he could have reacted so quickly." Leonardo paused. "Tell me Eugene, how long did it take for you to get to the house after the gendarmes received the call?"

"Gendarmes?"

"The police," Leonardo clarified.

"I'd say... two... maybe three minutes, tops."

"So, let us assume the worst-case scenario. Three minutes, and let us assume two minutes for the transmission of the call from here to the station, to the car. That amounts to five minutes. Hmm. Tell me Eugene, were the lights all out when you got to the house?"

"Yes. It's the first thing I noticed. It seemed pretty unusual."

"Hmm, interesting. Well, I strongly believe that someone must have planted a listening device in our home, and thus Mr. MacIntosh was expecting our call. He wanted us to find him as we did. I believe we have been hoodwinked," Leonardo paused again. "That explains why Plato no longer operates."

"You mean, they unplugged the computer?" Charles asked.

"Precisely." Leonardo confirmed. "Mr. MacIntosh has no more use for Plato. He has served his purpose."

"Wait a minute! I thought Plato was on our side," Leo protested, confused by Leonardo's statement.

"He was. However, I'm afraid Mr. MacIntosh got wise to us and probably suspected that we still communicated with the computer via the modem and that it was transferring intelligence to us. I suspect that by the time he discovered this, he felt that we had gathered sufficient information to act upon it."

"So, he set us up," Rodney completed Leonardo's thought.

"In a way. He probably heard our discussions and strategies. All he had to do was wait for us to come."

"So, you think our house is bugged?" Eugene asked his mind reeling with the one hundred and eighty-degree turn of events.

"Unmistakably," Leonardo responded. "I have found one located under my work desk, and another in the telephone receiver."

"What about the TV room?" Rodney asked, fearing that he might have been heard when he declared the true identity of the hostage.

"I have looked and found nothing."

"But tell me Leonard, if there are only two rooms in that basement, where did MacIntosh hide Collins?" Charles asked, persuaded he'd found a flaw in the Master's evaluation of the events.

"I must admit that I was puzzled at first. But Plato helped me to find the missing piece." He paused. "You see Charles, there is a door at the end of the corridor. I am willing to wager with you that there is some sort of underground tunnel that can serve as an escape route in times of danger."

"Yeah, there's a door. I saw it. It's locked," Eugene confirmed.

"I would assume that Professor Collins was still sedated when Mr. MacIntosh moved him. So he probably placed him in the secret passageway while the search went on in the house. Mr. MacIntosh was rightfully convinced that once the police found him, they would stop their search since they had found the so-called hostage." He stopped and paced momentarily to gather his thoughts. "Tell me Eugene, did they take Mr. MacIntosh anywhere after they found him?"

"To the General Hospital."

"So, once he came to, the police were probably shocked to find out his real identity. Mr. Macintosh probably explained his predicament as the foiled attempt by some punks to rob his home," Rodney concluded.

"There is some merit to your theory," Leonardo agreed.

"What about Collins?" Charles asked. "We're back to square one. We need to talk to him if we want to get to the bottom of the Spear affair."

"You've got that right!" Rodney agreed. "We don't have much choice guys. If that's really Collins locked up in there, we have to find a way to pull him out of that hellhole."

"Yeah, but how?" Leo asked.

"We don't have many options left," Rodney said. "The test flight of the M-4-0 is only a week away. We have to get to Collins if we want to get to the bottom of this."

"What about the bugs," Charles asked. "How are we going to get rid of them?"

"We won't," Leonardo suggested. "If we are to be successful in our initiatives, we cannot let on to whoever is listening to us that we are aware of their ploy."

"That's going to be hard to do, won't it?" Eugene asked.

"Perhaps, but we must succeed."

10

Remote Control

The stone and cast-iron fence shielding 245 Holditch connected to a stone utility building bearing the same Victorian architectural attributes as the mansion.

From a car parked one hundred yards away on a dimly lit side street, Leonardo and Eugene watched as three of the four young men dressed in dark clothes climbed the perimeter wall. Leonardo sat strategically so that he could see any threatening activity in the vicinity. Eugene lay back in an inclined position on the driver's side.

Charles, still standing at the foot of the fence, threw a bag to his accomplices, then adroitly climbed the fence and jumped to the other side. He took three flashlights out of the bag and handed them to Edmond, Rodney and Oscar. Rodney had called him, hoping that he would join them in their efforts to get the prisoner out of Jake MacIntosh's mansion. On the one hand, he felt that there was safety in numbers, and since Leo had had to work that night, they were somewhat shorthanded. Then, there was the fact that Oscar was very strong, which would surely be an advantage, given the task at hand. After being brought up to date on the situation, Oscar had of course accepted. This was a great opportunity for action after the somewhat quiet summer that he had spent in his hometown.

While Oscar explored the area, Rodney walked over to a side window on the utility building and pushed the head of the lamp flat against the windowpane to maximize the lighting inside and reveal the contents of the building. Against the far wall were a riding lawnmower and an old pick-up box that had been transformed into a trailer. On the right side of the room, Rodney could make out a workbench with an impressive collection of tools on and around it.

Oscar came out of the darkness. "I've found the door," he announced in a whisper. His three friends hurried to his side.

"Where is it?" Charles asked.

"Around the corner. But there's a light over it."

"Let's go in through the window, then. We won't be as visible and the trees will hide us from the house," Rodney suggested.

They walked back towards the window. Edmond pulled a pair of work gloves from the bag and put them on. Without consulting his friends, he punched his fist through one of the windowpanes. Using the butt of his flashlight, he then broke off the jagged ends and reached for the window lock. When he turned around and saw the shock on the faces of the witnesses, he smiled and shrugged.

"Are you enjoying yourself, Ed?" Oscar asked sarcastically.

"I've seen this done in movies," he defended. Then, annoyed by his friends' silent disapproval, he protested. "I've never done this before, I swear!"

"Obviously," Charles responded, trying to pull his friend's leg. "You could've cut yourself the way you did that."

One after the other, they slipped into the building through the window and turned on their flashlights.

"Leonard thinks the passageway leads to this building," Rodney explained. "Now all we have to do is find the door."

Four beams of light wandered in various directions, light rays crossing periodically as they searched for the opening.

"I don't see any other door," Charles said.

"Over here!" Oscar called. He pointed his light to the floor between the tractor mower and the trailer. "It's a trap door," he said.

He reached down and grabbing the handle pulled the door up in one strong motion. He leaned it against the trailer beside him.

"And there's the stairs to the secret passageway," Charles declared as they shone their lights inside the open hole.

"This reminds me of Young Frankenstein. Remember the part where they're going through these passageways looking for the secret room, and you hear the violin in the background? What was her name?" Oscar said reliving the scene of the movie.

"Here we are breaking into a fortress, and Good Old Dude is thinking about the Young Frankenstein movie," Edmond chuckled.

"Would you guys be quiet!" Rodney chastised, as he started going down the stairs leading towards the tunnel. His comrades followed. As they entered the tunnel, Oscar noticed a light switch and flipped it on. The action prompted a simultaneous reaction of panic among the other men, who all about-turned to face danger.

"I found the light switch," Oscar whispered, almost apologetically.

His announcement was met with a collective sigh. The four intruders continued down the long straight and narrow corridor until they reached a door at the other end.

"That must be the door."

"Good observation, Ed," Oscar retorted.

"I thought Eugene said it was a wooden door," Edmond whispered.

"It's probably made of wood, but it's been covered with a piece of sheet metal on this side, probably to protect it from humidity damage," Charles explained.

"There's another light switch," Oscar informed.

"As Eugene said, we need a key to get in," Rodney pointed to the lock. "It's one of those locks with key barrels on both sides." He reached for the door handle and slowly turned it. To his surprise the door opened. He closed it immediately.

"It's unlocked," he whispered. "Kill the tunnel light."

Charles reached for the switch.

Rodney reopened the door slowly. The corridor on the other side of the door was in full darkness. He pointed his flashlight to the floor, and noticed a toolbox on the floor and a roll of sheet metal that had been placed on top of a stack of firewood.

"I guess they're going to put sheet metal on both sides," Charles assumed.

The four men entered the hallway. The four beams of light resumed the search for doors.

"This must be the door," Edmond attracted his friends' attention by pointing his flashlight to a door with a dead bolt on the outside.

"There's light in the room."

He unlatched the bolt and opened the door. Bill Collins sat on a bed, holding a shot glass in his hand. His hair was tousled and his face unshaven. An open, half-empty bottle of scotch whisky was sitting on a small table in front of him. Collins struggled to get on his feet.

"Who are you?"

"Shush!" Oscar said quietly, putting a finger to his lips.

Charles stepped forward and smiled at the older man. Collins was looking bewildered.

"We're here to get you out," Charles whispered.

"Who are you? How did you get in here?" Collins asked not recognizing Charles.

"You'll soon find out," Charles answered. He pointed to the bottle. "I thought you gave that up?"

"I've found a lost true love," Collins reached for the bottle and cradled it in his arms like a father picking up his first newborn.

Charles yanked the bottle out of his hands and grabbed his arm. "Come on," he said firmly. "Let's get you out of here!"

He and Oscar each took one of the Professor's arms and brought him out of the room. Everyone stopped for a moment when they heard footsteps coming down the stairs. No one said a word, but the tension was climbing. Edmond signaled to the others to go ahead while he shut the door to Collins' detention room and locked it with the dead bolt as his friends half-carried, half-pushed the drunken Collins into the secret passageway. Edmond followed them, making sure to carefully close the door behind him and hurried to join his friends in the unlit tunnel. They climbed up the stairs to the trap door. It was shut. Rodney tried to open it and cursed.

"Damn! The door is jammed."

"Let me try," Oscar said as he pushed his way to the top of the stairs. He bent down, pressed his back under the door and braced his feet on the steps below him. He tried to lift the door using the brute force of his legs, grunting under the strain. Nothing budged.

"Someone's blocked the door," he said. "What the hell's going on here?"

Something was definitely wrong. Looking for a solution, Edmond turned around. It was then that he saw a light under the door between the tunnel and the hallway. Danger was imminent. He dashed in the direction of the light, convinced that he had to react quickly. Opening the door slightly, he saw a man who was pushing a mass of something into the tunnel and then pouring the contents out of a container onto the pile. Then, Edmond saw the spark and the light of a match that was thrown on the heap setting it ablaze.

"Fire!" he screamed in panic as he scrambled up the stairs.

His friends turned and saw the red glow under the door at the bottom of the stairs.

"Help!" they screamed as they pounded and pushed on the trap door, desperately trying to open it.

Smoke was starting to billow into the stairwell. Rodney desperately looked around him for anything that could save them. He finally pulled off his shirt and put it to his face, indicating to the others to do the same. They kept pounding on the door and calling for help.

When Leonardo and Eugene had seen the light in the utility building come on, and then off a few minutes later, they knew that it was an indication of trouble. They quickly scaled the wall, Leonardo impressing Eugene with his agility. They ran towards the utility building and found the open window.

"Something's burning," Eugene cried out when he smelled the smoke. He jumped through the window and fell to the floor. As he scurried to get up, he heard the crash of the entrance door as it gave way to the tremendous force with which Leonardo had pushed it. Eugene ran towards the door and flipped the light switch on.

They found the trap door and were horrified when they saw that smoke was seeping through the cracks around it and that the tractor-mower had been parked on top of it. They could hear coughing coming through the door.

"Eddy, Rod, we're gonna get you out!" Eugene hollered.

The two men pushed the machine off the door. The trapped men were still pounding and pushing, but the door didn't budge. Seeing that the deadbolt had been slipped into place, Leonardo reached down and quickly dislodged it. Immediately, the door flung open and Oscar's arms and torso bolted through the opening, along with a dense cloud of smoke. The two rescuers reached down to pull the victims out and bring them to safety. Eugene and Leonardo grabbed Professor Collins and Oscar, still gasping and coughing, motioned his friends towards the now gaping opening of the door and helped them over the fence.

"We've got to get out of here before anyone sees us," Charles commanded.

"Where am I? Bill Collins had passed out during the escape from the burning tunnel. "I need a drink

"Professor Collins, do you remember me?" Charles asked.

"Get me a drink, and…and I'll remember who you are. I promise."

"It's me, Charles. I'm one of your students. I worked with you on the M40 project."

"Very nice to meet you. Now get me a drink."

Rodney came out of the house with Leonardo and walked towards Charles. He grabbed Charles' hand.

"So you found them!"

"Yessir! And I think we have them all, so they shouldn't be able to overhear our conversations anymore. It's safe to go back in the house," Rodney said.

"How were you able to find these?"

Rodney nodded his head in Leonardo's direction.

"Plato was of great assistance," Leonardo answered.

"I should've guessed. Can Plato cook too?" Charles asked sarcastically. He paused and ran his hand through his thick mane of hair. "I'm sorry, Leonard. I guess I'm just tired. If you don't mind I'd like to get a bit of shuteye. Is it okay if I use your spare bed, Rod?"

"Go right ahead. We'll sit with the professor for a while."

Charles got up and walked into the house.

"We should take Professor Collins into the house, too," Rodney said to Leonardo.

The Master agreed. He reached down for the professor's arm. In one swift motion, he hoisted him over his shoulder and headed into the house. Rodney laughed, once more taken by surprise by Leonardo's unpredictability. He followed them through the kitchen and into Leonardo's quarters. Leonardo lay the professor on the chesterfield. Collins offered no resistance. Oddly enough, he had fallen asleep during his transportation.

"Rodney. You need some sleep. Get some rest. We can discuss this later. I shall keep a vigilant eye on our guest."

"Well, I sure could use some sleep. Are you sure you can cover?"

"Go in peace. I would like to get acquainted with the professor."

His head the only part of his body not totally submerged, Rodney lay in the bathtub, enjoying the therapeutic effect of the water that poured steadily out of the faucet. It was an excellent way to replenish his energy.

The bathroom door opened and Edmond entered in his typical unhurried way.

"Hey, Rod. You're having your monthly bath, I see. I thank you. No, we all thank you for that." Edmond pinched his nose.

"As a matter of fact, I'm finished," Rodney answered as he rose in the bathtub. "It's a wonder what three cups of bleach will do. You see I'm all clean."

"Collins is up and about."

"How's he doing?"

"Other than the fact that he's severely hung over, puking every few minutes and dying for a drink, I'd think he's doing very well. At least, his memory's come back. Charles is having a talk with him now. I guess he's giving him the latest news. Collins mentioned the defect in design that Plato identified and Charles told him how we managed to get that corrected. Boy, that really blew his socks off! I suppose that now Leonardo and Charles are going to introduce him to Plato."

Edmond paused and leaned on the bathroom sink. "I think he could stand a bath, too."

"Well, why don't you and Charles bring him up. It'll do him a whole lot of good. Get him some of Eugene's clothes. They wear about the same size. I'll be done in two minutes max."

"They've been locked up in there for more than a day," Leo told Eugene. The consummate eavesdroppers stood by the door.

"What are they doing?"

"I'm not sure. It's been a roller coaster of emotions over the last few hours. At times you hear Collins cursing and begging, and at others, you hear him laughing."

"What's Leonardo saying to him?"

"Come to think of it, I don't remember hearing his voice. Oddly enough, Collins seems to be doing all the talking."

"Hmm, that's strange. I wonder what Leonardo's up to."

"He probably got the professor plugged like Plato. Maybe he's programming him. Imagine this. Collins, activate," he said mimicking Leonardo's voice. "Collins activated," he mimicked the computer's voice. "Please estimate the value of pi at the millionth decimal."

Edmond chuckled. They moved away from the door and entered the TV room.

"What's on the tube?" Edmond asked.

"The news, I guess." Leo switched on the television. "Let's get the local news," he suggested as he tuned to the station.

"Boy, it's sure been an eventful summer hasn't it?" Edmond commented.

"You can say that again. I hope that we'll come back to a more regular life. You know: women, beer, women, sports, beer, beer, women, sports..."

"Speaking of beer, why don't you be a nice boy, and get us a few cold ones," Edmond suggested.

"Go right ahead and get yourself one. You know where your fridge is."

"I'm fresh out."

"So am I."

"Do you always leave empty beer cans in your fridge? You can get a nickel at the friendly store for empties, you know."

"You've been in my fridge again. Damn. I'll have to put a lock on it," Leo growled in mock anger.

"Please Leo, get us a good cold beer," Edmond batted his eyes mimicking a child's whining tone.

"Well okay, if you put it that way, Uncle Leo will get you a cold one." He got up and walked out of the room.

Edmond turned to the television.

"...Mayor McNeil said that the item would be addressed in the next municipal budget." The news anchorman glanced at his notes and continued. "The final test flight of the Sparo Spear M40 is scheduled for next Monday. The president of Sparo Aeronautics called a press conference today to address some of the rumors that have been circulating regarding the viability of the project. Myla Mason is reporting." The screen showed some footage of a previous Spear flight as the voice of the reporter explained.

"Rumors abound about the Sparo Spear project. Many questions and suspicions surround the upcoming final test. You will recall that the Federal Government has announced that it will end its financial support of the project next month. The survival of the project will depend on the result of next week's final test flights. Potential clients will be on hand to witness the flight and orders are pending, should the test be successful. Jake MacIntosh, the president of Sparo Aeronautics had this to say:"

Jake MacIntosh, standing at a podium with the Sparo logo behind him and a scaled down model of the Spear M40 to his left, appeared on the screen.

"As you all know, rumors have been circulating that Sparo Aeronautics, and more precisely, the Spear M40 project, is close to collapse. Let me assure you that the test flight scheduled for Monday at fourteen hundred hours will quash all rumors. Sparo Aeronautics is and will remain a leader in the aeronautical industry well into the twenty-first century." MacIntosh spoke forcefully and with conviction.

"Mr. MacIntosh, there are people saying that the fire at your home the day before yesterday may have been an indication of the Sparo project's fate. It is the second incident involving your house in a matter of days. What are your comments on this?" a reporter asked.

"I fail to see the relationship. Officials believe that it was vandals who have twice broken into my house. This last time, the day before yesterday, they set fire to an old mattress that was stored in my basement. I'm convinced that there is no connection whatsoever with the Spear project. The police investigation confirms this. The rise in crime in this city has nothing to do with Sparo's challenges. It's important that you understand that all is well with the Sparo Spear M40 fighter and it will technologically be a leader for many years to come."

"We know better, Jake baby! We're going to get your ass, buddy," Edmond shouted at the television.

The rapping of knuckles on the door echoed from the hall.

"Who could that be?" Rodney asked.

"Someone new, obviously. Nobody I know would knock before entering." Getting up from the easy chair, Leo put his beer down on the coffee table and went to greet the stranger.

"I'm here to see Edmond," Rodney heard the female voice announce.

"Please come in," Leo said and yelled, "Ed, someone's here to see you."

"I'll be down in a minute," came the answer from upstairs.

"Please follow me," Leo said. "You can wait for him in the TV room."

Rodney watched as Leo escorted the tall curvaceous brunette into the living room. He recognized Rhonda Scott from the Spear project.

"Hi Rhonda, what a nice surprise," he greeted her with a handshake.

"Hi Rod, how are you," she pulled him towards her and kissed him on the lips.

"And I'm Leo," Leo intervened, reaching for her hand and hoping to get the same treatment.

"Pleased to meet you Leo." She didn't kiss him.

"Edmond mentioned he was dating a gorgeous woman by the name of Rhonda but I had no idea you were the one."

"What! You don't find me attractive, Rod? You'll get over the shock. There's life outside of Sparo Aeronautics, you know." She paused. "And what sort of things did you hear about me?" she asked with a coy smile, changing the topic.

"Nothing bad," Rodney laughed nervously. Looking down at her hand, he noticed that she wasn't wearing her engagement ring.

"It's okay, Rod, I'm single now. And I promise to treat your friend real nice," she said in a sexy tone, when she saw Rodney's point of focus.

Rodney was at a loss for words.

Rhonda reached for Rodney's hand and pulled him towards her. "I could always reconsider and make myself available for you, Rod."

"Pfff!" Leo spat his sip of beer.

"Would you like to add something, Leo?" Rhonda queried, amused by his reaction.

Leo shook his head as he tried to regain his breath and composure.

"I see you've met Rhonda," Edmond said as he entered the room.

"Yessir," Leo grinned. He and Rodney stood uncomfortably, refraining from uttering anything, for fear of looking any more stupid.

"Well, shall we go?" Edmond suggested, sensing his friends' discomfort.

"I'm ready. Hope to see you guys soon," she bade farewell and followed her young escort.

The two friends stood, looking towards the portico, until the couple was out of site.

"Do you get the feeling that Edmond is taking on more woman than he can handle?" Leo asked.

"I think he's in for a hell of a ride," Rodney predicted, but remembering that Edmond had said that she had initially come on to him, he was thinking, *"What the hell is she doing?"*

"So what's the scoop?" Eugene asked as he repeatedly tossed and caught the tennis ball.

"Well, Professor Collins is slowly but surely recovering. Leonardo has been spending day and night with him. They seem to have formed some sort of bond. Collins feels physically ill because of his withdrawal from booze, but his mind is practically back to normal," Charles replied.

"So I guess we can take him to the police and put an end to all of this," Eugene concluded.

"Assuming he remembers the details of his incarceration," Rodney specified.

"He's gotta remember that he was kept locked up in that basement," Eugene argued.

"Oddly enough, he doesn't. He doesn't remember his experience in MacIntosh's basement. He doesn't have any idea how he got there. All he remembers is feeling ill one night, going to bed, and then regaining some sort of consciousness, here in this house," Charles explained.

"What about the booze? He was as drunk as a skunk when we found him in that basement."

"I've got a feeling that someone made sure he got hooked on the bottle again. Somehow, I feel they were going to put him back into circulation in a drunken stupor, knowing that he's suicidal when he's on the bottle," Rodney reasoned.

"That sounds farfetched," Eugene doubted.

"Until you find me a better explanation, I'll stick to that theory."

"Were you able to get anything from him on the tampering with the Spear project?" Edmond asked.

"Collins thinks like us when it comes to MacIntosh. He knows that Jake doesn't have the project at heart and he's pretty sure that he'll sabotage the project somehow. Now that the plan to sabotage the casing has been uncovered, Collins thinks that he's going to find another way," Rodney said.

"Yeah, but does he know how and why?" Eugene queried.

"How, we're not sure. And why? Well, I think there's something in it for him if the project doesn't come through."

"You seem convinced of that." Charles looked at Rodney inquisitively.

"When is MacIntosh due for retirement?" Rodney asked.

"Not for a while. He's in his early fifties and only in the third year of a ten-year mandate," Charles answered.

"Well, I have it from a reliable source that MacIntosh is planning an early retirement. He expects to come into a lot of money, soon."

"How will he get that money?" Edmond asked.

"I don't know where the money's coming from, but I'll bet that it'll probably come from the M40 project's going down the tube. But we'll worry about that at another time. We have a more pressing matter at hand."

"The only thing we know for sure is that whatever fate is reserved for the Spear, it'll happen on Monday," Charles added.

"What are we going to do? That's less than four days away and we don't even know what we're looking for!" Eugene pressed.

Bill Collins and Leonardo came in the room. The professor's face showed fatigue and strain. His complexion was gray and he was perspiring heavily.

"Good to see you up and about," Charles greeted.

"Tell that to my body," Collins answered.

"Rodney, William and I require your assistance," Leonardo interjected.

"Name it."

"I would like you to speak to the gentleman that you and Charles met when you did your test flight simulation."

"James Knoll?"

"Yes, that's correct.

"James Knoll is a friend of mine and he owes me a few favors," Collins intervened. "I need you to find a way for him to meet you here. Could you try to arrange that?"

"I'll get my brother to help me with that one. He's a friend of his. But what do you have in mind?"

"We need access to the Spear M40 flight simulator. Leonard has convinced me that we can take over the controls of the simulator remotely. We need to have the right instruments to monitor the plane during its flight and identical controls that will permit us to override the actual controls, if need be."

"You're kidding!" Eugene exclaimed. "You guys are crazy if you think you can take over the controls of a high-tech plane from a distance!"

Bill Collins' face turned red. "Young man, I was instrumental in the design of this fighter plane. Nobody knows it better than I do. I designed the computer program that flies this fighter plane and I am convinced that Leonardo and I can pull this off!" he said vehemently. He paused, knowing he had made his point and took in a deep breath. "Now. We have less than ninety-six hours to put this together. We will need everyone's cooperation."

"You've got it!"

"You're out of your bloody mind," James Knoll. "You're asking me to break the law."

Bill Collins walked towards James and sat beside him on the chesterfield. The doors to Leonardo's quarters had been closed to ensure their intimacy.

"Jimmy, how long have you known me?"

"Eight years."

"How would you evaluate me?   Do you think I would ask such a big favor unless I was absolutely certain of what I was doing?"

"You haven't in the past, but..."

"Listen. Jimmy. You were instrumental in the programming of the Spear. Do you want all your efforts to be for naught?"

James Knoll got up and paced the room. "Bill, you're asking me to put my ass on the line. I've got a family. My wife takes care of the kids at home. I've got no savings and I can't afford to lose my job."

"Well then, tell me what the hell am I supposed to do? Should I let close to ten years of my life go down the tubes? You don't know me well if you think I won't put up a fight. I need your help. The livelihood of Sparo Aeronautics, your main client, is at stake. All I ask is that you give me unlimited access to the simulator."

James Knoll pondered the request. He ran both hands through his hair repeatedly, his fingertips scratching his scalp at every stroke. There was tense silence in the room.

"I've got some tests booked for the next few days," he said finally, as he raised his head and looked at Collins.

"Can I get access to it at night?"

"I guess I could get you a clearance."

"Can you shut down operations in the hangar during the test flight?"

"Yeah, I could probably pull that off. I could schedule some maintenance on the machine during that afternoon. But we still have a problem, Bill."

"What's that?"

"Who'll take the commands should the test flight go wrong?"

"Do you have any suggestions?"

"I could probably get one of the trainees to do it for us."

"No, that would be too dangerous. We can't afford to have a leak," Collins rejected the suggestion. "Can you train any of us here?"

"We don't have much time. I don't think I could get anyone to do this in such a short time."

"What about you?"

"Bill, you know I can't. With my bad heart, I'd probably croak in that seat. Hey, wait a minute! What about that kid who called me?"

"Rodney?"

"Yeah, Rodney. He's got great potential. It's a long shot, but with intensive coaching, there's a chance that he could pull it off. Maybe I can sit in with him, in the gunman's seat, but he'll have to be the lead man."

"It's a go?" Collins asked.

"It's a go. But we'd better get Rodney into the saddle as quickly as possible. He's got quite a crash course in flying to go through."

Rodney sat facing Bill Collins who was in the Lay-Z-Boy chair in Leonardo's quarters. Leonardo sat in front of his computer working on last minute adjustments.

"Professor Collins. May I speak to you for a few minutes? "

"Sure. As long as you call me Bill. What's on your mind?"

Rodney leaned on the armrest of the chesterfield.

"Jake MacIntosh and you used to be friends?"

"Yes, indeed we were," Bill Collins exhaled deeply as he answered.

"I guess you guys didn't see eye to eye on certain things about the project. I know that more than anyone, you want to see the Spear project succeed. "

"The M-four-zero is one of the two most important things in the world to me," Bill Collins admitted.

"Yes I know. But we know Jake MacIntosh doesn't have the project at heart, right?"

"Right."

"Why?"

"Hmm. It can only be explained with one word," Bill responded.

"What?"

"Jake MacIntosh has fallen prey to one of humanity's worst sicknesses - greed."

"Greed." Rodney repeated.

"You see Rodney, Jake is a great engineer and he earned his way up the ladder. That's how he got the job as President of Sparo. He got that big salary with all the perks that he always dreamed of."

"How does that make him greedy? I'd like to be a big boss in business, someday. Does that make me greedy?" Rodney asked.

"No, it's normal that you should have goals for yourself and that you want to make maximum use of your capacities. But Jake has been at the top for a while and he's convinced himself that he's worth much more than what he's paid. As far as his salary at Sparo is concerned, he knows that he has peaked.

"Yeah, but I'm sure he's getting a hell of a pay," Rodney interjected.

Bill Collins sighed. "You've heard the expression, living beyond your means, Rodney?"

"Well, yeah, sure!"

"Jake has always lived that way, and he's always needed the promotions and pay increases to pay for his accumulated debts. When it comes to spending, Jake is incorrigible."

"But what does this have to do with the Spear project?" Rodney wanted to know.

"He still finds ways to spend more than he earns, even with the high salary he's getting."

"So he's accumulated more debts," Rodney concluded.

"Precisely."

Rodney scratched the back of his head. "If Jake's salary's peaked, how is he covering his debts?"

"Well, Jake is a resourceful man. He's found a way to milk some more money from the project. He got some of the government loans channeled into a company owned by his wife, some five million dollars. You see, the company is under her maiden name, so it can't be traced, and because she's a manic-depressive who is presently institutionalized, he's got full signing authority. Believe me, though, she had absolutely nothing to do with it." Professor Collins suddenly became sad and for a few moments, looked in the distance, absorbed in his thoughts.

Rodney was absolutely fascinated by what was being revealed to him. He let all the information sink in, then turned again to Bill Collins. "That's really amazing. But how did he pull all that off?

"Jake needed some inside help. He managed to get Ned and Simpson on board with a promise that they'd get a cut of the action. With this inside help, it was easier to get the whole thing through without raising suspicions. Everything was under control, until the Feds advised Jake that they were sending in the auditors to look at the books. You see, they started getting suspicious about some cost overruns."

"Five million dollars in overruns, I'll bet they were curious! When are the Feds coming in?"

"Jake has been able to keep them at bay for a while. He told them that with the tight deadline and the importance of the upcoming test flight, he wants all his staff dedicated to the common objective. He's played the political card, hinting that any interference could make the difference between success and failure."

"And by them agreeing to this, he's been able to buy some time."

"Oh, he bought himself more than that," Bill replied.

"What do you mean?"

"Well, if the test flight is a failure, the government will pull the plug on the project and the M-four-zero will be history, and so will Sparo Aeronautics, which means…"

"Which means that the Government will have egg all over its face and will want to put the whole thing to rest as soon as possible. That means no audit by the Federal Government," Rodney inferred.

"An audit would be unlikely," Bill Collins agreed.

"So Jake and the boys would run off with five million and the case is closed."

"And Jake would receive full severance pay and pension," Bill added. "However, there is a loose end."

"You?"

"That's right. You lads put the proverbial wrench in his gears when your rescued me."

"But, can't we bring this to the government's attention?" Rodney suggested.

"What will you bring to their attention?"

"Everything you've told me."

Bill glared defiantly at Rodney. "I will deny everything."

"Why?"

"I have too much to lose, and by doing this, we would put the whole project in jeopardy."

"I don't understand."

"I'm asking you to have faith in me. It's important that we bring things to light only after we have foiled Jake's plans. These are my conditions for helping you. Jake has too much at stake to let this project succeed. We have to stop him. This is the best way to neutralize him, and that means you can get my collaboration for this and nothing more. I will come clean after the test flight, you have my word."

"But why do we have to wait before we tell anyone?"

"If we tell, the Government will investigate and stop the project, which means that the test flight will be delayed, which means that the project will be killed, and then everybody loses. Is that what you want?" Bill Collins said angrily.

"Are you sure that's what's going to happen?"

"I'm not going to sit around to find out!" Bill shouted as he sprang out of his chair.

"Remember the Pazzi Conspiracy," Leonardo interrupted, manifesting his presence and interest in the conversation.

Both men turned towards the Master who kept on working at the computer. He had been so quiet that they'd forgotten that he was there.

"What's he saying?" Bill asked.

"He's talking about greed." Leonardo had made his point once more. "I'll tell you later." Rodney brushed off the comment with a movement of the hand.

Bill Collins' bad temper had been diffused by Leonardo's comment. He marveled that Leonardo was able to perform intricate tasks while listening to the conversation. Rodney, for his part, was used to it.

Rodney took in a deep breath. He was uneasy about how to bring up a very delicate subject. "I know that you're the one who issued the work order to modify the jet engine casing. I'm sure you knew that it would lead to disaster, but you still ordered the modifications to the plans and gave the orders to carry on the work." He paused. "Why did you do it?"

"I thought I didn't have any choice. It was stupid. But I feared for..."

Bill Collins stopped. He couldn't believe that he'd admitted his guilt and he was disturbed by what he was about to say before he caught himself.

"Did this have anything to do with Mrs. MacIntosh? "

Bill Collins was manifestly astounded by Rodney's question.

"What did you say? "

"You're in love with her, aren't you." Rodney's statement was matter of fact.

Bill Collins' face had paled. "Why do you say that?" he stammered as he got up from his chair and faced the window, his back to Rodney.

"I sort of suspected it, but I wasn't sure of this until a few moments ago. Your reaction confirmed my suspicion," Rodney admitted.

Bill Collins heaved a sigh. "You're very perceptive for one so young." Bill Collins said sadly. He bowed his head, then straightened up again and told his story, occasionally glancing over his shoulder at Rodney, but mostly looking out the window, as if he was speaking to himself.

"You guessed correctly. I met her... at a detox center. You see, after my wife died, I believed that I had no reason to live. My only friend was the bottle and it almost destroyed me." Collins pulled off his glasses and wiped his tears. "Betty MacIntosh helped me to get through this. She had an addiction to drugs and she was at the same clinic as I was. We helped each other through our respective problems. We became very close. At first, it wasn't anything physical, you know. We just cared deeply for each other and supported each other through our ordeals. I know that she's the reason that I was able to put my life back on track and get involved in the Spear project. I'm eternally grateful to her. The irony of it all is that she introduced me to Jake."

"Did MacIntosh find out about you and his wife?"

"He did, about a year ago. Betty was going through a depression at the time and she told him about her love for me. Before long, I stopped getting calls from her. Then I found out that she had been institutionalized, where, I was told, she was being kept under heavy sedation. I, of course, hurried to her side. For a while, I saw her every week. Then Jake told me that he knew about my visits and that he had left strict orders to bar me from going to see her. However, some time later, when I told him I suspected that he was tampering with the project, he tried to pull the wool over my eyes, and in a calculated gesture of magnanimity, allowed me to visit her again, but under strict conditions. By the time my suspicions were finally confirmed and I confronted him with it, he had realized that he now had the upper hand."

"Betty? "

"Precisely. He threatened to remove all my visiting privileges permanently. I knew that if he did, Betty would probably become a vegetable." Bill Collins paused and with his hands behind his back, stared blankly out of the window. After a moment, he turned to Rodney.

"You see, Rodney, I love that woman. Jake knows that I owe my life to Betty. Without her, I would have found the bottle again. Therefore, he manipulated me into helping him. He will stop at nothing to get his way," he said, fearing that Rodney may have doubts about his character. He took a deep breath and paused for a moment. "Undoubtedly, Jake MacIntosh has all the reasons to want the project's failure."

"He's got the five million riding on it!"

"Hmm! Yes. But, that's only the tip of the iceberg. If the project fails, he can peddle the technology to competitors who are willing to give their souls to benefit from the Sparo Spear technology. Jake stands to personally gain several more millions of dollars."

"So, what made you change your mind?" Rodney asked.

"What do you mean? "

"You obviously decided at some point to fight Jake MacIntosh."

"Betty has given up on life. Jake got the better of her and he was getting the better of me through my collaboration with his scheme. In fact, he was destroying everything that I hold dear. One day, I came to my senses and decided that I could not let him manipulate me anymore. It became evident to me that the only way that I could help Betty was to stop Jake."

"So you stood up to him. You became a threat. That's why he went through that elaborate scheme to get you hooked on booze again."

Bill Collins nodded affirmatively as he moved slowly back toward his chair. He slowly let himself down in it and, with his head thrown back on the headrest, allowed himself to weep.

The lights from the instrument panel lit up like a video arcade game.

"Tower to Zulu 081, you have clearance for 4G turn at forty thousand feet."

"Zulu 081, Roger. Turn will occur to starboard," Rodney informed.

With a controlled motion of his hand, he pushed the joystick steadily to the left. The G forces of the sharp turn gripped the pilot, bringing him to an unprecedented adrenaline high. His heart beat at a frenetic pace with the excitement and the strain of the gravitational pull. He felt lightheaded, but his mind rushed at the opportunity of living on the edge, sitting on the fence between life and oblivion.

His hand slowly responded to his mind's warnings that it was time to take the fighter out of its body crushing turn. The magnificent bird leveled and resumed a straight-ahead thrust.

Rodney's lungs strained to recover the oxygen that had been squeezed out of his body during the strenuous test.

"Zulu 081 returning to base. Please advise on coordinates." He sighed, relieved that he had been able to again survive the stress. He looked to starboard as the T-138 chase plane found its position.

The control panel lit up with multiple lights flashing.

"Mayday, Mayday, Mayday. I've lost all power. The plane is out of control. It's in a nose dive," he calmly informed the control tower.

"Eject, Rod. Don't be a hero," Charles' voice came through his headset.

Rodney reached for the ejection seat activator and pulled. The canopy exploded away from the plane and the pilot waited for the seat to follow.

"One thousand one, one thousand two, one thousand three..."

The seat didn't eject. He looked at the scenery below him. The details of the forest took on new dimensions with each passing second.

"...One thousand twenty, one thousand twenty-one, one thousand twenty-three..."

He braced himself for the unavoidable.

Rodney rose violently from his nightmare, his hair and face drenched with sweat, his chest heaving. He glanced at the clock to his left. Three thirty-one a.m..

He blew air out of his lungs and took a deep breath.

"Less than twelve hours 'til test time," he reminded himself.

The voice on the central P.A. system convened all non-essential personnel to leave their work post and witness the test flight that would determine the fate of the Spear M40. Every employee had received a copy of a memo from the president of the company thanking them for their energy and devotion in meeting the deadlines and helping make the Spear M40 project a viable one. This was a first since Jake MacIntosh had taken over the reins and in most employees' opinion, a long overdue gesture under the circumstances.

Clear skies and moderate winds were once again ideal conditions for testing. The bell announced the approaching time of the flight as the workers exited the buildings and quietly marched towards the designated area along the tarmac. Excitement had given way to tension and anticipation.

Four black limousines, led by a security patrol car, drove onto the tarmac, and stopped near the stage behind a roped-off area. Jake MacIntosh and the invited dignitaries stepped out of one of the limousines. He was carrying a box that he set down beside the podium on the stage that had been set up for the presentation. Meanwhile, the guests were escorted to their reserved seats. Jake Macintosh smiling and radiating an air of confidence, walked to the podium.

"My dear friends and colleagues. It is with great pleasure that I come here today for the most important test flight of the Sparo Spear M40. I would like you to join me in extending a warm welcome to the Honorable Mr. Burnett, our great nation's Minister of National Defense, and to our future clients who will share with us this important day in our company's and country's history. "

The crowd politely greeted the guests with brief clapping.

"I take this opportunity to thank each and everyone of you for your invaluable contribution in creating and producing the most advanced jet fighter in the world. You were instrumental in Sparo Aeronautics' rise to the forefront of the aerospace industry. This wonderful piece of technology is yours." His comments were acknowledged with a loud cheer and an animated round of applause.

"At this time, I'd ask Captain Michael Mazenkowski, the pilot for this memorable flight, to join me on the podium."

The Captain approached the podium, cheered on enthusiastically by his friends and colleagues.

"Captain Mazenkowski, it gives me great pleasure to present this helmet to you, as a memento for this great day," he said as he handed him the pilot's helmet that he took out of the box he had carried onstage. The pilot accepted the gift with a handshake and placed it on his head, the oxygen mask clipped to one side. This gesture generated an even more enthusiastic response from the crowd that knew the fate of the project now rested in his capable hands.

"Now, I'd ask Mr. Burnett to say a few words and call for the start of the test flight."

The crowd politely applauded.

"Thank you Mr. MacIntosh. First of all, I wish to thank you for inviting me today. I'm aware of all the work that the employees at Sparo Aeronautics have put in this project, and I salute you. This is an exciting day for all of you, and I know that you're looking forward to the test flight, so I'd ask that the Sparo Spear M40 be brought onto the tarmac at this time."

The doors to the hangar opened. An airport tractor pulled the jet fighter onto the tarmac and positioned it behind the stage. The appearance of the sleek mechanical bird drew a loud cheer from the animated crowd. The dignitaries and the pilot were invited to stand beside the plane and pose for a group photo, the pilot's attire standing out among the business suits. As the photographers, cameramen and journalists recorded the newsworthy event, everyone put on a good face.

The crowd watched intently as Captain Michael Mazenkowski climbed the tall boarding ladder to the cockpit. Being senior pilot for the company brought many responsibilities and a lot of pressure, but never had the stakes been so high. He was all-the more determined not to let the project down. He eased himself through the front canopy, and with the assistance of two members of the ground crew, fastened himself into the giant bird. He completed the before-start checklist as usual and got his final instructions from ground. Engine start was normal.

"Ground, flight one-zero-two ready to taxi to runway one-zero-eight," he advised ground control.

"Flight one-zero-two, you're clear to taxi runway one-zero-eight, winds one-six-zero, ten to twelve knots."

Mazenkowski taxied the Spear and completed his after-engine-start checklist along the way to the take-off hold position on the strip. From a parallel runway, two chase T-138 fighters took off and circled the airport, waiting for the Spear's takeoff.

The Sparo control tower gave clearance.

"Flight one-zero-two clear for take-off, runway one-eight, winds one-six-zero, 10 knots. Contact departure three-two-five-point-six-five," they informed.

The pilot positioned the plane for takeoff on the runway. With impressive acceleration, the fighter streaked down the runway and took to the air.

"Spear M40 has taken off at 14:19 p.m. and cleared to company tower," the controller's voice sounded in Mazenkowski's earphones. The crowd, watching from the ground, broke out into a thunderous cheer as they witnessed the successful takeoff.

As it did on every prior test, the aircraft climbed to 18,000 feet at a speed of 500 knots. The pilot reset the altimeter to 2992 and activated the plane's after-burners, thrusting it into a steeper climb. At 40,000 feet, Mazenkowski leveled the craft and maintained altitude until the two chase planes reached him.

"Everything normal from starboard," the first pilot informed over the airwaves.

"Chase plane number two checking in at eight o'clock. Situation normal," said the pilot of the second chase plane.

"Roger," Michael responded. "All information on panels indicates normal operation. I'm now activating fly-by-wire mode and taking fighter into 5G turn, at Mach 2.1"

"Roger. All systems clear. You have clearance for maneuver." The control tower gave clearance.

Michael activated the A.F.C.S. control. As the afterburners kicked in, the pilot felt the G forces caused by the extraordinary acceleration of the fighter. When it reached Mach 2.1 the plane banked into a sharp turn to starboard. The pilot was a mere passenger, experiencing the gravity forces without interfering with the controls.

"Piece of cake!" he exulted after the turn. "It's performing as required! This baby is maintaining altitude and speed as required!" He was unable to stifle a yawn, which he attributed to his body's need to shake off some of the tension. He shook his head and regained composure.

"That's a Roger. Way to go Michael," the control tower voice echoed.

"Now I will deactivate fly-by-wire and go solo. It's time for me to show those people on the ground what this baby can really do."

"Flight one-zero-two, clearance at level three-one-zero and five-one-zero.

The canopies of the two-passenger simulator cockpit were closed. The simulator cockpit reacted to the climb as did the plane, its nose pointing to the warehouse ceiling. The pilot and his guide in the gunman's seat sat inside, concentrating on all activities on the control panels. From the headset in their helmets they listened to the exchanges between Michael Mazenkowski and the air-traffic controller. The video representations on the screens were identical to the information received during the conversation.

"I'm taking the plane into a climb to 45,000 feet at Mach 2.5," the pilot informed.

"That' a Roger. You have clearance."

The numbers on the simulator's altimeter climbed and the horizon line disappeared on the screen. The pilot's labored breathing murmured in through the simulator's pilot headset.

"Hee-haw! Thirty-nine thousand feet and climbing!" Michael's giddy voice informed.

The simulator pilot then heard a distinctive yawn. The altimeter, and the plane, continued their climb.

"Forty-three thousand five hundred feet. He should be leveling off by now," the simulator pilot muttered in his oxygen mask. "Forty-six thousand feet and still climbing." Suddenly the altimeter leveled off at forty-nine thousand feet where it stayed suspended for a brief moment before it plunged into a fast-paced dive. The simulator reproduced the rapid ascension and the momentary leveling off before going into a tumbling and uncontrollable roll.

"Remote override!" the simulator pilot ordered as he grabbed the control stick. "Kill communication with tower. The plane is without power."

James Knoll responded swiftly to the request. "Manual override activated. You have full control, Rod."

"Activate remote computer for possible override," the new pilot commanded.

"Plato, activate," the muffled voice of the co-pilot instructed.

"Plato activated."

The remote pilot felt resistance from the control stick as the simulator mechanically reproduced the gravitational force of the free fall. He extended his arm to the control panel and activated the engines once again.

"Thirty-eight thousand feet and falling," James Knoll informed from the technician's booth.

"Engines are started," the remote pilot growled as he struggled with the controls. "Thirty thousand feet." He felt the engine's resistance to kick into action.

"Twenty-nine... twenty-seven... twenty-five...come on...twenty-three...twenty-one...twenty…nineteen…eighteen…I'm leveling off!" he cheered and exhaled in relief.

"Good work Rod and Leonard! Take her home," James congratulated.

"I'm taking the baby down for an instrument landing. Activate communications from simulator to tower."

"Control tower, this is Flight one-zero-two requesting permission for pass over air field at altitude two-five before landing." Leonardo asked for clearance.

"That's a Roger. That was some pretty crazy flying you did there."

"Hey I can't get enough of this bird," Rodney interjected trying to sound like Mazenkowski. Leonardo's request hadn't been part of the scenario and had taken him off guard. He switched off communication with control tower to stop any other verbal intervention from the Master while on air.

"Pretty slick, there, Leonard. I gather you want to take this baby for a spin," he addressed the Master.

"The thought has crossed my mind. This is as close as I shall ever be to really flying," Leonardo defended.

"Are you out of your bloody mind?" James Knoll protested.

"Come on, James. Where's your sense of adventure?" Rodney prodded.

The pilot heard James Knoll's loud sigh in his headset.

"Ah, what the hell! After the things I've seen this old geezer do over the last few days, I say, let him go, Rod," James Knoll gave his blessing.

"Who's old?" Leonardo protested.

"Define old," Rodney replied.

"Ah, to soar like a kite," Leonardo exulted. "Watch this old geezer fly!"

The two chase fighters joined the aircraft and in formation, they descended in the clear skies back toward the launching airport.

The Spear, tailed by its two escorts, made a spectacular pass over the airport. Near the end of the runway, the two other fighters peeled away and assumed position for landing. The Spear went on for one last and final climb. The crowd watched its every move with awe and cheered loudly when it climaxed into a graceful roll. The aircraft then descended and aimed itself at the runway where it came to a soft and controlled landing, to the onlookers' exuberant approval.

"Rod, I believe the pilot is regaining consciousness," James informed.

"Communicate with him on a closed circuit and give him instructions."

"Line is open. Captain Mazenkowski, are you all right?" James Knoll asked.

"Yeah, what happened? Who... who is this?"

"I'll explain that later. All I can tell you is that you lost consciousness and we were able to take control of the plane remotely."

"How did you manage that?" the pilot asked.

"It doesn't matter. Now listen to me. We've landed the plane for you, but we will need your assistance to taxi it. When you do, we want you to take it to hangar 203."

"Why 203? It's at the other end of the runway."

"Since there's been problems, Hangar 203 is the closest to the end of the runway. A crew is waiting for you there."

"Roger." The pilot took control of the plane and followed instructions. When he reached the hangar, the doors opened and Bill Collins and Charles rushed towards the plane followed by a crew of technicians.

11

Déjà Lived

"Yo!" Edmond cheered as he popped the cork on a bottle of bubbly wine. "We've done it!"

Six glasses were raised in a toast.

"We saved the Sparo Spear project and we've put MacIntosh's butt behind bars," Charles jubilated. "And you know what the best part is? No one at Sparo knows that we're behind this."

"I'm sure MacIntosh knows," Rodney cautioned. "And since he'll most probably be released on bail, we'd better keep a low profile until the trial."

"Jeez, Rod. Don't be such a wet blanket. MacIntosh is as guilty as sin. You know it, we know it and he knows it. He can't get off the hook. With all of us knowing what we know, he's a sitting duck," Charles retaliated.

"Hey, Leonardo!" he called out, seeing that the Master had come in to join them. He got up, gave him a hug and kissed him on the cheek. His friends chuckled when they saw Leonardo's embarrassment.

"And if we succeeded, we owe all of it to this guy!" Charles said, keeping one arm around Leonardo's shoulder. He picked up the bottle of sparkly, poured some into an empty glass and handed it to Leonardo. "Thanks Leonardo," he said, looking directly at him and raising his glass.

"Leonardo?" Rodney repeated, surprised by Charles' identification.

"Yes, Rod. Leonardo. Like in Leonardo Da Vinci. I know all about him, now."

"'Who told you?"

"Collins. Leonardo opened up to him and told him who he was and about his incredible travel through time." Charles raised his glass again. "To Leonardo," he toasted.

Rodney relaxed. Charles obviously didn't know about Rodney's travel back in time and about his own death in the other time.

"Hear, hear, to Leonardo!" they all echoed as they raised their glasses to join Charles. They formed a circle around the Master, some patting him on the back, others rubbing their hands on his balding head. They'd grown very close to him over the last few weeks and he had time and time again proven to be a loyal and reliable friend.

"So Rodney, give us the whole story of what happened in the plane," Edmond requested.

Rodney obliged. "Well, the pilot lost consciousness while he was attempting a steep climb, that's where we had to take over the controls and..."

"How did he pass out, do we know?" Eugene interrupted.

"Well, once the plane landed, Charles and Bill Collins inspected the plane, inside and out. They checked the oxygen supply and cabin ventilation and couldn't find anything."

"Yeah, we were stumped for a while," Charles continued. "We knew that the pilot had fainted and that there was a chance that the physical strain may have been a factor. So the pilot was sent down for a physical examination. The only thing the physician mentioned was that the pilot had particularly bad breath. We thought that we'd come to a dead end, until I remembered the ceremony before the flight."

"What happened at the ceremony?" Leo asked.

"MacIntosh gave the pilot, Captain Mazenkowski, a new helmet and headgear for the flight. I noticed that MacIntosh had brought the helmet in a box in his limo and that he carried it onto the stage himself."

"That's strange. You'd think a big shot like him would've gotten one of his employees to do that," Edmond interjected.

"Precisely. No one else but Jake MacIntosh got close to that helmet. So we sent it to the lab for analysis and that's where we discovered that the oxygen mask had been laced with an anesthetic substance. That's what had given the pilot bad breath. All the evidence pointed to MacIntosh and that's what landed him in jail."

"But if the substance was in the mask during the whole flight, why didn't the pilot pass out sooner?" Leo asked.

"He almost did. When we listened to the black box recording of the flight, we detected that he'd started to feel some of the effects of the anesthetic during the routine 2G turn. But as the plane leveled off, so did the drug. You see, the anesthetic had been placed in the sponge padding inside the oxygen mask. At ground level and under normal flight conditions it didn't have any effect. But when the G forces on the body increased, so did the pressure to the mask. So you can imagine that at the speed the M40 was going, it emitted dosages strong enough to put out a horse. The doctor said that the anesthetic and the physical exertion to resist the forces is what made the pilot giddy at first and then knocked him out"

"MacIntosh took a hell of a risk," Leo concluded.

"That is debatable," Leonardo objected. "Had we not intervened, the aircraft would have plummeted to the ground and exploded in a ball of fire. There would have been no evidence to find."

"Yeah, the crash would have been attributed either to pilot or technical error. Either way, the whole project would have been dead in the water," Rodney added.

"Boy, I feel like we've just lived in a James Bond movie or something," Oscar said, shaking his head.

"MacIntosh must be pissed off. Because of us, he lost millions and may spend a long vacation in one of our country's finest prisons," Leo said with pride.

"He's not in there yet. There's a long way to go before that," Rodney cautioned.

"How the hell did you guys get clearance to inspect the plane after the flight?" Eugene asked.

"We got a bit lucky," Charles replied. "As you know, we got the plane taxied to a remote hangar where Collins and me were waiting. This bought us some time to do our search before any of the big wigs reacted."

"Yeah, but didn't any of the employees in the hangar object?"

"Nah. When they saw that Bill Collins was leading the search and that the pilot was helping him, they didn't say a word. And let me tell you, it's a good thing we were there after, because Mazenkowski was pretty confused about the whole thing."

"How'd he react when you told him about your remote flying of the plane?" Leo inquired.

"We didn't," Rodney replied. "Well, we sort of explained it to him, but we didn't go into too much detail, and asked him to keep it to himself. Since he doesn't want the company to know that he passed out while flying a half a billion dollar plane - which could cost him his job, seeing that not everything is out in the open yet - we had no trouble convincing him to cooperate."

"But how did you get the cops to throw the book at MacIntosh?"

"We told the cops that the pilot wanted us to do a verification of his air supply, because he felt dizzy whenever the G forces increased. He put this in his flight report to be on the record. The rest was left to us," Charles said.

"Yeah, but that still doesn't incriminate anybody," Oscar noted.

"That's true," Charles conceded. "However, Bill Collins called in a favor from an old friend, Detective Burrows from the police. He invited him and one of his colleagues to come and witness the flight first hand with him from Hangar 203."

"Credible witnesses," Oscar interjected.

"You've got it! Collins made sure that they heard the pilot's testimony."

"The elaborate version about him losing it?" Edmond asked.

"Nope. Who'd believe that?" Charles replied. His listeners chuckled. "Mazenkowski's testimony raised enough suspicions for Detective Brown to follow our search attentively and then start an investigation when we got the test results."

"Yeah, but that still doesn't tie in MacIntosh," Leo challenged.

"All we need is reasonable doubt," Rodney replied. "Detective Brown has proof that there was sabotage, and that's classified as attempted murder. As for the culprit, we have video clips of MacIntosh walking out of the limo all the way to the podium with the helmet. We see him hand it over to Mazenkowski. As for motive, I think that's an easy one, don't you?"

"We'll make sure of that," Edmond supported.

"So what's next?" Leo continued.

"We'll probably have to testify in court against MacIntosh. But I don't think that's a problem for anybody here. We've got all the nails for his coffin."

"You've got that right, Rod!" Oscar said.

"And, as for the immediate future, we're organizing a mother of a big party tomorrow night," Edmond cheered. "Who's with me on this?"

"Yo!! Only if there's wall-to-wall women," Eugene replied.

"Count on it!" Leo promised.

The party was a great success. Debbie leaned on the front porch's guardrail, receptive to the multiple aromas of the late summer night. After a while, she turned and looked at the congestion of bodies in the main corridor inside the hall of 230 Anderson. She saw Rodney appear in the midst of the crowd. Seeing her, he smiled and continued to wind his way through the revelers to get to her, tightly holding a drink in each hand. Then she saw that someone's hand had gripped one of his arms. He turned and was face to face with Rhonda, who smiled at him as she grabbed him by the waist and pulled him towards her. Rodney seemed surprised when she kissed him passionately. He stood there, momentarily helpless and taken aback by Rhonda's come-on. Rhonda released her grip and winked at him. In a seductive sway, she climbed the stairs to the second floor.

Rodney looked embarrassed by the unsolicited advances. He turned towards the portico and joined Debbie on the porch.

"You know her?" Debbie asked, visibly upset by what she'd witnessed.

"Yes. But it's not what you think."

"She seems to like you."

"She likes Ed. They've been dating." He sighed and handed Debbie her drink.

"Rod, that woman is trouble. Take it from me. You should get her out of here!"

"Now, now! There's no reason to be jealous. And by the way, who are you to tell me who I can or cannot invite?" he teased.

"You think I'm jealous," she retorted, annoyed by the comment. "You really don't know me do you?" She took a deep breath. "Goddam it, Rod, you're not listening to me. I'm telling you, she's bad news," her voice vibrated with emotion.

"What do you mean? Do you know her?" Rod asked concerned by Debbie's reaction to Rhonda.

"Of course I do. She's..." Seeing that Rhonda was approaching, Debbie stopped talking and looked away.

"Is there a problem?" Rhonda asked as she put her arm around Rodney's neck. She kissed him on the cheek, her eyes glancing at Debbie, obviously trying to provoke her.

Debbie broke away and ran off the porch and onto the street.

Rodney glared at Rhonda who seemed to be enjoying Debbie's reaction and broke away from her unsolicited hug.

Debbie had bolted for her car, reaching in her jean pocket for her keys as she ran. She hurriedly unlocked the car door and jumped into it. Rodney grabbed the door before she could close it.

"What the hell's wrong? What's gotten into you?"

"Let me go! I've got to go!" Debbie slammed the door and started the car. "Be careful, Rod!" she pleaded through the half open window.

The engine growled and the car peeled out and up the hill.

Sporadic red, white and blue lights suddenly invaded the evening sky. The intruding rays cut the path along which a police cruiser traveled. It was déjà vu. The vehicle was destined for 230 Anderson and Rodney knew that they were responding to a complaint.

"Of course. I'm reliving the party!" he muttered. His heartbeat doubled in intensity. He sensed imminent danger.

"Here you go, fellas," Rhonda said as she walked into the living room, adroitly holding a tray covered with beer mugs, a collection gathered from various unsuspecting local taverns and all filled with frothy brew. "I thought you might appreciate your beer in a mug."

Rhonda strutted to Edmond and kissed him on the forehead provoking a collective "Woooooo," from the other fellows. She then presented her tray to Rodney. He took a glass. She looked at him seductively and smiled. He raised his glass in her direction in response, looking at her warily. He sat on the living room sofa and watched the self-appointed waitress' every move, Debbie's warning ringing in his ears. The repetition of the events was flagrant. There was trouble up ahead, but this time, he was ready to take it head on.

"Where's Leonardo?" Edmond queried.

"He's been invited out by Professor Holmes. I don't think we'll see him until the morning. He doesn't like crowded rooms."

Rhonda left the room, carrying a tray covered with the empty beer bottles that she'd cleared from around the room. Once she was out of sight, Rodney inconspicuously poured the contents of his beer mug into a potted plant beside him.

"I've got my eyes on you, Rhonda," he muttered, remembering the party previous to his time travel.

"He's out for the count," Sergio proclaimed as he lifted Mark's arm. "Another victim has succumbed to excessive beer consumption at the festivities!"

Sergio placed an unlit cigarette between Mark's lips. The sight of Mark fast asleep, with a cigarette hanging from his lower lip, generated some tired laughs from the few still awake.

"We kicked butt. We sure showed that Jake guy," Charles slurred, the effects of stress and alcohol having taken their toll. He sat on the floor next to Professor Collins who leaned on the sofa beside him, fast asleep. He hadn't been drinking alcohol all evening, as a matter of fact, when Rhonda had gone around taking everyone's order, he'd asked for ginger ale. Evidently, the events of the last days had exhausted him and he'd also passed out.

"I really like being with you guys," Charles blubbered, tears streaming down his cheeks.

"What's this guy talking about?" Sergio asked, confused by Charles' babbling. "Cheer up, Charlie, we're having a party."

"That Leonardo guy sure is amazing. Isn't... he?" As the words left his lips, Charles fell back against the sleeping professor and joined him in the magical world of dreams.

"Ho-humm. His name is Leonard," Sergio replied in a yawn.

Rhonda had quietly witnessed the conversation. She got up from the easy chair she had occupied for the past hour and grabbed Edmond, who was still struggling to stay awake.

"Come on. It's time for us to go to bed," she commanded, as she took his arm and pulled his one hundred and eighty-pound body to its feet.

Sergio and Rodney observed the ease with which she handled their friend. They looked at each other, impressed by this demonstration of strength and balance.

"Good night, fellas," she said over her shoulder.

"Do you need any help?" Sergio volunteered.

"I'll be just fine," she reassured.

"You should ask Eddie if he'll be okay," corrected Rodney. "I think he's biting off more than he can chew," he added, fully aware of the scary truth of his comment.

Rhonda turned her head towards Rodney and blew him a kiss followed by a wink in appreciation of his comment.

"I'm just a pussycat," she replied and led Edmond up the stairs.

"Wow, what a woman!" Sergio said to Rodney. "How did he manage to get her?"

"Bad luck, I guess," Rodney replied.

Sergio yawned uncontrollably, mouth wide open. He dropped his cigarette in an empty beer bottle and lay down on the chesterfield, his feet hanging over the end and his head resting on Eugene's lap.

"I'm so tired all of a sudden." He yawned again. "It's hitting me, just... like..." He didn't finish his sentence. Like his buddies before him, Sergio was out like a light.

Rodney looked around the room at all the motionless bodies. He listened closely for any sound coming from upstairs. He heard one of the bedroom doors close softly. Edmond's door he assumed. Light footsteps carefully traveled across the second floor, then came down the stairs and headed for the living room.

Rodney closed his eyes. He felt the movement of air in the room and smelled the perfume as the night visitor walked from one sleeping body to the other. The aroma became more distinctive when Rhonda stopped in front of him. Her warm hand reached for his face and gave him two small pats on the cheek.

"Out like babies," she murmured softly. "Now the sand lady is going to take good care of you." Rodney listened to her footsteps as she swiftly walked out of the house.

He rose from his position and discreetly walked towards the window to see what she was up to. She'd opened the trunk of a car parked in front of the house and was pulling out a belt bag that she fastened around her waist, the pouch positioned in front. She then put on a pair of latex gloves. Her movements were swift and precise as she filled the pouch with various items and closed the zipper. She bent into the trunk and took out a plastic gasoline canister that she carried with her towards the house. Rodney returned to the chesterfield and resumed his position.

He felt her as she came back into the living room. Through slit eyelids he watched as she cleared the coffee table and put a small, rectangular box on it. She lit the surface of the table with a pocket flashlight that she placed close to the box. He saw her pull a glass vial with a needle and syringe out of the box.

"Gentlemen, this is bad stuff. This is what bad trips are made of," she squealed with perverse delight. The black widow planted the needle of the syringe into the vial and extracted some of the lethal potion.

"Okay, who wants to try the goodies first?" She pivoted and looked at all her helpless victims and arrested her choice on Rodney.

"My dear, dear Rodney. You look like you need a little boost. Jake is very disappointed in you. You've caused him hardship," she cooed. "But Jake won't have to worry about you anymore, not once I'm finished with you."

She bent down and kissed him passionately. "Get ready for your last trip, love. I'll transmit your best regards to Debbie."

She rolled Rodney's sleeve and tied a rubber band above his elbow, then she grabbed his arm and directed the needle to his arm.

"Sweet dreams, Rod."

Rodney's response was a kick and a push that landed her on the floor. She swiftly reached into her pouch and pulled out a small pistol.

"Stay put, Rod. Don't force me to make it messy," she growled as she sat up. "Now pick up that needle. Rodney didn't. "Pick it up!" she yelled, waving the gun in his face. He thought it better to comply and gain some time.

"See what you've done?" Rhonda continued. "Now you'll have to use it on yourself. That'll save me some dirty work, though. Come on, honey, do it!"

Rodney pretended to bring the needle to his arm, then taking advantage that her attention was morbidly drawn to what he was about to do, in a swift motion he bolted and jumped through the living room window. The sound of three successive shots followed that of the shattering of glass. Rodney fell to the ground, looked up and saw his assailant pointing the gun in his direction. In a desperate, he thought futile, attempt, he rolled sideways on the ground, towards a bush that seemed yards away. Three more shots rocked the peaceful neighborhood. Rodney gasped. After a moment or two, he realized that apart from the pain of the cuts and bruises that he'd gotten from his stunt out the window, he wasn't hurt. He took a deep breath. Then, he heard the sound of quick successive footsteps coming from the street. He got ready to bolt again.

"Oh my God, Rodney. Are you alright?"

"Debbie?" He stopped and rolled to face her. She stood beside him, pointing towards the window with a smoking gun that she held in her right hand.

"Did you hit her?" he asked.

"I don't think so. She probably took cover inside." Relieved to see that Rodney was okay, she sighed. "I told you she was trouble."

"You weren't kidding." He paused. He rose to his feet clutching his sore shoulder. "Can I borrow this?" he asked, taking the gun from Debbie's hand. "I think I should try to find her. Maybe, you'd better stay here," he added.

Debbie nodded. "Please be careful," she said, now shaking from the aftermath of having used a gun.

In a crouched position, holding the gun rather ineptly, Rodney cautiously went to the front door. When he crept into the portico, his heart was pounding erratically and his body was shaking. He dashed down the hallway across the doorway to the living room. In a tentative move, he peeked inside the room. Rhonda was not in the room. With his back to the wall he walked towards the kitchen.

Three more gunshots echoed from the back yard. Rodney froze. There was silence. "Rodney!" Debbie called out from behind. He turned quickly and pointed the gun in her direction. She stood facing him, her hands up in the air. "Debbie, move back," he ordered.

A thumping noise was heard coming from the kitchen, followed by a muffled scream. Rodney jumped around and through the doorway, he could see Leonardo holding Rhonda with her back against the wall. He had both hands above his head and around her neck, so that her feet were dangling quite a distance from the floor. Rodney could hear the gurgling noise of the choking woman as her windpipes were being crushed by Leonardo's powerful grip. She was still holding the gun in her right hand, her fingers still pulling on the trigger by reflex, but she had spent all her rounds. The gun suddenly fell to the ground. Leonardo dropped his victim, who collapsed in a corner.

Rodney and Debbie were stupefied by Leonardo's display of strength. Silence reigned for a few moments, but Rhonda's gasping for air soon broke it.

"Good timing, Leonardo," Rodney said, relieved.

Leonardo was catching his breath after the extraordinary physical exertion. He looked at Rhonda who lay unconscious in the corner. "To quote your friend Sergio... I am happy to be living in quiet times... where violence is a less integral part of society," he quipped.

"And you believed him," Rodney replied.

Leonardo shook his head. "I'm happy to see that you're all right, Rodney," he confided.

"What were you doing in the back yard?"

"I felt there was still impending danger. I remembered that you had told me about Charles being found hanging in the kitchen after such a gathering, so I kept a vigil in the back yard, away from everyone." He sighed. "My intuition did not fail me," he concluded.

Rodney walked towards Leonardo and gently put his hands on the Master's shoulders. "Thanks, Leonardo," he said. "I don't know if we could have made it if you hadn't been there. I'll go see how the others are doing."

Rodney turned away from Leonardo and went on to the living room. Everyone was sleeping, blissfully unaware of the events that had gone on around them. When he returned to the kitchen, Leonardo was nowhere to be seen. Debbie was leaning on the doorframe, keeping a vigilant eye on Rhonda.

"What do you know about her?" he asked Debbie, as he gently took her hand in his.

"As you know, her real name is Miranda Scott. She was first hired at Sparo as my stepfather's executive assistant." Debbie shivered and moved closer to Rodney. "More recently, she's become his mistress and love interest. She helped Jake put my mother in that mental hospital. Jake promised that he'd marry her if she did."

"Which explains the engagement ring that she was wearing," Rodney said.

"She's also a weight-lifting fanatic."

"Yeah, she's really strong. You should have seen the way she carried Edmond around. I wondered what she was doing in his life all of a sudden. Now, I see that Jake probably put her up to seducing Edmond, just to infiltrate our group. She's a pretty tough cookie, judging by what she was ready to do here tonight. But I guess she won't be hurting anyone else for a while, though. The police will make sure of that." He paused. "Since when do you go around carrying a gun?"

Debbie blushed. "I don't usually," she explained. "It was my father's, one of the few things that I have to remember him by. I kept it for sentimental reasons, but tonight, I'm sure happy to have it. I was able to help someone special with it." Debbie took a deep breath trying to undo the knots tied up inside her. "I just knew that something was wrong. When I got home, I couldn't stop thinking about her being here and all. I figured that Rhonda's being here probably had something to do with all the questions you were asking me about Jake MacIntosh. Then, I got to thinking about Jake's arrest and had a feeling that you had something to do with it. And I was right, wasn't I? Rhonda and Jake are two of a kind. They'll stop at nothing to get their way. It became clear to me that if she was here, it was probably because she was up to no good. So I loaded the gun, just in case, and came back. Good thing I did, too."

"Yeah, good thing you did. Thanks Deb... for hmm... letting me stick around Earth a little longer." He took her in his arms and gave her a long, soft hug.

"Are your friends okay?" Debbie asked finally.

"Yeah. I suspect they've been sedated."

Debbie looked at Rodney doubtfully.

"I think Rhonda spiked their drinks to knock them out. She did mine too, but I didn't drink it. When she thought all of us were out, she was going to give us an overdose of some bad drug." He pointed to the gasoline canister by the entrance to the living room. "I suspect she was going to use that to burn down the house afterwards. It would've looked like a bunch of students got high and set fire to the place. Anyway, I'm pretty sure that's what the coroner would have concluded." He remembered the officer's conclusion after Charles' death.

"How do you know this?"

"Hmmm. Déjà lived, I guess. It's a long story that I'll be happy to tell you real soon," he said, as he slipped his arm around her. "She sure would've gotten your stepfather off the hook if she'd succeeded." "No witnesses."

"What do you mean?"

"Just think of it. There's no case against Jake MacIntosh without our testimony."

Debbie turned towards Rodney and kissed him.

"What's that for?"

"I'm just glad that you're safe. And I'm grateful to you for getting the monkey off my mother's back, not to mention mine."

"I hope there's more where this came from," Rodney hinted.

Debbie kissed him again. "Plenty more."

The sound of sirens was heard in the distance. Rodney and Debbie walked to the living room window to look at the police cars accumulating in front of the house. Leonardo had undoubtedly called them.

Leonardo was wearing his red embroidered tunic and fuchsia cloak, looking like the Renaissance man that he was. He and Rodney sat alone in the living room, which had been reorganized into the Master's quarters after the party. Order had been restored since that night, and life had come back to normal. However, on this night, they both had an overwhelming urge to spend some time alone together. They sat across the room from each other and smiled. In the few months that they'd spent together, they'd shared so much. Leonardo had discovered a whole new world and Rodney had been in the physical presence of his mentor. Most importantly, they had become friends.

No words were exchanged. What could they say? Neither knew for sure what exactly would happen next, but they both had a pretty good idea. Rodney felt like a son waiting for his father to leave him and pass on to another life. The experience was perplexing. Leonardo was the perfect picture of health. *"He could be around forever,"* Rodney thought. *"Not likely,"* his gut told him.

"Professor Holmes is getting suspicious," Leonardo said finally.

"That doesn't surprise me. He's been snooping around here a lot lately. Do you think he knows who you are?"

"No. He thinks I'm a... what did he call me? A counterfeiter. He believes I spend my time reproducing masterpieces. Great works of art such as Michelangelo's, he told me. Can you believe the nerve of that man, comparing me to that deformed, grotesque man?"

"He was a great artist."

"Granted. But this man, Holmes, felt that my style was more reminiscent of Michelangelo's than my own. And he considers himself an authority on Renaissance work!."

"Self-proclaimed, perhaps."

"Perhaps." Leonardo smiled at his young friend. "You show great promise, Rodney. You have an inquisitive and logical mind, as well as strong beliefs and integrity. Most of all you listen to this," he said pointing to his heart. "You have good intuition. Never lose sight of that."

"I had a great teacher."

Leonardo, shirked the compliment. "Most of all, you have good friends. That is worth more than all the gold in the world."

"You're a great friend, Leonardo."

The two men sat, quietly. Many thoughts ran through their minds, but neither would address the idea that they would soon be parted.

"I finally got to fly," Leonardo said suddenly.

Rodney smiled. Of all the things by which he'd remember Leonardo, the flight in the Spear M40 would be the most memorable. For Leonardo also, because this flight had been the fulfillment of a dream that had started almost a half millennium before. He had caused the plane to soar like a kite, as he had imagined it so many times.

"If you don't mind, Rodney, I would like to retire."

Rodney stood up, as did Leonardo. They stood facing each other momentarily. Teary-eyed, they hugged in a manifestation of the unbreakable bond between them, one that neither time nor distance could ever sever.

"Thank you Leonardo." Rodney sighed, fighting back tears. "Good night." He slowly walked out of Leonardo's quarters and climbed the stairs to his own room.

The clear, blue sky was showing little contrast apart from a few white cottony clouds floating on the atmospheric canvas, resembling the background of a Renaissance masterpiece. Near the river, the young man bade farewell to the older one as the kite approached from the distance. The powerful bird of prey opened its claws as it descended toward the bearded man. The youth observed in awe as the master of the skies clutched its precious cargo by the shoulders and lifted him into the air with the beating of its powerful wings. The extraordinary passenger remained passive, his light red embroidered tunic and fuchsia cloak fluttering gracefully in the wind. From behind, his white beard expanded in volume on both sides of his head, giving the young man the impression that it acted as secondary wings. Hypnotized by the sight, the youth sat on the riverbank and looked into the distance until the kite and its passenger had disappeared.

The portico door vibrated from the agitated pounding of early-morning visitors. Edmond ran down the stairs to meet them.

"Hey, Sergio, Professor Holmes," he greeted them. He yawned loudly and stretched.

"Where is he?" Holmes said as he barged inside the corridor.

"Whoa! Where do you think you're going?" Edmond said as he restrained the rude man.

"I need to speak to that… that counterfeiter Leonard."

"What about?"

Rodney scurried down the stairs, dressing hastily, followed by Eugene and Leo.

"What's going on here?"

Edmond shrugged nonchalantly. "He seems to have a bee up his ass."

Holmes reached for the door handle to Leonardo's quarters.

"That old bastard has taken back what is rightfully mine," Holmes yelled, struggling to get out of Edmond's strong grip.

"The paintings have disappeared," Sergio explained.

"What paintings?" Rodney asked.

"The ones Leonard sold him."

Holmes broke away from his oppressors and barreled into the room followed by the residents.

"Where's the painting?" he asked.

"On the wall." Edmond stopped dead in his tracks. "It's gone!"

Everyone gathered in the room. With sad surprise, they saw that the mural painting of four students bathing had vanished. The wall had regained its old complexion of tired peeling paint on plaster and the poster of the young woman with the bare bottom again covered the cracks. Holmes, vociferating some threat about reporting to the police, with Sergio in tow, left the house in a huff. Eugene and Leo rushed out of the room and bolted up the stairs to Leo's room.

Rodney walked over to the desk where Leonardo's computer set-up remained intact.   Leonardo's communication headset had been conspicuously placed on top of a folded sheet of paper. It was the sheet with the computer coordinates and the handwritten notes that had been at the root of the adventure. Rodney delicately picked them up and almost reverently, put on the headset.

"Plato, activate," he commanded.

"Plato activated for Rodney," the computer acknowledged in a voice identical to Leonardo's. The screen lit up to a black background, displaying a constellation from which the outline of an object resembling a bricklayer's trowel with two holes on its flat face stood out.

"Black hole, white hole, worm hole, space!" Eugene read some labels from the graphic screen presentation. "What's that all about?"

"I think it's Leonardo's theory on our travels," Rodney concluded. There were tears in his eyes.

Eugene and Leo came back into the room.

"He's gone isn't he?" Eugene said, teary-eyed.

"The notebooks are gone too?" Rodney asked knowing the answer.

"Yeah," Eugene replied.

They bowed their heads and for a few moments, silently shared their grief for Leonardo's departure. Then, straightening up, they looked at each other. As if of one mind, they headed out of the room.

"You get the beer, Eddie," Leo said.

"I'll go put on some music," Rodney called out as he climbed the stairs.

Less than thirty minutes later, Leo, Rodney and Edmond were all sitting in the bathtub, each one holding a beer. The Doors' "Break on Through to the Other Side" was blaring through the speakers.

"Hey. Where's Eugene?" Edmond asked.

As if on cue, Eugene came in, holding a drawing pad and some charcoal. He closed the bathroom door behind him and leaned against it. He ceremoniously opened the pad to a blank page and while darting glances at the men in the tub, he started to draw. The others all laughed at the scene, fondly remembering the original one.

"Hey, Eugene! You're not going to go weird on us are you?" Edmond called out, splashing some water in his direction.

"Weird? Who're you calling weird?" Eugene answered as he threw down the pad and charcoal. He hopped towards the bathtub as he took off his clothes and with a great flurry that sent water sloshing over the edge, took his place in the bathtub with the others.

AGMV
MARQUIS
Québec, Canada
2000